Bolt
Cou

D1137368

WI...
LOVE

&

THE MAVERICK WHO RULED HER HEART

BY
SUSAN CARLISLE

HEART OF MISSISSIPPI

Hot sultry nights with delicious docs—
in the heart of Mississippi…

Kelsey and China Davis grew up with dark secrets
that rocked their once steady family foundations.
While China wants to stay in Golden Shores,
Kelsey can't wait to leave…

But neither sister expects to meet the two gorgeous docs
who have come to Golden Shores searching for a fresh
start. And once the fireworks begin it's not long before
pulses are racing and temperatures are rising!

**Find out just how hot things can get in Mississippi
with Susan Carlisle's fabulous duet:**

THE DOCTOR WHO MADE HER LOVE AGAIN

and

THE MAVERICK WHO RULED HER HEART

THE DOCTOR
WHO MADE HER
LOVE AGAIN

BY
SUSAN CARLISLE

MILLS & BOON

First published in Great Britain 2014
by Mills & Boon, an imprint of Harlequin (UK) Limited,
Eton House, 18-24 Paradise Road, Richmond, Surrey, TW9 1SR

© 2014 Susan Carlisle

ISBN: 978-0-263-90788-9

Harlequin (UK) Limited's policy is to use papers that are natural,
renewable and recyclable products and made from wood grown in
sustainable forests. The logging and manufacturing processes conform
to the legal environmental regulations of the country of origin.

Printed and bound in Spain
by Blackprint CPI, Barcelona

Dear Reader

For many years I've spent a week here and a week there on the Gulf Coast. I've been to a number of places in the world, but the beaches of the Gulf are the most beautiful. Clean white sand, radiant sunshine, friendly people—pure pleasure. When I placed China and Payton in this setting I knew it would be a wonderful backdrop for their romance. Their love story has been great fun to write. No two people could be more different and more alike at the same time. It was joy mixed with frustration trying to get China and Payton together while they were fighting to stay apart.

On a personal note, my heart goes out to anyone who has been touched by cancer. My family and friends certainly have been. I look forward to the day when this ugly disease is eradicated for ever. I'd also like to add a special thank you for the quality help I received from the staff of the Crestview Nursery in Crestview, Florida. All the plant information was much appreciated. I love you all.

I hope you enjoy Payton and China's story. I like to hear from my readers. You can find me at www.SusanCarlisle.com

Susan

Dedication

To Zach
I love you, Z.

Susan Carlisle's love affair with books began when she made a bad grade in math in the sixth grade. Not allowed to watch TV until she'd brought the grade up, she filled her time with books and became a voracious romance reader. She has 'keepers' on the shelf to prove it. Because she loved the genre so much she decided to try her hand at creating her own romantic worlds. She still loves a good happily-ever-after story.

When not writing Susan doubles as a high school substitute teacher, which she has been doing for sixteen years. Susan lives in Georgia with her husband of twenty-eight years and has four grown children. She loves castles, travelling, cross-stitching, hats, James Bond and hearing from her readers.

Recent titles by Susan Carlisle:

SNOWBOUND WITH DR DELECTABLE
NYC ANGELS: THE WALLFLOWER'S SECRET*
HOT-SHOT DOC COMES TO TOWN
THE NURSE HE SHOULDN'T NOTICE
HEART SURGEON, HERO...HUSBAND?

NYC Angels

CHAPTER ONE

WHAT WAS THIS guy doing? China Davis waited for the driver to park so she could take the space next to him. She watched appalled as the red-hot-off-the-line foreign sports car straddled the parking line.

Really? This person was going to take up two spaces in the far-too-small parking lot during morning rush hour?

Disgusted, China observed the driver do just as she'd feared. She would have to go around the building and park in the strip mall parking lot. She'd be lucky if she could juggle the donuts and coffee back to the car without spilling one or both all over her scrubs.

China glanced at the tag on the slick vehicle as she passed. Illinois. It was a little early for the summer crowd to be showing up. Still mid-May, she'd been looking forward to another few weeks of peace before the beach mob invaded.

Living in a small southern coastal town had its advantages but there was a downside also. Four out of the twelve months the locals had to contend with the influx of people. It didn't help that here was only one main road into town, which had no choice but to end when it met the water of the gulf. From there the driver had to choose east or west along the beach.

Dolly's Donuts was located on the main road. As the

local morning hangout for the senior citizens, it was also the place in town for quality donuts. China's mom had pointed out more than once to her that patience was a virtue. That might be so but China had promised hot donuts, and she didn't like to disappoint.

As she hurried into Dolly's, she mentally reviewed her order list. She glanced at her wrist watch. Yes, she was going to be late. Something that had never happened before. The line at the counter was four deep when she slipped into the tight glassed-in space that was Dolly's customer area. The place still had the feel of a fifties-era coffee shop, with a few metal stools with orange seats facing a long narrow counter.

China studied the tall man in front of her with the wide shoulders. His dark hair was cut supershort, as if it had been shaved off and was beginning to grow out.

One customer down, three more to go.

Her attention returned to the man. He wore a salmon-color polo shirt that fit him loosely but contrasted nicely with his dark coloring.

She peeked around him to see what was happening with the next patron. The man gave her a pointed look and she straightened, finding her place in line again. Her father had used that same look to make her and her siblings fall in line.

Another down. China stepped forward. Thankfully the man ahead of her was next.

"What do you consider your best donut?" he asked.

Oh, no! He was going to get Roger started on donuts. She'd be lucky to make work by lunchtime.

Dolly's husband stated in a voice of authority from behind the cash register, "We sell a lot of these." He pointed to a tray of glazed. "But the best, I believe, are the double chocolate. We make a special…"

China zoned out as Roger went into a monologue on how the dough was prepared.

"I'll get you some fresh ones from the back."

"That sounds great," the man in front of her said, as if he had all the time in the world. He probably did, but she sure didn't. They were expecting her at the clinic and she needed to be on time. She worked hard not to receive complaints about her actions; she wanted no conflict.

When Roger ambled off, China leaned around the man and said in a low voice, "You're not from around here or you'd know better. Don't ever get Roger started. It goes on forever."

The man pinned her with a dark look of disapproval that made her chest tighten as she shrank back into her place. He turned his back to her again. She wouldn't be saying anything further to this guy.

In the brief moment she'd seen his face straight on she'd been able to tell he was thin. No tan line marked his temple from eye to ear where sunglasses might have been. In fact, he looked as if he could use a little time outside. Still, he had an interesting face. Not handsome in the Hollywood leading man sense of the words but more in an attention-grabbing way.

"Here you go," Roger said. "How about coffee?"

"Black," the man said in one deep syllable.

Roger turned away and a full minute later slid the coffee container across the counter and quoted the man his total.

With relief, China moved closer, anticipating her turn. As she did so the man rotated and bumped against her.

"Excuse me," he said, with an air of authority.

"I'm sorry," China said, sliding to the side to dodge his coffee cup and moving well out of his way. She didn't want to cause any more of a scene. It had been on impulse for her to have spoken to him to begin with.

He strolled by her before she turned to placed her order. While Roger bagged it she looked out the glass doors at the broad back of the exasperating man. He headed straight for the fancy sports car. *I should have known.*

The man was one of those who thought he was entitled because he was handsome and drove a fancy car!

Payton pulled the Mercedes into a parking space behind the clinic to face a wall of greenery that was overgrown. In his other life it would have been another row of cars in a spiraling parking garage. He looked at the 1940s wooden house that had been converted into a treatment center. The Golden Shores Walk-in Clinic in Mississippi. It was nothing like the state-of-the-art facility he was used to, nothing resembling the highly charged ER in Chicago where ambulance sirens blared every few minutes.

Truthfully, nothing about Golden Shores was like the place he'd called home his entire life. Here the buildings went no higher than three levels when he was used to skyscrapers and glittering glass. Two-lane roads were the norm. None of those eight-lane interstates with cars whizzing by. If he got behind a truck pulling a boat then he had to sit back for the ride. Everything moved slower and people spoke with a drawl. But this was what he wanted. The easier pace, the chance to enjoy life. A place to recover. He'd moved nine hundred miles from family and friends to find his own destiny. Cancer had taken its toll and now it was time for him to take control. Create the life he wanted.

He hadn't counted on the cute but weird local who had been behind him at the bakery. She'd certainly not been tuned into the idea of a relaxed pace. Donuts weren't his usual fare for breakfast so hopefully the chance of running into her again were slim to none.

Payton gathered his coffee and donuts and got out of

the car. Unsure where to enter the building, he spied a sign stating it was the employees' entrance and started toward it just as a compact car whipped into the lot. He pushed the door open and found himself at the end of a passage that ran the length of the house.

Closing the door behind him, he headed towards the voices coming from the front. The floor creaked in places as he walked down the wooden plank hall. No serviceable white-tile floors of a hospital E.R. in sight. Along the way he passed small rooms located on the left side. Those had to be the exam rooms. Directly across from the third one was a small room that looked like an office. Next to it and just before the waiting room was an alcove that appeared to be the lab area. *Can you say go back in time thirty years?*

The end of the hall opened into a waiting room with a waist-high counter to the right that served as the reception desk. Chairs that looked like hand-me-downs from the hospital business office were pushed up against the other walls.

All talking stopped as he came into view. Three pairs of eyes fixed on him as he said, "Hello. I'm Dr. Jenkins, I hope you're expecting me."

Suddenly each woman started speaking. Finally, the middle-aged one with the red spiky hair waved a hand and the other two stopped. "Hi, I'm Jean, the office manager. This is Robin." She indicated the young woman to her left, who appeared to be fresh out of college and was smiling at him as if he were a candy bar. "She's one of the nurses. And this..." she pointed to the middle-aged woman sitting at the desk "...is Doris. She handles Reception. We heard you were coming and we're glad to have you."

"Thanks. I'm glad to be here. So we handle everything with one nurse?"

"Well, no. I don't know where China is but she should be here in a minute. It isn't like her to be late."

"Hey, someone give me a hand," a voice that was vaguely familiar called from the door through which he'd just entered. "You wouldn't believe the idiot in front of me at Dolly's," the disembodied voice said, dripping aggravation.

Down the hall came the woman who had been at the donut shop. Her attention was focused on maneuvering her way in the narrow space and she seemed to be struggling to keep several bakery bags and the purse that was slipping off her shoulder in place. Her chin-length, straight brown hair swung as she walked. She had a petite frame that made her almost seem fairy-like, especially dressed in hot pink scrubs.

The voice grew closer. "He took up two parking spaces. Asked Roger questions. Everyone in town knows not to ask Roger—" She came to an abrupt halt and her cocoa-colored eyes grew wide. "You!"

"Yes, I would be the idiot," Payton said in a voice that held a hint of humor.

There were soft chuckles from the other women.

"Wh…What are you doing here?"

"I'm Dr. Jenkins. The new doctor."

Eyes the same shade as the deepest part of the ocean twinkled at China.

Jean stepped forward. "I see you two have already met. Let me help with those."

China handed her the sack of donuts and the paper tray with four coffees. "I said I'd bring donuts," she murmured, unable to take her eyes off the doctor. How had she missed that shiny car in the parking lot? Because he'd made her late and she hadn't been paying attention.

"I can see," he said crisply. He looked at the coffee Jean

held. "It looks like it was a good thing I stopped and got my own. You hadn't counted on me."

China's face heated. No, she hadn't. Why did he have to sound so gracious about it? To make her feel more guilty? The door behind him buzzed, preventing her from apologizing. She had never been so happy to see a patient.

"Dr. Jenkins, let me show you the office," Jean said. "Robin will put the patient in exam one. When you're ready we can get started for the day."

The doctor gave China an unwavering look for a second before he followed Jean down the hall.

With relief, China sank into a chair next to Doris.

"Auspicious way to start the day," Doris quipped.

"Only you could use a big word to sum up total and complete embarrassment."

"Aw, honey. Such is life. Go do your job and all will be well."

The buzzer announced another patient. China opened the bottom cabinet and stored her purse. "I guess I'd better get busy before I look worse. Donuts and coffee will have to wait."

After Doris had taken the information from the mom of an eight-year-old boy, China led them to examine room two. There she took the child's vitals and noted the mom's recitation of his symptoms.

"The doctor will be in to see you in a few minutes," she said, before stepping out into the hall and placing the chart in a tray beside the door. As she turned to go to the front, she ran smack into a wall of male chest. A large hand cupped her shoulder to steady her.

"Are you going to be running into me all day?" a voice asked from above her head.

China stepped away and looked up at the insufferable doctor. "No. I'm sorry. I didn't mean to." China pulled the chart from the tray and handed it to him. "Your patient is waiting."

His low chuckle followed her down the hall. She shook her head. Obviously making good first impressions wasn't her thing.

China waited as Dr. Jenkins examined the boy and told the mom, "I'm going to have the nurse do a strep test and see what we've got. I'll be back in after we know for sure." He smiled reassuringly.

She followed him out of the room.

"It's China, isn't it?" he asked.

She nodded.

"Exam two needs a strep test. Where do I find those?"

"I'll take care of it."

China moved by him, taking special care not to make contact. She went into the lab and he followed. "They're right here." She opened the cabinet. "I'm, uh, sorry about calling you an idiot."

He shrugged his shoulder. "It's okay. Sometimes I am."

Now he was being charming. She hadn't expected that.

"Thanks. I'll get this done." China held up the pre-prepared swab with its plastic cap. "I'll let you know the results right away."

Doris came down the hall. "China, your mom's on the phone."

She wished she could make it clear to her mom not to call her during work hours. "Please tell her I will call her back."

"I'll take care of the test if you need to get that," Dr. Jenkins offered.

"No, I'll do it."

China waited for the doctor to come out of the exam room where Robin had placed another patient. When he stepped out she said quietly, "The boy has strep."

"Thanks for letting me know."

The rest of the morning passed in much the same way. At lunchtime China and Doris took their meals brought from home outside to the table. Robin and Jean would eat later.

"So how is Dr. Jenkins working out?" Doris asked.

"He seems to have a solid medical background, is great with the patients and thorough."

"Well, that was certainly a clinical evaluation," Doris remarked.

"I guess it was but I've not seen him do anything past strep and stomachache."

"Jean said Administration at the hospital told her he's from Chicago."

"Why would he want to come down here and work?" China picked up her drink and took a sip.

When Robin joined them China gathered her leftover microwavable lunch. She had to be on duty while Robin ate.

Jean called from the door, "China, Dr. Jenkins needs you in exam two. We have a boy with an open wound."

"On my way," she responded. "This may be where I get to see what he can do," China remarked to Doris as she hurried away.

China entered the exam room to find Dr. Jenkins with a lanky boy of about eleven years old sitting on the table and a mom perched on a chair with a troubled expression on her face.

"China, I'm going to need saline, a pan and a suture kit," he said, without looking up from his patient.

"Yes, sir. Right away."

He glanced up and gave her a quizzical look. A sharp tightness shot through her chest honed from childhood. What had she said wrong?

China left to gather the supplies. Returning, she found that Dr. Jenkins had turned the boy around so that he could place the pan on the pull-out footrest. There he would be able to pour the saline over the wound so it would run into the pan. China set the supplies on a small metal surgical stand that was stored in one corner then pulled it out to within easy reach of the doctor.

She opened the bottle of saline and handed it to him. He began to pour the liquid over the wound. When the boy winced Dr. Jenkins said, "I'm not from around here so tell me about this skimboarding you were doing."

The kid relaxed noticeably.

"It's done with a thin oval board. You throw it down and jump on it and ride it along the surf coming in on the beach."

"That sounds like fun. Are you any good?"

By this time Dr. Jenkins was preparing the local anesthesia to deaden the wound and the boy was taking no notice. The doctor had skills.

"Pretty good."

China had never learned to do anything like skimboarding, surfing or the usual water sports common for someone who lived near the water. Her father had become more controlling after her brother had left home at sixteen when given the ultimatum to straighten up or get out. China had learned early in life to do as she was told or she too might not have a place to live.

After her brother had left her father hadn't wanted China or her sister hanging out with the crowd down at the beach or doing much that wasn't under his watchful eye. Her mom, devastated by losing one child, had left most of the parenting to China's father. He'd had to know where they were at all times. "Might get into trouble. Too many drugs and alcohol. That's where your brother got

into trouble," he'd say. China soon found that it was easier to just go along with what her father had wanted, to do
whatever had kept the peace.

For Kelsey it had been much harder. As soon as she'd
finished high school she'd been out of the house. Sadly,
China didn't hear from her outside an occasional card or
phone call. She missed Kelsey and wished they had a better relationship. Kelsey's hadn't spoken to their parents in
years, which meant that her parents, especially her mom,
clung to China.

"Do any tricks?" Dr. Jenkins asked, drawing China's
attention back to what was happening in the room.

"I can turn around," the boy told Dr. Jenkins proudly.

"Wow. Do you think I'm too old to learn?" The doctor placed the needle at the edge of the boy's laceration.

"Naw, heck anyone can do it," the boy said, squaring
his shoulders in pride.

"You think you could teach me?" Dr. Jenkins made the
first stitch and the boy didn't even flinch.

"Sure."

"What do I need to know or buy?"

"It's no big deal. All you need is a board. You can get
those anywhere around here."

"Do I need a special size?"

Was he really going to try skimboarding? That was
for kids.

With a grin the boy said, "As far as I know, they only
come in one size."

"Any certain weight I need to get?"

The boy gave him a perplexed look. "Not that I know
of."

Dr. Jenkins tied off the last of the nine neat stitches he
had placed in the boy's leg.

China had to give him kudos for a quick, perfect suturing job and keeping the patient calm. He had a wonderful way with the boy. She'd seen none do better. Actually, he was the best she'd seen.

Dr. Jenkins pushed the stool back and stood. "Would you teach me?"

He sounded serious.

"Sure, why not?"

"Great. I'm going to let Nurse China bandage you up. I want you to come in one week from now to have the stitches out. Then we'll make a date for you to show me how to skimboard."

"Okay," the boy said, with a huge grin.

He spoke to the mom. "Just see that it remains dry and clean. No swimming or skimboarding until the stitches are removed."

China began opening the sterile bandage package.

From behind her Dr. Jenkins said, "Let's not use that one. It needs a four-by-four."

That tightness in her chest was back. Was this doctor going to be hard to please? "I'll get one right away." She left and returned with the required gauze.

Dr. Jenkins stuck out his hand. The boy hesitated a moment and then took it. The doctor smiled. "See you next week. I'm going to hunt for a board today. I'm already looking forward to the lesson."

Who was this guy? He sounded like he'd moved here for the recreation instead of a job. He had an excellent bedside manner but would she be able to work with him?

Leaving the clinic for the day, China still had grocery shopping to contend with before she could go home. She hated it, hated it. The word wasn't too strong. She made a point to be in and out as quick as possible. Some people didn't like to clean bathrooms but shopping for food was her issue.

She maneuvered the buggy with the knocking wheels at a brisk pace through the aisles, snatching what she needed from the shelves. She tended to buy the same things so she didn't worry about studying the prices or nutritional value. It had been a long day, starting with the trip to the donut shop, and she just wanted to go home, maybe do some gardening.

With everything on her list except the trail mix she favored, she pushed the buggy through the produce department. She reached out to pick up the plastic bag of nuts, chocolate candy and oats.

"So, not after donuts this time, I see."

She looked up to find Dr. Jenkins grinning at her. She wanted to groan. Was he going to be around every corner she turned?

He moved his nearly full cart along beside hers. "I guess food is our common denominator."

"I don't think it's so surprising that we meet here since we've only shopped at the two busiest places in town."

"Still testy over this morning? Are you prickly to everyone when shopping for food or is it just me?"

His grin fed her annoyance. "Hey, I'm not prickly." She pushed her cart forward. He followed. "I just don't enjoy grocery shopping."

"You know, if I was a psychiatrist I might find some hidden meaning in that statement."

She was afraid he just might. The job of shopping and cooking had fallen on her at far too young an age. She hadn't complained. If she'd wanted to eat then she'd needed to fix it. Now every time she entered the grocery store it brought back unhappy memories. That's why she made a point to do most of her buying once a month. She picked up the small items she might need at a convenience store at other times.

China winced when he peered over into her basket, "Not much of a cook, are you?"

She glanced at all the prepared food piled there. "No. In fact, I hate it."

"I love to cook. Our cook, Ruth, taught me all I know. At least now that I've moved here I'll have time to enjoy cooking a meal."

Our cook. They'd certainly come from two different worlds. She'd been the family cook. If you could call theirs a family.

More from intimidation than need, China picked up a few apples and put them in a small clear bag. She tied it off and placed them in her buggy. Payton had managed to make her feel at fault twice in the same day. Once over calling him an idiot and now over her eating habits.

"At least *they* look like a healthy choice." He nodded toward the fruit in her buggy.

Obviously she didn't meet the grade with his man. "So do your doctoring skills extend to reviewing everyone's grocery cart?" she asked flippantly.

He chuckled. "No, but I do believe in eating right and encouraging others to do so also."

"Well, it must be working. You are so slim and trim."

He blanched then said, "I'll let you finish your shopping. See you tomorrow."

China watched him walked away. They hadn't gotten off to the best of starts. Maybe she wasn't giving him the chance he deserved. She looked down at the items in her cart. He hadn't been wrong about her meal choices at all.

Payton opened the door to his house, which was built in the old Florida architectural style with wide verandas and seemingly never-ending white stairs up to the front door and another along the side to the kitchen. The property was located along West Beach Road well outside of town. He'd specifically asked the realtor for something private, well away from the summer crowds, with large windows. The woman had done her job well.

The master bedroom faced east, giving him a bright morning wake-up call. The house was well worth the amount of money he'd invested in it. Payton had hired a decorator long distance to furnish it. He'd wanted it livable when he arrived but it still lacked the personal touch.

He sighed. His parents didn't understand his need to leave Chicago. In fact, his father was so disappointed that he could hardly speak to him. He no longer met his parents' expectations. Having lymphoma had made him re-examine his life. His new goal was to find out what he wanted. His parents still held out hope he would change his mind and come home. He was just sorry that his actions had put a wedge between them. He'd changed, and they couldn't deal with it.

The house was huge and Payton had no one to share it with, but that suited him fine. Janice wouldn't have enjoyed it here anyway. Too hot, too many bugs and *too* far from social engagements. She'd complained he wasn't the man she'd fallen in love with. Did she think people who feared they might die didn't change? The second she'd found an opening she'd been gone.

Pushing the side door open, he placed the first load of bags on the counter then he headed out for more. Ten minutes later and proud he was no longer puffing after walking up stairs like he once had, Payton had all the food in the kitchen. He hadn't totally regained his strength but it was quickly returning. China had reminded him that he hadn't completely found the robust man he'd once been yet. Some swimming and sailing would solve that issue.

Today had been the first time he'd worked a full eight

hours in months. He'd been the one in med school who everyone had envied for his ability to work on little sleep. Not anymore, though, and especially not tonight. Good dinner, short swim then off to bed was his plan.

After putting the groceries away, Payton pulled out a skillet. He'd prepared a simple stir-fry, planning to eat outside to enjoy the weather. Unlocking the door to one of the many porches, he picked up his plate and drink then stepped out. He sank into a wicker chair with a comfortable-looking pillow. With a sigh, he propped his feet up on the small table in front of him, which matched the chair.

The cell phone resting against his thigh in his hip pocket vibrated. It would be his mom. She'd already called a number of times during the day and he'd been too busy to answer. Because she was a mom she worried. The old saying that you were always your mom's baby, no matter how old you got, was no truer than when you were sick. His mom had more than jumped into caretaker mode when he'd required help. Now he needed her to let go, for his sake as well as hers. Still, he couldn't bring himself to tell her to back off. That was one of a number of reasons he'd wanted to leave Chicago.

Some time later, his meal finished, he pulled his phone from his pocket and pushed the speed-dial number assigned to his mom. His chest contracted at the sound of relief in her voice when he said, "Hi, Mom."

"Honey, it's so good to hear from you. How're you doing?"

Payton told her about his day, the house and the town. He left out his two meetings with China.

"Well, at least it sounds like a nice place."

Payton watched as the sun became a half circle on the horizon. "It is. I'll call you in a few days."

"Okay." The wispy tone in her voice said she was still

holding out hope that Payton would return to Chicago. That wouldn't happen. All he wanted right now was to regain all his strength and make the most of life. He'd start by calling the marina and seeing if his sailboat had arrived. On his first day off he would be on it. It had been far too long.

Gathering his plate and glass, he took them inside. He'd call around to see where he might go parasailing. He hadn't done that since he was a kid. It would be fun to try again. He'd be looking for a skimboard tomorrow.

He hadn't missed the surprised then disapproving look on China's face when he'd been asking the boy about learning to skimboard. It would be the first of many new things he planned to experience.

The corner of his mouth lifted. China had made his first day at work in Golden Shores memorable.

The next morning Payton rose early to take a run on the beach. The distance wasn't what he could have done months ago but he was pleased with his effort. He felt invigorated and ready to face the day. His mom had admonished him not to overdo it but Payton was determined to get back to peak health as soon as possible and put having cancer behind him.

As he came down the hall of the clinic an hour and half later he heard the women talking but there was also a deep voice mixed among them. Payton placed his coffee and sack lunch in the office and walked to the front.

Jean and Doris were sitting behind the desk. Standing beside China in front of them was a tall, lanky man dressed in blue scrubs.

"Good morning, Dr. Jenkins," Jean said.

"Please, make it Payton." He looked at everyone.

"Payton it is," Jean said with a smile. "This is Luke."

She indicated the guy beside China. "He's one of the nurses that rotates in when either China or Robin have a day off."

Luke extended his hand and Payton took it. "Nice to meet you."

"You too," Luke said. "We're glad to have you around here."

The front door opened and a patient entered, ending their conversation. Over the next few hours Payton saw a steady stream of people, the highlights of which were a stomachache, severe sunburn and a twisted ankle. He loved it. This was nothing like the high-pressure, impersonal work he was used to. This was the kind of medical-care work he wanted to do. At least when a patient returned to see him he would recognize a face, maybe remember a name. Everything his parents couldn't understand. He no longer wanted to be one of *the* doctors in Chicago.

It was late afternoon when China handed him a chart. "The patient is complaining of vomiting, running a low-grade fever and weight gain."

Payton's chest constricted. It sounded so much like his symptoms. The ones he'd put off addressing, along with the swelling in his neck, until it had been almost too late. Deep in his gut he'd known it was cancer, but fear hadn't let him admit it. That was behind him now. He had a new lease on life, and he planned to make the most of it.

"Dr. Jenkins? Are you okay?" Concern underscored her words.

China's hand resting on his arm brought him back to reality. "I thought we agreed it was Payton."

She looked at him far too closely. Could she read his apprehension?

He moved his arm and her fingers fell away. He'd had his fill of concern months ago. "I'm fine," he said, far too sharply. "What room is the patient in?"

China stepped back and her eyes flickered with a look of what struck him strangely as fear before she said in a businesslike tone, "Exam three."

Why would she be scared of him? He'd spoken more harshly than he should have but not enough to bring that type of look to her eyes.

Thankfully the patient had nothing more serious than an infection. Was he always going to overreact when someone came in with the same symptoms he'd had? For a second there he'd slipped and the all-too-perceptive nurse China had noticed. That couldn't happen again.

CHAPTER TWO

Two DAYS LATER, China came in on the one to seven shift. Evening shifts were her favorite. Busy, with often interesting patients but it allowed her to get some gardening done in the morning. Her plants were where she put all her energy outside of nursing. It had been her way of escaping the unhappiness in her house when she'd been growing up and it had become her way of coping. She was a member of a couple of garden clubs in town and made the most of what she learned.

"Hi, there," she said to Robin and Doris as she approached the front desk.

"Hey," they chorused absently.

"So what's been going on today?" China asked, as she put her purse away.

Jean leaned toward her. "Nothing special. Robin's been mooning over Payton. She thinks all doctors are good looking, especially if they drive a nice car."

China sputtered in an effort to contain her humor. Evaluating a man's looks wasn't China's usual thing and particularly if it was based on a car, but she had to admit Payton was attractive beyond the average male. Something about him intrigued her. She'd dated but had never let a guy get really close. When a guy started making demands she backed off. She'd had enough of that in her life. Could a man ever understand her need to be a partner, feel secure? It certainly wouldn't be someone like the sports-car-driving, silver-tongued, charismatic Dr. Jenkins. Her mother had warned her about becoming involved with men like her father. More than once her mother had said she wished for her daughters an easier life than the one they would have with a man like their father.

Robin's shoulders squared and she gave Jean her indignant look. "That might be so, but it doesn't change the obvious. He's got the hottest car in town."

The sound of a throat clearing came from behind them. "I'm not sure that's a compliment as it sounds like I have a four-wheel personality," Payton said from the doorway of his office, before he stepped into it.

Robin and Doris giggled.

"We really do need to quit talking about him. He seems to always catch us," Doris hissed.

China had learned her lesson way before now.

Payton strolled up to the desk. "Robin, how would you like to go for a ride some time since you seem to like my car better than me? I'll even let you drive."

The young woman's face lit up. "Really? You mean that?"

"Sure."

"If anyone else wants to come along…" he looked at Doris and then China "…you're welcome too."

Robin said with a huge grin, "You have a date. I'm off now but will be back at seven when you close up here."

China and Doris laughed as Robin almost skipped down the hallway with pleasure.

"I wish I could make all the women I know happy that easily," Payton said, as he picked up a chart.

Was he talking about a girlfriend? It didn't matter. It wasn't her business.

At present there was only one patient at the clinic, a pre-teen with a possible broken arm. As China walked down the hall to check on the boy, the low rumble of male voices caught her attention. Larry Kiser, the doctor Payton was relieving for the day, was in the office with him. Why was she able to distinguish Payton's voice so clearly from Larry's, which she knew much better?

She entered the exam room and spoke to the mom, reassuring her. As she exited Payton stepped out of the office.

"I understand that the patient needs to go to the E.R. for a cast," he said.

"Yes. I'll take care of the paperwork right away and let the E.R. know they're on their way."

"Thank you, China."

"You're welcome, sir."

"You don't have to speak to me like I'm a drill sergeant. Yes, is fine."

"I was taught to say 'Yes, sir' and 'No, sir.' My parents told me it was a sign of respect."

He nodded. "I appreciate that. But it makes me sound old and rigid."

"I'm sorry. It's sort of ingrained in me. I'll make an effort not to, but I can't promise it won't slip out."

"Where I come from, 'Yes' suffices."

Maybe the reason he rubbed her up the wrong way was because they were from such different parts of the country. "I'll try," she said, heading down the hall and mumbling, "sir."

"I heard that."

She grinned. There was something about Payton that brought out the devil in her, as her father would have said. She so rarely let that happen but it felt good when she did.

Robin and Doris left for the day, with Robin once again promising she'd be back at closing time. Payton pulled his keys out of his pocket and jingled them. "They're here, waiting for you."

The patient flow increased then eased around dinnertime, which gave China a chance to catch up on some charting and clean out a supply cabinet that sorely needed it. At five Jean had to run out for a few minutes on an errand. As China worked she could hear the soft rumble of Payton's voice as he dictated in the office.

She was standing on a small metal stool on tiptoe, stretching to reach a box of alcohol wipes that had been pushed to the back of the shelf, when Payton said, "China, do you—?"

China jerked back, her foot slipping off the stool, and she fell backwards. Strong arms caught her around the waist and set her safely on her feet.

Shaking, she quickly moved out of his hold. "You scared me."

"I didn't mean to. You aren't hurt, are you?"

"No, I'm fine," she muttered.

"Good."

He sounded indifferent and she was still recovering from his touch. "Is there something you need?"

"Wanted to know if there's more printer paper somewhere."

"Yes. Jean keeps it stored in her office. I'll get it."

"Just tell me where it is and I can find it."

"I don't mind." China headed into Jean's office.

"Do you always have to be the one who helps?" His voice had a tone of exasperation. "I've noticed you're the first to say you'll do it."

She turned and placed her hands on her hips. He really was far too critical. "You gained all that knowledge from just knowing me a few days?"

"Yes. It's okay to let people manage for themselves."

"I do. But it is also nice to help when people need it. And while we're at it, do you feel the need to tell everyone how to live or am I just special?"

He raised a brow, which gave him a perplexed look. "What're you talking about?"

"I'm talking about you complaining about my eating habits, my speech and now my behavior. Is that something that people from the North feel compelled to do?"

"I'm a Midwesterner."

"Whatever you are, we're here in the *Deep South* and we consider it poor manners to criticize others, at least to their faces." She'd lived on an unraveling rope most of her life where disapproval was concerned and she didn't want to come to work every day thinking it would be there also. She turned and stalked into Jean's office. With a clap of the cabinet door closing, she returned and thrust a ream of paper into his chest.

Payton gave her a bemused look that upped her anger a notch.

"Don't worry, I won't be doing another thing for you outside what's required as a nurse." Having no place to go, she hurried down the hall and out the back door into the humid evening air.

What was wrong with her? The man made her mad enough to punch something. Of all the nerve!

Payton wasn't sure what had just happened but he'd give China this—she had passion. He'd seen her aggravated at him at the donut shop, had recognized her being impressed with his skills with a patient, had seen her apologetic over her grocery cart contents but he'd never have guessed at the depth of passion that was bottled inside her.

He had just been teasing her when the conversation had started but she'd taken it and run. He'd hit a nerve somewhere and she'd exploded. That would be an understatement. He didn't think TNT came in smaller or more combustible packages. Did that translate into any other areas of her life? The bedroom perhaps?

Payton huffed. He'd gone far too long without a woman to be thinking like that. Janice had left him and then he'd been so sick. China didn't even like him. She'd more than made that clear.

He'd returned to his office when the door from the outside opened and closed. Seconds later the water ran in the small kitchen sink. After a while China passed his door, carrying a water can, and was headed for the front of the building. He'd noticed her the other day caring for the large, lush ferns on the front porch and the tropical plant in the waiting room. She even took care of the plants.

Being cared for was something he wanted nothing of. He was determined not to make dependency a crutch in his life, become a burden. That was part of the reason he'd moved to Golden Shores.

He and China finished the rest of the evening in the professional politeness of "Yes, sir" and "No, sir" on China's part. Instead of the "sir" being an address of respect, it grated on Payton's nerves. It didn't have the ring of sincerity to it that it had once had.

He ushered his last patient out and found China talking and laughing with Jean and Robin.

"I'm ready when you are, Payton," Robin cooed.

Payton almost groaned. He may have done the wrong thing by asking Robin out on a ride. He'd have to make it clear this was a friendly trip. China excused herself, saying she had to clean the exam room before she left.

Fifteen minutes later China was coming out of the back door as he and Robin drove away. She called China's name and waved from his open convertible. He didn't miss China's weak smile and half-lifted hand in response.

For the next week they circled each other in polite indifference. It did help that they each had a different day off. On the day they both returned and were assigned the morning schedule together, China gave him a civil smile and went about her job with her usual competence.

Just about closing time Luke popped his head into Payton's office. "Hey, Payton, we're all going out to celebrate Jean's birthday tonight. She wants to do karaoke at Ricky's. Want to join us?"

If he had been in Chicago he wouldn't have been caught dead in a karaoke bar. His mom and father, his sister even, would've been worried that his picture might show up in the society column of the paper. Somehow at this point in his life karaoke sounded like the perfect form of entertainment. Plus he needed something more to do with his time. The people he worked with seemed like a good place to start cultivating friendships.

"Thanks. That sounds…interesting."

"Seven o'clock at Ricky's. You know where it is?"

"It that the place on Highway 13?"

"Yeah, that's it. See you there."

Payton and China had finished with their last patient and he was headed out the back door when he saw China stocking an exam room. "Aren't you coming to Ricky's?"

"What?" she said absently, as she continued to put bandages in a drawer.

"Aren't you going to Jean's party?"

"Nope."

What had happened to the "sir"? He'd been demoted. "You're going to miss Jean's birthday party?"

"I have a garden-club meeting."

"I don't believe you. Isn't there an age limit for those clubs? You look to be well under sixty-five."

"I'll have you know I'm a member of more than one garden club."

At least she was speaking to him. He hated to admit it but he'd missed their *discussions*. "You do surprise me. I guess Jean will get over you not being there."

A couple of hours later Payton pulled into the gravel parking lot of Ricky's. It was already filling up with vehicles. The red-brick building didn't look like much but he had the correct place. A large neon sign stood on the roof, flashing the name.

He pushed a button and raised the automatic roof on the car, got out and locked it. Maybe it hadn't been a good idea to buy such a conspicuous automobile. The car stood out among the pickup trucks and midsize sedans. A sports car fit his new found need to live on the edge, though.

Payton pushed through the glass door of the entrance and stepped into the dimly lit and noisy room. Not immediately seeing Luke or any of the women, he made his way to the bar. After ordering his first beer in months, he turned his back to the bar and watched the crowd. Just as he was getting ready to search further the door opened and China walked in with Luke at her side.

So she'd decided to come after all. His middle clenched. Were Luke and China dating? Why that would concern him he couldn't imagine. China had more than made it plain on at least one occasion that she wasn't awed by him on any level and barely tolerated him at work. Why he was giving it a thought he couldn't fathom. He had no interest in her and certainly no interest in being rejected again. Even if he let himself become seriously involved with a woman… He didn't think he'd ever let that happen.

Those that stuck with you through thick and thin didn't come along often.

Despite his conflicting thoughts, China held his attention. This was the first time he'd seen her in anything but scrubs. She wore a simple blue sundress that made her look more like a waif than a siren. But somehow it fit her. Her shoulders were bare and her hair brushed the tops of them. Luke said something close to her ear. The smile she gave him was a little lackluster. Luke directed her toward the bar.

Payton stepped over to meet them. China's eyes darted from him to the crowded tables to the bar and back. Hadn't she been here before? Luke acknowledged him with a smile and a nod. China gave him a thin-lipped smile and looked away.

A waving arm drew their attention to a table near the front of the stage. Payton made out Jean's red hair. Next to her sat Doris and Robin. Luke led the way, making a passage for China. Payton followed behind. He couldn't help but notice the gentle sway of the fabric over her high rounded behind. She had nice curves that the scrubs had kept hidden.

Payton tore his thoughts away from China and concentrated on making his way to the table. Doris, Jean and Robin had large smiles of welcome on their faces as they reached them. He shouted, "Hello," over the din of music and melee and took the last available chair, which put him between Robin and China. Robin scooted closer.

Jean leaned over the table and spoke to China. "Thanks for coming. I didn't think you would. I know how you feel about these places."

Payton looked at China. She had a smile on her face but it didn't reach her eyes. Why didn't she usually come with them?

"Yeah, I was real surprised when she called me for a ride," Luke announced proudly, looping his arm across the back of China's chair. His possessive action made Payton tense.

The waitress came by and took their orders. Payton noticed that China ordered a cola, not alcohol.

He leaned in her direction to be heard. A sweet scent that suited her tickled his nostrils. Something floral. "You've never been here before?"

She turned toward him, which brought her lips within kissing distance. Her eyes grew wide and she stared at him. "No."

"Hey, who's going first?" Luke asked. His hand touched China's shoulder and she sat forward.

"First?" Payton asked.

"Yeah, to sing." Jean grinned.

"I'll do it if you'll sing with me," Robin said, looking at Luke.

"Let's go do it," he agreed, grabbing Robin's hand.

Minutes later they were on stage, crooning to a 1960s song from the karaoke machine.

Payton couldn't resist smiling at the horrible theatrics. He glanced at China. She had relaxed and eagerly clapped when they were finished. He wasn't sure if it was to be supportive or from relief that they had finished.

Luke and Robin returned to the table to a round of applause. As the night progressed others took their turn on stage. Payton found he was glad he'd come. This was as foreign to him as a visit to the moon would be, and he loved it. There was a freedom to laughing and enjoying himself without worrying about others' expectations. Close to eleven, Payton decided it was time to call it an evening and told everyone at the table.

"Oh, no, you don't. You haven't sung yet," Jean said.

"Yeah, everyone has to sing," Luke added.

"Come on," Robin joined in.

"I don't think…" Payton looked around the table. They all gave him earnest looks not to back down.

"We've all taken our turns at embarrassing ourselves, so you have to also," Doris said, with all the authority of a judge.

"Last call for karaoke," a man on stage said into the microphone.

Jean looked at China then back at him. "I guess that means it will be a duet. China, you haven't sung yet either."

Payton turned to China. She went pale and shook her head.

"Hey, we have a duet here," Doris called, raising her hand and pointing to Payton and China.

They shook their heads in unison. The man with the microphone said, "It looks like they could use some encouragement so let's give them a hand."

China's chin went to her chest and her shoulders slumped. Payton didn't even have to wonder if she was embarrassed. The crowd went into wild clapping, hooting and slapping the table. Payton leaned over and said to China, "I don't think we have a choice."

He stood and offered his hand. At least this would be one more experience he'd never had.

China looked at Payton's outstretched hand. Her heart drummed against her chest wall and her palms became damp. The crowd was still loud with its cheerleading. She hadn't sung in public since she'd been in the middle-school church choir. This was not the place she wanted to start again, and Payton was certainly *not* the person she wanted to share the moment with.

She arched her neck to look at him. His smile was

reassuring. "Come on, let's get this over with." He closed and opened his hand.

China placed hers in his and his large, strong fingers curled around hers. He gave a gentle tug. The crowd had died down some, but when she stood the noise level rose again. Payton led her to the stage, not releasing his grip. She gained confidence from the simple gesture. They'd hardly spoken other than about patient care, and now they had to do something as personal as singing together.

A spotlight circled until it came to rest on them. "I don't want to do this." Payton had to bend to hear her. She could only imagine the intimate picture they must be portraying. Panic crept through her.

"Come on, you look like you're going to a funeral. It can't be that bad." He grinned at her.

Payton looked comfortable with the situation. He probably frequented nightclubs regularly and did this sort of thing often. She was completely out of her element. She didn't go to clubs and certainly didn't make a spectacle of herself, singing karaoke. He acted as if this could be fun. Humiliating yourself wasn't fun.

Everyone in town would know about this by morning. Her parents would be horrified she'd even stepped foot in this place. They would be upset when they found out. This had been one of Chad's hangouts. One of those places she'd been forbidden to go after he'd left.

Some of her friends had used fake IDs during high school to get in. In college she'd been invited on weekends but she'd always made an excuse about why she couldn't. The only reason that she'd come tonight had been because she'd let Payton dare her into it. Now the worst was happening. She'd disappoint her parents after working so hard not to add to their pain.

The first strain of an old love ballad began. Could it be any worse? "My Endless Love."

She groaned loudly enough that Payton glanced at her. He no longer had a sappy grin on his face. In fact, he looked a little green. With rising satisfaction, she grinned. This might turn out to be fun after all.

The words to the song began to scroll on the monitor. Payton's tenor voice sang smoothly. "'They tell me…'"

He'd surprised her again. The man could carry a tune. She picked up the next line and he took the other. Soon China forgot that she was in front of a group, singing with a man she wasn't sure she even liked. She had became so caught up in the sound of Payton's beautiful voice. They harmonized together on the chorus.

On the second stanza, Payton grinned at her when it was her turn to sing. She slipped on the first word but pulled herself together and gave it her best effort. The noise in the room gradually ceased as they finished with a long drawn-out note. The crowd went wild. China glanced at Payton. A smile of pleasure brightened his face. She'd not seen that look in his eyes before.

Payton wrapped an arm around her waist and pulled her against his hard body. She circled his waist with a hand. Briefly she noted she could feel his ribs.

"I think they liked us," he said near her ear. "We should bow."

She nodded, overwhelmed by being so close to him and how much she'd enjoyed singing with him. Who would have thought? He led her into a bow.

"Ladies and gentlemen, I do believe that was the best we have heard tonight," the emcee announced. "Are you two a couple?"

China shook her head vigorously and stepped out of Payton's hold.

"Well, you could've fooled us," the man said, as China headed off the stage.

She made her way back to the table, not looking left or right, to pick up her purse. She had every intention of walking straight out the door. China pulled up short when she realized Luke was no longer sitting there. He was her ride home. Where was he?

China searched the area, horror making her heart beat faster. She needed to get out of here.

"You were great." Doris, Jean and Robin spoke in unison.

"Thanks. Where's Luke?" She looked from one woman to the other.

"He was on call. He had to go in," Robin said. "We're going over to the Hut and see what's going on there for a little while—want to come?" Robin asked.

China had no interest in going to another nightclub. "No. I think I've had enough excitement."

"I can take you home," a voice she knew far too well said from behind her.

Did she have a choice? A taxi would take too long. Walk? Her house was too far and it was too late. "I would appreciate the ride."

"Okay, let's go."

Payton seemed as anxious to leave as she was. Picking up her purse and saying goodbye, she made her way to the door. Payton stayed close behind her.

China took a deep breath as she entered the night air. The wind gusted around her, a sure sign that it would rain before morning.

"I'm parked over here," Payton said.

He strode through the parking lot but not so fast that China couldn't easily keep up. At the end of the row they walked between two cars and were at his vehicle. With a soft beep the doors unlocked. Payton opened the passenger-side door for her.

"You know, you really don't have to hold the door for me."

"I'm just being a gentleman."

"Thank you, then." She slipped down into the low seat. "I may need more help getting out than in."

He chuckled softly. "I can do that too."

Payton closed the door and went around to get in behind the wheel. Starting the car, he pulled out of the parking space and asked, "Which way?"

"Back toward the clinic. I only live a mile or so away."

Payton's vehicle really was nice. She ran a hand over the smooth leather of the seat. China knew luxury cars. Rob had had one when he'd wheeled into town. He had been a big-time real-estate man from Los Angeles, looking for investment property. He'd come by the clinic and taken a liking to her.

Always a bit of an outsider, Rob made her feel wanted, had filled her head with promises of being the center of someone's world. Just as quickly as Rob had arrived, he'd disappeared, leaving China crushed. Lesson learned. She rubbed the seat again. Payton's car and hers were one more thing they didn't have in common. The feel of the leather reminded her not to pin her hopes on someone. The small-town life, white sands and blue waters and especially her wouldn't hold a man. She'd accepted what her life was and would be.

She and Payton rode in silence as if they were both glad to have a reprieve from the noise inside Ricky's. Leaning her head back, she closed her eyes.

"Hey, don't go to sleep on me. I'll have to take you to my house if you do."

Her eyes flipped open and she sat up straighter. "Make a right one block past the clinic."

"So I'm guessing you don't want to go home with me."

China wasn't going to comment on that statement. She wasn't up to their usual conversation. He made the turn she'd indicated. "Go three blocks and turn left and the house is the second on the right."

Payton smoothly maneuvered through the tree-lined streets and pulled into her drive.

China opened the car door. "Thanks for the ride."

"Hey, wait a minute. I'll help you—"

"I've got it. See you later."

She was out and gone before he could open his door. He watched in the illumination of the headlights as she bypassed the walk to the front entrance of the bungalow and continued toward the detached garage further down the drive. Her dress blew in the wind that was picking up. He caught a glimpse of trim thigh before she pushed the hem back into place. Reaching the stairs, she started to climb them.

So China lived in the apartment above the garage. Flowerpots lined the steps. She really loved plants and seemed to have a green thumb. Maybe he'd been a little harsh with his comment about garden clubs. The plant care he was familiar with was done by someone who showed up in a van and brought new plants to replace the brown ones. Neither his mom nor Janice would ever damage their manicures by messing in dirt.

China was nothing like the other women he knew. She was a dependable nurse, helpful beyond necessary, gardener, a darned good singer, and she had the prettiest brown eyes he'd ever seen. What more was there to discover about Little Miss I-can-hold-my-own-in-a-battle-of-wits?

Payton waited until the light flickered on inside the area above the garage before putting the car in reverse and backing slowly out of the drive.

China was the most interesting woman he'd met in a long time. Did he want to discover more?

CHAPTER THREE

NEAR LUNCHTIME, ON TUESDAY of the next week, Doris stuck her head inside Payton's office and said, "Hey, Jean needs to talk to everyone. It's a slow day, which doesn't happen often around here so we're going to eat and meet at the picnic table out back."

She headed down the hall without waiting for a response. That might have been the longest invitation he'd ever received to lunch and he came from a society family who made them a regular affair. Doris, he'd learned, was the mother hen of the group. Robin the precious child they all tolerated, Jean the leader who used a kitten-soft hand but everyone heeded, Luke the fun guy who popped in, and China... He smiled.

Monday morning she'd arrived at work with no comment on their duet on Friday night. He'd overheard the other women teasing her but she had not said a word to him that hadn't been professional in nature. He would have thought she'd softened toward him after their evening out, but not China.

Still, it was a nice day and he looked forward to taking his meal outside with the others. He was slowly feeling more a part of this close-knit group. There had been none of the same camaraderie at the large E.R. he'd left. The staff had come and gone with too much regularity. Golden

Shores was slowly turning into a place he could belong. To make life even better, he'd just received a much-awaited phone call that his boat had arrived. Sailing topped his agenda for his next day off.

Payton stepped out into the bright sunshine and breathed deeply. He felt better just by being in it. He couldn't remember a time when he'd ever done anything like have lunch with co-workers, other than grabbing something from the machine on the way through the snack room. He wanted to live differently and this certainly qualified. There would have been no "Let's go out back to eat" if he was still in Chicago.

"Hey, Payton, we saved you a spot." Jean shifted around on the cement bench, giving him a place to sit. Doris sat next to her and moving around the table was Luke and beside him China. As he maneuvered his leg under the table his knee hit China's leg. Her gaze jerked to his before she lowered her gaze and pulled her leg out of contact with his.

He glanced at her lunch. She had a sandwich and raw vegetables. At least she didn't have one of those nasty prepackaged microwave meals with all the preservatives. When she noticed his interest, she moved her meal more squarely in front of her but didn't meet his look. He couldn't help but grin. She was self-conscious.

"We've been asked to cover the medical tent at the concert Saturday night. I'm sorry that I couldn't give you more notice. I only do what the higher-ups ask. For your trouble you will all be awarded the next day off."

Everyone but him groaned.

"It's Sunday. That's our day off anyway," Luke said.

"I was hoping you wouldn't notice that." Jean smiled. "Our shift will be from eight until."

"Until?" Payton asked.

"Until it's over," everyone, including China, said in unison.

"Where's the venue?" Payton asked.

"On the beach near the state park. They put up a large stage and in comes the crowd," Luke offered between bites of sandwich.

"How do they charge and control the crowd?"

"Don't. This one is to encourage tourism around the Gulf area to help the economy after the tornado that came through last spring," Luke said.

Payton remembered it. He'd seen a little of the TV reporting when he'd been in the hospital, recovering from pneumonia.

"People are bused in from parking lots out of town. It's a big deal. And a lot of fun."

Jean held up a hand. "Now that Luke has given us an enthusiastic overview of the event we need to get down to the medical particulars. We should expect the usual. Too much to drink, falls, turned ankles, the occasional black eyes from hands being slung during dancing. I've already spoken to Larry. He and Robin will take the early shift."

She looked at Payton then China. "You two will have the late shift. You'll need to be at the tent no later than nine o'clock and stay to see that the tent is dismantled. That means bringing everything back here afterwards. Remember I said you get the next day off." She gave them a bright smile. "Doris and I will be splitting up to help with the paperwork. Let's plan for the worst and hope for the best."

China had always enjoyed working the concerts. She loved music and it was a great way to enjoy some of the best.

The artists were world class and they were giving of themselves to help others.

An hour before she'd been assigned to arrive she stepped off the hospital shuttle bus. She'd left her car parked behind the clinic. China headed for the area where the medical tent was located. The warm-up act was already on the stage and the noise level was rising. Crossing the section of the beach highway that had been closed, she made her way to the entrance gate and showed her badge. As she walked, she passed food venders, T-shirts sellers and trinket hawkers. The excitement and intensity in the atmosphere grew the closer she moved to the stage. The medical tent had been stationed on a concrete area with easy access to the road in case an ambulance was needed and just far enough away from the major activity that it was easy enough to talk without shouting too much.

Larry and Robin were seeing to a patient as she entered. To her surprise, Payton was already there. He wore a polo shirt that hung loosely from his broad shoulders across his chest and a pair of tailored khaki shorts that made her think of preppy men and tennis matches. This was no T-shirt with a slogan and slouchy pants kind of guy, the kind she tended to notice. If she had to pick a word for Payton's looks it would be classy and they had an appeal.

Her familiarity with guys like him was little to none. No wonder Payton seemed to rub her the wrong way so easily. She had no concept of his kind of guy, didn't know how to react to him. As long as he kept his criticism to himself, she found he had some positive qualities.

Payton was patiently putting a small bandage on the moving target of a two-year-old girl's finger. The mom was blissfully watching Payton, not her child. He seemed oblivious to the woman's admiration.

China had to admit it made an almost Norman Rockwell moment. Payton's dark head, leaning over the little girl's blonde curls, had her wondering if he'd ever thought about being a father. He was good with kids.

Had he ever gone skimboarding? The boy had returned to have his stitches removed but she'd been with another patient and didn't know if they had really made plans. Not wanting to step over the line into personal space, she'd not asked. It was unlike her to be standoffish but every time she and Payton moved beyond the professional—Jean's birthday was the biggest example—things got too personal. Too uncomfortable. Payton seemed to be from the same mold as her father. She wanted no part of that.

Anyway, he was just another co-worker, and tonight he was more so as they would be partners.

Larry and Robin were still seeing to a patient when Payton finished.

"You're certainly here early," China remarked.

"Yeah. I wanted to see what was going on. I've never been to a concert on the beach. There really is a crowd."

"Yes, there is. I never did things like this either."

"Why? You live right here."

"I was too busy doing other things."

Cooking, cleaning, washing clothes. It had needed to be done and she had been the one to do it. Her mom had been locked in her grief over not knowing where her brother was to the point she hadn't been able to function.

Payton glanced around the tent. "I haven't had a chance to look around. We're not busy now and Larry and Robin are here for another thirty minutes so how about you give me a tour?"

"You go on. They…" she nodded to the others "…may need help."

"Come on, China. Quit making excuses. I'm not going to bite."

She huffed. "I know that."

"So have mercy on the new guy and show me around."

Not wanting to cause a further scene, China nodded her agreement.

"Even though you're not on the clock yet, carry a radio in case we need you," Jean said, from where she sat at a small table with a laptop.

Payton took the radio she offered.

China headed out of the tent. Why did he always manage to goad her into doing something she wasn't sure she wanted to do?

She circled and weaved behind the back of the throng toward the ocean.

"Hey, wait up," Payton called. "A tour guide is supposed to stay with the person she's guiding."

"And the group is supposed to keep up." She headed down the middle of the beach.

"Where're we going?" he asked, catching up.

"This is the best way to see things otherwise we'll always be fighting the crowd."

They walked through the sand until they got about halfway to the stage and she stopped.

"This is part of the state park area." She swept her hand around. "I guess you've seen it when it is empty. That over there…" she pointed "…is the Beach Hut. The wildest place on the beach. They have mini-concerts and dancing all the time."

"Do you go often?"

Her head whirled and she glared at him. He was serious. "I do not."

"You've never been?"

She shook her head. That had been more Kelsey's scene. They were as different as daylight and darkness but Kelsey loved her dearly. Missed her daily. Wished they had the relationship that they had once had as girls.

His look was one of pure disbelief. "Not once? Didn't sneak in as a teen?"

"No." That had been Kelsey's specialty. Thank goodness she hadn't gotten caught. It would have killed her parents.

"Well, well." He pursed his lips and moved his chin up and down.

"Just what does that mean?"

"It means that I thought you might be a goody two-shoes and you have just confirmed it."

Compared to him, she probably was. He struck her as someone who went after a good time, and she was the one who found a peaceful evening at home exciting. Kelsey would like him. "Someone needed to be the good kid in my family."

She suddenly had all his attention. "Why is that?"

Heaven help her, she'd said too much. She didn't want to talk about the past now or even later with this man.

"Come on, I'll show you the stage area." China started moving again.

They walked further down the beach and far enough that the crowd swelled out. They began to have trouble moving around without running into someone. China stumbled when the smooth sand rolled under her foot. A hand grabbed her arm, steadying her. Payton's hand.

"Thanks," she mumbled. When they reached the barriers the security guard stopped them. They flashed their badges, and he smiled and walked away.

"This really is a major production. I had no idea how large it was," Payton said.

"And it's a really great thing these celebrities do for the

coast. They not only bring money in, they get us noticed in the headlines. We need to start back."

He nodded.

When they'd come up off the beach and had reached the area where the concessions were located, China sat on the low curb and begin taking off her tennis shoes. Payton followed suit and they emptied sand out of their shoes. Done, and standing again, Payton said, "Hey, let's grab a bite to eat before we go to work. I bet we won't have a chance later."

"You mean this type of food?" She waved her hand around at the tents and food trucks lining the way. "These menus rely heavily on frying, which might not meet the specifications of your discerning palate."

"My, do I sense some sarcasm in that question? Just so you know I can eat good, unhealthy food with the best of them on occasion, come on, I'll buy." He headed down the lane.

"I don't think so."

"You know you want some. It's just your type of food," Payton called back over his shoulder.

"Please don't imply that you know me so well."

He stopped and looked at her. "Oh, I would never make that mistake. Okay, if I can't convince you to eat with me then at least suggest which truck might be the best."

She pointed toward the bright orange moving-van-sized truck with slide-up sides. A large shrimp was painted over most of the passenger-side door and overlapped onto the hood.

"Sid's is the best."

"Then Sid's is the place. What do you recommend?"

She looked at him as if he had three heads. "No self-respecting Gulf coaster would have anything but shrimp, hush puppies and fries. Ours is the best in the world."

Payton stood amazed at how animated China became about eating at Sid's. This was obviously serious business to her. For once she wasn't uptight around him. He liked this China a lot, wished he saw more of her.

"Are you sure you don't want me to get you a basket?" Payton asked.

"I'm sure."

"Okay, but it sounds like your loss."

He stepped to the window but before he could place his order a man almost too large for the space he was standing in said in a booming voice, "Hey, my China doll. Come to have some of Sid's famous shrimp?"

"Not tonight, Sid."

"But you are my best customer," the man complained. His smile was so large Payton felt such there wasn't a single tooth in his head that wasn't showing.

"I know, but my…" she hesitated a second as if searching for the right word "…friend would like to have your shrimp basket."

So now China considered him her friend. He'd certainly moved up in the world.

"Shrimp basket coming up." Sid turned around.

"So I'm your friend now, uh?" Payton asked in a teasing tone.

"Only as long as you like the same kind of food as I do." She grinned at him for the first time ever where it really reached her eyes. He couldn't help but stare.

A flash of yellow caught his attention out of the corner of his eye. Flames filled the space in front of where Sid stood. A curse word ripped the air as the blaze grew. Sid backed away, at the same time dropping the metal frying basket. He held his hand and doubled over in agony. A guy in the truck with him rushed to the fryer with a fire extinguisher. After a couple of blasts from the container the flames died out. Steely-colored smoke billowed out the serving window. The smell of sodium bicarbonate filled the air.

"Sid!" China's shout of alarm added to the chaos.

"China." Payton caught her before she rushed inside the truck. "Run to the med tent and get us two bottles of saline and bandages."

She didn't argue or question, was gone before he could say another word.

Payton hurried to the end of the truck and entered the doorway left open for ventilation. As the air cleared he could make out Sid, holding his hand wrapped in his apron. He moaned with pain.

"Sid, I'm Dr. Jenkins. Let me have a look at that."

The man's face, which had been rosy minutes before, had taken on a pale pallor. Payton's lips tightened into a tight line. Burns like this hurt like the devil.

"Push that stool this way," Payton barked to the young guy pinned in the truck because Payton and Sid filled the space between him and the door. The young man did as directed.

"Sid, you need to sit. I don't need you to pass out on me."

The man took the seat, moaning softly, his face contorted in pain.

Payton glanced at the helper, gaining his attention. "Get some cool water, not cold. A lot. We need to get Sid's hand in it."

The guy did as Payton said without question, thankfully. The helper handed Payton a cooking pot filled with water.

"Okay Sid, I need to see your hand. Be careful when you take it out of the cloth. We don't want you to lose that skin covering your wound."

Carefully Sid unwrapped his hand from the apron.

Payton examined the red injured skin. There was no blister present. A second-degree burn at least. "I don't think this is going to require a trip to the hospital, but you were close."

They had just finished submerging the hand in water when China returned.

She entered and unceremoniously placed the supplies bundled in her hands on the counter. "I also brought some dry clothes."

He glanced at her. "Good girl." A look of surprise and then satisfaction flickered across her face. "We need to get the hand clean and dry. We'll have to work fast because it will hurt like hell when it is out of the water."

Payton sat on his haunches in front of Sid. China brushed Payton's shoulder with her thigh as she maneuvered around him in the tight space.

"How are you doing?" China put her hand tenderly on Sid's forehead, pushing the tuft of almost nonexistent hair back.

"I've been better," he said through clenched teeth. "This is the worst burn I've had in a long time."

"We'll have you fixed up in no time, and you'll be frying shrimp for me again," China assured him.

Payton watched the interaction with interest. China cared about this man. But, then, China cared about everyone. She tried to make things better for each person she met. His mom had shown that same type of compassion until he'd announced that he wanted to do something different with his life. Then she'd not been pleased.

"Okay." Payton brought their attention back to him. He nodded toward the young man with the stricken look on his face. "Sid, we're going to let your help step out of the truck before I get started."

China brushed past him again as she exited so the helper

could get by. When the man was gone, China returned, her thighs brushing his shoulder again. The space was unquestionably too tight.

"China, get a pan and fill it with soap and lukewarm water. We're going to have to get all the oil off. We'll do this once and do it well, so put plenty of soap in the water."

China went to the tiny sink and did as Payton asked. Bringing the pan back, she maneuvered around the other pan and placed the one she carried on the floor.

"Sid, I can't lie. This is going to hurt, bad. As soon as I'm done, back into the cool water it'll go," Payton said.

Sid nodded. Sweat covered his forehead.

"Okay, China, hold the soap pan up."

She put a knee on the floor and bent the other, picking the pan up she'd just prepared and holding it steady. Payton lifted Sid's hand out of the water and placed it in her pan. Sid hissed.

"Hang in there, Sid." Payton begin to scoop water over the angry wrinkled skin of Sid's hand until all the grease had been removed.

A long sound of discomfort came from Sid as the air hit the wound.

Payton placed the hand back in the cool water. China sat the pan down on the floor, splashing soapy water on one of his shoes. She stood and put a hand on Sid's beefy back, slowly moving it in a reassuring pattern over his shoulders.

"Sid, I'm sorry but we'll have to go at it again," Payton said. "I have to run saline over the area just to make sure it is clean. We can't have it get infected. When you're ready, let me know."

China picked up the soapy pan, went to the sink and emptied it. She returned with the pan and grabbed the two dry towels off the counter where she had left them. Going down on one knee, she placed the towels on her leg and held the pan in position to catch the saline.

Payton gave her a nod and a reassuring lift to his lips. She returned a thin-lipped smile. "This time we're going to dry it off and bandage it. Dry and clean is the ticket to no infection," Payton explained to Sid.

He nodded and lifted his hand out of the water. "It's easing some."

The look on his face was telling a different story. "I'll give you something for pain in a minute and then write you a prescription for something a little stronger to take if you need it." Again the man bowed his head.

Slowly Payton poured the saline over the hand, making sure it went between the fingers. He took a towel from her thigh. She was the most intuitive nurse he'd ever worked with, having everything prepared and within reach. He patted Sid's hand dry and examined for broken skin.

"Believe it or not, it looks good. The pain should ease and it should heal well."

The man had his mouth so tightly pursed that his lips were white.

China took the pan to the sink and left it there. She returned and placed a hand on Sid's shoulder again and squeezed. It was a soothing gesture, not over-the-top dramatic. Janice hadn't been capable of doing something as simple as that, just being there for him. China didn't even have to say anything to let Sid know she cared.

She handed Payton the roll of gauze and he begin wrapping Sid's hand, making sure he went between each finger. He finished by encasing the complete hand in gauze. With a grunt Payton stood and stretched. He'd been in a squatting position for too long.

"Can I still work? This is one of our biggest money events of the year."

"I don't think you need to be the fry cook but you could sit here and give orders." Payton offered him a smile. "But that hand must remain clean and dry."

"That's the best you can do, Doc?"

"Yeah, that's it. And I want you to stop by the clinic on Monday morning and let me have a look at your hand."

"You'd better do as the doctor orders," China said, giving the man a hug. She wasn't showing pity but practical concern.

China wasn't someone who ran from a storm but stood against it. He appreciated that about her. In fact, he was finding a number of things he liked about China.

"I promise," Sid said softly, giving her a one-handed hug back.

China gathered the leftover supplies. When she had them together she leaned over and kissed Sid on the forehead. "I'll check on you tomorrow."

Sid gave her a weak grin. "You don't have to do that."

"I will anyway."

Payton stepped out of the trailer and China followed. China stopped when they were a few feet from the truck. She had an earnest look in her eye when she said, "Thanks, Payton. I'm glad you were there when it happened. That man is important to me."

He shrugged his shoulder. "You're welcome. So how do you know Sid?"

"He was my father's best friend when I was a kid." She walked on as if she'd said all she was going to say. There was more behind that statement, he just didn't know what.

China and Payton were late arriving for their shift but it was for good reason. Sid's burn issue could have been far worse if Payton hadn't been on the scene to care for it so quickly and carefully. He'd been proactive and sure of himself. In an emergency he was just the type of person needed in a leadership position, someone you could depend on.

Her heart had soared at Payton's praise. They had been partners, each appreciating the other's abilities. He'd moved up in her estimation.

When they arrived at the medical tent there were three patients being seen and another two waiting. It was much like that for the next three hours until the concert wound down and the crowd made their way home. Even then Security brought a middle-aged woman who had slipped and twisted her ankle when trying to load a bus. It took another half an hour to stabilize the joint by wrapping it. Security saw that the woman and her husband got to their car.

She and Payton still had to pack medical supplies and break down the portable examination tables and chairs and return them to the clinic before they could go home.

"You ready?" she asked Payton thirty minutes later.

When he didn't immediately reply she glanced at him. She was worn out but even in the dim light his shoulders slumped and he was moving more slowly. He was exhausted.

"You okay?"

"Sure." Payton lifted a large plastic box into the back of the van. Minutes later, with everything packed, he closed the doors of the van. "I'll drive," Payton said.

China climbed into the passenger's side before he offered to help her. The extra time they'd spent with their last patient had allowed the traffic to lessen and they made it back to the clinic in good time, but it was still well past midnight. They unloaded and she put away the medical supplies while Payton stored the folding chairs and exam tables in a small storeroom near the back door.

She was more than ready to go home. They'd had a

busier night then she'd expected. They'd not even had a chance to grab something to eat or drink. Done, she walked to the back of the building to see if she could help Payton. It had been quiet for some time so she expected to find him waiting in the office. He wasn't there when she looked so she continued toward the back door.

Payton sat on the floor with his back against the door-jamb, as if he'd slid down the wall. She rushed to him, kneeling beside him. "What's wrong?" Instinctively she reached out to touch his forehead. He turned away, not allowing contact.

"Go away. I'll be all right," he growled.

"Did you fall?" China looked for any obvious bumps or bruises.

"No, I didn't fall. Go on home. I'll be right behind you." He still refused to meet her gaze.

"I'm not leaving you like this."

"I don't want your help," he hissed.

"You might not, but you're going to get it. I'm positive you need it."

"I don't need anyone fussing over me."

"I find you sitting on the floor, and you think I'm fussing over you?" she asked incredulously. "What kind of nurse would I be if I left you here?"

His eyes were diamond hard when he said, "Go away. I'll be fine in a minute."

"No. So what happened?"

"I'm just tired and hungry."

"It looks like more than that to me. I think I should get you to the E.R."

CHAPTER FOUR

PAYTON WISHED CHINA would just leave. He felt humiliated enough as it was. Why wasn't he surprised that the stubborn woman wouldn't do as he asked? "I am not going to the E.R. for a little dehydration." His voice held a touch of disgust. "I was dizzy, that's all."

"Dizzy?"

"Is that the new nursing practice? Repeating everything the doctor says?" What would it take to get her to leave? Could he make her mad enough that she'd just go?

She blinked. Climbing to her feet, she said, "I'll get you a sports drink out of the break room. Then I'm going to examine you."

"I'd appreciate it if you would leave me some pride," he mumbled as she left. He hated being weak. How had be managed to let this happen? Not being used to warmer weather and no food had taken its toll and here he was in a pool of mortification. He'd worked hard to put those days of illness behind him, had started over with a vengeance. Yeah, right. That was working well at this moment.

Less than a minute later China returned with the drink and a stethoscope circling her neck.

"I'll drink this and be able to drive home. It's late. You need to be in bed." He took a swallow of the liquid.

"I'm not leaving you until I know you can get home safely."

"Go home. Doctor's orders."

"Really? That's the best you've got?"

The woman had spunk. He took another swallow of the drink. The quicker his electrolytes stabilized the sooner he could gather his pride.

China placed her hand on his forehead. Her fingers were cool and dry. Somehow he felt more invigorated by her simple touch.

In complete nurse mode, she picked up his wrist and checked his pulse. How many times in the last year had that been checked? He'd been poked and prodded until he couldn't stand it anymore. He'd turned into a nasty patient but he'd been unable to stop himself. Fed up, angry with himself and life, he'd lashed out.

"It's a little fast but within range." She pulled the stethoscope from around her neck. "I'm going to need to listen to your heart." She started undoing the second button of his shirt.

"Why, China, I had no idea you cared. You've hidden it so well."

She fixed him with a look meant to quell him. Instead he enjoyed it. A sure sign he was starting to recover.

China removed another button then slipped the stethoscope under his shirt and listened. She was so close she could smell the salt from the ocean in her hair. One breast brushed his arm as she moved the stethoscope around on his chest. Oh, yes, he was undeniably feeling better.

The look of concentration on her face made him question if she'd heard something out of the ordinary. Done, she pulled the stethoscope away.

Her eyes widened slightly. She'd seen it. She was close enough that he heard her suck in a breath. Seconds later she released it and it warmed his neck. She'd seen the small blue tattoo on his chest. Now she knew what he'd never planned to tell.

"You've had radiation." She stated it in a matter-of-fact way. There was no pity, no sadness, just plain acceptance of fact.

"Yes."

"How long ago?"

"Months."

She leaned away from him but didn't stand. "Why didn't you drink more tonight? Say you needed to eat? You have to take better care of yourself. You should have said something. Asked for a minute to get something to drink."

He grabbed the door facing and pulled himself up. "You sound like my mom." China jumped up and reached an arm out to help him. He shook it off. "Are you about done with the lecture? We were swamped and you expected me to sit down and enjoy a meal. Give me more credit than that. I'm going home, China. You should too."

Payton placed a hand on the wall to steady himself and took another draw on the sports drink.

"You're not driving yourself home."

"How do you plan to stop me?"

"I'll call the police if I have to." She gave him a determined look that made him think she just might.

Too tired, too out of sorts and desperately wanting his bed, he nodded his agreement. "Okay. But you have to promise not to tell anyone about this or that I've been sick."

"Agreed. You wait here while I turn off the lights."

Payton did as he was told, no longer up to fighting with her. Soon she was back and they headed out the door. She offered to help him but he refused. It was bad enough she had to drive him home. He wasn't sure how he'd face her on Monday morning.

When China started toward her car he said, "No way am I going to fold into that tiny car. You drive mine."

She looked a little unsure for a minute then nodded. He dug out his keys and handed them to her.

As she pulled out of the parking lot she asked, "Where to?"

"West Beach Road. Five point three miles on the right. Three-story facing the ocean."

As he leaned his head back and closed his eyes he heard her low whistle. "Nice real estate."

Payton didn't know how long it took China to drive him home because he slept the entire way. It wasn't until he felt a gentle shake on his shoulder that he woke.

"I think you're home. Is this it?" China asked, looking out the front window.

"Yes." Payton reached for the handle and pushed the door open. "See you later."

"I'm coming up. With all those steps I want to make sure you don't fall."

Payton said a sharp word under his breath. "You're determined to emasculate me."

"I don't think that's possible. Your self-esteem and women's reactions to your good looks won't let that happen."

"So you think I'm handsome?"

"I'm not having this conversation at one a.m."

He stepped out of the car and started up the staircase. The thump of China's feet told him she was close behind. Guilt washed over him. She had to be every bit as tired as he was and she was babysitting him. He flipped the mat back and pulled the house key out from under it. Opening the door wide, he went in and flipped on a light. "Okay, now you have seen me home you can go. I'll get a ride in tomorrow and pick up my car."

"You plan to get a shower?"

"Why? You want to join me?"

She looked at him with a smirk. "No, but I don't want you to fall and have no one here with you."

"How do you know there is no one here?"

With satisfaction he watched her turn red. "I don't. I just assumed because you have never mentioned anyone…"

"China, there's no one here. You don't need to feel any obligation to stay. I'll be fine getting a shower. Go on home."

"I'll just wait."

After a huff of impatience he moved closer to her. "I want you to leave me alone."

"I will when I know you're safe."

He shifted so close that her breasts were only inches from his chest. She sucked in a breath and her eyes widened. "You can't intimidate me."

"I'd bet I can." Payton wrapped an arm around her waist and pulled her against him. His mouth caught the small sound of astonishment that escaped her lips before he covered them with his. Her lips were warm and full, wonderful. Her hand grabbed his shirt at his waist as if she needed to steady herself. After a few seconds she leaned toward him.

Payton let her go almost as quickly as he'd held her. He looked into her eyes. "I may be sick but I'm not dead. It has been a long time for me so don't come and check on me before you leave unless you plan to stay."

The next morning the sun was high enough in the sky it was becoming warm as China drove Payton's car toward his house. Had she gone crazy? Unable to stand not checking on him, she tamped down her nervousness. She'd made up her mind it was necessary and started driving.

He'd actually kissed her the night before. Why? Had she pushed him too far? Had he been trying to scare her so she would leave him alone? If that was the answer it had worked. He was walking down the hall when she tore out the back door. She'd run like the proverbial rabbit.

She had worried all night that something might happen to him and now she'd made a fool out of herself by checking on him. In order to stall, she'd stopped to buy donuts. Before leaving home, she'd pulled some of her homemade chicken soup out of the freezer. If he wasn't into the questionable nutrition of donuts, maybe he'd appreciate the soup for lunch.

The sports car's tires crunched against the shell drive as she pulled in and stopped beside the stairs. Turning the vehicle off, she rested her forehead on the steering wheel in an effort to gather her wits. What was she going to say? *I was worried about you.* He wouldn't like that. He'd made that clear. Maybe *I just thought you might like breakfast. I brought you your car back. I loved your kiss, and I came out for more.* No, she *wouldn't* say that.

She raised her head, took a fortifying breath and opened the car door. As she placed a foot on the drive, a deep voice said in a sarcastic tone, "I was beginning to wonder if you were ever getting out."

China jumped. Her heart racing, her hand went to her chest before her gaze jerked upward, "Oh, you scared me."

"What're you doing here?"

He wasn't happy to see her. Okay, what was her plan? "I thought I may as well drive out and return your car. You can just take me home."

"Is that nurse-speak for 'I'm here to check on you'?"

"Yes. No. Maybe."

"You couldn't help yourself, could you? You have to make sure everyone is all right, taken care of."

China started up the stairs again. "Here I was trying to be nice and considerate. I brought your precious car back in one piece and brought you some donuts, plus chicken soup."

"Chicken soup? So you do think I'm an invalid. I don't need your pity, China."

She reached the porch where he stood glaring down at her. He was dressed in a pair of sport shorts and a T-shirt that had seen better days. Despite that, he looked heartier than he had the night before. She kind of liked the not so buttoned-up version of him, despite the snarl on his face.

"Please, don't mistake my concern as pity. I pity people I don't know. You're too aggravating to pity. So you can get over that idea."

His lips lifted slightly.

"I'll leave these for you." She indicated the donut box and bag with the soup in it. "I'll also call someone to come and get me. I'll just put these on the kitchen counter. You'll never know I was here."

His eyes moved slowly upward to meet her gaze and down her body again. "I doubt that."

Heat filled her. Was he referring to last night? China didn't know how to respond or if she wanted to, so she opened the door they'd used the night before and went inside. She placed the food on the counter. Was he trying to frighten her away? She refused to react to his poor behavior.

"Sorry to be such a grouch." He stepped over and picked up the donut box. "How about sharing these with me? Or I'll take you home, if you want."

Why didn't she jump at the chance? Maybe because she found this proud man interesting? He certainly kept her on her toes mentally. Since he'd come to town it had been one usual day after another.

"I guess I could have a donut since you asked so nicely."

"Good. Then why don't we eat these out on the porch? You want something to drink? Coffee's made."

"I'd just like a glass of water. I'll get it if you'll tell me where to find a glass."

"On the right side of the sink." He headed out the door. "I'm starving."

China found a tumbler, ran water into it and put in a couple of ice cubes. She considered the large kitchen area. She'd not paid much attention the night before, having been more concerned about Payton. The room was beautiful, decorated in a beach motif with a modern twist. It had bright blue round placemats on the oversized table that would accommodate a large family. Yellow and white striped curtains adorned the windows but didn't block the light. She liked it.

Picking up her glass, she went out to the porch. Payton sat on a settee with his legs stretched out over a table and the box of donuts on the cushion beside him. He had a blissful look on his face.

China took the chair to his right. He picked up the box and offered it to her. She pulled a donut out and gazed out toward the water. This area wasn't overly populated, like her part of town. She now knew why he had chosen to come out here and eat. The view of the ocean was amazing, wide and unobstructed.

Neither of them said anything. In some ways it was the most pleasant morning China had ever spent but in other ways it was the most disconcerting. The undercurrent of awareness between her and Payton made her feel edgy, insecure.

"I like your view," China finally said.

"Thanks. I've never really thought about it."

"How could you not?"

"I liked the house because it was far enough out to be private."

"Well, you sure got a view whether you value it or not. I've lived in Golden Shores my entire life and never had one this wonderful."

"Feel free to stop by and enjoy it any time."

She wouldn't be doing that. At least, not when he was home. "The house is plenty big enough for your family to visit."

"I don't see them coming down."

For a second a look of regret cross his face but he soon recovered. The tone of his statement had her thinking that was a subject he didn't want to talk about any more than he did about having had cancer.

"You and your family are pretty tight, aren't you?" he asked.

"I am with my parents. I don't see my sister regularly." That was an understatement. "Do you see your parents often?"

He looked away and out toward the ocean. "I did when I was in Chicago but now that I'm down here obviously not much. I talk to Mom off and on, though."

"What about your dad?"

"He's not really speaking to me these days." He raised a hand, palm up, stopping further questions. "Which is something I'm not going to discuss."

So that was a touchy subject as well.

"Payton, why did you decide to move to Golden Shores? Outside of tourists, we aren't on anyone's radar."

"I wanted to make a change in my life."

"Because you've been sick?"

"You can call it what it is, China. Cancer. Lymphoma."

"Okay, because of the cancer." She still had a hard time saying the word.

"That and other things. The cancer made me see that I wanted to live life instead of spending my time climbing the career ladder at work or the social ladder outside work."

"Well, you've come to the right place for that. The only ladders I know of around here are the ones behind the sheds of people's houses."

Payton threw his head back and laughed. China joined him.

He slowly recovered. "That statement is just the reason why I am here." He looked at her long enough to make her squirm before he said, "You know, I think that's the only time I've ever heard you laugh. You should do it more often. You have a beautiful one."

Suddenly the conversation had turned personal and China wasn't as comfortable.

He continued, "I just want to work and put the cancer behind me. I moved down here to make a change for the better. I don't want people to feel sorry for me and I don't want to be treated differently."

"If you are talking about last night, we all need help some times. It isn't a bad thing to let others in."

"I had no intention of doing so. I would have never told you if you hadn't seen…"

Time to change the subject. "I put the chicken soup in the refrigerator. If you don't want it, just throw it out."

Payton looked at her. "I thought you didn't cook."

"I never said I didn't cook. I just don't like to cook." China took a bite of a donut.

"I see."

"It's my grandmom's recipe, if you must know. I make a batch up and freeze it. So it was no big deal to bring it."

"I appreciate you thinking about me."

Warmth filled her. He did sound grateful. There was

a first time for everything. "You look like you're feeling much better. Did you have any trouble last night?"

He pierced her with a look that made her glow inside. Had he thought about their kiss? "Um, do you think you could take me home now? I'm supposed to be at my parents' for lunch."

"Sure, give me a minute to change. I'd planned to go sailing today anyway." He stood and gathered up the donut box.

"Do you think you should? After last night?"

A horrified looked marred his handsome features. "I'm fine, China. I just got a little dehydrated, that's all. Please, don't make more of it than there was."

"I just—"

"I know. You just can't help yourself." He moved around the table and passed her in one lithe movement that implied he was in perfect health.

China had to admit that over the past week he look like his skin had taken on a golden hue. As ridiculously aggravating as she found Payton at times, she liked him. He'd added excitement to her rather dull life.

"Let me get my shoes and gear. I'll drop you by your house on my way to the boat."

"You own a sailboat?"

His eyes lit up. "Yeah. A thirty-footer that is so sweet."

What would it be like to have Payton look at her with that same gaze of happiness? Why would she care? They just barely tolerated each other. The only time they seemed to work seamlessly was while caring for patients, and kissing. She shouldn't think about that.

"You need to be sure to drink plenty of water and wear your sunscreen. You don't want to relapse."

"China…" his gaze locked with hers "…stop it. I'm fine. I'm not one of your projects."

"I'm sorry. It just comes out sometimes."

"Forgiven this time. I'll get my stuff and be ready to go."

While Payton had disappear into his house, China took her tumbler inside and put it in the kitchen sink. Unable to control her curiosity about the rest of his home, she moved to the archway that separated the kitchen area from the living room. It was the most beautiful room she'd ever seen, with all the glass windows bringing in not only the sunlight but the view of the Gulf.

She ran a hand along the arm of one of the two blue overstuffed sofas accented in red. They faced each other in front of a framed large-screen TV above the fireplace. The high ceiling and slow-moving fans gave it an overwhelming feeling of comfort. Her breath caught as she moved further into the room. Before her was a grouping of comfortable-looking chairs covered in a sand-color fabric that faced the ocean. Stepping over to one, she marveled at the one-eighty-degree view.

The only thing missing to make the room perfect was greenery, something living. In her mind's eye she placed a Hawaiian ti near the chairs, crotons in a bright spot on the end table and a majesty palm in the corner. She smiled. Perfect.

"Hey, I was looking for you. Ready to go?"

Payton looked healthy in his white knit shirt and navy shorts. He wore docksiders on his feet. The quintessential yachtsman, if she'd ever seen a picture of one.

China glanced down at her pink T-shirt and blue jean cutoffs. They were definitely from two different worlds. She would go shopping this week and do better with her dressing.

"Just waiting on you."

"You had a funny look on your face when I came in. Is something wrong?"

"Just daydreaming."

He came to stand beside her. "I wouldn't have taken you for a daydreamer. I see you as far more practical than that."

"Maybe I'm full of surprises."

He wrinkled his brow in thought. "Maybe you are at that. Uh, about last night. I know I overstepped the boundaries with that kiss. I hope you don't think that's going to happen again. I'd like us to be friends. I don't what that to stand between us."

She swallowed. Obviously he hadn't reacted to that moment like she had. China mentally shook herself. Payton was a co-worker and the type of man she needed to be involved with on a personal level. They were professionals and it needed to remain that way.

"How about we start over and try for friends?" Payton offered.

That sounded safe enough. She smiled. "Friends sounds good to me."

Payton wasn't so sure he was completely comfortable with China's ready agreement to them just being friends. He shouldn't have kissed her but, still, he had enjoyed it. It was just as well they didn't become more involved. She knew too much about him. What if he started to care and she realized she couldn't deal with his health issues? No one would have that kind of power over him again. Remaining friends was a good plan.

He pulled into China's drive. "Who lives here?" Payton indicated the house.

"Mrs. Waits."

Payton studied the yard and the lush greenery around the house. "You do her gardening for her, don't you?"

Taking on a bashful look, China said, "I help her."

"You have a green thumb. The yard is beautiful. Would you consider helping me with my place? Pick out a few plants?"

A glow to compete with the lights of New York on a clear night came over her face then faded. "I don't think I can."

She didn't need to get mixed up with him. Despite appearances, he might leave just as quickly as he'd arrived. What kind of person just picked up and left everything they knew and loved? Her brother had but, then, he'd just been a kid. Kelsey had in every sense of the word, except the physical. Did the fact she was still in town give her a chance to get to know her sister again?

"Why not?" Payton demanded. "I can see you want to."

"You can't."

"China, can't you help out a guy that's clueless?" He made a pitiful face. "We could go shopping on our next day off. Have a friendly outing."

"Outing? That sure is an old-fashioned word."

"It's a friendly word. Like one friend helping another pick out plants."

"You're not going to give up on this, are you?"

"I'd rather not."

She grinned. "Okay. I'm off Thursday. How about you?"

"Yep."

"I promised to help my mom that morning but I'm free that afternoon."

He tapped the steering wheel with his palm. "Then it's a date. I mean, a friendly outing."

China looked as if she might back out for a moment before she said, "I'll be ready." She opened the door and stepped out but leaned down again to look at him. "See, it isn't so hard to ask for help."

"Are we back to that?" He didn't want to talk about what had happened last night.

"I just don't want you to get into trouble."

He grinned. "So what you're saying is that you care about me."

"No. What I'm saying is that even I would stop and help a dog if it was hurt."

Payton couldn't contain the laugh that burst from him. "So is that a move up or down, in your estimation?"

She glared at him. "Bye, Payton."

Payton was disappointed to hear the car door click closed. The sudden silence wasn't as peaceful as it had been before China had come into his life. He drove away with a feeling flooding him he'd not experienced in a long time—happiness.

He'd made the right decision. Their kiss the night before hadn't been his smartest move. China was the type of woman he had no business trifling with. She was permanence, stability, and he'd just come out of a hurtful relationship with no intention of returning to one any time soon. China, of all the females he knew, wouldn't accept half measures. She was marriage, a house, car and two children sort of person. He wasn't that guy, at least not anymore.

At one time he'd believed that he and Janice would settle down together and have a family. His illness and her inability to deal with it had ended that dream. Now all he wanted was to make the most out of life, live to the fullest. To stay away from anything more emotional than how he felt about his boat. If he did get involved with China and they became serious, she'd be the type to stay with him out of guilt if he became sick again and he wouldn't accept that, on any level.

The next morning Payton arrived at the clinic feeling better than he had since he'd been told he had cancer. Yesterday's sail in the bay had been stimulating. It had felt good, being active again. Despite his aggravation with China, he'd done just as she'd instructed and made sure to drink plenty of fluids and wear sunscreen.

Leaving his lunch in the office, he made his way to the front to check in for the day and was disappointed to find that China wasn't standing at the counter, as was her habit.

"Good mornin', Payton."

"Morning, Doris. Any patients for me this morning?"

"Not yet, but I'm sure we'll have one soon."

"Hey, Payton," Robin called, as she came out of Jean's office.

"Good morning." He worked to keep his regret off his face. If Robin was working the early shift, China wouldn't be in until two.

Going through his usual routine for the day, Payton caught himself checking his watch more often than he was comfortable with to see if it was time for China to come in. He'd managed to ask discreetly if it was her or Luke who would be there that afternoon.

His heart beat faster when China's voice carried down the hall from the front as he came out of an exam room. This wasn't good. The woman had become an infatuation he couldn't afford. He was making more of a few cordial moments on his porch the day before and his ability to convince her to help him buy plants. For heaven's sake, he'd never cared about a plant in his life. Had all that chemo affected his brain? He was enamored with China and he was acting like a schoolboy on Valentine's Day.

He had to put a stop to it. Someone who was easy and uninvolved was what he was interested in. That didn't describe China. He didn't want to hurt her, and he would if he continued on this path. So why had he been looking forward to seeing her with such anticipation? It was time to find some female company that wasn't China. Plan made, he was out of the clinic in thirty minutes.

Payton was on his way to the front desk when a booming voice said, "My China doll."

Sid. Payton couldn't help but grin. The man was a character.

"Come on back," China said. "I'll find Dr. Jenkins and let him know you're here."

Payton met them coming down the hall. He had to force himself to take his gaze off China. He was going out tonight to meet some women. "Hi, Sid. I thought I might have to go to the restaurant to check on your hand."

"China told me to wait until she was here. She said you'd still be around."

"Good. Come on in here and let me have a look." Payton headed into an examination room. Sid followed and China came in behind him. "So, have you been keeping it clean and dry?"

"The best I can," the older man said in a noncommittal tone.

Payton gave him a pointed look.

"I've not been cooking, I promise. I do have to take a bath sometimes, but even then my wife made me wear a plastic bag over it."

Payton smiled. "Understood." He turned to China. "Please get some antiseptic liquid. I'd like to rinse Sid's hand in that just to make double sure it doesn't get infected. Then I'll rebandage it."

China nodded and left.

Sid watched China leave. "That's a good girl there. She sure hasn't had it easy."

"I'm afraid I don't know her that well. Let me see you hand."

Sid swore and lifted his injured hand. "With China

what you see is what you get. Pure goodness through and through."

"She is nice." Payton found that he meant that. Too much so. China had been great to him when he'd been sick and had cared enough to go out of her way to check on him yesterday. Against his better judgment, he liked her attention.

"Smart too. Top in her class at nursing school and while taking care of her family."

Panic filled him. *China has a husband? Children? No one had ever said anything. Had he kissed a married woman?*

"I didn't think China was married." The statement came out with a little waver in his voice.

"She's not, but her parents depend on her. Still do. Far too much, in my opinion. Since she was twelve until she moved out last year, she's pretty much held the family together."

Relief filled Payton as the last of the gauze dropped into the garbage can. Seconds later China entered with a plastic bottle in her hand and bandages in the other.

"It looks like you hand is healing well. Continue doing what you're doing, Sid. China, I'm going to let you handle washing Sid's hand and the rebandaging," Payton said.

At China's surprised "Okay," he glanced at her. Hadn't she ever been trusted to do more?

"We good?" he asked her.

She straightened. "I'll take care of it."

Payton headed toward the door. "Good to see you again, Sid."

"Hey, I want to give you these." The man handed Payton some cards. "A couple of free meals on me in thanks." He nodded his head toward China. "Maybe you and China can come in together."

"Sid." China tried to shush him.

Had China told Sid about Payton kissing her? No, that wasn't something she'd share.

"Thanks Sid, I might just do that. Take care of yourself."

CHAPTER FIVE

A FEW MINUTES later Payton joined China in the hall as Sid headed for the front door.

"How does it sound if I pick you up at two on Thursday?"

China looked behind her. Had anyone heard? She didn't want the others to know that she and Payton were doing something together. They would make more of it than there was.

"You're not thinking of backing out on me, are you?"

She was but she didn't plan to tell him that. "Uh, no. Two sounds fine."

"Good, I'll see you then." He strolled toward the employee entrance.

China groaned when Robin came out of the back room. Telephone, telegraph, tell Robin. Now everyone would know she and Payton had plans.

"So, you and Payton have a date?"

China managed to turn a groan into a low moan. "No date. He just wants me to help him buy some plants for his house."

"Well, that's a new twist on 'let me show you my etchings'. I thought you didn't even like him."

"I never said that. Anyway, it doesn't hurt to be nice to a new person in town. Show some southern hospitality."

Robin gave her a knowing grin. "If you say so."

Against China's better judgment she was starting to like Payton, far too much. That kiss that gotten her to thinking what if... More than once Payton had proved that he wasn't the controlling person that her father was. Just now he'd handed over Sid's care, believing she could handle it without him looking over her shoulder. It was a simple thing that signified what he thought of her abilities and that meant the world. She'd grown up with a father who'd ruled with a thumb firmly on her, no trust. She smiled. Payton trusted her at least with his secret and patients.

China still had that smile hovering around her lips when Doris said, "I hear you and Doctor Hunky have a date?"

"Doctor Hunky? When did you start calling Payton that?"

"So you think he's hunky too?"

Doris was watching her far too closely for her reaction. "I didn't say that!"

"You didn't have to. You knew exactly who I was talking about." Doris grinned at her.

Jean came out of her office. "So what's this I hear about you and Payton dating?"

China put her hands on her hips. "It's not a date. He asked me to lend a hand in finding some plants for his house."

Jean nodded. "Well, he asked the right person."

China could have kissed the woman. She at least accepted the idea of her helping Payton without any strings attached.

"Have you ever been to his house?" Doris asked.

China hated to lie but she'd promised Payton she wouldn't tell anyone about the cancer. If she admitted she'd been to his house they'd want to know why. "No, but I guess we'll go there before we go to the nursery."

"I heard it's the big yellow one down on West Beach Road. I've always wondered what it looked like inside."

"Then maybe you should come for dinner some time," Payton said from behind them.

All their heads swivel to the sound of Payton's voice.

"I thought you'd left," China blurted. What had he heard of their conversation? Her lie?

"I forgot my lunch box. I just stopped back to pick it up."

Doris shook her head. "This is the last time I'm going to talk about you without letting you know first, or maybe I should put a cowbell around your neck so I'll know when you're coming."

Payton chuckled. China liked the sound.

"I'll try to stomp my way up the hall from now on. About that dinner. How about Saturday night at eight?"

Embarrassment covered Doris features. "I can't have you do that."

"Would you agree if I invited you all to dinner?"

Doris looked at her and said, "China, you'll come, won't you?"

She didn't know how to gracefully say no, and Doris was giving her a pleading look.

"I guess. I usually spend time with my parents on Saturday night, but I can change it to another night."

"Great," Payton said. "I'll see if Jean and Robin can make it. Maybe Luke and Larry."

The more the better as far as China was concerned. That way the larger the buffer between them. He'd given her one more reason to like him. Payton had to stop that. What was she going to do when she had to be alone with him on Thursday?

By the time Payton arrived to pick China up three days later she'd worked herself up into a nervous tizzy. She'd changed clothes five times. Even more times she'd picked her phone up to call to say she couldn't make it. Instead, she made up her mind that she was an adult and could do something as simple as going to a plant nursery with an attractive man.

She was sitting on the bottom step of the stairs to her apartment, waiting, when Payton pulled into the drive. Her traitorous heart fluttered as he grinned at her when he climbed out of the car.

He wore jeans that had seen better days, a blue collared shirt and his docksiders. His hair had grown to more of a military length. Pink colored his high cheekbones. He'd been in the sun earlier in the day. Payton looked the picture of health, and she'd never wanted to kiss a man more.

Wow, those unruly thoughts would get her into trouble. Instead, she returned his smile as she stood and walked toward him.

"Hey, I thought I might have to knock on the door and beg you to come out."

She leaned her head to one side. "Why's that?"

"I know I make you nervous."

"You don't make me nervous." That was the biggest bald lie she'd ever told. He did make her jittery with awareness. His simple, far-too-short kiss had awakened something in her that she'd never felt before.

"Okay, it's too fine a day to fight. Friends?" He stuck out his hand.

China took it. His fingers wrapped around hers, strong and confident, as if cocooning them. She mentally shook her head. *Quit the dreamy teenage girl stuff and get with the program.*

She tugged her hand free. "Friends." She looked at his car then back at him. "I think we should take my car. Yours is too perfect and you'll not want to get dirt in it. I have mine set up to transport plants."

"Okay, if you think I can get into it," he said, in the most agreeable tone. "You're the boss."

He went up a notch in her estimation. It was her experience that men want a woman to do as they asked. Her father certainly believed that and the men she'd dated had wanted her to be agreeable all the time. She pursed her lips and cocked her head in question.

"What?" he asked, in complete innocence. Maybe he was sincere.

"I would have thought you'd fight me about going in my car."

"Why? You're the leader of this outing, and I bow to your knowledge."

She laughed and he joined her. For one of the few times in her life she felt carefree. It was nice, very nice.

"Okay, since you're up for Mr. Congeniality then I guess you don't mind me driving either."

"Not at all."

That's right. He'd let Robin drive his car. It had surprised her at the time. Her father always did the driving. Woman couldn't do as good a job, he'd say. Payton seemed perfectly content with the idea. They walked toward her car, which was parked along the street. "When I first met you I took you for one of those males who thought a woman should be two steps behind him."

He grinned as he opened the passenger door. "Well, you never know what surprises I have in store."

That zing of awareness in her middle grew stronger. Did she want to find out? Yes. But should she?

China left Golden Shores behind and headed up the four-lane highway northward. Payton hadn't said much, seemingly glad to sit back and be chauffeured. He been raised with a cook, did he have a chauffeur too? He smelled wonderful, sort of like warm earth.

"So where're we going?" he finally asked.

"To a nursery about ten miles from here. They have the hardiest plants around."

At least now she could concentrate on what he was saying instead of how good he smelled. She'd never be able to get into her car again without thinking of him. She groaned. His scent was sure to linger for a long time.

"You're really into plants, aren't you?" Payton rather liked the way China's eyes lit up when she spoke of going to the nursery. What would it be like to have China's eyes shine in anticipation of seeing him? Somehow the challenge and the idea that it could happen gave him a rush he'd not experienced in a long time.

"Yeah, I'm really into plants."

"Why?"

She jerked her head toward him. Her look was one of shock, as if he'd discovered something he wasn't supposed to see. What was she hiding?

"I starting gardening as a preteen with a neighbor and it grew from there. Pardon the pun." She gave him a smile. "I like growing flowers and that turned into growing tomatoes, and then a full garden patch."

"Interesting."

"What do you mean by that?"

"Just that it's interesting that you turned into a gardener at such a young age."

"I didn't know there was an age limit."

"I'm just making an observation." Time to change the subject, which obviously had an agenda behind it. "Tell me about your name. Where did it come from?"

"My parents."

He smirked. "Funny. How did your parents decide on the name?"

"My father said I looked like a china doll. So there you have it."

"It makes me think of something fragile," Payton said.

"Don't be mistaken by my name. I'm no pushover."

"Believe me, I never thought you were."

"How about the name Payton? It's an interesting name." She made a right turn down a long straight road.

"Oh, I'm from a long line of Paytons. Father, grandfather, great-grandfather, etcetera, etcetera."

"Sounds impressive."

"Yeah. There are some that think so."

She glanced at him. "Not you?"

"I'm proud of the heritage but there is also baggage and pressure that goes with it that I'm not a fan of."

"Oh, poor little rich boy."

He made a scoffing noise. "Not funny."

"Then don't you mean expectations instead of baggage and pressure?"

How had China managed to read between the lines so clearly? He couldn't seem to get his parents to understand why he'd had to get away. Why he had to find his place in the world. Janice certainly wouldn't understand. His name and position had been what had drawn her to him in the first place. It hadn't been true love. The type that stayed with you through thick and thin, in health and adversity. After his illness he had to know that someone wanted him for himself and not his family name.

"Yeah. Expectations."

"I know about those too," she said, so softly that he almost missed the words. "Okay, here's the nursery."

China drove into the packed sand lot and parked. Payton grinned as he stepped out of the car. She was already picking out a child's red wagon that sat among six near the door of a long half-moon shaped building with black netting covering it.

"You pull and I'll pick." China lifted the handle, indicating it. "I'm sorry. I didn't mean to sound like I was ordering you."

"I don't mind taking orders." The smile she gave him was one of relief. Where had she gotten the idea that she wasn't allowed to speak her mind? He took the wagon handle. "What's this for?"

"To put the plants in." She left off the "dummy" her tone had implied and headed off through the door, leaving him to follow. Payton couldn't remember feeling more out of his element. He'd never been to a plant nursery or been so completely dismissed by a woman for something as mundane as a plant.

He grinned, looped his fingers through the hole of the handle and went after her. This was one more of those new experiences he'd hoped for. He seemed to have a number of them when he was with China. They started down the rows of tables filled with green plants and then up the one with flowering plants. They all looked the same to him.

As they went China's cheeks took on a rosy hue in the heat.

She stopped and looked at him. "I have some suggestions, but do you know anything you might want?"

He was clueless but he'd never admit it. "I'll trust your judgment." And he found that he did.

Payton watched has China moved though the sea of plants in an almost butterfly method. She flitted from one plant to the next, picking up this one and putting it on the wagon, discarding the next and moving on down the line. In no time the wagon was full and she was leading them to the door.

Falling behind, he called, "Hey, is this like going to

war? Where you can't speak in case the enemy might hear us?"

She stopped and looked back at him. "What?" Her look implied that she'd almost forgotten he was there. He didn't like that idea at all.

Stepping closer, into her personal space, he asked, "Remember me?"

She blinked, her eyes going wide. Good, at least she knew he was alive.

China stepped away. Payton had been too close. Near enough for her to smell his warm masculine scent with a hint of spice.

"Of course I know you're here." She went back to looking at the plants. "I don't see any Crotons or Hawaiian ti so I need to ask. It would be perfect in the living area and any rooms that face the same direction."

"Like my bedroom."

Payton might not have intended the words to come out gravelly and suggestive but they sounded that way to her.

His bedroom. What was it like? As beautifully decorated as the rest of his home or had he put his own stamp on the space? She didn't think she'd ever know. That was one place she didn't plan to explore.

"We have to find the plants that can handle the direct light. If they don't have them here we can go to another nursery that I know of, if you have time."

"I've got all the time in the world." He acted as if he was perfectly content to do whatever she asked until an unsure expression covered his face for a second. He quickly smiled again. Had he been thinking about having cancer and how close to death he'd been?

"I'll pull these to the checkout counter while you find someone to ask about the others."

A few minutes later China joined him. She was here with Payton. That thought gave her a warm glow. "They don't have what I'm looking for."

"Then off to the next place we go."

"It's about a half an hour up the road," China said as she pulled out of the parking lot.

They road in silence for a while before Payton asked, "Have you lived in this area all your life?"

"Born and bred here."

"Ever thought of moving?" Payton asked.

"Not really. My parents are here. My sister also."

"I have a sister too."

"Really? You close?"

"We were at one time. At least, until I moved down here."

China waited on a car so she could make a left turn. "My sister and I went two different directions a long time ago."

"Why's that?" Payton asked. She didn't have to look at him to know he was studying her profile.

"When my brother ran away at sixteen it changed everything." Why had she told him that? That was one subject she didn't discuss with anyone and certainly not with someone who was almost a stranger.

"What happened?"

"It's too long and too ugly story to go into now." With relief she saw the nursery sign. "Anyway, we're here. We won't be long. If they don't have what I'm looking for then I'll look for it online."

The nursery had one of the types of plants China was searching for. As she was talking to a salesperson Payton wandered over to some brightly painted Italian motif pots. "What about getting a few of these to put some of the plants in?" He picked up a medium-sized one.

China had to admit he had great taste. The pots would be perfect, incorporating all the colors in his home.

"They're rather expensive for the number we need."

He raised a brow. "I think I can handle it."

China didn't doubt that he could.

"How many should we get?"

China kind of liked the sound of *we*. There was some hint of permanence in the word. As if Payton would be around for a while. Payton was making all the noises of someone who could be counted on. He certainly acted like it where his house was concerned. Could she do the same? She wanted to and that was the first step.

She added up the number of Crotons and Hawaiian tis she'd decided he needed. "Eight should be enough. We can come back if we need more."

He pulled a neglected cart over and started placing pots on it. "What do you think about this one?" Payton lifted up a yellow pot, unlike the rest.

"I like it. Do you have a yellow room?"

"I do now," he said with a grin.

When he'd gone through and picked out all he wanted Payton grinned at her and said, like a cute little boy who had just gotten his way, "You know, I like shopping with you. I might do it more often."

She laughed. "But remember I don't do grocery stores."

"Maybe what we need to do is make a deal that I do the grocery shopping and you do everything else. With me tagging along, of course."

"That just might be a plan." Especially as it sounded like a relationship. Were they slipping into one despite her efforts not to?

"Great. Let's get this paid for and get back. I'm beginning to get into this plant stuff."

Fifteen minutes later they were headed down the road.

When they passed the sign to the ferry Payton said, "Is that the ferry that comes in at the end of West Beach Road?"

"Yes."

"Do you get seasick?"

"No."

"Then why don't we take the ferry back?" Payton asked.

She didn't want to, but she couldn't tell him the reason. "Okay."

Forty-five minutes later they were waiting in line when the ferry rolled and frothed the water as it docked.

"I can't remember the last time I rode a ferry. Maybe as a child but I'm not even sure I did it then," Payton said.

China couldn't help but smile. He sounded like he was really looking forward to the ride. "I've not ridden it in a long, long time."

Slowly she drove cross the ramp onto the ferry, pulled to the spot the crew member indicated and turned off the engine. Another crew member came to the window for the fare. Before China could get her purse, Payton handed the man money.

When the man had gone she said, "I could have gotten that."

"Don't be unreasonable. You drove your car and you're helping me out so the least I can do is pay the fare." Payton opened the door. "Come on, let's get out and watch."

China reluctantly followed him up the stairs to the observation deck. "I haven't been up here in years."

"Why not?"

Now she was sorry she'd brought it up. "I don't know."

He looked at her. "Give. There's more to it than that. I can tell by the tone of your voice."

"Hey, you don't know anything about the tone of my voice." She took a step away from him.

"I know it gets high when you're aggravated with me,

soft and gentle when you are caring for a child and hard as nails when you believe you're right. But all that's beside the point. So answer my question."

He wouldn't let it go so she had to say something. "This was Chad's favorite thing to do."

"Chad?"

"My brother." She looked at the horizon, where the sky was darkening then back to the white-capped water. "Yes."

"Why did he leave?"

"He'd gotten in trouble with the law. Father gave him an ultimatum: follow his rules or get out. The next morning he was gone."

She looked at Payton and found him studying her with eyes that were shadowy with compassion. "Have you heard from him since?"

"No. And I miss him every day." She shivered from memories and from the wind picking up.

Payton stepped closer and put an arm lightly across her shoulders. "Why don't we just pretend this is a first for both of us?"

China felt warmed. He was referring to the ferry ride but, still, the statement sounded more intimate then it should have. She glanced at Payton. He was looking off into the distance.

"Do you ever see dolphins here?" he asked.

"I have seen them. A storm is coming in so they might not be around."

They stood side by side, looking out over the water, barely touching. Somehow the pain of the ugly memories she'd experienced when she'd driven onto the ferry were being replaced by the pleasure of spending time doing something as simple as looking for dolphins.

"Hey, isn't that one?" Payton let go of her and leaned over the rail.

China grabbed his arm. "Don't get too excited. You might go over. Show me where."

Payton stretched his arm outward and she followed the direction he pointed. Seconds later she saw the fin and a glimpse of a silver back coming out of the water.

"There they are again," Payton said with wonder in his voice.

"Yes. Aren't they beautiful?"

"Yes. Beautiful."

His breath whispered across her cheek. She glanced at him to find him watching her. The sun was covered by clouds, but her cheeks were warm, as if it were high in the sky on the brightest of days.

The grinding roar of the engines going into reverse broke the moment. They were coming in to dock.

"We'd better get in the car or we'll have people honking at us," Payton said, taking her hand and helping her down the metal stairs. They ran to the car, laughing, and climbed in. China started the car just in time to take her place in line.

As they bumped over the docking plate Payton said, "We need to do this again soon."

China couldn't disagree.

CHAPTER SIX

IN THE LAST HOUR, Payton had unloaded plants and pots, hauled them up the stairs and helped China place flowers in hanging baskets and containers. He'd had about enough of greenery but China seemed more than happy to continue.

She was a dynamo where plants were concerned. She'd dove headlong into plotting and placing the greenery as soon as they'd arrived at his house. Now she was busy arranging flowers in the living room. The baskets for the porches would have to wait until he bought hooks to hang them from.

Payton washed his hands in the kitchen sink, which had been a no-no when he'd been growing up. Taking two glasses from the cabinet then adding ice and pouring tea into them, he carried them to the living room. Sweet iced tea was one of a number of things he was quickly learning to love about living in the south.

"China, leave those and come watch the storm with me."

"What?" She looked at him in surprise.

"I like a good storm. Come watch it with me."

"It sounds like a good way to get electrocuted. The storms down here are nothing like the ones you're used to."

"We have plenty of terrible weather in Chicago. Remember it's flat there also. Come on. That can wait.

If I have learned anything in the last year it's that stuff can wait."

China looked up from where she knelton the floor and gave him a long searching look. She rose slowly. "Let me wash my hands and I'll meet you outside."

Payton nodded and strolled toward one of the doors to the front porch. Minutes later China stepped out and hesitated. Her gaze moved from him to the dark sky off to the west. She was beautiful with her hair blowing around her face and her chin raised against the wind. This was a formable woman who could stand against a storm in life. He'd never seen that in Janice but he had seen it in his mom when she'd so fearlessly cared for him when he'd been at his worst. China had that same backbone.

She moved to take the chair nearby. Payton patted the extra spot next to him on the love seat. "You can see better from here." After a moment she took the spot he'd indicated but acted as if she was making sure she didn't touch him. He propped his feet up on the low table in front of them and ran an arm across the back of the settee. China sat forward stiffly.

"Relax, I'm not going to bite, and the storm isn't going to be that bad."

The wind grew and whirled around them, whistling around the corners of the house.

"I think I'd better go." China moved to stand.

Payton lightly placed his hand on her shoulder. "You can't. I need a ride to your house to pick up my car, and I'm not ready to go."

He had her there. China's nature wouldn't let her leave him without transportation. She had to always be taking care of someone. This time he rather liked being the focus of her attention and he was going to make the most of it.

"Lean back and watch. Haven't you ever watched a storm coming?"

"Not really." She shifted toward him slightly.

He removed his hand from her shoulder, placing it on the back of the settee.

"Have you always been a thrill-seeker?"

"What do you mean?" He was truly puzzled by her question.

"You wanted to learn to skimboard, the fast sports car, moving so far away from home." She waved a hand around. "Sitting out in the middle of a storm."

"I just want to experience new things. I've never had the time or inclination to just watch a storm come in. I thought it would be fun."

China looked at him closely for another few seconds. The desire to kiss her, take her, shot through him like the bolt of lightning flashing in the dark clouds just offshore. But he didn't. If he acted on his desire he might want more. He'd already made up his mind that friendship was all he could handle. Plus, they'd had a great day and he wasn't about to ruin it.

"Check out the lightning," he said softly, knowing she couldn't resist the suggestion.

As she became enthralled with the show before them, she shifted toward him and leaned back. Payton was tempted to gather her into his arms but he held fast. Watching the storm was building one in him.

When a fat drop of rain landed on China's cheek she squealed. Payton laughed. A full-bodied sound that came from deep in his gut with an "everything right with the world" quality. He'd never laughed when he'd been with Janice.

"I'm not getting wet!" China moved to stand.

Payton pulled her back. "You can't miss the best part. Stay here and I'll be back in a sec." He went into the house and retrieved a largest beach towel from the bath. Returning, he said, "Here, cover up with this."

Taking the towel, China pulled it over her so that it covered her front like a blanket. Payton took his seat again. She lifted a corner of the towel, offering him a place under it. Payton couldn't care less if he got wet, but he wouldn't pass up an opportunity to snuggle with China. Not for all the gold lost in a Spanish galleon during a Caribbean storm. When the towel didn't quite cover one of his legs she moved in closer, giving him more of the material. The rain blew in earnest but they remained dry and warm.

China glanced at him during the angriest part of the storm. "You know, this is rather fun."

"I thought you might like it." He hugged her to him.

Soon the sky was cloudless again, and the only noise came from the water dropping off the eaves. A few silent moments went by before Payton whispered, "This is the best part. Take a deep breath through your nose."

They did so in unison.

"So what do you smell?" he asked.

"Freshness, salt, the scent of the sea grass."

"I smell life," he said softly.

China removed the towel, turned enough that she could meet his gaze "Why, Dr. Jenkins, I do believe you're a closet poet. Thanks for insisting I stay."

"You're welcome. Now I think it's time you take me to my car."

China blinked as if amazed by his remark. She sat up quickly. "Uh, yeah, it's time for me to go. I mean us to go." She headed along the porch toward the stairs. "I'll just wait for you in the car."

* * *

China sat staring out the windshield at the newel post of Payton's staircase. What had she been thinking to become moony-eyed over Payton? She'd almost kissed him on the cheek despite her desire to find his lips. She wasn't that forward. They'd shared a pleasant afternoon, and she'd almost ruined it by making a fool of herself. Heck, she wasn't sure how it had happened but she was beginning to like the good doc.

They really had nothing in common. He lived in this big house. She lived in a tiny apartment she didn't own. He had a car that people looked at when he passed. Hers blended in with all the others in the parking lot. He was all about skimboarding and sailing and she favored plants. They only shared medicine. And kisses. Those they unquestionably had in common.

Payton joined her minutes later. They spoke little during the short ride to her house.

As she pulled into the drive he said, "I appreciate your help today. The plants look great. Now all I have to do is not kill them."

"Just water as the little tabs direct and you'll be okay. I'm sorry I didn't think about getting hooks so we could hang the baskets."

"Not your fault. I didn't think about them either. I'll pick some up tomorrow after work. You want to come out and help me hang them?"

China shook her head. "Sorry, I have to take my mom to the doctor. Don't forget that larger pot in your bedroom. It likes that particular type of light."

She'd already spent too much time with him. He was addictive. The hour spent at his house had her rattled. She needed to think, put some space between them. Was he always as wonderful as he had been this afternoon, or would he turn into one of those men who had to have control when you got to really know them?

"Yes, ma'am." He smiled. "Look, now you've got me doing it."

She laughed. "You're becoming a true southerner."

"I guess I am." He touched her arm. "Thanks for your help today. I really enjoyed my afternoon."

"You're welcome."

China turned off the engine and they both climbed out of the car.

"Well, I guess I'll see you tomorrow."

"I'll be there. Good evening, Payton." China headed toward her apartment. She felt his gaze on her as she climbed the steps to her door. Would these conflicting feelings for Payton still be there in the morning? She was afraid they would be. She was already counting the hours until she saw him again.

At the clinic on Saturday morning, just before lunch Payton asked, "China, would you come in my office for a minute, please?"

What was going on? They had been cordial with each other since getting to work, but she'd seen to it that they were never alone. Not that she didn't trust him, it was more like she couldn't trust herself. She'd stayed up far too late into the night thinking about Payton, looking forward to coming to work so she could see him. She didn't like it.

Payton headed toward his office, and she followed slowly. She entered to find him waiting beside his desk. He said, "If you don't mind, would you close the door?"

She started to say that, yes, she minded, but Payton would never embarrass her or do anything she wasn't in agreement with. "Okay." She pushed the door until it made a soft click. "Is something wrong? Are you feeling sick again?"

"No, I'm fine." There was a harsh edge to his tone.

She straightened. "All right, then. So what did you drag me in here for?"

"I asked you, I didn't pull you in here by your hair."

"Look—"

Payton put a hand out, palm up. "Let's not fight. That's not why I ask you in here." He ran the hand through his short hair, mussing it.

China hadn't seen him this unsure before, not even when he'd admitted he'd had cancer. What was going on?

"I think I've bitten off more than I can chew."

She grinned. He'd been using more casual sayings over the last couple of days.

"I'm not sure I can handle the dinner tonight by myself. I've cooked for two but never six. I know this is a lot to ask, and I know how you feel about cooking, but I have no one else to turn to. Would you come early and help me?"

He'd said the words so fast that China had to think about what he'd asked. She wasn't sure how she felt about the statement. Despite her better judgment and her vow to keep space between them, she didn't have the heart to turn him down. "I'll go home and change, and be there as soon as I can."

His smile of relief made her middle flutter.

"Thanks so much, China. I owe you big time. I've already done the shopping so you don't have to worry about helping with that. Now we'd better get back to the patients."

His abrupt end to their conversation somehow disappointed her. Had she expected him to express his undying gratitude by kissing her? That was more like wishful thinking.

* * *

Hours later China knocked on the kitchen door to Payton's house. At the faint sound of "Come in," she opened the door.

All she could see of Payton was his backside encased in navy knit running shorts. She had to admit he had a fine behind. Seconds later his head came out from inside the cabinet. Standing, he grinned at her and placed a large boiling pot on the counter. "Hey, there. I was hunting a pan."

"Well, I hope so, otherwise putting you head inside a cabinet would be rather strange."

"You wouldn't be surprised, though, would you?"

"In order not to start an argument I'm going to take the high road and not answer that."

Payton raised his head heavenward. "Thank you for small miracles."

China couldn't help but laugh, something she found that she was doing more often around Payton. When she'd first met him she'd never have guessed they would ever be friends. She could work with anyone but to her great surprise she like spending her off time with him as well.

"I'm a little behind. Would you mind being my second-in-command and chop up the onions and potatoes?"

"I need a knife. What're we having?"

"A beef loin in puff pastry with braised potatoes, salad and a fruit trifle."

"Wow. That sounds wonderful. No seafood?"

"I thought everyone probably got all of that they wanted any time. I wanted to do something different. Besides, it's my specialty." He pulled a bowl out of an upper cabinet.

"So you've made it before."

He handed her a knife. "A number of times."

She put her hands on her hips and glared at him. "So you got me here on false pretenses."

Payton looked directly at her. "Well, yes and no. I can use the help and I find that I rather like spending time with you," he said matter-of-factly.

China's heart thumped against her chest wall. All she could do was stare at him. "Uh, where's a cutting board?"

"It's under the cabinet to the left."

She turned her back to him to go after the board.

"One thing I've learned is that time is precious and I'm not going to waste any more of it. I think you like me also. Or at least your kiss said you do."

China reached for the cutting board and when she turned around Payton was already concentrating on the meat he was preparing. "The potatoes and onions are in the pantry." He nodded toward a door.

Payton had turned all business. Had he really said what she thought he'd said? She found the vegetables and brought them to the island.

"Come and work over here in front of me. There's plenty of room. Next to the windows and porches, I like this kitchen best. It's made for cooking together and entertaining."

"It's wonderful. Nothing like the small one I grew up cooking in."

"When did you start cooking?"

"When I was twelve."

"I came to it much later in life. Ruth, our cook, thought I needed to know something about preparing a meal before I left for college. So I hung out in the kitchen and fell in love with cooking."

"I might have enjoyed it more if I hadn't seen it as a chore."

"Why is that?"

"Just that I had to help out at home."

"I'm not surprised."

"What does that mean?"

"Just typical for you. Helping out."

She stopped chopping and looked at him. "You didn't say that like it's a compliment."

"Don't get mad. It's just an observation."

"I suggest that you keep your observations to yourself unless you have something nice to say." She made a cut into a potato with more force than required.

"You have the most beautiful brown eyes I've ever seen."

China felt the heat flow up her neck to her cheeks. Her heart fluttered. Never in a million years would she have dreamed that Payton Jenkins would ever flirt with her. Somehow it was empowering.

Payton grinned but kept his head down and pretended to be concentrating on wrapping the loin in pastry. He'd gotten China's attention with his remark about her eyes. They worked together in silence for a while but he was aware of every movement she made.

She was aware of him too. He dropped a knife and she jumped. Tension as deep as the gulf filled the room, and he was enjoying having her a little off center. China put up such a wall where he was concerned that it was nice to see he was making a chink in it. He wasn't sure what the future held for him or if he had the right to be involved with anyone, but where China was concerned he couldn't help himself. She intrigued him.

He slipped the roasting pan into the oven. "Are those potatoes and onions ready?"

"I have one more to cut."

"Great. I'll get them started and then we can set the table. I've already made the trifle and have it in the refrigerator. After we finish the table I'll change and then we can put together the salad."

She nodded and a minute later said, "I'm done. Hand me the pan and I'll put these in it."

He did as she requested. With the same efficiency he admired in her nursing, China cleaned the area and washed her hands.

"Okay, where are the plates, silverware and napkins?"

"I'll get the plates. The silverware is in the drawer to the right of the sink, the napkins in the third drawer down."

Payton was putting the plates on the table when China said with amazement in her voice, "These are all cloth napkins."

"Yes. So?"

She turned and looked at him. "That's all you have?"

"It is. Bring the green ones."

She reached in the drawer and counted to make sure she had all that were required. "I've never known someone who only uses cloth napkins."

"You make it sound like a crime. We only used cloth at my house when I was growing up."

"Yeah, and we only used paper. If my parents own cloth ones, I've never seen them." China brought the napkins and a handful of silverware to the table.

"Well, enjoy using mine tonight."

"I think I will."

Payton glanced at the clock on the wall. "If you don't mind finishing up here, I'm going to take a quick shower and change."

"I'll finish. Do you want to use the regular glasses or do you have something else in mind?"

Payton stopped at the doorway to the living room. "Those are fine. There are some wineglasses up there also." He pointed in the direction of a cabinet she'd not looked in before.

China started placing the silverware around the plates.

"Hey, China."

She looked at him.

"Thanks for your help. Really."

She smiled. "You're welcome."

Payton pulled his shirt up over his head as he went down the hall with a smile on his face. Maybe the being friends idea was overrated. It was fun to tease China. Nice kissing her too and he wanted to do it again. He was starting over in life so why not have some fun? No one said their time together had to last forever.

With the table set and wineglasses waiting, China went outside to check the plants. Payton had hung the orange lantana around the porches. It contrasted well with the yellow of the house and looked beautiful. Any home always felt more comfortable with plants around, or at least she believed so. After checking the dampness of the soil in a couple of baskets, China returned to the living room to look at a pot there. The faint sound of water running told her Payton was still taking a shower.

A buzz from the kitchen drew her attention. She went to see what it was for. Turning the timer off on the oven, she opened the door and checked the loin. Not sure what to do and not wanting Payton's meal to be ruined, she closed the stove door and turned the oven off.

There was no choice. She was going to have to ask Payton what needed to be done. Bracing and reminding herself she was an adult, she headed toward the sound of water. At his bedroom door she called his name. Hearing no answer, she stepped further into the room. What was she going to do if he stepped out of the bathroom naked?

Have a heart attack? That was silly. She saw half-naked bodies all the time in her line of work.

Yeah, but none of those were Payton's.

Squaring her shoulders, she walked across the room and knocked firmly on the open bathroom door. "Payton."

That heart attack might not be such a far-fetched idea. Payton's walk-in shower was made of clear glass blocks. She could make out the shape of his body on the other side. He had his hands raised as if he was rinsing his hair. The fleeting idea that she should avert her gaze crossed her mind but her eyes wouldn't cooperate.

"Yeah?"

"Sorry to bother you but the buzzer went off, and I was wondering if I need to take the loin out."

"And I was hoping you had come in to join me."

"In your dreams."

China watched as his silhouette moved to the end of the blocks. Was he going to stand there naked in front of her? Would she look away? Not likely.

Instead, he stuck his head around the edge of the wall. His gaze held hers. "You are."

"Come on, Payton, stop teasing me and tell me what to do about the meat. I should just let the meal get ruined."

He grinned. "You're much too nice a person to do that. Pull it out, please. It needs to rest for ten minutes."

Without another word, China headed back to the kitchen. She searched for the hot pads. Her hands trembled at her first try at taking the heavy pan out. Payton had rattled her. She didn't like it. Control was something she usually managed to maintain, had needed to keep a tight grip on since her brother had left. Someone had to. China took a deep breath and tried again, successfully. This time she sat the pan on the granite counter top with a thump.

Done, she looked up to find Payton standing behind her.

She hadn't seen him enter the kitchen but she known he was there just the same. The fresh smell of soap and something that was Payton's alone circled around her.

He leaned over her shoulder to study the golden brown pastry. "Mmm, looks and smells perfect."

She couldn't disagree. "It does look amazing. Impressive, in fact."

He stepped around her and pulled out a basting spoon from a drawer. She'd moved but she'd had to touch him to do so. That she refused to do.

Payton only wore a pair of buff-colored slacks, no shirt and no shoes. A towel hung around his neck. She'd never been more aware of a man in her life.

He dipped the spoon into the juice at the bottom of the pan and brought it to his lips. She watched as his tongue reached out for the fluid. "Perfect," he breathed. "Want a taste?"

She knew he was talking about the liquid but her focus was on his lips.

"China," he said in a soft, rusty voice, "stop looking at me that way. I don't think you want all the staff at the clinic to find us sprawled across the kitchen counter. Which is going to happen in about three seconds if you don't stop."

She blinked and pushed back, which made her brush his bare chest. The sound of the spoon dropping to the pan came just before Payton's hand caught her upper arm and pulled her gently back toward him.

"Let's see if what we were both thinking is true," he whispered just before his lips met hers, gently at first. But he soon pressed deeper. Payton tasted of beef and salt. His lips requested and promised something wonderful at the same time.

China stepped closer, bringing her hands up to Payton's waist in the hope that there she'd find a way to steady herself. She opened her mouth and Payton accepted the invitation. She wrapped her hands more tightly around his waist, enjoying the warmth of his skin. His arms held her securely. He entered and retreated and entered her mouth again. Heat and desire rose in her until she was sure the earth had tipped out of orbit.

Bit by bit her hands ran across the planes of his back as Payton deepened the kiss.

At the sound of the doorbell chiming, China jerked away and out of his hold. "I'll get that while you dress."

Payton chuckled. "Saved by the bell. This time. China, don't think for one minute this is over. I will kiss you again. That's a promise." He headed toward his bedroom.

"Not if I don't want you to."

Payton stopped, turned and looked at her before he said, "But you do." Just as abruptly he turned again and walked off.

She groaned. Heaven help her, he was right. She did want him to kiss her again. But she wouldn't let him.

CHAPTER SEVEN

PAYTON WAS PLEASED that his dinner party was turning out to be such a success. Doris and Jean had arrived together. Both had given China suspicious looks when he'd stepped into the room fresh from the shower. Neither woman said anything but he could tell that China was uncomfortable about what they might be thinking. To ease her worries he came right out and said, "I asked China to come early and help me with the preparations. She was a great help."

He winked at China. Her cheeks turned rosy.

By the time Robin and Luke arrived and then Larry and his wife, the party was in full swing. He couldn't remember attending a more boisterous and loud social gathering outside the frat parties he'd gone to in college.

When Doris and then Jean asked if they could see his place, he took everyone on a tour. He noticed that China brought up the rear when they changed rooms. It wasn't until the group reached his bedroom that she stepped out of the crowd. She went over to the Hawaiian ti, which he'd placed close to the window. She lovingly touched a leaf before looking at him.

He smiled and she returned it with warmth in her eyes. It was as if they were sharing a special secret. Somehow it made him stand taller. As if making China happy made him happy.

"Man, you have a beautiful view," Larry's wife remarked.

"Yes, I do." He was looking at China instead of out the window.

"Okay, enough of this girly stuff. Let's eat. I'm starving," Luke stated.

"I have to get things on the table," Payton said. He'd finished the salad and potatoes while China, Doris and Jean had enjoyed the view from the porch. China had offered to help but he'd declined it.

She assisted him placing the food on the table after he'd called that dinner was ready. The conversation during dinner was lively and everyone was complimentary about his culinary skills. A couple of times he looked down the table to see China watching him. It hadn't passed his notice that she hadn't chosen to sit beside him. She was on Luke's right and Robin sat to his left.

Over dessert everyone laughed and told bad medical jokes. He watched as China lifted a spoon full of trifle to her mouth. His groin tightened at the thought of kissing those lips again. As if she'd sensed his interest, she glanced at him as she pulled the spoon from her mouth. Was she teasing him or enjoying the trifle? Either way, he was turned on. That was something he'd not been in some time. It felt good to lust after a woman again. And hunger for China he did. More so every day.

Near eleven, Larry pushed back from the table and said, "I hate to be the one to bring this party to an end, but I have to work tomorrow, unlike some others in this room." He looked pointedly at Payton.

"I appreciate that and will think of you while I'm sailing."

Larry stood and smiled at him. "You know, I'm not sure I like you despite your ability to cook."

Payton rose and walked to the front door with Larry and his wife.

"We enjoyed it, man," Larry said, as he shook Payton's hand.

"Glad you did. Come again." Payton meant it. He liked having people around. He'd pushed them away when he'd been sick and had never really appreciated dinner parties even before that.

Doris and Jean came up behind him. "We've got to go too. Thanks for having us."

"Anytime. I'll see you both on Monday."

"I'll see you on Monday too," China said, as she joined them on the way out the door.

"You're not staying to help clean up?" Payton asked in mock surprise.

Before she could answer Robin said, "I can. I'm a great dishwasher. China, would you mind giving Luke a lift home? He rode with me."

At Payton's stricken look China said in a too-cheerful voice, "Not at all."

"Great. Then I'll get started," Robin said, turning toward the kitchen.

"Luke, I'm ready when you are," China called.

"I'll be right there."

China had stepped out on the porch when Payton grabbed her elbow. "Go sailing with me tomorrow," he said, low enough that only she could hear.

"No."

"Why not? Scared?"

"Of what?"

"Being alone with me. Don't trust yourself, do you?" Payton said, close enough to her ear that it might look like he was kissing it.

"I'm not afraid of you," China hissed.

"Then maybe you're afraid you'll jump my bones."

She moved away and said in an indignant voice, "I am not. Where did the let's-be-friends rule go?"

"What're you two talking about?" Luke asked, striding up to them.

"Nothing. Come on, it's been a long day." China started down the stairs. Luke shrugged as he went by Payton and followed China.

If he let her leave without her agreeing to go sailing there would be no way to convince her over the phone. He had to get her agreement in person. "Hey, China, wait a minute."

She stopped halfway down and turned to look at him. As if Luke was his wing man, he said to China, "I'll wait for you in the car."

Payton stepped down to her. "I've decided rules are made to be broken. I'd really like to take you sailing as a thank-you for your help with the plants and dinner."

"You don't have to." She moved down a step.

"I know you don't, but I do. If you're worried, I'll kiss you again. Then you have my word as a gentleman that I won't." Even in the yellow glow of the porch lights he could see her warring to make a decision. "I promise you'll have good time."

"I'm not much for water sports."

"If you don't enjoy yourself, I'll never ask again."

She took so long to answer he feared she was going to say no. "All right. What time should I be ready?"

"Nine o'clock too early?"

"No." She headed down the steps.

"Bring sunscreen and something to swim in. 'Night, China."

The next morning China again wondered what she had gotten herself into. She couldn't seem to say no to Payton, regardless of how hard she tried. Maybe she just needed to go along and stop fighting him and her feelings. She couldn't remember when she'd last taken time to just enjoy a day, spent it doing nothing constructive.

Before she could talk herself out of going, Payton pulled his car into the drive. The sudden realization that she was going on a date with Payton hit her. This wasn't her helping out a new person in town but them spending personal time together. She didn't date often and she sure didn't date guys like Payton. Her father had her told her more than once to watch out for the smooth-talking, fast-car type of man because they would get her into trouble. She was in over her head—way over.

China swallowed the knot in her throat as she watched Payton walk toward her. Tall, with a tan, he appeared virile and full of life. Dressed in a white collared shirt with his shirttail out, navy shorts and deck shoes, he could be a member of the classic yachting crowd. His broad smile was white against his skin. Payton was breathtaking and so out of her league. What could he possibly see in her?

"Ready?" he asked, reaching down for her beach bag.

She grabbed it, stopping him. "Something has come up. I'm not going to be able to go."

He pinned her with a look, his mouth thinning. "Just this second? Like what?" He snapped his fingers.

"I don't have to tell you."

"Yes, you do. I think that if you break a date with someone they deserve to know the reason. Especially if it's at the last minute."

"I just can't go."

He sat down beside her. "Why, China?"

"Because you and I have nothing in common."

Payton took one of her hands. His thumb ran slowly across the back of her hand as if he was trying to soothe a wild animal. "Oh, I think we had plenty in common last night."

"But that is all we have, sexual attraction."

"So you admit it. You're attracted to me?"

"I think you know I am. I don't go around kissing every man I see." She looked down at her toes, which she'd polished bright pink just minutes before he'd driven up.

"I'm glad to hear that. I had hoped I was special."

"Now you're making fun of me."

"No, I'm not. I'm just trying to find out why all of a sudden you don't want to go sailing with me."

"I just don't see where this is going."

"All this is right now is one friend talking to another and taking that friend sailing to say thank you." Payton caught her gaze. "This is not a NATO pact affecting millions of people. This is two people having fun together and getting to know each other better. Nothing more, nothing less. Go with the flow for once. You might find out you enjoy yourself."

Put that way, her argument sounded rather silly.

"Come on, China. Let's have some fun. I think you take life far too seriously. Enjoy it some. If you don't like sailing I promise to bring you straight in." He put up three fingers. "Scout's honor."

She took a deep breath. "Okay, I can use a day away."

"As far as I'm concerned, you can sunbathe to your heart's content all day long."

"That does sound nice."

Payton stood and helped her to her feet. He didn't let go of her hand as they walked to his car, as if he was afraid she would bolt. Settled in for the ride as they made their way down the East Beach Road to the Golden Shores Marina, China had to admit it was fun having the wind blowing through her hair, the sun on her face and a handsome man at her side. This was what every woman dreamed of. Maybe that was the problem, it seemed too good to be true.

"Were you really a Boy Scout?"

Payton looked at her and grinned. "Eagle Scout, in fact."

"That figures. An overachiever."

"Is that a bad thing?"

"No, I think that's one of the reasons you're such a good doctor."

"My goodness, I'm going to blush. Two compliments in less than an hour. Are you running a fever?" He reached over to briefly touch her forehead.

China slapped his hand away. "Funny doctor. Don't give up your day job to be a comedian." She laughed.

Payton joined her. It was nice to be around someone with a sense of humor. He was right, she was far too serious. Maybe it was time for that to change.

Payton had broken out in a sweat when China had said she wasn't going sailing. For some reason it was important that she come along, see his boat. Friendship was the order of the day. They would spend the day together just getting to know each other better. He loved being on his boat and wanted to share that feeling with China. If she let loose he'd bet she would be a lot of fun. He'd seen hints of if before. A day out on the water might be just the ticket to seeing her less serious side. Problem was that mastering his basic instinct would be the order of the day.

He pulled the car into a parking spot near his slip. Climbing out, Payton grabbed a large brown sack out of the trunk and met China, who had just closed her door. He grinned. "Ready?"

"You really love this sailing stuff, don't you?"

"I do. Nothing like it. I can't believe you've lived here all your life and never been."

"After my brother left, my parents discouraged us from doing anything dangerous. I think they were afraid of losing us."

"I wouldn't consider sailing dangerous. Still, I won't let anything happen to you. Nothing but fun stuff today." He took her hand. "Come on, let me show you my baby."

"Baby?"

"Yeah." He gave her hand a tug. "My baby."

They walked down the gray wooden dock.

"This is almost picture perfect. The gleaming white boats against the blue water," China said.

"See, you're already glad you came."

"I guess I am."

"Don't get too excited." He stopped near the end of the dock where his boat bobbed gently in the water.

"Free at Last," China read out the gold script letters paint on the transom. "I know little about sailing but I thought a boat was supposed to be named after a woman."

"Some are. Since I don't know a woman to name mine after, I just put how I feel when I'm on her."

China pursed her lips and nodded her head as if she'd learn something significant. "Interesting."

"I'm not sure that's a positive response but maybe you'll understand after you take a ride." Stepping onto the edge of the boat, he held his hand up to help China board.

She placed her hand in his and carefully stepped onto the boat then down onto the deck.

"You can have a seat on that bench. I've got to untie us. I'll be right back."

Payton jumped to the dock and glanced back at China. She sat stiffly on the green cushioned seat with a look of unease marring her features. "Hey." She met his look. "I'm not going to let anything happen to you. I really do think you'll have fun."

"I'm all right."

"Then smile."

She gave him a bright but unconvincing smile. Hurrying to the bow, he released the rope securing the boat to the dock and returned to the stern to do the same. Climbing aboard again, Payton started the small motor and put it into gear. Slowly he maneuvered out of the slip. He glanced back to find China watching with interest as they put distance between them and land. Her body had lost that tense appearance. She was coming around.

China raised her face to the sun, closed her eyes and basked in its warmth. The sound of water lapping against the side of the boat had her drifting off. When was the last time she'd napped?

The sharp snap and flutter of a sail catching the wind brought her eyes wide open. She couldn't see Payton, but sounds of movement in front of the cabin said he was there. The wind whipped her hair into her mouth and she gathered it in one hand and pulled it to the side. She stood, swaying as the boat shifted in the water. Bracing her feet apart and holding on to the edge of the roof of the cabin, she looked over it. Payton was leaning over a winch, winding up rope at a rapid speed.

She had a fine view and time to enjoy it. Payton's muscles flexed with his effort. His legs were strong and sturdy. He was a man in his element, confident and in control. As he straightened and turned to adjust something she was presented an unobstructed view of his firm butt.

Payton turned. His gaze met hers as if he knew she'd been ogling him. A self-assured smile slowly spread across his face as he came toward her. Her lips lifted as if of their own accord. The man had that kind of effect on her.

Looking down on her from the top of the cabin, he said,

"Hey, sleepyhead, you'd better sit down. I'm come down to bring the boom around. I wouldn't want you to go swimming without me."

Captivated, China could do nothing but stare at him. With the sun at his back, his hair tousled by the wind and his white smile for her only, she had to remind herself to breathe. It was beyond her wildest dreams that she could be off sailing with such a gorgeous man.

He lithely made his way along the narrow companionway between the side of the boat and the cabin to join her. "China, you okay?"

She blinked and sucked in a breath. "Yeah, why?"

"I've been talking to you, and you've been ignoring me."

The problem was she *hadn't* been ignoring him, she'd been fixated. "What did you say?"

He took her elbow and led her to the bench. "I'm going to let you handle the rudder while I take care of the boom. We need to tack soon so I can show you my favorite new spot."

She shook her head. "I don't know anything about the rudder." China was afraid her apprehension was showing again.

"You don't have to. It's easy and I'm going to show you how." He took her hand and pulled her toward the seat again. "Sit down."

She took the same spot she been in earlier.

"This…" Payton put his hand on the shiny, well cared-for wooden handle that was just behind the seat "…moves the rudder." He demonstrated by pushing it back and forth. The boat shifted to the right and then to the left as he moved the handle. "Now you put your hand right here."

China put her hand where he indicated and Payton

placed his palm over it. "Now, all I want you to do it hold it steady."

"I don't think—"

"No thinking required. You'll be fine. Relax and enjoy. I'm letting go now."

Her heart hung in her throat as his fingers left hers.

"See that point of land straight ahead?"

She nodded.

"Keep us headed in that direction. We aren't going to leave the bay so there shouldn't be much more wind than this. I'm going to get the line to the boom." Payton moved to leave her.

"Don't go."

"I'll be right back. You just adjust the rudder back and forth and keep us headed for that point."

Payton disappeared from sight. She looked at her hand to find that the knuckles were turning white. She eased her grip on the wood and took a slow deep breath. Payton wouldn't have left her with his pride and joy if he didn't trust that she could handle it. Finding the point of land again, she moved the rudder and brought the boat in line again. A sense of pride washed through her. She was controlling this huge sailboat. She'd felt out of control so much of her life that it was invigorating to feel some power.

She smiled up at Payton when he returned.

"You're starting to enjoy yourself, aren't you?"

She lifted her chin and let the wind blow in her face. "I have to admit, I'm having fun."

Holding a rope in his hand, Payton came to sit down beside her. "I was hoping you would."

The earnest look he gave her said that it had really mattered to him that she enjoyed sailing. Why?

"Okay, here's the important part and the dangerous one

if you don't pay attention and listen. I don't want you to get hurt."

Suddenly the confidence she'd felt ebbed away.

"When I bring the jib around you have to duck. If you don't, the boom with hit you in the head. So when I yell 'Duck', you'd better do it."

Her poise returned. Surely she could do that without any problem.

"You ready?"

"I'm ready."

"Okay, here we go."

Payton couldn't help but grin at the determination in China's voice. She approached sailing just as she did her nursing and gardening: head on. He found it refreshing. Found her extremely desirable. Would that passion be just as intense in her lovemaking? With every fiber of his being he wanted to find out. To see her come alive beneath him. Why had he ever agreed to make this a friendly trip?

He pulled the rope and the boom began to swing toward them. It gained momentum during the movement. When it was almost parallel with the boat, Payton yelled, "Duck."

They both leaned over, bringing their heads close together. After the boom passed by them, he positioned it and the jib sail caught the wind. The boat jerked and moved swiftly across the water.

He looked at China. She wore a smile from ear to ear. A surge of delight filled him, like none he'd felt since being told he was in remission. China was bewitching him. We're just friends, he had to keep reminding himself. "You're having fun?"

She glanced at him. "This is amazing. I'm so glad you insisted I come."

"I'm glad I did too. You're beautiful."

She stared at him with questioning eyes and parted lips. The desire to kiss her made his chest ache, but he'd promised it would be a sociable day, no pressure. Instead, he laid his hand over hers and adjusted the rudder. "Don't forget we have to head toward that point."

China pulled her hand out from under his and pushed his off the rudder handle. "I've got this."

"Aye, aye, Captain Bligh."

China's laughed intertwined with Payton's. The sound made her chest constrict. She liked sharing something simple as a laugh with him. What would it be like to have that in her life all the time? She was still smiling half an hour later as she ducked on Payton's command as they tacked their way across the bay. She couldn't remember when she'd had more fun.

"Okay, we're going to anchor here. I need a swim." Payton handed her the rope.

"What am going to do with this?"

"Just hold it for a minute. I'm going to unfurl the sails and drop anchor." He climbed around the cabin. Soon the jib sail was coming down and next the mainsail collapsed. The boat began to drift. A few minutes later Payton returned.

"You can let go of the rudder and the rope now," he said in a voice full of mischief.

She placed her hands in her lap. "Are you making fun of me?"

"I would never do that."

"I should hope not." She used her most indignant voice.

Payton reached for the hem of his shirt and pulled it up. "You can change in the cabin if you wish."

"I don't think I'm going to swim."

He stopped midway through removing his shirt and gave her a pointed look. "You do swim, don't you?"

"I do."

"Then why not?"

China could think of any number of answers to that question. *I've not swum in years. I don't want you to see me in a bathing suit. I might jump your bones if I see you in yours.* "I'll just wait for you here," she finally murmured.

He let his shirt drop back into place. "If you don't swim I'm going to throw you in clothes and all."

"You wouldn't dare." She glared at him.

"Do you really want to try me?"

Payton stood above her with his feet braced against the gentle roll of the boat and a determined look on his face. "Well, I guess I'll change."

"Good choice."

Dipping her head to enter the cabin without hitting her head, she stepped into a narrow space with a bunk filling one side with cabinets above and below it. On the other side was a counter with a mini-sink and equally small refrigerator below. At the end of the aisle was a door that must lead to the bath.

The sound of water splashing drifted in. Payton must be in the water. Taking a deep breath, China pulled the far-too-tiny pink pieces of her bikini out of the beach bag. Why hadn't she gone out and bought a one-piece? She didn't wear a bathing suit often. Her two-piece was years old. She liked to sunbathe sometimes so she'd chosen a bikini for that reason, with no intention of wearing it in front of someone like Payton.

Someone like Payton? Someone she was attracted to.

Groaning, she slipped into the suit and was grateful there was no mirror for her to review how she looked. It was best she just get into the water as soon as possible.

She braced herself with another deep breath and gathered her towel. Stepping into the sunshine again, she looked out across the expanse of water. She had to admit it was wonderful to be so far away from all responsibilities. There were a few other boats around but they were just dots in the distance. She and Payton were alone.

"Hey, slowpoke. Come on in," Payton called from below her.

She moved to the side so she could see him.

A wolf whistle rent the air. She didn't have to look in the mirror to know that she was as pink as her suit after that sound of appreciation. China glared at him. "Stop." She had to get in the water soon. "Is there a ladder I can use?"

"Just jump. It's plenty deep here."

She dropped her towel and hesitated a moment before she leapt through the air. Seconds later, she came up, sputtering salt water.

"You're supposed to close your mouth before you hit the water," Payton remarked from where he had his hands wrapped across a plastic float.

"I know that," she barked, as she pushed her hair out of her face and kicked her legs at the same time.

"Come here and share my float. You'll get tired, treading water."

Payton's smile was large and inviting. His damp shoulders glistened in the sunlight. The urge to run her hand over the contracted muscles almost got the better of her. The man was making her crazy. She wasn't sure it was a good idea to get close to Payton when he was fully dressed but barely clothed and wet was clearly a bad idea.

Did she have a choice? She couldn't tread water forever. Slowly, she paddled toward him. He didn't move, making no effort to meet her halfway. When she was close enough to touch the float he shifted to the other end so she had plenty of space and they were in no danger of coming into contact. At least he was keeping his promise not to touch her, kiss her.

She wanted him to. Every fiber of her being screamed for him to do so. If she let go, gave in, what would happen?

Hot sex, a few days, weeks, maybe months of good times, but it would end. It always did. Her family had been fun to be a part of at one time. A family together, and then it had been over. Her family dynamics had taught her that if you messed up you were out. She wasn't going to set herself up for that kind of hurt. She'd do something wrong and Payton wouldn't want her anymore.

A few minutes went by with neither of them saying anything as they drifted along next to the boat. She glanced at Payton and he was looking off toward the shore as if he had no idea she was around. Here she was, half-dressed, and he acted as if she didn't exist. She was so aware of him her body hummed.

What would it be like to touch his water-slick body? Feel those muscles. Be held against him? She needed to get a grip. She couldn't stand the tension that was building like a rogue wave. She had to ease it or she would be swept away.

"I think I'll swim out a little." She didn't wait for Payton's response.

With nice smooth strokes remembered from childhood swimming lessons, she moved away and parallel to the boat. She'd not gone far before she saw Payton keeping up with her stroke for stroke.

She continued on and he did also. When she'd gone as far as she could without resting she stopped. He did too.

"Are you following me?" she asked in a playful tone.

"Yes."

She started back toward the mattress left floating in the

water. Payton joined her but remained just out of touching distance. She stopped again.

"Stop following me." She cupped a hand and pushed water toward him. It splashed him in the face.

"So that's the way you want it to be." Payton returned a handful of water.

This time China dared to get closer then sent water flying his way. He returned it. Not to be outdone, she charged him, placing her hands on his shoulders in an effort to push him under.

When she made a move to retreat, Payton captured her wrist and pulled her to him.

"I thought you were going to keep your hands to yourself."

"You touched first. All's fair now."

The heat of his desire pressed firm and erect against her stomach. He hadn't been as immune to her as she'd believed. A hot longing filled her. Payton's hand skimmed more than stroked her as it followed the curvature of her hip over her waist to stop just under her arm. A tiny part of her brain registered that he must be standing on a sand bar. His other hand cupped her behind and held her securely against his length. The thumb of his other hand pushed against the material covering her breast, finding its way underneath. She moaned. Payton's fingers moved out from under her suit to the back and pulled at the strings holding it secure, leaving her top to float around her neck.

"Wrap your legs around my waist."

In a haze of need China did as he requested, bringing herself into a position where his length teased her center.

His voice was husky and low as he demanded, "Hold on to my shoulders and lean back. I want to see you, touch you, taste you."

She came out of the passion-filled daze long enough to say, "I don't think—"

"Sweetheart, it's only you and me for miles. Look at me."

Her gaze came up to lock with his. His eyes were dark with need, and looked like the stormclouds they'd watched roll in days earlier.

China's heart skipped a beat. It was a heady feeling to know she'd put that look in his eyes. She did as he asked. Titillated, excitement flowed through her veins. Hypersensitive to every movement of Payton's hands across her belly, over her ribs until they cupped her breast, she shivered.

His dark head slowly descended. She held her breath as his tongue flicked her straining nipple. China moaned. Her core tightened as heat coiled in her. She shifted against him. Payton made a throaty sound of passion. She'd never before felt such blistering, intense need. Allowing her no time to adsorb what was happening, he brought his lips down to her breast again and sucked. Her hips flexed, pushing her core against him.

Payton groaned as if in pain but his focus didn't leave her breast. His wet tongue circled her nipple and China moved forward again. His mouth released her and he mumbled between fleeting kisses across her chest, "Sweetheart, you're killing me," before his mouth captured her other nipple.

China's fingers bored into his shoulders, clinging for dear life in the middle of the emotional storm Payton was creating within her.

She wanted, wanted… She wanted Payton. Forget all her "should nots." She had to have him.

His hand slid along her back and between her shoulders to cup the back of her head. He brought her mouth forward to meet his lips.

The kiss was one of reassurance. Deep, slow and searing.

The heat in her exploded into a raging fire.

His other hand lowered, his finger found the edge of her bikini bottom and pushed beneath. China's heart tapped out of control. Instinctively, she loosened her grip on his shoulders, giving his prying hand better access.

He didn't hesitate to take her offering. His fingers circled her thigh until they reached the jointure of her legs. Pushing aside the narrow scrap of material, he teased her center.

The throbbing built until she squirmed. She had to have his touch. Begged for it. He had to stop the ragging need that clawed for release. China flexed her hips in invitation.

Payton softly chuckled as his mouth brushed over her jaw. "Not yet, sweetheart." His dipped his finger into her center but just enough to find the wet warmth that was her and not the Gulf.

When she whimpered in complaint, he reentered as far as he could. With a sigh of rapture, China squeezed her legs around Payton's waist, arched her back and let the sensation of pure, perfect, pleasure overtake her.

CHAPTER EIGHT

PAYTON HAD NEVER seen anything more stunning. He'd traveled all over Europe. Studied the most famous of paintings, visited the Alps in the winter, but noting came close to preparing him for what China looked like with her breasts raised to the sun and coming apart in his arms. He gave thanks that he'd lived to see it. China in her glory was the essence of what being alive meant.

He'd stepped over the line. There was no turning back now. He wanted more. All.

China had touched him and that had been all it had taken to send him over the edge. He'd tried to keep things friendly. Had given her space on the float. Had swum far enough away they wouldn't accidentally brush against each other. Then she'd come after him. He wanted that fire, that passion.

Payton pulled her to him and held her close. He waited until her breathing evened and her legs were no longer circling his waist and dangled in the water. Holding her around the waist, he let her stand. He took her hand. "Can you swim to the boat?"

She didn't answer.

"China, please look at me, sweetheart." She finally lifted her gaze to meet his. "Thank you."

"Why? You didn't…"

"No I didn't. But you were the most wondrous thing I've ever seen. Now, if you think you can swim, I'd like to go back to the boat and spend some more time in private exploring you."

"I can swim."

"Turn around and let me tie your top."

She presented him her back. After he'd fixed her top in place he stepped close enough to let her know that his desire hadn't diminished. He placed a kiss on the ridge of her shoulder.

They walked to the end of the sandbar hand in hand. As the water became too deep, they swam. At the boat, Payton lowered the small ladder at the back and climbed aboard. He took China's hand and helped her to the deck. She started to pull her hand away but he held it fast. He took her into his arms and gave her a soft kiss that should leave her no doubt she was desired.

The subdued and no longer forthright China had him worried that she might be regretting what had happened in the water. He didn't want that. Quite the contrary, he wanted her as hot and bothered as she'd been earlier.

Seconds later her arms came up to circle his neck. Her mouth opened and his tongue intertwined with hers. His manhood pulsated for release between them.

Payton pulled his mouth away. "Sweetheart, it has been a long time for me. I'm not going to last much longer. You deserve better, but could we go inside the cabin where I don't have to worry about sharing you with the world?"

She raised her big doe-like eyes to meet his gaze and nodded slightly. Releasing her, he took her hand and led her into the cabin.

Slow down, man, or you're going to scare her.

Taking a deep breath in the hope of calming his libido, he turned to face China. Her eyes were wide. They held a hint of anticipation mixed with uncertainty. That was one of the many aspects of her personality that he found appealing. She seemed to be confident and sure one minute, needy and naive the next.

Payton cupped her face, brushing his thumb across her cheek. "You're beautiful."

Her gaze left his for a spot somewhere on the bunk.

"Look at me, China." Her look met his again. He said softly, "I don't lie." She blinked as if in acceptance.

Payton ran the pad of his thumb over her kiss-swollen lips and she smiled. It was one of a woman who suddenly grasped her power.

China placed her hands on his chest. With exceedingly slow movements she trailed her fingers over his skin, touching and circling his nipple before moving on follow the ridge of his pectoral muscle. She skimmed her palm across his chest like a gentle wind, making his skin tingle in her wake. Stepping closer, she placed a kiss on his neck and nipped his skin before going up on her toes. She brushed her body against his already straining erection.

Could he take much more? Afraid to touch her for fear he'd push her against the bath door and take her without thought, he kept his hands tightly fisted at his sides, giving her time to feed her need.

As she kissed his jaw her hands traveled down over his ribs to his waist until they reached the top of his swim trunks. There she ran her fingers around the line of his waistband. At the back, China pushed a finger under the material but quickly pull it out again.

He groaned and moved a half a step closer. The woman would be the death of him.

"Not much fun to be teased, is it?" she murmured next to his mouth.

He wasn't answering that question because if he did it wouldn't be with words but actions.

She went flat-footed again and began to explore his chest with her tongue. One hand left his waist to brush against his manhood.

That did it. In one swift motion he sealed her mouth with his, tongue finding her warm sanctuary as he picked her up, turned around and fell to the bunk.

Payton rolled so that he didn't crush her. China's legs were entangled with his. He ran a hand up the expanse of the creamy silken skin of a thigh until he found the bottom of her bikini. Tugging, and with her help, he removed them. Just as quickly he had her top on the floor. Standing, he pushed his wet bathing suit down. He glanced at China. She'd rolled onto her side with an arm hiding her breasts from view as she unabashedly watched him.

"Like what you see?"

The corners of her lips rose. That small action was enough to make him feel ten feet tall. No longer feeling like a victim of cancer, he found his previous male swagger returning under her admiration.

If she wanted a show he'd give her one. Turning slowly, he presented her with his back as he dug into the backpack he kept hanging on a peg. With relief he found what he sought. Just before he turned around, the touch of a finger moving over one cheek of his backside had his blood heating to boiling.

"I've been wondering what that butt looked like without clothes covering it."

His heart rate went into hyper mode. With a rumble deep in his throat he opened the package and prepared himself. Turning, he came down on her and at the same time pushed her back against the bunk. Nudging her legs apart, he looked at her. China reached for him, pulling him to her as he pushed forward and found her hot, waiting center. She lifted her hips in welcome.

China was so incredibility accepting and responsive to his every touch. He leaned down and kissed her, and to his great satisfaction she shuddered in his arms. He followed with his own release to collapse next to her, one leg resting possessively across one of hers.

While ill, he'd not felt like having sex. Being dumped hadn't helped and he'd never been into mindless encounters. But never had he had such mind-blowing sex.

But that wasn't accurate either. It was lovemaking when shared with China.

China looked at Payton lying beside her. Her head rested on his outstretched arm. She was snuggled close and one of his legs was entwined with hers. Moving would be impossible even if she wanted to, which she didn't.

When she'd met Payton never in a million years would she have believed that she'd end up in his arms. A fleeting touch of lips along her ear said that he was waking. She turned her face into the crook of his neck and inhaled the warm, musky scent of him. No matter how long she lived she'd remember this.

China didn't know if it had happened when she'd called him an idiot and he'd taken it so well, or had it been when they'd watched the storm roll in, but she had let this man charm her, and she liked it.

Payton's hand brushed back her hair from her face. "You okay?"

"Ah-ha."

"You might want to look at me so I know for sure."

China raised her head and smiled. "I'm better than okay."

"I'm sorry things were rushed. I'll do better next time."

More brazen than she'd ever been in her life, China shifted out of his hold and turned so her arms crossed and rested on his chest. "I'm not complaining. I thought you rather excelled at being rushed."

His grin was slow and sexy. "Those kinds of compliments can get you almost anything."

"How about something to eat? I'm starving."

"That I can do." Payton gave her a quick kiss before he stood. "I brought a picnic lunch. Nothing fancy."

"I don't need fancy. Just substantial."

"Here." He handled her a long thin piece of glossy floral fabric that had been hanging from a peg on the wall. "You can put this on while your bathing suit dries."

"I'm not putting on some other woman's sarong, am I?"

"Yes."

"Yes?" she shrieked, throwing her legs over the side of the bunk and grabbing the blanket to cover herself.

Payton grabbed her shoulders, stopping her. "I kind of like you jealous." He placed a swift kiss on her lips. "It's my sister's. She left it here the last time she came sailing with me."

China relaxed.

Payton opened a small cabinet above the bunk, giving China a full view of his physique. The urge to reach out and run her fingers over his tight abdominals had her hand trembling. He had gained some weight over the last few weeks. If she hadn't known he'd been sick she would have never guessed.

He must have sensed she was admiring him. "If you don't stop staring at me like that, you're going to be really hungry by the time we get to food."

China swallowed hard. Was she brave enough to call his bluff? Maybe not a few weeks ago but now... She reached out and let her hand drift over his warm skin. It rippled beneath her touch. She watched in fascination as his manhood grew and stood proudly before her.

Payton growled, dropping the shorts he'd been holding to the floor. "Now you've done it. No food for you."

China didn't mind at all.

Payton laid out on the deck a sheet he'd retrieved from the drawer under the bunk. Of the few supplies he'd brought with him from the house, a tablecloth hadn't been on the list. He set the sack he'd carried aboard in the center.

He'd left the cabin so China could dress and have a few moments to herself. He needed them too. The afternoon had been intense, amazing and totally mind-blowing. China took so long to join him that he worried he might have to go in after her. Maybe giving her some space had been a bad idea. The one thing he didn't want her to do was withdraw. He wasn't ready to let go of what he'd experienced in her arms.

He cared too much about her. But could there really be more? What if he got sick again? Was he willing to put her through that? If he took a chance, would she leave him like Janice had?

"Hey," China said, bringing him out of his dark thoughts. With the sun as a backdrop, she looked sweet, fresh and well loved. His heart swelled. He'd never seen a woman look more desirable. With great restraint, he stopped himself from grabbing her and taking her again.

"Hi." The simple word came out rusty. He cleared his throat. "Come and have some lunch." Payton stood and stepped to meet her. Offering his hand, he was pleased when China took it. He led her around one side of the cabin to the bow of the boat.

Her gasp made him look at her. "Is something wrong?"

"No. This is just so…wonderful. I hadn't any idea you planned to eat up here."

Payton smiled, pleased with his surprise.

She visibly relaxed.

"Come sit down. I think you'll like my other surprise as well."

Payton helped her sit on a cushion and took his place, making a point not to come into contact with her. He was afraid if he did the food would be forgotten one more time. Opening the brown bag, he pulled out a smaller white one with the name "Sid's" printed in red on the side.

"You stopped by Sid's."

The sound of amazement in her voice made him smile. "I did," he said proudly. He opened the bag, pulled out a sandwich in a wrapper and handed it to her.

"A shrimp po boy. My favorite."

"I know. I asked."

She looked at him with a shocked expression. "What's wrong?"

"It's just that I don't think anyone has ever gone to the trouble to ask what I like."

Why? Hadn't someone, her parents, ever cared enough to be interested in her likes and dislikes? "Well, I did." He grinned. "I also found out that you like hush puppies almost as much as you do chocolate." Payton pulled his sandwich out of the bag then offered China a canned drink from the small, soft-sided cooler he had nearby. He removed the wrapping from his sandwich and took a bite. "This is good." He shook the thick sandwich slightly in the air.

"You didn't think you'd like it?"

He chuckled. "I guess not, but I should've known better." As they ate he looked out over the water. Finishing his sandwich, he remarked, "It must have been nice to live in such an ideal place. Small-town USA. The beach nearby. Everyone knowing what you like to eat."

Had China flinched?

She didn't look at him as she said, "Sometimes things aren't as ideal on the inside as they appear on the outside. Even paradise has its problems."

"That's mighty cynical."

"You never know what towns, families, people are like until you're a part of them."

"My family is pretty tight-knit. Or at least they were until I left. I'm close to my sister, but then again she is about the only one not mad at me. Her husband and kids are great. The tough part about being in a family is that it doesn't go well when you don't go along with the 'family plan.'"

China put her sandwich down on a napkin and looked off into the distance. "I can hardly remember what our family plan was"

"Why's that?" Payton asked softly.

China didn't understand it but for some reason she wanted Payton to know, to tell him the whole story. "I had a solid family. You know, the kind that everyone looks at and says, 'That's the perfect family.' A father who had a good job, a mom who was home for us, three kids and a dog." She put her hand up and made quotations marks in the air. "The perfect American family."

"Something happen to that?"

"My brother turned sixteen and it was as if everything exploded. The band that had held us tight popped off. Chad had always been headstrong but as a teenager he really started bucking the rules. Began running around with the wrong crowd. Or at least it wasn't the crowd my parents wanted him to be involved in."

She paused. Did she really want Payton to know all her dirty laundry?

"And?"

With a sigh of resignation she continued. "Father got wind of it and cracked down. Hard. He suspected Chad was drinking and doing drugs. He had Mom search his room regularly. Dad forbade him to go out at night. Told him who he could see and not see. My brother rebelled big time. Things got difficult at home, his grades dropped and his relationship with Father went from bad to worse. There was screaming all the time, doors slamming. Mom and Father couldn't agree about how to handle Chad and they fought. Mom isn't a strong person and she finally gave up and let Dad have his way." China took a sip of her drink, easing her dry throat.

"When the police called…" she hesitated but then blurted it out "…to say they'd picked up Chad on the beach, smoking pot with a group of other teens, my father went ballistic. Mom tried to calm him down but he wouldn't listen to reason. Chad stayed in jail overnight. Father didn't even drive him home."

"And he ran away."

She nodded, hating to see the look of pity on Payton's face, but as she'd gone this far she might as well tell him everything. She said softly, "Mom and Father blamed each other for Chad's behavior. She said he was too hard on him and he believed she went behind his back and let Chad have his way too much. I don't know which it was. My parents still struggle with not knowing what has happened to him. Everything in our lives became either before or after Chad left. Not that we ever talk about it."

"That had to have been tough."

"Yeah, it was. Still is. Our family came apart like an old rag. Mom and Father are still married but they never really talk. My younger sister doesn't speak to them. She was close to Chad and blames them for pushing him out. I even have to work at it to get her to have anything to do with me. She wanted out of the house and I just wanted what we had before my brother left—my happy family back. Kelsey managed to get through high school without getting into any real trouble. I ran interference most of the time when I thought Father might really blow his top."

"Where's your sister now?"

"Oh, she lives here in town."

"And you don't see her?"

"It does sound bad when you put it like that. I see her at Christmastime mostly. Even then I have to beg her to meet me somewhere. She refuses to go to our parents'. Won't have anything to do with them. I might see her on an occasional birthday. I send cards on hers but she doesn't do that in return. She's a nutritionist at the hospital. There were a few years there I didn't think she would finish school but she did." China looked away from Payton. "I shouldn't have dumped this on you. I'm sure you know more now about my family than you wanted to."

"I'm glad you told me." He brushed his thumb across her hand. "I want to know everything about you."

She gave him a weak smile and removed her hand.

"Have you ever looked for your brother?"

"I think Mom did for a while without Father knowing it but the most I do is check the paper and see if he is ever in it. I think at this point on some level even Father would like to know that he isn't dead. I certainly would." She picked up her sandwich again. "Enough about my life. Hadn't we better be getting back?"

"Are you ready to be captain again?"

"I kind of like being in control."

He gave her a suggestive grin. "I'm going to keep that in mind."

She heat crawl up her neck. "I didn't mean it like that."

He cupped her cheek. "Don't apologize. I rather like the idea. And you're right. We should be thinking about getting back."

Together they gathered up what was left of their meal and stored it below. She changed into her top and jeans before leaving the cabin. Payton was coming in as she was going out. He pulled her to him, taking her mouth in a sweet and tender kiss. China wrapped her arms around his neck and leaned into him. A heavenly minute later Payton broke away with a groan.

"If we don't stop here, I'm going to take you again right out here on the deck when I have a far more comfortable bed at my house."

She gave him a pointed look. "Are you assuming that I'm going to join you?"

"Sweetheart, with you I don't dare assume. The best I can do is hope. You always seem to surprise me." With an exhalation he stepped away. "I'll get the mainsail up," he called. "You want to man the rudder again while I handle the jib?"

It was dusk when China watched as Payton maneuvered the boat into the slip at the marina. She had to admit this had been the best day of her life. Perfect. But could it last? Could he be her safe haven?

She had so much baggage. Payton did too. Did he even want more than a sexual relationship? Could she or would she agree to anything further if he did? She needed security and he had just moved to town, had a new job and was trying to figure out the direction he wanted his life to go. Payton didn't sound like the man for her in the long run.

China studied his profile. Straight backed with wide

shoulders, Payton looked as if he'd been born on a boat. His ability to make her come alive when he touched her made her shiver to think about it. China smiled. She really couldn't resist him.

Payton showed her how to tie the boat firmly at the bow and had her do it at the stern, guiding her through the steps. China waited while he hopped aboard again and got their lunch trash. He climbed back onto the dock, tossed the bag in a nearby garbage can, took her hand and they walked toward his car. They passed a group of deep-sea fishing boats along the way. On one, a couple of men looked as if they were working on some fishing gear.

"Have you ever been deep-sea fishing?" Payton asked.

"N—"

The air was suddenly scorched by a four-letter word. They both stopped and looked back.

One of the men was holding his hand up and jumping around.

"Pete, stand still and let me have a look," the other man said in an annoyed voice.

"Wh'ta you need to look for? You're the one who pushed the damn hook through my finger."

"I've got to get it out," the other man said in a high voice.

"You're not touching me. You'd kill me," Pete yelled.

"Then I'll take you to the emergency room."

"That'll cost too much. No insurance."

China and Payton walked over to the boat. "Can we help? I'm Dr. Payton Jenkins and this is China Davis. She's a nurse."

Peter stopped pacing, his face contorted in pain. "Yeah." He held up his meaty finger for them to see. Between the first and second knuckle of his index finger the bright gold eye end of a nook jutted from his skin. There wasn't any blood but the tight white line around Pete's mouth told it was painful.

"You have a first-aid kit?" Payton asked.

"Yeah," the man without the hook in his finger said.

"Get it, please."

"Right away." He disappeared into the cabin of the boat.

The dimming lighting along the pier necessitated that Payton and China climb aboard in order to see. The light of the cabin overhang was better, otherwise she would have insisted that Payton work on the dock. Compared to Payton's immaculate sailboat, this one was a trash dump. He stepped onto the boat then helped her. In short order, which China was astonished by, the man returned with the first-aid kit. Apparently things were more in organized inside the cabin.

"Okay, Pete, you need to sit down." Payton looked around as if unsure where that would happen.

The man pushed the stuff piled on a raised captain's chair off onto the deck with a clatter. Pete dropped into the chair without question, looking far too pale in the faint light.

With a raised eyebrow of bewilderment that was almost comical Payton said, "All right, then, let's see what we've got." Payton took the man's hand in his and examined the wound site. He looked at Pete. "You know I can't pull this back. The barb will get more securely stuck in your finger. That will require surgery."

"I was 'fraid of that," he said in a tight voice as he glared at his friend.

"I'm going to have to push it though. The one promise I can make is that it's going to hurt like the devil."

"Just do it, Doc. I can't walk around with this." He glanced at China as if reminding himself to watch his language. "Blasted hook in my finger."

"I'm going to need some wire pliers. Got any?"

"Sure," Ralph said. "What kind do you want?"

"The sharpest will suffice."

"Coming up."

Payton turned his attention back to Pete. "I'm going to clip off the eye end of the hook and use that end to push it through." Payton rubbed the spot on the finger where the hook should come through. "The skin on our fingers is some of the toughest of the body. Yours is especially thick because of the type of work you do. This won't be fun."

"Never thought it would be," Pete announced stoically, but a look of fear showed through his bravado.

"So, Pete, how long you been a fisherman? China, would you see if you can find some alcohol that we can use to sterilize this with?" Payton was referring to the hook.

She opened the kit and located a few alcohol pads.

"Aw, about twenty years or so," Pete answered.

The other man returned with the pliers and handed them to Payton.

"China, open one of those and wring the liquid out over the hook and the pliers. It may take two."

She tore the alcohol package and did as he instructed over the hook. As the liquid ran over Pete's finger he winced.

"Now the pliers," Payton said.

China squeezed all she could out of the first pad and then opened another.

"Okay, we're ready to start. China, hold Pete's hand down against the arm of the chair."

She moved around beside Payton and took Pete's wrist securely in her hand.

"I think I'll go see about something in the cabin," the friend stated.

"Yeah, that's just like you, running from a little blood."

Pete looked at Payton and nodded his head toward the man. "He faints at the sight of blood."

Payton stopped what he was doing. "Go into the cabin. I don't need to have to stitch you up if you hit your head." Payton waited for the man to disappear into the cabin. "All right, Pete, you may feel a tug when I cut off the eye."

"I'm ready when you are, Doc."

Payton snipped off the end of the hook quickly and surely. Pete let out a yelp.

"Okay, this is going to be the hard part. China, hold him tight. Pete, grip the armrest. Here we go." Putting the flat of the pliers against the top of the hook Payton pushed. China watched as his chew tightened in his effort to not hurt the man and still get the hook to move through the skin.

Pete hissed. Payton leaned into the effort. Time seemed to creep by before the barbed end of the hook made a bump in Pete's skin and then popped through. Pete had turned white.

"Oh, hell," Payton said.

"What's wrong?" China asked, looking at the hook.

"The tip of the hook is missing. It may have broken against the bone or been that way before it went in but either way it's missing."

"What's the problem?" Pete asked in a tight voice.

"It means that I have no choice but to take you to the E.R. It has to be x-rayed."

"I can't pay."

"Let's not worry about that now. You could get an infection and it could kill you if that tip stays in your finger."

"Come on, Doc. Is there no other way?"

"No." Payton said the word as if he was a general giving orders. "China, we'll take him in the car. Let's get the finger covered and get moving."

China pulled out what bandage and tape she could find in the kit and used them to cover the finger, hook and all.

"Hey," Payton called into the cabin to Pete's friend. "We're going to have to take Pete to the E.R."

"What?" the man stuck his head out of the cabin.

"I've got to go to the hospital, man. Come pick me up," Pete said.

"Hold your hand up above you heart and it will help the throbbing," China told Pete, as they walked up the pier. Payton had jogged ahead to get his car and meet them at the entrance of the pier. Payton was pulling up when Pete started to sag beside her. She put an arm around his waist but with his girth she had little chance of holding him upright. The car screeched to a halt and Payton came running to help.

Together they steadied Pete and helped him into the back seat of the car.

"Let's go before he does more damage to himself or one of us." Payton took his seat behind the steering wheel.

With Pete seated and his head lying back against the top of the seat, China said, "I'll ride back here and make sure he doesn't pass out." She climbed into the backseat.

Payton didn't break any laws but he didn't hesitate to move as fast as possible through the traffic. At the hospital, he pulled under the covered emergency entrance. China had her door open and was coming around the car to help with Pete by the time Payton was opening the door. Together, supporting Pete on each side, they walked into the building.

As one of the nurses came toward them Payton announced. "I'm Dr. Jenkins from the walk-in clinic downtown. I need an exam room."

"This way," the nurse said, and directed them to a space.

With Pete's help they were able to get him on the bed and settled.

The E.R. doctor on service that evening entered the room. "What we got here, Payton?"

"Hey, Rick. This is Pete and he had a fish hook in this finger. He needs an x-ray to find the tip."

China was already in the process of removing the bandage as they spoke. When she had it off both men looked at it.

"Well, you're in luck. We aren't busy tonight and therefore neither is X-Ray. Should be able to do one right away. We might want to finish getting that hook out first, though," Rick said.

"Hey, Doc." Pete looked at Payton. "I'd like you to do it."

Payton looked at Rick. He shrugged. "Sure, Pete. If that is what you want."

"I'll get the supplies," China said, and started across the room to the cabinets.

"When's the last time you had a tetanus shot, Pete?"

"Heck, I don't know."

"Then you'll need one before you're released. I'll add it to the chart."

China joined them again and placed what Payton would need on the stand beside the bed. Payton picked up the needle with the lidocaine in it. "Pete, I'm going to deaden your finger then we'll get this hook out of it."

Pete flinched and moved away. "Hey, I don't like needles."

"You'll like the alternative less. I need you to lay your hand on the bed and look out into the hall. And don't move."

Slowly Payton pushed the thin needle under Pete's skin near the hook. To Pete's credit he didn't cringe and Payton was soon finished. Picking up the pliers China had brought from the supply cabinet, Payton said, "Okay, let's get this done." Payton seized the angry end of the hook with the nose of the pliers and pulled.

As soon as the hook was removed, China placed one of the alcohol pads over the wound.

Pete flinched but didn't jerk away.

Payton dropped the hook in the red biohazardous box. "How are you doing, Pete?"

"Fine." There was a thin white line around Pete's lips.

"Now off to X-Ray. Hopefully we got it all."

"If not, what happens then?"

"I'm afraid surgery." At the puckering of Pete's lips, as if a complaint was forthcoming, Payton said, "Let's not worry about that until we see what an x-ray shows."

The X-ray tech wheeled Pete off.

Twenty minutes later Payton entered the exam room, where China was bandaging Pete's finger. "Well, the radiologist says everything looks great. No foreign objects visible."

Pete's buddy entered the room with a searching look and wide eyes.

"Well, I see your ride is here. When the desk nurse is finished with the paperwork you're free to go."

"Thanks Doc," Pete called, as she and Payton were going out the door. "You ever want to go fishing, me and my buddy are the ones to come to."

Payton waved a hand above his head in acknowledgment.

"No way I'm I getting on that tub again," he whispered to China.

"Thank goodness. I was afraid you might invite me along."

They laughed. Minutes later, Payton opened the car

door for China and she slid into the seat. An air of uncertainty settled over her as he drove through the almost empty parking lot. Would he ask her to come home with him? Did she want to? At the exit Payton paused and looked at her for a long moment before he said, "China, I won't assume but...would you come home with me?"

All that confidence Payton had shown just a few minutes earlier as he'd handled the removal of the hook had gone out the window. He was as insecure about their relationship as she was. Somehow that reassured her.

She nodded. A huge smile covered his face as he took her hand and placed it on his thigh before he pulled out into the traffic.

Somewhere after midnight Payton rolled over and kissed her shoulder before his mouth found hers. His hand cupped a breast, teasing the nipple. This time their lovemaking was slow and easy. Later, much later, China curled up next to his warm body and inhaled deeply. Her eyes slowly closed on an exhalation.

Life could be safe and secure.

"So, do you want to go parasailing with me today?" Payton asked, as he placed kisses across her belly midmorning of the next day.

"What?"

"You know, where someone pulls you behind the boat and you're attached to a parachute and you go up in the air."

She rolled her eyes and said in a sarcastic voice, "I know what parasailing is. I just wanted to know why you would want to do it."

"Because I never have."

"Do you have a death wish or something?"

Payton tensed.

"I'm sorry. I didn't think. It hard for me to imagine you having had cancer. You seem so hearty."

"I am hearty."

"You know what I mean."

Payton sat up and looked at the majestically beautiful woman before him who had no idea how much she affected his world. "I know. I just like giving you a hard time."

"Will you tell me about it?" she asked softly.

Payton hesitated. Did she really want to know all the gory details? She deserved to. With a resigned release of a breath he said, "I worked long hours in the E.R. in the largest trauma center in Chicago. I didn't mind. I loved what I did. Everything gave me an adrenaline rush. I'm from a long line of doctors. In fact, my great-grandfather was on the board when the hospital opened. My father sits on the board today."

"You were headed that way too," China said, as a statement of fact.

"Yeah. I was on the fast track with the in-crowd ticket. But I got sick. I didn't see it coming or maybe I didn't want to admit it. I started feeling tired. Then I found the lump in my neck."

He couldn't miss the soft intake of China's breath. To her credit, she didn't say anything.

"I couldn't ignore any longer that something was seriously wrong. If I had been one of my patients I would've chewed me out for not going to the doctor sooner. I went to see my best buddy and…" Payton grinned "…he did chew me out. There was a biopsy, the bad news radiation and chemo. My parents came unglued. My fiancée handed my ring back."

"Not much of a person, in my opinion." She sounded like a warrior fighting for her family. He liked the sound of it.

"Thank you. I agree. It hurt at the time but in hindsight I don't think we would've made it anyway. She was far more interested in my family name and its influence than me."

China smiled at him. "Well, I'm glad she let you go, otherwise I might not have met you."

He gave her an appreciative kiss. "Thank you. I feel the same way about you."

"So how did your family react to your diagnosis?"

"The same way they do to everything. He'll overcome this.' My mom became my major caregiver. I'll forever be grateful to her."

"I hear a but in there."

"Well, Mom almost became oppressive with her help. She was worried about losing me and I understand that, but when I began to get better she had a hard time accepting I needed her to back off."

"I'm guessing she didn't take it well when you decided to move down here."

"No, and neither did my father. They wanted me close because they love me and are concerned about me but they were also upset that I would give up all they considered important, like my position at the hospital, my influence in the community, to move down here to nothing." When China stiffened he was quick to say. "Sorry, those are their words, not mine. To say they didn't understand I had changed or I needed to move my life in a different direction would be an understatement."

"I know that this isn't any of my business but are you seeing someone regularly for check-ups?" The note of concern in her voice didn't escape his notice.

"Yes, Nurse China. I'm taking care of myself. I have regular bloodwork done. I'm going to Chicago next month for a checkup." His look met hers. "Hey, why don't you go with me?"

China was surprised to find at she rather liked the idea of meeting Payton's family. "How about we see when the time comes?" If she made that step, she would be trusting that there was something more between them than just being bed friends.

"Okay, I'll let it go for now but what about that parasailing?"

"How about I watch you?"

"It would be a lot more fun if you went up with me. We could make out, maybe try a little something else."

China laughed and swatted him playfully. "You're trying to live dangerously again."

Payton ran a hand from her foot up along her calf and smiled when she shivered. "Yes, maybe I am, but it sounds like fun, doesn't it?" He dropped his voice to a sexy persuasive tone.

She smiled. "I could just kiss you before you go up."

"That's not the same. Come on, China. I think it would be fun." He gave her a pleading look.

"Okay, if I agree to do that, what are you going to do for me?"

China felt her cheeks growing warm in reaction to Payton's wolfish grin. She swallowed the lump of anticipation in her throat. "That would be nice but I really had something else in mind."

He narrowed his eyes. "Like what?"

"Like going to a botanical garden."

His look became unsure, as if spending the day looking at plants wasn't his idea of fun. To his credit he said, "Sure. How about Tuesday? We're both off."

"How do you know that?"

"I checked the schedule."

"Are you stalking me?" She gave him a dubious look.

Payton moved in close, becoming predatory. "And if I were?"

China liked it that he'd been interested enough to check on when she worked. With hooded eyes she said, "I guess I don't mind."

"Since I can't talk you into going parasailing with me today, how about we spend the day on the beach? Maybe try some skinny-dipping?"

"That sounds like fun but I make no promises about the skinny-dipping."

"Given time, I bet I can convince you it would be fun." He grabbed her and tugged her to him, suppressing her giggle when his lips found hers.

CHAPTER NINE

PAYTON HAD TO admit the day had been more interesting than he'd anticipated. China had almost hummed with her excitement over visiting the Beaumont Botanical Gardens. Her reaction mimicked his to the thoughts of going sailing or, better yet, having China beneath him. He could appreciate that delight.

He'd picked her up early Tuesday morning. They'd stopped by Dolly's for donuts and coffee on their way out of town. "So, do you have directions?"

"I do. It's only about four hours away."

"Four hours!"

"Did I forget to tell you that?" she said in a sugar-sweet voice.

He chuckled. "I think I've been had. I'm glad we don't have to be at work until two tomorrow. We're going to make a day of it and a night." At least he'd have China to himself for a good long time.

"I didn't bring anything to stay overnight."

He wiggled his brows. "You won't need it."

"Now I think I'm the one being had."

"Oh, I plan to."

China turned pink before she leaned back and gazed out his sunroof. "Looks like we're going to have a nice day. The last time I went to a botanical garden it rained. It was still wonderful but I didn't enjoy riding home damp."

"You walked around in the rain to see a garden?" Disbelief filled his voice.

"Sure, why not? It's a different world when it rains."

She did truly love this stuff. He was learning a different facet of China. Would he ever learn them all?

Payton enjoyed the drive. His family had always flown when taking vacations. Making long road trips had never really been his thing but he'd taken pleasure in the freedom he'd had when driving down from Chicago. He given credit to his smooth-driving car for making that trip fun but spending time with China on this one was far better. It was also fascinating to see the miles and miles of swamp as they motored through Louisiana. He'd seen pictures of the land but nothing compared to the view from bridge after long bridge over untamed acreage.

He and China chatted about nothing in particular, argued over what was the best fast-food restaurant, both agreeing that a chicken sandwich was far better than a hamburger. They even sang along at the top of their lungs with the radio, like two college students escaping on spring break.

The more time he spent with China the more he discovered he enjoyed being around her. That was in bed as well as out. All in all it was a pleasant morning and far more entertaining than he would have imagined.

But could it continue? Should he let it? Would she leave him if he got sick? No, but China had such a caring heart that she could become like his mom about his illness. He didn't want that. It would kill their relationship just as surely as if she walked out on him. Right now he was going to make the most of their time together.

Just before lunch he drove into the paved parking lot of the botanical gardens.

They were on their way to the entrance when China asked, "Are you hungry? If you are, we can get something at the vending machines."

He took her hand. "I'm open to whatever you want to do. This is your day."

She smiled up at him with such happiness in her eyes that it hit him like a fist to the chest. He'd like to always be the one to put that look on her face. Heaven help him, was there ever a better feeling? He returned her smile.

"Okay, then. I want to look. Those donuts I had are still with me." China took his hand. It was the first time she'd ever initiated a contact in public. He liked knowing she felt he was hers to touch.

"Maybe you should have thought a little longer about having that third donut."

She stopped and glared at him. "What're you trying to say? I'm getting fat?"

Payton put a hand over his heart. "No way." He slowly looked at her from the top of her head to her feet. She looked breathtaking in her light blue dress that showed her legs off. "No, I'd say you're just about perfect."

She giggled. A sound he treasured.

"Thanks. I do love it when you pour on the charm."

They started walking again. He lowered his chin, giving her a disbelieving look. "I put on charm?"

"Sure you do. You play Jean like a fine violin."

Payton brow wrinkled. "What does that mean?"

"That you sweet-talk her into getting your way." She glanced at him. There was a twinkle in her eyes.

"I do not."

China stopped and put her hands on her hips. "You

didn't think she wouldn't mention that you'd talked her into changing your schedule?"

He had the good grace to look contrite. "Well…" He drew the word out. "I might have done that. But in my defense, I wanted to spend the day with you."

China squeezed his hand and grinned.

Oh, yeah, he had it bad.

"Thanks. I think that's the nicest thing anyone has ever done for me."

They'd reached the information stand.

"There's no charge?" In his Chicago world he was charged for everything.

"Nope. Plants lovers, you know." China pulled a map of the gardens out of a rack.

Payton looked over her shoulder. "So, have you decided what we're going to do?"

"I have. We're going to take this path through the formal gardens, then down to the water gardens, and around this way." She used her finger to show him the path.

"Maybe I should have said stop by the vending machine after all. That looks like I might need to fortify myself for the trip."

"Come on. If you pass out I promise to leave you and come back for you later," she said in a kidding tone.

He chuckled. "You're a hard woman, Ms. Davis."

"No, I just don't want to miss a minute of the gardens. I've been trying to come here for years."

"Why haven't you?"

"I guess time, and my parents needed me." She shrugged. "I didn't have someone to enjoy the gardens with."

He looped her arm through the crook of his. "It's not parasailing but I'm glad I came."

They'd started down a path between knee-high box-woods when China said, "I'm glad you did too."

Some time later they entered a wooded area. "These are pretty. What type of plant is this?" Payton asked.

"Southern azalea. There're thousands of varieties. They come in all colors—pink, red, white. Many more."

"My mom would love these. She'd have the gardener planting some at her house if she only knew."

"It would be a waste of the gardener's time. They don't grow well that far north."

She reached out and touched a petal of a flower gently.

It suddenly struck him that China would make a wonderful mom. "Okay, lesson learned."

"Well, that's a first. I taught the smartest doctor I know something."

Payton squared his shoulders and puffed out his chest as if he were a peacock, strutting. "I'm the smartest doctor you know?"

"Don't let it go to your head, Doc. But you are the best I've seen. You were great with Pete."

He leaned in close, as if he was going to tell her a secret. "You're not just saying that because you like other things about me?"

She pushed him away. "Please." She grinned. "You do think highly of yourself."

"Those little noises of pleasure you make at just the right moment might make me believe you think I'm pretty nice." She did have a way of making him feeling special. Something no other woman had ever done. Because of her admiration his male ego was in fine form.

A blush covered her cheeks and she looked away. "Quit trying to embarrass me and let's go and see the water garden. The pictures of it remind me of Monet's water lilies paintings."

"Now, those I know. Mom has one hanging in the living room."

"Figures," China muttered, as she led the way.

By midafternoon they'd found a small café that offered sandwiches and a shady place to eat. China took a seat at a small rod iron table for two under a huge oak that was part of the patio area belonging to the café. She watched as Payton joined her with a heart filled with happiness.

Payton's hair had grown over the weeks. There was a slight wave to it now. It felt warm and soft in her fingers. That she knew well from the number of times she'd run her fingers through it. He wore dark glasses against the sun but behind them were eyes of pure blue that twinkled when he teased, and he did that often. Her family wasn't that type. It was seductive to have someone notice her enough that they teased her. Payton had a way of making her feel important, not just being around because she was needed to help.

He put down the tray with the food and sat. They ate quietly, each lost in their own thoughts. Payton was really a fine-looking man, nice, caring, divine lover...

"You're staring at me. I really don't mind beautiful women doing that—"

"Sorry."

"What were you thinking?"

"That I should say thank you for bringing me today."

Payton took her hand and squeezed it then let it go. "It has been my pleasure and I mean that. You might have something with the 'stop and smell the roses' idea."

She grinned at him. "I hope that wasn't just a pun."

"No pun, just a thought."

"So you found out that you can feel alive without an adrenaline rush." She picked up her sandwich.

He met her gaze. "Was today about proving a point?"

She shook her head. "No, but it didn't hurt if I did. I don't think life is about what we do but about who and what we love."

"I love to sail."

"Yes. But why? What is there about sailing you love?"

Payton looked off into space a moment before returning his gaze to hers. "I love the way the water laps against the hull when I'm lying on my back, looking up at a blue sky."

"That—" her voice had a snap of awe in it "—is what living really is."

"Okay, Miss Know-it-All. What's really living for you?"

She almost blurted out, "Being with you," but she caught the words before they passed her lips. "When I put my hands down in rich soil and feel it crumble between my fingers. Or smell the wholesome goodness of where the sun kissed it."

"You didn't even have to think about your answer."

She met his gaze. "No, I didn't. I recognized that a long time ago. It's where I feel like I belong. Where I feel happy and secure."

"Security is important to you?"

"Yeah, I guess it is. I never really had it after Chad left. I was always afraid I'd mess up and Father would be telling me to get out. So, what are you looking for?"

He took a long moment to think. "I really don't know."

"You want to know what I think?"

"I don't know. Do I?"

She smirked. "I think you're looking for contentment."

"You're starting to sound like one of those Eastern gurus."

China picked up her drink cup. "I'm no guru. I just know that you can't always be chasing something to feel alive. The simple, slow-down method works for me. I think you need to look at why you need adventure or danger to feel alive."

"You might be getting a little preachy now."

She wrinkled her nose. "Sorry. That wasn't what I meant to do. How you spend your time really isn't my business anyway."

He captured her hand again and her gaze. "I'd like to be your business."

China's heart thumped faster.

"I think we have something special here, China. I'd like to believe that I'm your business and you're mine."

She gifted him with an easy smile of acceptance. "I'd like that too."

Payton leaned in and gave her a gentle kiss that assured her he meant every word.

Three hours later, he pulled the car to a stop in front of a magical, historical hotel in the French Quarter of New Orleans, complete with filigree rod iron balconies, huge green shutters and a wooden, cut-glass door. A young man dressed in red livery circled the car to stand at Payton's door.

"Payton, this is too much," China said in a voice breathy with amazement.

"Why?"

"I would've been comfortable with a roadside hotel."

"You would have but I wouldn't. I've stayed here a number of times. They had a room open, we needed one, so here we are."

"Figures." Payton moved in a more affluent world than hers. There was his need for adventure also. She wasn't always comfortable with either of those. Kelsey would appreciate his need for fast living. *Kelsey.* China missed her.

Wished she could share some sister time and tell Kelsey about Payton and the way he made her feel.

Payton had stepped out of the car and leaned down to look at her. "How's that?"

"You get what you want."

"Sweetheart, all I want right now is a hot bath and you, and not necessarily in that order."

She didn't miss his satisfied grin of male pride before he flipped the valet the keys and came round to help her out of the car. He offered her his arm and they walked into the lobby.

"It's unreal." China looked past the polished oak registration desk to the open courtyard beyond with a bubbling fountain.

He smiled indulgently and said, as if he were speaking to a child, "Go on out and look at the plants. I know you want to. Our room is across the courtyard so I'll meet you out there."

China gingerly touched the palm that towered over her head and studied the ground cover, which had been carefully cared for, until Payton joined her. He took her hand without comment, led her up the outdoor staircase and along the open walkway above the courtyard until they reached a door located furthest from the busy street outside the hotel.

Payton placed an old-fashioned skeleton style key into the lock and swung the door open. Taking one long step into the room, he tugged her in after him and pushed the door closed.

"Wha—?"

"This is what!" His mouth took hers as his hands lifted and brought her up against his sturdy body. The evidence of his desire stood thick between them. China wrapped her arms around his neck. Payton's hands cupped her behind.

He backed to the bed, bringing her down on top of him as he lay on the mattress of the canopied oak four-poster bed.

Her lips left his. She tilted back, still straddling his hips. "Beautiful bed."

Payton growled, "Forget the decor. I'm going to show you how comfortable it is." He rolled her over and took her lips again.

Once again his life had been turned upside down. Payton smiled. At least this time he was enjoying it. To have China wake in his arms was the height of satisfaction. They had spent the entire night in New Orleans in bed making love and sharing room service. He owed her another visit so they could get out and be tourists for a while. They'd returned to Golden Shores in enough time to change and get to work on time.

Payton was grateful they were busy. Every time he met China's gaze her eyes held this dreamy look that remind him of the time they'd spent together and he wanted her all over again. She'd give him a Cheshire cat grin as she passed him in the hall and he'd be hard for her.

Did she feel the same way? What if he got sick again? The questions went on and on. What he did know was that he was going to enjoy every minute he could with her.

They both, thankfully and disappointingly, had opposite shifts the rest of the week. They shared the weekend off and spent the time sailing, swimming, tending plants and, best of all, making love. He should have guessed by China's spirited attitude that she might be rather aggressive in the bedroom but when she'd become the aggressor during their lovemaking he'd almost embarrassed himself by losing control.

On the Monday afternoon after their amazing weekend Payton flipped a chart closed and stared out into space.

He had sworn that after Janice he'd never let himself truly open up to a woman again. He'd started over in a new place with a new chance at life, a dream home and a place to live life to the fullest. Then what happened? China.

He glanced at his watch. One-thirty. China would be in at two. To his great woe he and China were working opposite shifts again all week. She'd insisted that he take her home the night before. It had almost killed him but he'd done as she'd requested. Her reasoning had been that she needed her sleep and he wasn't letting her have any.

It had been so long for him and he found China irresistible. She hadn't complained and she was always eager to please. Maybe he'd demanded too much. She'd seemed reluctant to leave him during their long kiss that had had him hot for her again before she'd climbed the stairs to her apartment. In fact, if he hadn't been afraid he'd sound pathetic, he would've beg to go up with her.

Heaven help him, he had it bad. If he didn't pull it together he'd pounce on China the second she entered the clinic. Robin, Jean and Doris would appreciate that show but he had no doubt that China wouldn't. He glanced at his watch again. With a snort of disgust he pulled another chart off the stack.

Payton sensed China before he looked up to find her standing in the doorway.

"Hey," she said almost shyly.

"Hey." He grinned and came around the desk. To his disappointment, Larry came up behind her.

China didn't know what she was thinking when she stopped by Payton's office. That wasn't her habit when she came in for her shift but she'd been dying to see him. Even her gardening hadn't interfered with her daydreaming about him. She'd relived every moment they'd spent together, had even started to believe they might be building something lasting. Still, the closer she'd come to work time the more insecure she'd become. Maybe he'd just wanted her because she'd been available. He'd been sick, she was the first girl…

With nervous jitters, she'd approached his door and spoken. She had been relieved to see Payton smile and heat had come to his eyes. The same disappointment she felt showed on his face when Larry stepped up behind her. Just a look as simple and unsolicited as his made her stomach flutter. A warm, mushy feeling washed over her.

For all her believing she'd never let it happen, she'd fallen hopelessly in love with Payton.

"Hi, China," Larry said, as he squeezed by her into the office. "I'm not interrupting anything, am I?" He glanced at Payton and then at her.

"No," she and Payton said in unison.

Larry gave them both curious looks. She lowered her eyes and said, "I'll let you two talk."

China took a report from Robin then headed down the hall to speak to the two patients who were waiting in the exam rooms. Payton met her coming up the hall. He glanced around then grabbed her arm and pulled her into an empty exam room. Closing the door, he leaned back against it and brought her against him.

"I'm not leaving without this." His lips found hers.

Any concern she'd had that Payton might not still be interested in her vanished. His mouth was hot and heavy, asking, begging and taking. She tugged his knit collared shirt from his pants and slipped her hands underneath, finding his warm skin, letting her fingers trail around to his back.

One long delicious kiss later China pulled away. Payton's eyes held an intensity that said he wanted more. He desire pressed thickly against her. She sighed. Nothing had changed.

She said softly, "Payton, this isn't the time or place."

He let his forehead rest against hers. "I know. Can I see you tonight after you get off?"

"My parents are expecting me for dinner tonight."

He let her step away but didn't release her. "I'd love to meet your parents."

Was she ready for that? That wasn't a step forward she was sure she could make. What would Payton think of them?

"I don't know."

"Why? I've got to meet them some time. Come on, China. You're not ashamed of me, are you?" He grinned.

How could she say no? The man she loved should know everything about her. Especially her parents. "Don't be silly. If you want to go then be here at seven."

Payton was sitting in the parking lot talking on the phone with his friend and physician when China slipped into the passenger seat. He smiled in welcome.

"Yes, John. I'll have it redrawn tomorrow first thing."

"This won't wait, Payton. None of that pretending it will go away stuff. There may be nothing to it but I'm not taking any chances at this stage."

"I understand. I'll be a model patient, I promise."

"That'll be a change for the better."

"Funny, buddy, very funny."

"Tomorrow. No excuses."

"I got the message. Later, John."

Concern marred China's features. "What was that all about?"

"Nothing. Just a friendly reminder to have my blood drawn."

"That's all there is to it, isn't there?"

"Yes." He leaned over and gave her a quick kiss on the lips before starting the car.

She gave him a suspicious look. "You would tell me if something is wrong?"

"China, stop fussing. I'm fine. Leave it alone," he said, more sharply than he'd intended.

"I only asked because—"

He took her hand and squeezed it. "I know you care. Okay, which way to your parents'?"

"They live out the Bay Road but we've got to stop by the grocery store first."

He backed the car out of the parking spot. "What? You don't do the grocery shopping?"

"Mom needs a few things and she asked me to stop by and get them."

"Is she sick?"

"No. Why?"

"I was just wondering why she couldn't do her own shopping." Payton pulled into the main street and headed toward the store.

"She mentioned she needed to pick up a few things and I offered to get them for her. Do you have a problem stopping?"

"No, I was just surprised, that's all."

Forty-five minutes later Payton turned the car into the crushed shell drive China indicated. It was a simple board and batten house on stilts, facing the bay. Painted a light gray and trimmed in white, it was similar to the other homes lining the road. It had a long green manicured lawn that met a pier that stretched out into the water. Plants graced the porch that wrapped around the place on three sides. It was obviously a well cared-for home.

Payton gathered the grocery bags from the trunk and followed China up the steps to wait beside her at the front door. A woman with short gray hair and world-weariness about her mouth greeted them at the door. She offered a smile that didn't reach her eyes. How long had it been since she'd been truly happy?

"Hi, honey, come on in." Mrs. Davis stepped back and allowed China and Payton to enter.

"Mama, this is Payton Jenkins."

"Welcome, Payton. China told me she was bringing a friend. It's nice to meet you."

At one time being China's friend had sounded good but now he wanted to be more. "Hi, Mrs. Davis. It's nice to meet you."

She closed the door and led them into a large, comfortable-looking room.

"China, I've waited for you to start dinner."

Payton looked at China. She seemed okay with the arrangement. Why wasn't her mom cooking? China had been at work all afternoon.

"Well, I'll get started on the potatoes. I guess Father will want pork chops. I'll add a salad as well. Father should be home soon, shouldn't he?"

"Yes, I expect him any minute."

"Payton, you can bring those in here." China indicated the bags he still held. He followed her through the living room into the kitchen. It was much smaller than his but efficient-looking. He placed the groceries on the counter.

"Why don't you go out and talk to Mom while I get supper together?" China reached for a bag and started to unpack it.

Leaning his hip against the counter, he said, "You don't want my help?"

"No, I'll get it."

What was going on? China hated to go grocery shopping

and wasn't that big a fan of cooking. He reluctantly left her and returned to the living room.

"Payton, come in and make yourself at home. China can handle dinner. Have a seat." Mrs. Davis indicated a chair across the room from the one she was taking.

Payton sank into the overstuffed chair. Further across the room sat a well-used recliner. It had to belong to China's father. On a table near by Payton saw a grouping of pictures of a boy at various stages in his life. The arrangement reminded him of a shrine. The pictures had to be of China's brother. His disappearance hung like a shroud over the family. Payton scanned the room and only found one picture of China and another of a girl that could only be her sister.

"So, Payton, are you from around here?" Mrs. Davis asked.

"No, I'm from Chicago."

She gave him a look of interest. "Chicago? Well, you're a long way from home."

"I am."

"Are you here on vacation?"

Before Payton could answer the question, what had to be the door from the carport area below opened and an average-sized man with thinning hair entered. He wasn't the big burly man Payton had pictured from China's description of him.

"Hi, Father," China chirped, in an overly happy voice.

"Hi. What's for supper?"

"Pork chops, of course. They're your favorite, aren't they?" She stepped out of the kitchen and kissed him on the cheek. "Father, I'd like you to meet Payton Jenkins. He works with me."

The man turned his piercing look to Payton as if interrogating him. For a second Payton almost squirmed under Mr. Davis's scrutiny but caught himself. He returned a level gaze. Hadn't China said her father was a rigid man? Payton was too old, had been through too much to let someone intimidate him. He rose and offered his outstretched hand to Mr. Davis, who took it in a sound handshake that made Payton believe he might have gained some respect.

"Father, supper should be ready in about fifteen minutes."

"Good, I'm hungry."

"Hi, hon," Mr. Davis said, stepping over to kiss Mrs. Davis on the forehead.

"I think I'll see if I can help China." Payton stood and headed for the kitchen. Was he imagining that the atmosphere had turned cooler and the women tensed when the head of the house had come in? The click-click of the recliner footrest cranking up told Payton that Mr. Davis had taken his chair.

Some time later, Payton helped China place the platters of food on the table.

"Supper," she called.

Payton saw Mrs. Davis rise from her chair. "Please, come join us, Jim," she said, low enough that Payton had the impression that she didn't want him to hear her pleading.

"No, I'll just eat here. I've had a long day."

Payton's mom might not have been the one to cook the meal but she'd seen to it that their family had always shared the evening meal together. That was one point his mom had never wavered on. Payton's father would have never gotten away with China's father's attitude.

"Mama, I'll fix him a plate. Come on and join us." China picked up one of the plates off the table.

Payton watched, amazed, as she hurriedly spooned

food in large portions onto it. China also worked all day and now she was playing server girl to her father? What had happened to the person who had stood up to him so many times?

China had just finished putting food on her own plate when her father called from the other room, "This pork chop is a little too done."

"I'm sorry, Father. You can have mine." China jumped up and headed to the living area with her plate in her hand.

Payton shook his head in disbelief. It took all his self-control not to take the plate from her and drag her out of the house. China had turned into a super-pleaser. Couldn't she see that her father was manipulating her? Had she been doing this for years?

When his look caught her mom's she smiled. Didn't she see what was going on? She acted as if China's actions were natural. They certainly appeared to be the norm in this house. He saw them as very dysfunctional and un-healthy.

China brought back her father's half of a pork chop on her plate. Going into the kitchen, she returned with no meat on her plate. She took her seat but didn't meet his gaze. He cut what was left of his meat and placed it on her plate. She glanced at him in surprise, as if everyone, including her, expected her to go without part of her meal.

"So, Payton, you were telling me what brought you to Golden Shores," Mrs. Davis said in an almost apologetic tone.

They carried on a conversation with no further inter-action with China's father. After dinner, Payton helped China do the dishes. When they left she kissed her father on the forehead. He acknowledged her with a grunt and continued to watch his TV show. Payton wanted to shake the man. Didn't he realize what a wonderful person China was? She deserved to be treated better by her family. Payton said good evening to the man, whose only response was to raise a hand briefly.

At his car, Payton opened the door for China then got in himself. He turned to her. "Exactly what happen in there?"

She gave him a puzzled look. "What do you mean?"

"The way you acted."

"How's that?"

"Like a servant. As if you couldn't speak up for yourself."

"They're my parents. I didn't do anything that I haven't always done. They need me."

What if he got sick again? Would she treat him the same way she had her father? Care for him more out of guilt than love? He wanted to be loved for who he was, not because someone needed to be needed. He couldn't, wouldn't put himself or China through that. They both deserved more. Janice may have hurt him but at least she'd been honest about what she could take. Could China bring herself to do that if he became ill again? Could he afford to take the chance of finding out?

"China, you actually gave your father your meal." He didn't try to keep his disbelief out of his voice. "Even more astounding is that he took it without argument."

"He's my father," she said in an ashamed voice.

"But that doesn't mean you should let him walk all over you. As strong a person as I've seen you be, not only with me but in medical situations, and you become a completely different person when you're around your parents. Why?"

"I don't."

"Yes, you do."

"They're all I have."

"No, they're not. You've got a sister."

"She doesn't have anything to do with us."

"After what I just saw, I'm not surprised."

"You're going too far now."

"I don't think so. I care about you and I know how you act around your parents isn't healthy. What're you afraid of? That if you're not the perfect child that your father will give you the same ultimatum he gave your brother and your mom will let it happen? You're an adult now. You don't have to have their blessing anymore. Don't you think it's time for you to have a life not controlled by them? When was the last time you told them you wouldn't be cooking supper when you came over? Do they even know that you hate the grocery store?"

"That's enough, Payton."

"China, you can't make up for the fact that they don't know where your brother is or ease their guilt. They have to learn to live with the past just like you do. You have to find security without living in fear of their rejection. What I saw tonight was you trying to keep the peace at all costs. That's not good for you or them."

"They've already lost two children. If I don't come around—"

"Then maybe they'll have to deal with each other and the way things are. They can handle life without you holding their hands."

She turned to him, her jaw clenched and lips drawn into a tight, thin line. "Well, it must be nice to sit on the outside and look in. To know what everyone else should do Mr. I-ran-away-from-home-because-I-couldn't-take-the-pressure."

"I didn't run away from home. I decided to live elsewhere. Take my life in a different direction."

"Some of us don't have that luxury. Like my brother... When life got too hard in one place, you just picked up and left. Sometimes you have to stay and deal with what is happening. I learned to deal the best way I know how. You haven't even made an effort to really talk to your parents, have you? Explain how you really feel? I don't see that we're all that different. What I know is that you can point out others' issues but you can't see your own."

That stung. More than he wanted to admit. "My parents have expectations, demands."

"And you don't think mine do?" she threw back at him.

"I know yours do but you don't need to let them make you feel like you're twelve again when all you want to do is please them so you can feel loved."

"I'm sorry I'm not who you think I should be." She opened the door. "I'll get Mom to drive me home. Thanks for a wonderful evening," she spat, and slammed the door.

Payton watched in disbelief as China stalked off. Had he just been hit by a Gulf storm? What had just happened? How could she not see what her parents were doing to her?

Surely when she calmed down China would come around. In the scheme of things, what they were fighting over was nothing. He knew life and death and this wasn't it. He'd give her some room to cool down and then they'd work it out. What they had together was too good to let go of just like that.

He slowly backed out of the drive. With one last glance back at the house he drove down the road, leaving an even bigger gap between them.

China couldn't remember a more uncomfortable discussion with her mom than trying to explain why she'd stomped back into the house and asked for a ride home. She'd didn't want to talk about Payton. He was wrong. She didn't do what he accused her of doing.

She spent a horrible evening, crying, and compounded it with tossing and turning before emotional exhaustion took her. Who did Payton think he was talking to? How had something so wonderful turned so ugly with only a few words? Payton had real nerve. Had she misjudged him just as she had another man she'd cared about? She'd been right about him in the first place.

As if the fates were ganging up against her, one of Larry's children had a school field trip and Larry had asked Payton to switch shifts with him. China managed to make it through the shift without interacting with Payton except when it had to do with a patient. He didn't seem any more eager to speak to her then she was to him.

China looked at her wristwatch. Only thirty more minutes. Her nerves were strung out tighter than a banjo string. She'd even snapped at Doris, which had got her a look of surprise. Thankfully a patient had come in and prevented Doris from asking questions.

At one minute to two China had her purse under her arm and was on the way toward the back door. She needed to plan something. Clear her mind. Figure out how to deal with Payton. How to fix things between them or at least learn to work with him without the burning hurt boiling over. Maybe she needed to see about transferring to the hospital.

"Yes, I understand." Payton's voice drifted out into the hall as she passed the office door.

She'd planned to keep on walking, not glance in his direction, but couldn't help herself. His shoulders were slumped and his elbows were propped on the desk with his dark-haired head in his hands. Something was wrong. Was he sick? Had he gotten bad news? She couldn't leave without knowing. They might be through but that didn't stop her from caring.

With her heart racing she asked from the doorway, "Payton, what's wrong?"

He raised his head. "Nothing."

The shadowed look in his eyes told her differently. She stepped further into the room. "What's going on? Are you feeling okay?"

"I'm fine."

"It doesn't look that way."

He stood. "I'm fine, really. I'm sorry if I hurt your feelings yesterday. I'm sorry if I'm hurting them now. But I think we have run our course."

She jerked back as if he'd slapped her. She'd expected this. He wasn't saying anything she didn't already know but she didn't like hearing it verbalized, especially in such a cold voice. She known it was over the second she'd seen that look of disbelief on his face. Not wanting to admit it, last night she'd had no choice but to face the facts. That didn't mean it didn't feel like her heart was breaking into a thousand pieces and being flung to the ends of the earth.

Refusing to run and hide, she choked out the words, "I agree."

For a second had there been hurt in his eyes?

"To make things easier, I'll see about transferring to another clinic or to the E.R."

Unable to say more, she nodded. Her greatest fear had come true. She didn't measure up. He'd said he didn't want her.

"I'm sorry."

China nodded again. With a force of will she hadn't known she had, she made her feet move. In a daze of pain, anger and disappointment and holding back the tears that threatened, she stumbled out the back door.

Payton closed the door to the office and sank into the desk chair. His head dropped into his hands. He'd been sick after chemo but he'd never felt as nauseated as he had when he'd seen the look on China's face. He'd known what he'd had to do, but that hadn't made it any easier. His bloodwork had come back abnormal. He couldn't, wouldn't take her on that ride with him if cancer had returned. China deserved a better life. A more secure one. She would spend her days caring for him, and he couldn't have that. He wouldn't let her sit by his bed and worry. His parents would be bad enough.

China would move on from him soon enough, he decided, but he wouldn't be so lucky. She wasn't someone he'd ever get over.

CHAPTER TEN

CHINA COULDN'T REMEMBER feeling more miserable than she had been in the last week. The only upside was that she didn't have to hold it together in front of Payton. He hadn't been at the clinic and she'd refused to ask why. She'd just figured that he'd managed to get a quick transfer or had taken a few days off.

She looked awful. No matter what she did—cold water to the eyes, drops, even cucumber slices—she still couldn't get the puffiness to recede from crying herself to sleep. She missed Payton's arms around her, his hard body against her back, his wit, his smile.

Doris and Jean had given her puzzled looks but hadn't asked questions. Robin wasn't as tactful. She cornered China in the supply room.

"So, what gives with Payton? You know where he is?"

China opened a cabinet and pulled out gloves, tissues and tongue depressors to replace those used in the exam rooms. "No. I haven't spoken to him."

"I thought you two were tight."

"Tight?"

Robin gave a disgusted snort. "Don't play dumb with me. We all know you and Payton were having a thing. You could see it any time you two were together."

China suppressed a groan. Had they been that obvious?

She closed the cabinet. "Well, if we did have a 'thing,' we don't anymore. I've not spoken to him in days."

"Jean did let it slip that he'd gone to Chicago. You think he's moving back there?"

China gathered the supplies in her arms. "You know, Robin, I really have no idea," she said, as she left the room.

Entering an exam room, she pushed the door closed with her elbow. She dumped the supplies in a heap on the table, sank into the chair and put her head into her hands before all the pain she felt flowed out. Some time later, she wiped the moisture away with the back of her hand and straightened her shoulders. It was time she pulled herself together. Got her life back to normal. Learned to live without Payton. She done it before he'd come to town and she'd do it again. Her parents were expecting her to cook dinner tonight, she'd focus on that.

China finished cleaning off the table and straightening her parents' kitchen. Her father was in his chair with the news on the TV but the volume down as he read the paper. Her mom focused on one of her many craft projects. There was no interaction between them or even China. They hadn't even asked about Payton. It was as if they were going through the motions of life but never really living it. She wanted more than that. Had lived it with Payton.

When had her family dynamics become so twisted? Was that why Kelsey never visited? Maybe it was time to ask her? See if she could reestablish some kind of solid relationship with at least one member of her family.

It had taken some persuading on China's part to get Kelsey to agree to meet. She'd not out and out said no. Instead, Kelsey seemed to have an excuse for being busy on every date China suggested. When China finally said, "This isn't about Mom and Dad. This is about me. Things I need to know," Kelsey agreed.

China watched Kelsey pull into the parking spot from the front window of the tearoom on Main Street.

Where China had dark hair cut conservatively, Kelsey was fair-haired with a trendy cut that stuck up on her head. China was petite and Kelsey was tall with an athlete's body. They couldn't be more different yet they had shared the same upbringing.

China stood as the bell on the door tinkled, announcing Kelsey's entrance. Opening her arms in welcome, China saw Kelsey's second of hesitation before she stepped into her embrace. They released each other. China smiled. "Thank you for coming. I've missed you."

Kelsey gave her a weary smile as they sat down in the antique wooden chairs at their table. China ran her hands across the tablecloth, as if smoothing out a wrinkle that didn't exist.

A middle-aged woman wearing a white ruffled apron came to take their order. After she left Kelsey said, "Please don't try to convince me I need to see Mom and Father."

"Like I said on the phone, I won't do that, but I would like to ask you some questions about them."

"China, I don't want to talk about them."

"The questions have to do with me. You're the only person I know to ask. I need to know."

Kelsey's brow wrinkled and she twisted her mouth upward. "What's going on?"

"I need to know…"

Kelsey put her elbow on the table and leaned toward China.

"Uh, a friend of mine said I act differently when I'm around Mom and Dad. Do you think that's true?"

"Hell, yes, you do!"

China jerked at the force of Kelsey's reply.

"I hated the way they treated you but I think I hated it more that you let them treat you that way."

"I didn't see it," China said softly, "until Payton pointed it out."

"Payton?"

"A friend."

The woman returned to serve them their tea then left silently.

Kelsey nodded. "Something happened to you after Chad left. You couldn't do enough to make Mom and Father happy, especially Father. You never stood up to them, no matter how unreasonable they were. You were always trying to make things better, smooth things over."

"Why haven't you said something before?"

"I was young, but I knew when you were trying to hide what I was doing from Mom and Father. You covered for me, and even lied for me on occasion, but I hated what I saw them doing to you."

Had her fear of stepping out of line and being rejected been that strong? "I didn't know they were doing anything to me. I just didn't want them to get mad at me."

"You were too young to recognize it when it started. I don't think they would have treated us like they did Chad. I think guilt and fear over him stopped them from threatening to put us out. I managed to hold it together until I could get out of high school but I couldn't take it anymore. By that time you were already the favorite child and I really didn't care."

"I wasn't the favorite!"

"Okay, maybe favorite isn't the right word. The more dutiful. I knew I needed to get away and it seemed like it was too late for you."

"So you just left and let me spend years being their

doormat. Why didn't you say something sooner?" China couldn't keep the anger and disappointment from surfacing.

"Would you have listened?"

"I guess not," China said thoughtfully.

Kelsey place her hand over hers for a second before she removed it. "Still, maybe I should have tried harder to make you see it. I'm sorry. So what has changed now?"

"I met someone and took him to their house for dinner."

"As in a man? Someone special?" Kelsey asked with a smile.

"Yes. A man. He told me he couldn't believe how I acted around them. That I shouldn't let them treat me the way they do. We had a big fight."

"Well, I hate to say it, but he's right. It's time for you to stand up to them. Stop letting them manipulate you. You don't have to please them anymore. You only have to please yourself. So tell me about this guy."

China blinked to keep the moisture from forming in her eyes. "There's not much to tell. We broke up. He's gone home."

"Home?"

"Chicago."

"Was he just here on vacation?"

"No, he was a doctor at the clinic. We fought and we haven't spoken since. He's not in town anymore."

Kelsey reached across the table and touched her hand. China looked at their clasped hands. It was the most sisterly thing Kelsey had done since she'd climbed into bed with her the night of the big fight between Chad and their parents. "So call him. Don't let our screwed-up family hurt your chance for happiness. Call him, find him, talk to him."

"I don't think he wants to have anything to do with me. He was so disappointed in me."

"Forget that. He'll get over it. Talk to him. If he cares about you he'll understand."

China squeezed Kelsey's hand. "Thanks for helping me see a few things clearer. I love you, sis."

Kelsey eyes glistened. "I love you too."

As they finished their tea they talked about Kelsey's new job at the hospital. Finally China felt like she had her sister back.

Standing on the sidewalk in front of Kelsey's car, China said, "Thank you for coming. I wish we could do this more often."

"I'm glad I came also."

"Can we get together again soon?"

Kelsey took a while to answer. "I'd like that. But no pushing me to see Mom and Dad."

"I promise. This'll be about us. I've missed you."

Kelsey stepped over and hugged her. "I've missed my big sis too." She let China go. "Now, go call that fellow and tell him you've come to your senses."

"I'll think about it."

"We have enough regrets in our lives. Don't add another."

China watched as Kelsey got into her car and drove away. Would Payton listen?

She had lived in fear of being rejected, of not being good enough. Had Payton ever made her feel that way? No. She'd managed to twist what he'd said to her about her parents. Hadn't he proved more than once he wasn't like that? They'd worked together with patients, bought plants for his house and cooked dinner together, and never once had he ever criticized or talked down to her. He'd done nothing but make her feel good about herself.

She was such an idiot. When she'd spoken to him at the clinic it hadn't been about her, it had been about how he felt. She would think about what she needed to do later. Now, she was due at the clinic.

Once again she looked for Payton to show up for work. She listened for his footfalls in the hall and heard nothing. Sitting behind the front desk, she scrolled through the lab work that had come in to see if any of the patients needed to be called for a return visit or updated on the results.

She scanned the numbers of each patient, looking for any abnormalities. Her finger pushed the "scroll up button when the white cell count of a CBC was too high. This patient would need to be notified. Checking the left-hand corner of the page, the name of the patient jumped out at her like a flashing neon sign—Payton Jenkins.

China sucked in a breath. Her heart beat faster. Payton's high white cell count could be an indicator that his cancer was back. Had that been what the phone call had been about? Or did he even know? She had to tell him. Had to talk to him. See if he was okay.

Weak-kneed, she walked to the doctor's office and closed the door. More than once she'd had to make a confidential phone call from there. No one would question the door being closed and disturb her. With a shaking hand she reached into the pocket of her scrubs and pulled out her cell phone. Scrolling down until Payton's number appeared, she touched the screen.

Would he answer when her ID came up on his phone? Would he be glad to hear from her? The phone rang and rang and rang. With each ring her disappointment grew. His voice telling whoever was calling to leave a message came over the phone. She slumped against the desk. His voice, oh, how she loved the sound of Payton's voice.

At the beep, she said, "Payton, it's China. Your bloodwork came through. You need to call the clinic." Even to her own ears the message sounded cool and official. Nothing like one lover speaking to the other. But they were no longer lovers.

Her phone rang seconds later. Her heart leaped. She dropped the mobile. Was it Payton? Would he be as glad to hear her voice as she would be to hear his? With a shaking hand it took two tries to pick the phone up off the floor. The knot in her chest eased. The ID read "Mom." She touched the screen. "Hello."

"Hi, honey. Could you stop by and pick up a few things on your way over this evening?"

"Mom, I'm not coming."

"Honey, why not?"

"Mom, I'm not going to be coming over for some time. Also, please don't call me during work hours anymore."

"China, what's wrong?"

"I just need to make some changes in my life."

"You know your father is going to expect those pork chops of yours."

"You can fix them, Mom. There's some in the freezer. I've got to go now. Bye." China ended the call.

It hadn't been easy and she would owe her mom more of an explanation later but she had made her first move toward pulling away from her parents. Now she had to move forward and create a life without Payton. With her sister in her corner and her new understanding of herself, she felt empowered to do just that.

Payton looked at the blinking light on his phone. He'd missed an incoming call. *China.*

He ached for her with every fiber of his being. His fingers itched to touch her silky skin, kiss her full lips, hear the soft sound of her breathing next to him in the middle of the night. Things had already been difficult between them before he'd received the news from John about his questionable lab work. Emotionally he'd run, and he had no doubt she recognized it. Now all he wanted to do was repair the relationship, have China back in his life—permanently.

Just days earlier he'd caught the first flight out for Chicago and had been back in the hospital, undergoing tests, that afternoon. The flight had given him much-needed time to think, and the reality that he might be sick again, this time possibly worse than before, had made him re-evaluate China's words, "Life is about enjoying where you are, the simple things." She'd taught him that lesson well. Watching a storm, planting a flower and seeing it flourish or just spending time floating on his boat, and most of all making love to someone you cared deeply for.

He'd been running from life just as she had accused him of doing. That had led him to Golden Shores in the beginning but now he knew without a doubt that was where he belonged, especially with China. It was time to stop and face his monsters. Try to make his parents understand. Was his relationship with them any less dysfunctional than China's was with hers?

In its own way, no. He'd deal with whatever problem he had physically then speak to his parents in the hope he could get them to understand. No matter how that conversation went, he would have made the effort to offer the proverbial olive branch. That was all he could do.

Even if cancer had returned, he wanted China in his corner, helping him fight. And she would, if he hadn't hurt her so completely that she refused to have anything to do with him. That he might never make love to China again worried him more than what his tests might reveal. As the wheels of the plane touched down at O'Hare airport, he had his plan in place and the resolve to see it through.

Later that afternoon Payton pulled out his phone as he

waited to have an MRI. He had to let his mom know he was in town. She would expect him to stay with her and his father. Payton would agree to stay with them, more in order not to hurt his mom's feelings than from need. When he'd spoken to John earlier that morning to let him know he'd be coming in, John had offered him a place to stay at his home.

Payton touched his mom's number and waited through the rings until her familiar voice came on the line.

"Hi, honey. It's nice to hear from you."

"You too, Mom. I just wanted to let you know I'm in Chicago."

"You are? Why didn't you let us know you were coming?" She paused then asked in a rush, "Are you coming home?"

She would think he was moving back but his home was now Golden Shores and China. "No, I'm here for some tests."

"I thought you weren't to have them until next month."

"My white count was high and John wanted me to come up for a look-see. I'm at the hospital now."

"Why didn't you call me sooner? I'm on my way."

Payton leaned forward in the waiting-room chair and propped an elbow on a knee. "No. I'm fine. Please, don't come to the hospital. I'll see you later this evening."

"I'll be there in a few minutes."

"Mom." He used a firm tone. "Do not come here. I appreciate your concern but I'm just having tests done. I won't know anything until tomorrow or the next day."

"I still think—"

"I know you care and I love you for that, but it's time we do it my way."

Her huff of resignation came over the phone. "You'll

be staying here, won't you?" It was less a question and more a statement.

"Yes, if you'll have me."

"I'll be waiting. Your father will be glad to see you too."

Payton wasn't as sure about that. "Nothing has changed. I'll be returning to Golden Shores."

"I know, honey. I know."

Payton hung up. For once he'd managed to get his mom to back down. She'd taken his requests far better than he'd expected.

A step toward real change. Not the hyperstimulating changes he'd sought when he'd moved south but the solid, life-altering ones that brought true happiness. China had improved his world. Guilt washed over him. Instead of supporting her, he'd criticized her family, her life. His parents had certainly had expectations and aspirations for him. Payton could understand where China was coming from. He'd dumped on her about her relationship with her parents when his hadn't been much healthier. Making it up to her was going to take more than flowers.

That evening the taxi circled the drive of his parents' home and stopped in front of the door. Before Payton could finish paying the driver, his mom was on her way down the steps.

"Hi, honey," she said, with a bright smile, but her eyes carried the worry he'd seen so many times during his battle with cancer.

He wrapped her in his arms. She and China were a similar size. What was the saying? "Marry someone like dear old Mom." Marry! Did he want to marry China? He smiled. Yes, he did, if he could convince her to have him.

"So how are you doing?" his mom asked, studying him closely.

"I feel fine. Never better, actually."

"I have to admit you do look wonderful. The tan, the smile on your face. Living in Golden Shores looks like it agrees with you."

"It does." He wrapped an arm around her shoulders and led her toward the house. "Why don't we go see what Ruth has planned for dinner and I'll tell you all about it."

"I think there may be more than sand and sunshine to talk about."

Payton hugged her to him. "Mom, you know me too well."

Dinner was a formal affair, nothing like the spirited ones that he and China had shared or even those around the picnic table behind the clinic. Changes had occurred in him that had nothing to do with living in a new house or learning new things. They went soul deep.

It had happened. Something he'd resisted. He was in love. He'd promised himself he wasn't going there again, then along came China. He'd not been running for her sake but his. Fearing he might get hurt, he'd turned into a coward where facing up to his feelings were concerned. He was no different than his parents not wanting life to change, but it had on so many levels.

His father was present but outside of surface-level conversation he had little to say. His mom carried the conversation by asking about his new house, Golden Shores and the clinic. When she specifically asked about the people he worked with he told her about everyone, including China.

"You like this China, don't you?" she asked.

He should have known that his mom would pick up on the inflection in his voice when he spoke of China.

"So you've found a local." His father made it sound like Payton was hanging out with criminals.

"Yes, and I intend to marry her, if she'll have me." That thought brought a warm feeling in his chest.

"She's from a good family?" his mom offered.

"Mom, don't you want me to have a wife I love and who loves me, instead of just someone with the right pedigree?"

His mom didn't have time to respond before his father said, "Your position at the hospital is still open."

Payton pushed back from the table. "Dad, I know you were hurt and disappointed by my decision to leave the hospital and move to Golden Shores. I can appreciate that. I made a drastic change, shocked you and Mom. I realize that. I don't think I would have made such a decision if I hadn't already been unhappy with the direction my life was headed. I was going through the motions. Janice leaving me when I needed her most shows that I wasn't making solid choices. I never wanted to be on the board of the hospital. What I wanted and what I still want is to help people and be happy. I've found that in Golden Shores."

"But you had a good position. A chance to make a difference here," his father said.

"I still have all of that in Golden Shores, plus time to sail, enjoy the beach and cook for friends."

His father huffed.

"You don't have to like my choices, and that's fine. I would just like you to respect that they are mine to make. I would like you to be a part of my life and hopefully my family's life. Having cancer did change my outlook on how I want to live. That I can't deny. I just want different things now and I'm sorry that they're not what you had planned."

"You weren't happy here?" his father asked in little less than a growl of disgust.

"Not like I am now. I hope you can come to terms with that. If you can't, I'm sorry."

During the rest of his stay things were cool between him and his parents. He'd done what he could to get them to understand, now it was up to them to decide what they wanted from the relationship. He hoped for the best but would accept what they decided.

Crossing the Bay Bridge into Golden Shores brought him back to the present. He had to get China to listen to him. His first instinct was to drive straight to her place but she probably wouldn't even allow him inside. He needed to think. On the water was where he could do that best.

"China, there's a man on the phone who wants to speak to you," Doris called from the front of the building as China was stepping out of the employee entrance. It had been the longest week of her life and all she wanted to do was to go home and try to get some sleep.

With a sigh she turned around and walked back up the hall. Reaching the desk, she asked Doris, "Who is it?"

"I think he said Pete."

Pete. She didn't know a Pete, yet the name sounded familiar.

China picked up the phone, "This is China. How can I help you?"

"This's old Pete. You were with the doc when he got the hook out of my finger, weren't ya?"

"Yes, I remember you."

"I can't find the doc and me finger is the size of a net buoy, and all red."

Great. The man had an infection. Would at least need an antibiotic. It had been over a week, almost two. It should have healed by now but that dirty boat… "You need to go to the emergency room. The clinic is closed now."

"I don't have the cash. Already can't pay the bill from last time. Can you come by and give it a look? I can't find the doc."

A stab of pain hit in the area of her heart. She didn't know where Payton was either. "You're going to need medicine for the infection. I can't give you that. You're going to have to go to the hospital."

"I can't do that. Sorry I bothered you." He hung up.

China placed the receiver in the phone cradle.

"What was that all about?" Doris asked.

"Just a fisherman with a hook in his finger."

Doris twisted up her face. "Ooh. That doesn't sound like fun."

"It wasn't." *But Payton had been wonderful.* "I'll see you the day after tomorrow."

China only made it as far as the car before she'd made up her mind to go to the marina and check on Pete. She'd worry about him until she saw the finger for herself. All the memories of the time she and Payton had spent on his sailboat came flooding back as she turned into the parking lot of the marina. The urge to circle around and leave filled her but she couldn't let Pete possibly lose a finger or worse.

She pulled out the emergency bag she kept in the trunk of the car and started down the long pier. Passing where she thought she remembered Pete and Ralph's boat being moored, she kept walking. Her feet faltered. Soon she would be passing Payton's boat. Squaring her chin, she planned to walk by it without looking but at the last second she couldn't help but do so.

Her heart thumped against her ribs and her knees went weak. She stopped short. The bag slipped from her hands to plunk against the wooden boards beneath her feet. The stern of the boat faced her and printed on the transom in large, gold script letters was *"China Doll."* Payton had said that people named their boats after someone they loved.

A man stepped off what looked like Pete and Ralph's boat further down the pier. He stood silhouetted against the sunset. That physique she would know anywhere. *Payton.*

He started toward her.

Her stomach fluttered. "Uh, Payton, I didn't expect to see you." She glanced toward Peter and Ralph's boat but saw neither man. "Pete called and said something was wrong with his finger."

Payton stopped within touching distance.

She glanced at the boat. "Why?" she finally got passed the lump in her throat.

He said in a solemn voice with a tone of conviction, "Because I love you."

She stared at him. He looked wonderful, better than that, perfect. All she wanted to do was throw herself into his arms but she had her self-respect.

"China, you're starting to make me nervous. Say something."

"I have to check on Pete's finger." She made to move past him.

Payton caught her hand, stopping her. "Pete's finger is fine. I asked him to call you. I didn't think you would talk to me so I thought maybe if I got you out here—"

"You could soften me up." She glared up at him. "You knew I'd come when Pete called, didn't you?"

"Yes. You have a soft heart. That's one of the many things I love about you."

She made a sound of annoyance in her throat. "How dare you talk to me about love. I don't even know where you've been for the last week. I saw your lab work. I've been worried sick. You just left. Someone who loves you doesn't do that."

Payton pulled her into his arms and brought his mouth to hers, effectively halting her tirade. His heart swelled when her arms slipped around his neck and she opened to greet him. She wouldn't make it easy on him but at least she wasn't immune to him.

He wanted her, had to have her, but on the pier wasn't the place. Payton broke the kiss but not the desire-filled fog China had wrapped around him. "We need to go aboard."

She looked at him with wide and dreamy eyes as if she'd forgotten everything but their kiss. He need to get her aboard before she came back to reality, which she would with a vengeance, he had no doubt. He wanted her relaxed and willing to listen when he explained.

Guiding China toward the boat, he let her go just long enough to hop onto the deck and then help her aboard. She came willingly. It wasn't until the clapping and wolf-whistling from the direction of Pete and Ralph's boat filled the air that she jerked out of her daze.

Payton swore under his breath. He pulled her close and dipped his head to distract her. She pulled away. It wasn't going to work this time. He would be paying the piper first. The talking would come before any lovemaking. "Let's sit here."

China waited until he sat on the bench and then she took a spot out of touching distance.

"Okay, go ahead and let me have it. I know I deserve it," he said, waiting.

"I have things to say but first I need to know about you. How you are feeling? What about your lab work?"

Payton reached to take her hand, which lay on the seat, but she placed it in her lap. "I'm fine. I'm sorry that I scared you. I shouldn't have run off like I did or lied to you about the phone call you overheard. You deserved better than that."

"So you went to Chicago?"

"Yes. I got back this afternoon. John, my doctor, wanted to run some tests just to make sure no cancer had reappeared."

Fear filled her eyes, which reassured him that she cared.

He smiled. "I got a clean bill of health. Apparently I had a sinus infection. While I was there I spoke to my parents, more specifically to my father."

She turned toward him, bringing one leg up to rest on the bench. "How did that go?"

Encouraged by having her full attention, he said, "I told him that I was sorry that I couldn't be who he wanted me to be and that I wasn't going to move back to Chicago. That I would be staying here and hopefully marrying you."

China's startled intake of breath filled the space between them.

"I told my parents that they'd have to accept that I had changed. They could be a part of my life or not, it was their choice."

She touched his arm briefly then removed it.

Skin that had suddenly been summer warm was abruptly winter cold.

"That had to have been hard to say."

"It was, but it needed to be done. And this needs to be said also. I shouldn't have jumped on you about your relationship with your parents. Family dynamics are difficult enough, without someone who isn't a part of the family giving a commentary."

China wasn't sorry. "No, I'm glad you did. It made me see things I hadn't realized. I actually told my mom I wouldn't be cooking dinner the other day and said no when she asked me to go to the store for her. A small start but a start."

"I'm proud of you."

His words of praise added to the joy of seeing him. "I had tea with my sister too. I asked her about how I acted around my parents to see if you were right. She said she'd seen it for years. It was one of the reasons she had stayed away. She hated what they had and were doing to me. Best of all, she has agreed to start meeting me more often. It's the chance to get my sister back. I have you to thank for that."

He grinned. "Is there a possibility I might get a thank-you kiss out of that?"

"Not yet. I'm still mad at you. You tricked me into coming down here."

Payton looked contrite but not repentant. "Yeah, I didn't think you'd see me if I came to your place and I sure didn't want to have this discussion in front of the three musketeers at the clinic."

"Hi, Doc. I see she showed up. Looked like she wasn't so mad at you a while ago," Pete said with a huge smile from the dock. Ralph was standing beside him with an equally large smirk on his face.

China jolted at the sound of Pete's voice and looked away in embarrassment.

Payton chuckled. "Yeah, she did seem happy to see me."

"Well, we'll let yoz get back to what yoz was doing."

The burly men chuckled like two teenage girls and walked off, slapping each other on the backs.

Payton looked at China as the two men left. "Let's go for a twilight sail. We could use some privacy."

Half an hour later Payton had maneuvered them out into the middle of the bay and turned off the engine. While he dropped anchor China took a seat on the bench and placed her hands in her lap. Payton gave her a curious look as he passed her. Did he recognize how nervous she was? Seconds later the running lights came on, glowing red and green.

Payton returned to sit beside her.

"I like the new name for your boat," China said.

He smiled. "I was hoping you would. I'm a little cool. Would you mind moving closer and keeping me warm?"

China giggled. Payton always had a way of easing her jitters.

He laid his arm along the back of the bench, giving her an opening to accept. China waited a moment before she shifted over so he'd have to wonder if he'd gotten back into her good graces. She finally moved next to his big, warm body. His hand cupped her shoulder and pulled her in close but that was the only overture he made.

China was disappointed. She wanted to be kissed, made love to. She had missed him. After his passionate kiss on the pier she'd expected him to take her to the bunk the second the anchor hit the water. Instead, Payton had said he wanted to talk. She snuggled close and enjoyed being in his arms again. They sat quietly for a few minutes, looking off to the west at the pink and orange sky.

Payton broke the silence. "You know, if it wasn't for you teaching me to enjoy the simple things in life I'd have you in that cabin, taking your clothes off." His voice was calm and unhurried. He continued to look at the sunset. "I'm in love with you, China. If you'll have me, I'd like you to be my wife. I know it won't be easy. It will be years before I'm considered cured. I've treated you badly—"

China cupped his cheeks. "Shut up and kiss me!" She brought his lips down to hers. Her hands went to his waist and pushed at his shirt until she was forced to break the kiss so he could remove it.

"I thought you'd want to see the sunset," he murmured, as she slid down onto the deck and pulled him with her.

"I'm more interested in seeing you."

Payton gripped her shoulders, making her look at him. "Not until you answer my question."

China grinned. "I never heard a question."

"Okay, smarty pants. Will you marry me?"

"Under one condition."

He looked uncertain as he asked, "What's that?"

"That you never, ever leave again without telling me. I have to trust you to be here."

"I promise I will never leave you again by choice."

China sighed. That's all she needed. The security of knowing he would be there for her. "Then the answer is yes, yes, yes! I love you too."

Payton lay on the deck and brought her down over him. "Then how about showing me under the stars just how much."

China brought her mouth to his, waiting and warm.

A short while later the sun gave away to the black of night. China lay in Payton's arms on the deck, with a blanket beneath them and one thrown over them.

He nuzzled her neck. "I know you've heard of the mile-high club. Well, how about we start a new one? The mile-from-land club." He kissed the sensitive spot behind her ear.

China turned her head and found Payton's lips. "I'm more interested in being a member of the happily-ever-after club. With you, I will be."

* * * * *

THE MAVERICK WHO RULED HER HEART

BY
SUSAN CARLISLE

MILLS &
BOON

First published in Great Britain 2014
by Mills & Boon, an imprint of Harlequin (UK) Limited,
Eton House, 18-24 Paradise Road, Richmond, Surrey, TW9 1SR

© 2014 Susan Carlisle

ISBN: 978-0-263-90788-9

Harlequin (UK) Limited's policy is to use papers that are natural, renewable and recyclable products and made from wood grown in sustainable forests. The logging and manufacturing processes conform to the legal environmental regulations of the country of origin.

Printed and bound in Spain
by Blackprint CPI, Barcelona

Dear Reader

Small beach towns have always held a fascination for me. I've often wondered what it would be like to live in one year-round, to watch the crowds come and go, or to have seventy-degree weather when others are living in zero during the winter months. What I *haven't* wanted to experience is a hurricane, which is also part of residing along the Gulf coast. Still, people choose to live and love in these towns where they might lose everything to Mother Nature.

My characters, Jordon and Kelsey, are a couple of these people. Kelsey has lived in the same tiny town all her life. She wants out. In fact that's all she can think about. Jordon has moved back to town after being gone for a number of years. It's the one place where he feels at home. Each sees living in Golden Shores from a vastly different perspective. Only through adversity do they manage to understand how the other feels and find happiness together.

I hope you enjoy Jordon and Kelsey's story, and the touch of sunshine the Gulf coast brings to it.

I love to hear from my readers. You can contact me at www.SusanCarlisle.com

Susan

Dedication

To Nick
Your mother loves you.

**Praise for
Susan Carlisle:**

'Susan Carlisle pens her romances beautifully…
HOT-SHOT DOC COMES TO TOWN is a book that I
would recommend not only to Medical Romance fans but
to anyone looking to curl up with an angst-free romance
about taking chances and following your heart.'
—*HarlequinJunkie.com* on
HOT-SHOT DOC COMES TO TOWN

CHAPTER ONE

JORDON KING COULDN'T decide if he was repulsed or fascinated by the tall, blonde woman with the spiked hair flit-
ting from one table to the next.

She greeted, smiled at and hugged each man as she
worked her way around the tables surrounding the dance
floor of the Beach Hut Bar and Grill in Golden Shores,
Mississippi. Maybe his issue was that she hadn't given any
attention to him. No, that wouldn't be the reason. Women
just weren't on his agenda right now. Getting his professional life back in order was.

Taking another draw on his drink, he placed the bottle
on the bar. What had it been? Fifteen years since he'd been
in the Beach Hut? Then he'd been underage and sneaking in with a fake ID. He surveyed the rustic room with
high wooden beams darkened from cigarette smoke before the no-smoking ban had been instituted. Very little
had changed, bringing back both good and bad memories
of the place.

Mark, one of his new colleagues at Golden Shores Regional Hospital, remarked as he looked toward the woman,
"Well, it looks like *she's* having a good time tonight."

"Yeah, it looks that way," Jordon said on a droll note.

"So, how do you like working and living in Golden
Shores?" Mark asked.

Jordon chuckled. "Well, I've not been here but two days, but so far so good. Thanks for the invite out tonight."

"No problem. I thought it might be a good way for you to meet a few people from the hospital."

That was the only reason Jordon had agreed to attend. Even in a small hospital there were people in departments he would never meet if it wasn't for some event like this. He watched as the blonde made a graceful movement, shifting one hip this way and then another as she made her way through the tight spaces between chairs toward the bar. There was something about her...

"Okay, everyone," the man on the stage said into the microphone. "It's time to get this party really started."

"For this next song I want you to find someone you either don't know well or don't know at all and bring them to the dance floor. Let's mix things up."

The blonde had been coming toward the bar and made a detour around a group, talking. It brought her out of the last set of chairs directly in front of him as the last of the instructions was given. Her gaze met his.

Never breaking their connection, she stepped up to him and said, "I don't know you. Want to dance?"

Even in the din her voice sounded low and raspy, like that of one of those old-time movie stars. Her eyes, which were almost too large for her face, watched him with an intensity that made him feel uncomfortable, as if daring him to turn her down.

Jordon shook his head.

She gave him a come-hither smile, crooked her index finger and beckoned him on. Had he met her before?

"No, thank you."

She stepped closer. "Oh, come on. It's impolite not to

accept someone's invitation to dance. Besides, you're the only guy in the place I don't know."

Maybe not. She didn't seem to know him. The woman really was a tease. Maybe the only way to get rid of her was to agree. He took another swig from his bottle and set it down, then nodded. Her smile turned brilliant, as if he'd given her the greatest gift. She headed for the dance floor and he followed.

This time he had an up-close view of her moving among the tangle of chairs and people. Her jeans fitted her perfectly, clinging to every single curve.

By the time he'd reached the dance floor, she was already turning to face him and starting to dance. Jordon joined her as she backed into the crowd and they were swallowed up. He was definitely more fascinated than repulsed when her hands went over her head and her eyes closed as she moved to the beat of the music. The woman was enjoying herself. She didn't need him there but he couldn't seem to turn away.

Dancing wasn't generally his thing but he did what he could not to embarrass himself. At one point she came out of her trance long enough to open her eyes and move into the light. He managed to catch a glimpse of her deep brown eyes. She jumped, startled for a second, then she gave him a weak smile. Where had all the earlier brightness gone?

One song died and the next one was building when she thrust out her hand and said, "I'm Kelsey."

She said the name as if she expected him to recognize it. He'd live in Golden Shores once for a short time as a teenager so maybe he should know her. He took her hand in his. It was warm, soft and small. Seconds later it slipped from his when a tall guy about the same age as him caught her attention. She turned to speak to him.

Jordon was forgotten just that quickly.

Who was that guy?

Kelsey had been racking her brains all night, trying to figure out why he looked so familiar. He leaned casually against the bar. With a solid appearance, trim hips and thick hair, he was by far the best-looking man in the place. She noticed him a number of times looking her direction with a censorious glare. One so familiar during her youth.

Dying of thirst, she'd managed to make her way to the bar. As the party planner and therefore designated hostess of the event, she'd spent most of her time making sure everyone was having a good time, especially the honoree and retiring employee, Patrice.

As if fate had taken her by the hand and led her astray, she arrived at the bar just as the emcee announced the dance. Her gaze locked with Mr. Handsome Glare.

She blurted out, "Do you want to dance?"

What had she been thinking? That was just it, she hadn't been thinking. To her surprise, and after major coaxing on her part, he'd agreed. She always loved to dance and, as if someone above was smiling down on her, they were playing her favorite song.

Out on the dance floor, where the light was brighter, she turned and looked at him. Her breath caught.

J-man.

That's all she knew him as. As a kid the name had sounded cool, maybe a little dangerous.

A ripple of nervousness went through her. Grateful she was dancing so that it didn't show, she kept moving after her initial falter. She'd never expected to see him again. Had grieved for him for months when he'd left without saying goodbye. In the middle of many lonely nights she'd fantasized about him returning to Golden Shores. Those had been preteen dreams. Long given up and forgotten. Still, the yellow plastic ring he'd given her lay in her jewelry box. What was he doing back here?

When she'd last seen him he'd been a thin seventeen-year-old with long hair that he'd pulled back at the nape of his neck. He had been her brother Chad's best friend, the one he'd gotten into trouble with.

For one stunned moment she looked into his eyes. A ripple of disappointment ran through her. He didn't recognize her. How could he not? He been everything to her at one time. But she'd only been one of his friends' little sisters. Someone they had to shoo out of the room when they got ready to talk. Still, it hurt that he didn't know her.

Kelsey glanced at him a couple of times. He wasn't the best dancer on the floor but he was making an effort. He wore a conservative shirt and khaki slacks. His jaw held a hint of five o'clock shadow that disrupted the perfect appearance.

As the song ended, Luke from the business office grabbed her arm and asked her a question. When she turned around J-man was gone.

Was he still going by that name? She couldn't imagine that he was. That label didn't suit him anymore. Searching the room, she saw his back as he headed out the door. Well, that was that, she probably wouldn't see him again. Maybe he was just a late summer tourist or, better yet, a figment of her imagination. Still, a sadness she didn't want to examine came over her.

On Monday morning Kelsey entered her office on the second floor of the hospital.

"Great party," Molly said.

Molly had been Kelsey's office colleague, roommate, and best friend since the eighth grade. "Thanks. It was a good one. I'll miss Patrice but I'm proud she has this chance."

"Yeah, she's been wanting to leave town since her divorce. The new job is perfect for her."

Kelsey wished she was the one leaving. She'd been trying to get out of Golden Shores for what seemed like forever. Away from her parents and the youthful reputation she couldn't quit shake clear of. If she landed the job at the hospital in Atlanta then they would be throwing her a party, hopefully in the next few weeks. She'd be free, with a clean slate.

"Hey, Kelsey." Marsha, a floor nurse, stuck her head in the door. "You're still doing the diabetic class this morning, aren't you? We've had a couple of calls about it."

"I am."

"The new hospitalist is going to stop by and introduce himself."

Kelsey wrinkled up her nose. "Who is it again?"

"Dr. King."

"Okay. I'll be on the lookout for him."

When Marsha left Kelsey said, "I guess a good nutritionist's work is never done."

Molly laughed. "I guess you're right."

Kelsey settled into the chair behind her desk and reviewed the patients she needed to speak to before they were discharged that day. She didn't have the most popular job with the patients but it was a necessary one. No one liked being told what they could or couldn't eat.

"Have you heard anything about this new doctor?" Kelsey asked. Not that it really mattered. She planned on being gone soon enough that it wouldn't affect her one way or another what type of person he was.

"All I've heard is that he's supposed to be excellent. I do know they didn't have to hunt him, he came looking for the position."

"Here? I wonder why? We certainly aren't a hotbed of cutting-edge medical care."

Molly looked at her. "Not everyone feels a need to live somewhere else, be at the cutting edge. Some of us are perfectly fine living with the sand, sea, and surf."

As a child Kelsey had been also. Now all she wanted was to put the ugly memories behind her. But she couldn't do that if she stayed in Golden Shores. She'd tried. She acted out to forget. "Still mad at me about applying for the job?"

"Yeah, can't you tell?"

"I may not get it."

"You'll get it and I'll be stuck with another office mate, be looking for a new roommate." Molly looked at her. "But I won't be finding a new best friend."

"I love you too, Moll."

"It's mutual." A second later she whirled round again. "Oh, I forgot to mention the word around the hospital is that the new doc is gorgeous. There's already a betting pool started on who he'll ask out first. Nancy in the business office, Charlotte in the lab, or you."

"Really?" Kelsey couldn't seem to live down the good-time-girl rep she'd gained as a high-school and college student. It was hard to convince people who had known her during those times to take her seriously now. She wanted to go somewhere she could start afresh.

"Yeah. I'm putting my money on you. I need a new bathing suit so do what you can to help me out."

"I don't think so." Both woman mentioned were very attractive and seemed to make a point of meeting and dating the newest and most attractive men at the hospital, from the emergency crew to the administration office to the latest unattached doctor. Kelsey had moved past those fun and games.

Kelsey checked the large round clock on the wall and picked up the folder she'd laid out the night before that included pamphlets and handouts for the diabetes class.

"Got to go. We going to meet for lunch?"

"Sure. Whichever one of us gets to the table under the tree first claims it."

"Will do."

Late September beside the coast made it pleasant to eat outside. She and Molly, along with other staff members, fought over the coveted table under the large oak tree where the sun wouldn't beam down on them at noon. The other tables and chairs placed around the area weren't always as lucky.

Kelsey gathered her folder to her chest and went out the door. "Later."

Jordon drove up Main Street on his way to the hospital. He remembered the road well. He'd traveled it hundreds of times with his parents. As an only child he'd done almost everything with them.

Golden Shores hadn't changed much through the years. It was still a sleepy beach town that grew even more relaxed after the summer crowd had gone home. The storefronts were neat and in good repair. Baskets of late summer flowers, blooming yellow, red and blue, hung from the light poles at each intersection. This small insignificant town had been the last place he'd felt like he'd had a real home.

Pulling his SUV into the palm-lined drive of the hospital and following the signs to the designated doctors' parking lot, he found an open spot. Stepping out of the vehicle, he inhaled deeply. The spicy scent of salt filled his nostrils.

After spending so many years in snow during the winter, it was going to be nice to live here.

Jordon rolled his wrist and checked his watch. He was due for a meeting in twenty minutes. Last week he'd spent an entire day in Personnel, being issued his ID and getting acquainted with hospital procedures. Thank goodness he had no plans to ever leave so he'd not have to sit through one of those again.

With a quirk to his lips he punched in the number he'd been given for the doctors' entrance. He'd left the high-tech world of a large northern Virginia hospital where swiping a card for entry was the norm to the simple but effective push-button code.

Twenty minutes and two wrong turns later, he found the education classroom he was looking for. He stopped and double-checked the plaque by the door. This was the correct place.

Inside, a soft raspy voice said, "Today I'm going to be sharing some tips on how to eat well and at the same time tasty."

Looking into the room through the open door, he saw a dozen or so people sitting in chairs arranged in rows.

A man almost as round as he was tall said in a gruff voice. "All I can tell is that I can have a half a head of lettuce and nothing about that is tasty."

Everyone in the room laughed.

The voice responded, "Now, Mr. Franklin. You know that should only be a quarter of a head."

Again everyone chuckled.

Jordon stepped into the room and came to a jerking halt. The woman from the party was standing in front of the room. It was her voice he'd heard.

They stared at each other. She looked very familiar for some reason. He'd thought about her a couple of times since their meeting, trying to figure out where he knew her from. Could she be one of Chad's sisters? What if she was? Would she recognize him?

What he could remember of the youngest was that she had been around all the time. She'd been sweet, cute even, but way too young. He'd thought then, if you were just a little older...

Today her hair lay along her head in a boyish cut. And she wore bangs, pink and black glasses with polka dots on them, a simple hot-pink shirt and black slacks. Above her shoulders she seemed to come from a more unconventional world and below them from a conservative one.

So Miss Goodtime was the nutritionist. She seemed to recover from her surprise quicker than he did. "Uh, can I help you? If you're looking for the dietetic class, this is the place."

"Then I'm in the right place."

She waved a hand in the direction of an empty seat. "Then please join us." Her words sounded calm but from the slight tremor of her hand he could tell his appearance had flustered her.

"Thanks. I'm Dr. Jordon King."

At the sound of her hiss his head jerked up to meet her gaze. Her face had paled. What was going on?

He looked out at the group, hoping to give her time to recover from whatever the problem was. "I'm the hospitalist who will be caring for you if you're ever admitted. I hope that doesn't happen but I'll be here if you need me. I'm going to stay for the class so if you have any questions just let me know."

He took a chair behind the last person in the room and settled in. It had been a long time since he'd had time to sit through a presentation on diet and nutrition. It would be a nice refresher.

Despite having been put off by the demeanor of the woman at the front of the room's at the Beach Hut the other night, he found her professional and competent during her presentation of what to eat and portion control. She asked if there were any questions. A number of hands shot up.

She pointed to a balding man about halfway back and said, "Mr. Rawlins."

"Can I ever have cake?"

"In moderation only. Think birthdays and special occasions. Not nightly with ice cream."

There were groans around the room but she smiled. "Look, I'm not the bad guy here. Diabetes is. We're talking about a lifestyle change."

That's just what Jordon was doing. He would never have dreamt that he'd be back in Golden Shores. He had been on the fast track up the professional ladder. Had even been touted as possibly the youngest chief of staff, but backing his girlfriend and partner hadn't only cost Jordon his job but his credibility, his self-respect and his confidence in his ability to judge character. He planned to regain all of that in Golden Shores. This was his chance to start over with a clean slate. The woman's chuckle brought him back to the present. He didn't even know her full name. As soon as the class was over he was going to find out.

"Maybe that's a better question for Dr. King."

He jerked his gaze to hers. "I'm sorry, I missed that."

"Daydreaming in my class, Doc?"

All the class turned to look at him.

"Just for a sec. My apologies. Now, what was the question?" He stood and looked around the room expectantly.

"I would like to know," a woman of about thirty asked in a quiet voice, "if there's a chance that I might come off insulin."

"It depends on what type of diabetes you have. Some

people can control the disease with weight, others can take a pill and others require injections. Speak to your doctor and let him or her know that you would like to try."

The woman smiled at him and said, "Thanks, Doctor."

The speaker drew the group's attention again.

"That's all for today unless someone else has a question." No one said anything. "Then I'll see you all next week. Please bring your list of what you ate for review. Thanks for coming."

Everyone stood and gathered their belongings. Jordon moved to the front as people headed toward the rear. When he reached the woman she was speaking to one of the attendees and he waited. When the final person was out the door he said, "This is the second time we've met and I still don't know your full name."

A look he would have called disappointment if he didn't know better flashed through her eyes. Should he know her? He'd not kept in touch with anyone who still lived in Golden Shores except Chad, and he no longer lived here.

"I'm Kelsey Davis. Hospital nutritionist." She started picking up the papers on the podium in front of her.

Davis. Maybe she was one of Chad's sisters? But which one? Then again, Davis was a common name: there were a lot of them in the world. Surely more than one family in Golden Shores had the name Davis.

"Nice to meet you, Kelsey. I look forward to working with you."

"Hey, Kelsey." A man stuck his head inside the door. He and Kelsey looked at him.

"Hey, Mike," Kelsey said with a smile.

"I'm sorry to interrupt," the young man, who had blond hair and the build of a weight lifter, said.

"Not a problem. I'm on my way out."

The man stepped into the room. As Jordon left he heard the man say, "Are we still on for tonight?"

Kelsey had never been more surprised than when the man from the party turned up in her classroom. More startling than that was the fact that J-man was the doctor she'd be working with regularly. She gotten over being nervous around boys along ago, but for some reason J-man, uh, Jordon made her stomach queasy. He'd been her first love. Now he didn't even remember her!

She'd not seen him since her brother and he had gotten arrested. Right before they had both disappeared. Jordon had been part of the reason her brother, Chad, had issues with their father. Only Chad had never come home. Part of the blame for why her family had become so screwed up was rooted in that long-ago night.

Where Chad was concerned she had a love/hate relationship with him. She'd adored him. He'd been the oldest to her youngest and she'd idolized him. When he'd left without saying anything to her she'd been devastated. As the years had gone by she'd grown to resent him too. Because of him her once happy life had crumbled and she couldn't seem to get all the pieces back into place. At least with China that was starting to happen. She wasn't even sure she ever wanted to make the effort with regards to her parents. Getting out of Golden Shores, closing the door on the past had always sounded like the best answer.

Now J-man was back as a doctor. Life really was crazy. If it hadn't been time for her to leave town before, it surely was now. Until the new job came through, she'd stay out of his way as much as possible.

At noon Kelsey carried her tray from the cafeteria to the table where Molly waited under the tree. She slid into the open spot next to her.

"Hey, how'd it go this morning? Did you meet the new doctor? He's the talk of the hospital." Molly picked up her sandwich.

"That's not a hard thing to be. This hospital isn't that big and most of the people who work here have known each other most of their lives." Except Jordon, who had no idea who she was or the part he'd played in her young life.

"So are you going to tell me what you think about him?" Molly studied her.

Kelsey was well aware of who Dr. King was. Too aware. She didn't want Molly to know everything she thought about him. "He's nice enough and seems to know his medicine."

Molly put down her fork and looked at Kelsey like she had two heads. "That's all you've got to say? Kelsey Davis, I've known you since middle school and that's the least I've ever heard you say about a male. He must have really done something wrong."

Molly had no idea. She'd moved to town the next summer. About Chad and how she'd felt about J-man were the only secrets she'd ever kept from Kelsey. "Okay, okay. What do you want? That he's the best-looking man I've seen. Dark hair, hazel eyes, shoulders from here to eternity and a butt to die for!"

Molly giggled. "That's more like it but I detect a note of cynicism. Problem?"

"No. He just reminds me of someone I used to know."

"Someone you didn't like."

She'd liked him too well. "I liked the person just fine but it was during a bad time in my life."

"Hello, beautiful ladies. Mind if I join you."

Kelsey looked up to see Adam standing there. He worked in X-ray and had gone to school with her and Molly.

"Sure," Molly said. She nodded toward the other bench.

* * *

Jordon followed Mark to the only outside table available. He took a spot opposite him, gave the food on his tray a dubious look and made a mental note to remember to bring his lunch as often as he could.

A loud burst of laughter came from the table to their left. Jordon knew without looking that Kelsey Davis was there. He'd noticed her along with another blonde with long hair, and he wasn't surprised to see a man sitting with them. Was every man drawn to her?

His mother had the same personality. People gravitated toward her, especially men. His father had proudly said more than once that "his Margaret was the life of any party." Jordon had loved to hear her laugh. It had always made him smile. Until that night when the sound had woken him. Her tinkling lilt had drawn him to her until he'd realized she'd been talking suggestively on the phone to a man other than his father.

He glared in the direction of the other table.

"Kelsey and Molly seem to be having a good time. They must be up to something."

"Up to something?" Jordon took a bite of his oven-baked chicken.

"Yeah, they're always planning a party or some outing or something."

Jordon grunted acknowledgement.

"You'll like working with Kelsey. She's a lot of fun."

"What's her story?"

Mark shrugged. "I don't know. The usual, I guess. Grew up here, lives here and will die here."

"You knew her before you started working here?"

"Yeah. We went to high school together. She has a bit of a reputation as a party girl. She enjoys having a good time but I never hear anyone saying anything but good things about her now."

"Does her family still live around here?"

"I don't know. Why?"

"She looks so familiar. I used to know some Davises, I just thought she might be kin to them."

"Why don't you ask her?"

"Maybe I will." He glanced at Kelsey's table again. But this woman *couldn't* be the young girl he'd once known. She giggled at something that had been said then turned, meeting his gaze. Time ground to a halt as they stared at each other before he forced his attention back to his unimpressive meal.

Either way, she wasn't someone he needed to get involved with.

That evening he was walking toward his car when he saw Kelsey getting into an aging small compact that didn't fit the persona he'd seen so far. It was nothing flashy, as he would've expected. She pulled out of her spot and passed him with little more than a glance. How could he be so aware of her when she didn't seem to even notice him?

CHAPTER TWO

MIDMORNING THE NEXT day Jordon's cell phone rang while he was familiarizing himself with some paperwork. Tapping the icon, he said, "Dr. King here."

"This is the E.R. clerk. You're needed here."

"On my way."

Rushing down the stairs, he made one turn and headed along a short hallway. He grinned as he walked. The last hospital he'd been affiliated with had been so large it had taken him five minutes to go from his office to the E.R.

He stepped up to the circular desk and said to the person sitting there, "I'm Dr. King. You paged me."

"You're needed in exam room three."

He look around.

The clerk pointed and said, "Down that way."

"Thanks."

Voices came from behind the closed curtain that hung across a metal rod. This was another reminder that he'd left a more modern facility behind. There the patient examination rooms would have had been enclosed. Golden Shores might not be up to date on their buildings but by all accounts the hospital provided excellent medical care and had a clean report as far as any medical malfeasance was concerned. He had no intention of letting what had happened in Washington occur again. He'd been embarrassed and publicly humiliated on too many levels for one lifetime. He'd make sure this time not to get involved with anyone or anything looking remotely illegal.

One of the voices coming from the other side of the curtain sounded familiar. Pulling the striped material back, he saw a woman who looked to be in her late seventies lying on the gurney. Kelsey sat next to the bed and held the older woman's hand.

Was she destined to turn up everywhere he went?

He raised a brow in her direction and made an effort to concentrate on the patient. Before he could ask a question a nurse rushed in.

"Dr. King, here's the chart."

He looked at the front page and said, "So what seems to be the problem Mrs.?" He glanced at the chart again. "Ritch."

"Young man, you may call me Martha."

He raised a brow. "Okay, Martha, what brought you in today?"

"I was playing bridge, as I always do over at Edith Hutchinson's house, and I just blacked out."

"Did you fall out of the chair?" he asked, concerned the she might have a concussion.

"More like slipped, Myrtice said as I was being put into the ambulance. Which is going to cost me my entire war pension."

Kelsey patted the woman's arm. "Now, Martha, that isn't the important thing. We'll take care of it."

Jordon cringed. That was what his lover and partner had said just before they'd arrested her for insurance fraud. He wouldn't take a chance on being involved in anything like that again. Jordon gave Kelsey a questioning look. Why was she here? She returned an unwavering gaze. Had she seen him wince at her words?

"Martha is one of my diabetic patients. She asked the nurse to call me."

He nodded. "So did you feel like your blood sugar had dropped?"

The woman hung her head. "I knew when I ate Sally's petits fours that I'd be in trouble."

"Martha! We've talked about this!" Kelsey exclaimed.

"I know, hon. But there's nothing like Sally's petits fours. You can't eat just one."

Jordon cleared his throat. "Well, then, young lady…"

Martha giggled. Kelsey smiled, which captivated him.

A few seconds later Martha made a huffing noise. "You do know I'm the patient, don't you?"

Jordon blinked and looked at her. "I'm well aware you are my patient. And apparently you don't follow doctor's orders. I'd like to keep you overnight and give you a good checkup just to make sure we have your blood-sugar level back in line." He looked at Kelsey. "I also would like Ms. Davis to give you a refresher course on what to eat and not eat. Just in case there's something that wasn't covered."

He noticed Kelsey stiffen but he wasn't sure why.

"I understand," Marsha said, with just enough humility to make him believe she might be more cautious about the number of petits fours she ate in the future.

"All right, I'll get the paperwork started to have you admitted."

"At least that isn't committed," Martha said.

Jordon chuckled. Martha reminded him of Ms. Olson, one of the patients he'd had to leave behind in DC. He'd miss her and what he'd worked so hard to build.

"I don't think your infraction was that serious but you can't keep eating petits fours. The nurse will be in to see about getting you admitted to the floor. I'll check in on you this evening before I leave."

Jordon pushed the curtain back and stepped out into the large open space of the ER. Before the curtain fell back into place Kelsey joined him.

"May I speak to you a moment, Doctor? In private."

She didn't wait for him to respond before she started out the double doors of the E.R. Left little choice, he followed her. She glanced back as she rounded a corner but continued on. He had a nice view of her high tight behind incased in blue pants that defined it to perfection. When he saw her again, she was standing beside a door. She pushed it open and entered as he approached.

Kelsey had no idea what she'd been thinking when Jordon had entered the small consultation room. Suddenly there hadn't been enough space or air. She hadn't been rational, she'd been too angry. She couldn't afford anyone to imply she didn't do her job well. He had inferred just that.

The chance of getting the job in Atlanta was far too important. If that got back to the administration of the new hospital she'd never have a chance at the position. It was hard enough to overcome the past, she didn't need anything else to stand in her way. Some of the administration staff had known her as a kid and still had a hard time seeing her as a responsible employee.

The second the door clicked closed Kelsey turned to face him and took a step closer, putting only a foot between them. Looking up at the tall and rather large man, she questioned her decision-making. He gazed at her with complete innocence, which fueled her ire to the point she gritted her teeth to stop herself from doing something far more stupid and unethical.

"Back there it sounded as if you might be implying that I hadn't done my job," she hissed. "That I am responsible when a patient doesn't follow dietary directions outside this hospital. I assure you that I instruct to the best of my ability but I cannot make anyone do what they don't want to do."

To her amazement, he looked surprised, maybe slightly annoyed.

"I didn't mean to imply—"

"Whether you did or didn't, it came out that way. You've not been here long enough to make any assumptions about my work. I don't need there to be any insinuations or suggestions that I don't do my job well."

"I didn't do either!"

"Just know I don't appreciate what you said. You're the new guy here and I'm going to let it go this time. If this happens again, just know we will be having another discussion. We have to work together and I'll be professional and I expect you to be the same."

He stepped toward her.

She'd made an uncalculated mistake. He stood squarely between her and the door. She wanted out and he was as formidable as a Stonehenge boulder.

"Are you finished?" he growled, his eyes narrowing.

Kelsey forced herself not to gulp.

"I don't know what you think I did," he continued, "but I assure you I didn't say that you were responsible. I know how rumors and unsubstantiated statements can damage a career. I would never do that to anyone. As for not appreciating something, I haven't allowed someone to harangue me in this manner since my mother caught me stealing money out of her purse when I was a kid. So, Ms. Davis, you can give it a rest."

He turned, jerked the door open and was gone before Kelsey could form a parting word. She scowled at the closed door.

* * *

Jordon drove home down Bay Road toward the house he'd rented in a "snowbird" deal. He would live there through the winter months while he looked for a place to buy. As a kid, his house had been a part of a subdivision located further inland. He'd always envied his friends at school who lived on the water so that was where he planned to get a place. When he'd returned to town he'd decided against one of the large condos on the ocean side and had opted for a place on the bay.

Pulling the SUV into the white crushed-shell drive and beside the one-floor bungalow, he turned the engine off and looked out at the water beyond. The sea grass waved gently in the wind. Yes, he'd done the right thing by coming back here. Not all the memories were great but the ones before his parents' divorce outnumbered those afterwards.

Hardy, his chocolate Labrador, barked his welcome as he climbed out. The dog already had a stick in his mouth, waiting for Jordon to play.

"Hey, boy." He leaned down and gave the dog a good pat on the side. "Let me change and we'll go to the water."

Opening the door to the house, he stepped straight into the kitchen area. The place had been built in the sixties and little had changed. Dark paneling, overstuffed furniture with wooden armrests and laminated floors in an unappealing green didn't deviate from the traditional décor of the times. The house wasn't attractive but it was clean and functional. The only concession made to change was the large TV on a stand in the corner. Jordon didn't plan to miss a single Washington Redskins' football game if he could help it.

He pulled his knit shirt over his head as he went down the hall to the larger of the two bedrooms. Throwing his shirt in the corner, he pulled on a well-worn T-shirt. It was nice not to have to wear a dress shirt and tie to work. The causal, more laid-back coastal lifestyle suited him just fine. Best of all, no white lab coat was required. Shucking his tan slacks and stepping into his favorite jeans, he pulled them into place, zipped and buttoned them.

Not bothering with shoes, he'd take his chance on not getting sand spears in his feet just to feel grass between his toes. He walked across the cool floor back to the kitchen to pour himself glass of tea. He'd always like sugar sweet tea and that was something he couldn't get north of the Mason-Dixon line. Back in the Deep South, if he asked for tea, it came sweet. One more perk about moving home, and that was just what he'd done—come home. He didn't plan to ever move again.

With glass in hand he called, "Come on, boy, let's go play fetch."

Despite it being late September, the weather was still plenty warm. Hardy pranced at Jordon's heels as he strolled to the dock where an Adirondack chair waited. Sitting facing west with a sigh of pleasure, he waited for the sun to set. Hardy dropped his stick to the wooden planks of the pier beside the chair and whimpered.

"Okay, boy. I'll play with you if you promise to watch the sunset with me." Jordon threw the stick out into the water. In a flash, Hardy sprang off the dock. Paddling, he reached the stick, grasped it in his mouth and headed back. Once on shore again, he shook himself and came running back to Jordon.

"Good boy." He patted the wet, wiggling dog and willingly took the shower of water when the dog shook himself again.

Hardy barked and Jordon sent the wood out over the water again. Hardy didn't hesitate before jumping from the dock and swimming toward his stick. A blaze of color caught Jordon's eye, pulling his attention away from the dog. A woman in a large pink-brimmed hat on her head strolled out onto a pier a couple of doors away. Jordon forgot the sunset and Hardy as he watched the woman pull off her cover-up and let the mesh jacket drop to the planks.

Yes, undeniably he was going to enjoy living here.

The hand with his drink in it stopped in midair as he studied her. She had smooth curves in all the right places. The tiny blue bikini she wore accented them perfectly. As she turned, then bent to adjust the lounge downward, he caught a glimpse of her face.

Kelsey Davis. How had he not recognized those curves from earlier? Maybe he'd been distracted by all that golden skin.

Did she live two doors down? Surely she was just visiting a friend.

As if she'd become aware of someone watching her, she glanced around. Her body stiffened the second she realized his gaze was on her. She hurriedly sat in the chair.

To his horror, Hardy came out of the water and didn't look right or left before making a beeline toward Kelsey's pier. As if in slow motion, Jordon stood and started moving as Hardy ran the length of the dock, dropped the stick beside Kelsey and shook himself. Water droplets filled the air, glistening in the early evening sunlight, to fall over Kelsey like rain.

Jordon ran and called Hardy, to no avail. He had made it to the entrance of her dock in time to hear Kelsey squeal then yelped when Hardy's wet tail ran across her thigh and up over her belly. In her effort to roll away from the dog, she toppled the lounge and fell to the pier. By the time he'd sprinted to the end of her dock, Kelsey lay on her side on the rough planks, pushing Hardy away, while the dog tried to poke his nose in her face.

"Hardy," he snapped.

The dog looked at him as if to say, Get your own girl.

Jordon chuckled.

"Are you laughing at me?" Kelsey's eyes had turned cavern dark in her anger. That emotion was familiar. He seemed to elicit it from her with little trouble.

"No, I'm just laughing at the picture you two make." Jordon grabbed Hardy's collar.

"It figures this monster would be yours."

He looked pointedly at her. "You don't like dogs?"

"I like dogs fine. I'm just not wild about showers given by them or sloppy kisses."

"I'll remember that."

Her eyes grew wide. Why had he said something so suggestive? He had no intention of sharing a shower with her, much less kissing her. She wasn't his type. Even if she had been, the sting of betrayal still smarted. It was best she remain on her dock and he on his.

Kelsey started to rise.

Jordon offered her a hand. "Here, let me help you."

After a second she took it and he tugged her upwards.

He sucked in a breath. As amazing as she'd looked from his dock, she was breathtaking up close. The bikini showed off most of her body but he still wanted to see more. Her breasts were full and high. His fingers itched to stroke them, just once.

"Can't you handle your dog?" Her eyes snapped as she glared at him.

"I guess he appreciates a pretty woman as well as the next male."

She squared her shoulders, which thrust her barely covered breasts upward. He couldn't help but stare.

"Surely you aren't flirting with me?"

Jordon couldn't pull his gaze away from the beauty before him. "What if I was?" he muttered. What had made him ask that? A half-naked woman had never made him lose his mind before. For heaven's sake, he was a doctor. Was his thirty-seconds-ago vow to keep his distance already going by the wayside?

Kelsey picked up the cover-up from the dock, giving him a fine view of her behind before she pulled the jacket on and tied it. "Don't."

Hardy bumped her leg. She leaned down and took his face in her hands. "So what's this guy's name?"

Jordon had to give her points for being a good sport. No other woman he'd known in the past or present would've taken Hardy's antics so well. "Hardy. As in Laurel and Hardy. Mr. Personality he is."

"You have beautiful eyes," she cooed.

How ridiculous was it to be jealous of his dog? Hardy seemed to melt like chocolate on a warm day under her ministrations. Jordon might have too, except he couldn't seem to get any positive attention from Kelsey.

"I had a dog almost just like you when I was a kid."

She stopped petting Hardy and straightened. It was as if her enthusiasm had suddenly waned. There was a sad note in her voice as if she'd remembered something she didn't want to. Had something happened to her dog when she'd been a kid? Wanting to change the subject, he asked, "So, do you live here?"

"Yeah."

"We're neighbors. I've got the place a couple houses over."

"Great," she said, with less gusto than he would have liked to hear. Why did it matter what she thought?

"Well, I guess we'll let you get back to your sunbathing or whatever you were doing. Come on, Hardy."

The dog looked from one to the other then sat beside Kelsey.

She said with a smirk on her lips, "I guess your dog likes me better."

Jordon picked up Hardy's stick and threw it in the direction of his dock. The dog jumped into the water.

"See you later, Kelsey," Jordon tossed over his shoulder smugly, as he walked up the dock toward the shore.

Back on his own dock, he threw the piece of wood two additional times for Hardy, in an effort to forget Kelsey only yards away. It didn't work. His attention kept slipping back to her. It wasn't just that she was a beautiful half-dressed woman within eyesight but Kelsey intrigued him on a number of levels. She was plain old-fashioned interesting. Something that women he was acquainted with weren't.

Hardy, finally worn out, lay down beside him. Jordon absently rubbed his ear. "Thank you for being such a turncoat."

The dog said nothing and Jordon continued to watch Kelsey as she read a book, the sunset no longer of interest. At dusk Kelsey folded her chair down, gathered her belongings and headed toward the house.

"Good night, Kelsey," Jordon said softly.

He stayed until the night swallowed up the last ray of light then made his way inside with Hardy at his heels. "I hope the view is as good every night," he said to Hardy, not sure if he meant of Kelsey or the sunset.

The next morning Kelsey tried her ignition switch one more time. Nothing. Was it just a dead battery or something more?

How was she going to get to work? Molly had a doctor's appointment and had left earlier. Great. It wouldn't look or sound good when her superiors were contacted by someone in Atlanta and they had her being late to work fresh in their memory. She needed a ride quickly. Looking two driveways over, she confirmed that the blue SUV was still sitting in the drive.

She grabbed her purse from the passenger seat, stuffed it under her arm and started in the direction of Jordon's bungalow. It would have been nice if one of the other houses around them was occupied but they were only used seasonally so she had no choice but to ask Jordon for help. She wasn't looking forward to asking him for a ride, but she had little choice unless she walked, and she would be late for sure if she did that.

She stepped up to Jordon's door. Her hand faltered before she knocked. Barking preceded the door being pulled open. Behind the screen door, wearing no shirt, stood Jordon.

"Well, good morning," he drawled in an exaggerated tone.

Why did the man manage to set her teeth on edge? Taking a deep breath, she said, "My car won't start. Can I get a ride with you?"

He grinned, "So what you're staying is you're not angry with me anymore."

"I knew you wouldn't be a gentleman about this."

Jordon clasped his hands over his heart. "That hurt. Of course I'll be glad to give you a ride." His grin grew and he pushed the screen door open and used his leg to block Hardy from exiting the house. "I'm almost ready. Want to come in and wait?"

Her gaze found his chest. "I'll just wait out by your SUV."

He shrugged and let the door slam. "Suit yourself."

The guy was so smug. What was it about her that made him so rude?

She'd been acutely aware of him behind her while she'd sat on the pier the previous evening. It had taken all her willpower not to glance behind her to see if he was watching her. She'd read the same three pages of her book five times and she still couldn't have told anyone what they'd been about. All she'd been able to think about had been what Jordon had been doing.

Refusing to give him the satisfaction of him knowing that he'd rattled her, she'd acted as unaffected by him as she'd been able. He'd completely ruined her plans for a relaxing evening. Wishing he would leave, she'd given up at dusk and packed her belongs. She had been grateful that he hadn't been sitting close enough to see her hands shake when she'd risen.

Had she heard "Good night, Kelsey" drift on the wind?

"Hey, you going to get in or daydream all morning?"

She blinked then focused on him. "I'm going to get in."

At the beep of the door being unlocked, she climbed into the vehicle and settled into the large comfortable seat. Jordon effortlessly took his spot behind the wheel. They didn't speak as he backed out of the drive and drove toward town. As they passed the blue house about a mile up the road Jordon commented, "I used to know a family that lived there. They were the Davises. Are you any kin to them?"

A sick feeling went through her. So he did remember. But there was no point in lying. "Yeah. Their daughter."

He jerked his head around to look at her.

"You might want to watch the road," she said.

"So you're one of Chad's sisters." He sounded utterly amazed.

"I am."

He nodded as if in thought. "Which one are you?"

She'd hung on his every word as a kid. She'd thought he'd been the be-all and end-all and he couldn't remember which one she was. That stung. "I'm the youngest one," she made herself say in a strong voice.

He pulled to the side of the road and turned to look at her. "So have you known all along who I was?"

"I recognized you while we were dancing."

"Why didn't you say something?"

She suddenly felt the need to defend herself. "I didn't even know your real name until you came into my class. You were always J-man to me. We need to get going or we'll be late."

He pulled the SUV back onto the road. "J-man. I've not been called that for years."

"Why did you move back?" Kelsey asked. There had to be something in particular to make anyone want to come back to Golden Shores.

The only indication he gave that her question might have disturbed him was the tightening of his hands on the steering wheel.

"It was time to make a change."

"But why here, of all places?"

"Because this is the last place I remember feeling like I belong," he said matter-of-factly.

Kelsey huffed. "And it's the one place I wish I didn't belong."

This conversation had gone way past a simple ride to the hospital. Kelsey was relieved when Jordon pulled the SUV into the hospital parking lot. She had to get out of there.

"Thanks for the ride," she said, opening the door of the SUV before Jordon had turned the engine off.

"Kelsey—"

She closed the door and headed for the employees' entrance, refusing to look back.

Answering questions about her family wasn't how she wanted to start her day. Jordon couldn't help but bring back unhappy memories. She missed Chad as much today as she had then. If she only knew if he was still alive.

Jordon watched as Kelsey entered the hospital and disappeared behind the metal outside door as if she'd pulled up the drawbridge. So she was Chad's sister. That sister. The one that he had wished he'd be around to see when she got older. Did she remember him as fondly as he remembered her?

Did she know where Chad was? Kelsey acted as if she didn't want to talk about anything having to do with her family. She'd not even looked at her parents' house when he'd driven by. He and Chad had been two unhappy teens who'd bonded and fueled each other's frustration. Leading up to his parents' divorce and afterward, he had been angry. Whatever his father had said, he'd done the opposite.

He'd started hanging out at the park with the wrong crowd, more to irritate his father than liking the kids who had been there. One night Chad Davis had shown up. He was a year younger but they'd seemed to hit it off. They'd started hanging around with each other at school, ditching classes together and otherwise becoming best friends. That had been until the night they'd been caught by the police, smoking dope.

Jordon climbed out of the SUV and slowly made his way inside. Did Kelsey know her brother was in the state prison not an hour away? When he'd visited Chad on the way to Golden Shores and told him about moving here, Chad had made Jordon promise that if he ever saw any of his family he wouldn't tell them where he was. At the time it was no big deal to make that promise. But now how long would he be able to honor that request? But trust, giving his word meant everything. Jordon wouldn't break his.

He'd certainly not wanted to discuss way he'd decided to move back to Golden Shores, with Kelsey or anyone else for that matter. Those events had been too painful. Shown how easily he'd been duped by someone he'd cared about. That had happened one too many times in his life. He would be careful about who he let his guard down to from now on.

In his office, he checked his messages. He was asked to be at a staff meeting at ten in the cafeteria. What was going on? Was some dignitary coming to town? He'd find out soon enough. There was just enough time to make rounds.

It was five minutes past ten when he entered the cafeteria. The room was packed so he stood against the wall. He hadn't been able to get there any sooner because Martha had kept asking him questions and telling him stories when he'd checked on her.

The CEO stood at the front of the room. "Most of you have been through this before, many of you more than once. Still, I want you to review your emergency procedures. In a few minutes you can get with your teams and update your contact numbers. The weather service isn't calling for the storm to hit here but we need to be prepared if it takes a turn our way. It's our job to work calmly and efficiently. Our community expects us to be here for them and we will be."

So they were preparing for a hurricane. Maybe he should have been watching the news instead of Kelsey last night.

"Dr. King?" He looked around the room.

Jordon gave the CEO a wave. "Here."

The CEO nodded in Jordon's direction. "I hate to put you on the ground running so quickly but you're to take over Dr. Richards's team. Everyone previously on Dr. Richards's team, please get together with Dr. King when we adjourn. I think that's all, folks. Check in with each other and keep your phones charged. On a positive closing note, we are going ahead with the hospital-wide low country boil picnic Saturday, unless the weather says something different."

Hospital picnic? He'd never been to one. The hospitals he'd trained in had been in metropolitan areas and far too large for such things. Another perk of living in a small town. A low country boil did sound good. He'd not been to one of those in a long time.

Having no idea who was on his team, he waited until he was approached by someone. Talk about being a fish out of water.

"Dr. King?" a balding man wearing a tie asked.

Jordon nodded. "Please, make it Jordon."

"I'm Jim. I work in the business office. I'll be handling the paperwork, communication and be your runner."

Jordon offered his hand. "Nice to meet you, Jim. So we are preparing for a hurricane?"

"Yeah, around here it isn't if we will have a hurricane but when."

"How many more are on our team?"

"Two more. Josh Little and Kelsey Davis."

Jordon almost groaned. She wouldn't like that any more than he did.

A tall man, dressed in nursing scrubs with golden hair and biceps that said he spent time in the gym daily, joined them.

"Hey, I'm Josh Little. I'll be your nurse."

The two men shook hands.

"I'm going to depend on you to keep me straight. I've never done this type of thing before," Jordon said.

"Nothing to it. Kelsey will be the boss," Josh said with a smile.

"Sorry I'm late. I was all the way across the room."

Jordon knew the voice that came from behind him.

He turned to look at her. She didn't appear any more enthusiastic about seeing him than he was to see her. "Glad you could join us, Kelsey. I understand you're the one who will tell me what to do."

She narrowed her eyes. "Our team does triage. You tell me which ones are the most urgent and I tag them. Josh handles care until you can see them. Jim will record everything."

"So where does this all happen?" Jordon looked at the group but the question was addressed to Kelsey.

"Our designated area is in the hospital lobby."

"What about supplies?" he asked.

"All that is taken care of. Housekeeping sets up and has the space ready to go if or when needed," Josh offered.

Jordon nodded his understanding. "Great. So all we need to do is exchange numbers?"

Kelsey said, "That's it." They all went through the process of telling each other their phone numbers.

"Who is responsible for doing all the calling?" Jordon asked.

"I do that," Jim stated.

Jordon looked at him and grinned. "So the plan here is to hope that I don't hear from you."

Jim smiled back. "That's the plan."

There was a buzz. "I've got to go. E.R. is paging me," Josh said.

"I've got to go too," Jim added.

As Kelsey turned to leave Jordon said, "Hey, Kelsey, will you tell me about the hospital picnic?"

She didn't look like she wanted to but she stopped. "It's held at the state park down on the beach. Food is provided and there are games. You know, the regular family stuff."

"You planning to attend?"

"I usually do."

"That didn't answer my question."

She looked at him for a second then said, "I haven't missed one in five years so I don't think I'll be missing this one."

"Mind if I tag along with you? I don't really know anyone."

It took her so long to answer he started to think she wasn't going to. Suddenly there was a look of triumph on her face.

"I have to be there early to set up. I'm on the committee."

"I don't mind going along and helping out."

"Good. I'm going to take you at your word. I'll pick you up a seven a.m. on Saturday. No, let me change that. You drive. You've got a bigger vehicle."

"Why do I think I've just been had?"

Kelsey grinned then walked off.

The weatherman had said the storm had stalled in the Gulf and wouldn't be coming ashore until early the next week. Saturday dawned sunny with a light breeze. The picnic was still on. Jordon pulled up into Kelsey's drive promptly at seven in the morning. He and Kelsey hadn't had much interaction in the last few days other than brief encounters over patients.

The door to her place opened. She stepped out and waved, indicating she needed him to come inside. He climbed out of the SUV and she called, "Hey, did you plan to sit there while I do all the work?"

"Sorry, I didn't know I was needed." He strolled toward the door. Kelsey had already disappeared inside again.

She pushed the door open and handed him a large box. "This needs to go, then come back and help me with the ice chests."

"Yes, ma'am."

Having stowed the box, he returned. The door wasn't open so he knocked and called through the screen door, "Kelsey?"

"Come on in."

She didn't wait for him to respond, disappearing down the hall.

Jordon entered. The interior was arranged very much like his place. The only thing different was that this bungalow had a feminine feel to it. Candles were arranged on the counter, bright throw blankets lay over the furniture and pictures of flowers adorned the walls.

"The coolers are next to the bar in the kitchen. I'll be there to help in a sec."

True to her word, she stepped into the room a few minutes later, wearing a tight T-shirt with something sparkling around the scooped neckline that gave him a hint of cleavage and cutoff jeans that showed off her legs to their best advantage. There was something raw and inviting about her. A woman who stood out in a crowd. He could see a touch of the young girl there too that he known so many years before.

Kelsey reached for a handle on one end of a large box cooler and he took the other. Together they carried it out. When they got to the rear of the SUV, they set it down while Jordon opened the doors.

"I'll take it from here." He lifted the cooler into the vehicle. "What have you got in this thing? Rocks?"

"Water balloons."

"Water balloons!"

"I'm in charge of the water-balloon fight."

"I'm glad I'm not signed up for that."

"You're too old," she quipped.

"How's that? My hair's not even gray yet."

"It's for the teenagers. That's how we get them to come to the picnic each year."

Jordon pushed the cooler further into the SUV. "Makes sense. Is that it?"

She turned toward the house. "Nope. There's another cooler."

"Why am I not surprised?"

Together they brought another cooler out to the SUV. "Just how were you planning to get these to the park if I hadn't come along?"

"Aw, I would have gotten one of the guys at work to help me."

That he wasn't shocked to hear. She seemed to always have some guy hanging around. Right now he wasn't much different but he'd keep his distance, if not in the physical sense the at least on an emotional level.

"Anything else?"

"I just have to get one more small cooler and a couple of bags. And my cake."

"Was I supposed to bring something?"

"No. Someone suggested we have a cake auction to raise money to help redecorate the children's wing. I was roped into baking one."

"I'll help you with the bags and you can handle the cake."

Ten minutes later they were in the SUV, headed toward town.

"Do you know where the park is?"

He gave her an incredulous look. "Yes. Remember I used to live here."

"That's right. I keep forgetting."

Something about the way she made that statement made him believe that wasn't true.

As he drove past her parents' home he watched out of the corner of his eye to see if she looked. Her focus remained straight ahead. He wanted to ask her if she knew where Chad was, what had happened after he'd left town, but today wasn't the right time. It would wait.

CHAPTER THREE

THE PARKING LOT already had a number of cars in it when they arrived.

Kelsey pointed. "See the white tent over there. If you could back up to it, we can unload easier."

Jordon did as instructed. Kelsey was out of the SUV and opening the back door before he moved the gearshift into park. A couple of guys he recognized came to help them. After unloading, Kelsey was still busy issuing orders as Jordon moved the SUV to a parking spot out of the way. He was locking up when he saw Kelsey's cake sitting on the floor of the passenger seat. She must have forgotten it. He picked it up and walked back across the parking lot to where she was helping set up tables.

"Kelsey," he called, "where do I need to put your cake?"

More than one person stopped what they were doing and looked at her.

A red hue covered her face and by the thrust of her chin she left no doubt she was not pleased with his question.

"Kelsey, you baked a cake?" one woman asked.

"The last one you put salt in instead of sugar," another commented with a grin.

"I thought you'd just buy one and put your name on it," the guy helping Kelsey put chairs around a table said with a chuckle.

Kelsey took a proud stance. "Hey, look, I can bake with the best of them I just choose not to on most occasions." She tossed her head and went back to work.

"I think we need all the cakes we can get for the auction," another woman offered. "Maybe the fact that the winner of the cake gets to share it with the baker will make Kelsey's the highest earner."

"Thank you, Carolyn. You're a true friend." Kelsey said, then looked around at the crowd. "Unlike everyone else."

Kelsey put the last chair around the table, stalked over to Jordon and all but snatched the cake out of his hands. "Thanks," she hissed.

"I didn't know you were hiding it," he said, for her ears only. "Sorry."

"Forget it."

Jordon had no idea her baking was such a sore point. Where she was concerned, he kept making mistakes. "Can I help with something?"

"We still need to put up the tables for the games." She pointed toward a woman with a blue ball cap on her head. "Pam over there will tell you what to do."

Jordon was a little disappointed she was fobbing him off on another person, but he didn't need to be spending any more time with her than he presently had. He'd had to fight the urge to jump in and defend her baking skills. She wouldn't have appreciated that and he was even more perplexed by the idea that he thought he should.

The hours flew by as he helped first Pam then Max and finally Roger to get the large burner and pots ready to cook the meal. At around ten, cars began arriving one after another. It was a family event, so kids showed up in all shapes and sizes. As the morning went on he only caught glimpses of Kelsey from a distance but he seemed to search her out every so often as if she was his to watch over. Which she certainly wasn't.

One time he saw her hugging a petite woman with shoulder-length brown hair. Kelsey smiled at the tall man who had a possessive arm around the woman's waist. Something about the interaction indicated these people were important to Kelsey. Who were they?

"Hey Jordon, how about helping us with the cooking? We need some muscle," Roger, who Jordon had learned worked in the lab, asked.

"Sure." Jordon knew nothing about cooking a low country boil but it was nice to be asked and included. Plus it kept his wandering mind off Kelsey.

At around twelve-thirty he, along with half a dozen people, helped pour buckets of corn, new potatoes, onions and shrimp over newspaper-covered tables. There were plenty of paper towel rolls available and everyone took their places at the picnic tables and dug in. With his job done, he looked for Kelsey. She was sandwiched between Josh and some other guy Jordon hadn't seen before.

One of the nurses from the E.R. called to him and moved down enough that he could join her table. The food was excellent and the conversation lively. He was glad he'd attended.

Before the first table could finish their meal and leave, the CEO stood and said through a bullhorn, "I'm glad you all could make it today. I'd like to say thanks to the picnic committee headed by Kelsey Davis for this fine event."

Kelsey had said nothing about being in charge. She'd implied she was only helping.

The CEO continued, "The games are about to begin. Please don't forget to go by and check out the silent cake auction. As an added bonus you get to share the cake with the cook. And the money goes to a good cause."

Jordon spent the next half hour making a circle around the area to see what was happening. There was apple bobbing, bingo and three-legged racing through the sand that brought smiles and laughter from everyone. A beach volleyball game was beginning when he walked up.

One of the nurses from the geriatric unit called his name and waved him over. "Come on, Jordon, we need another player."

"Sure." He took his place on her side of the net. He'd played some volleyball in the early years of high school and had been pretty good at it but his skills were rusty. What he might lack in ability he more than made up with height. Two volleys later he was able to return the ball over the net for a point, which built his confidence.

"Okay, we need this point," one of his teammates said, when it came time for him to serve.

He didn't know about getting a point, he just wanted to get the ball over the net without embarrassing himself. He gave the ball a solid hit and it did as he'd hoped. It was volleyed back. The other guy on his team returned it for a point. Jordon served again.

The number of spectators around the sandy court grew. Those in the crowd took sides and cheered for their team. This was the type of team sport experience he had missed later in high school. He'd been far too busy being angry at his mother. During the year he'd spent in military school he'd not qualified to play on any teams because he'd not attended long enough. He rather liked feeling a part of a unit, something he'd not had since his parents' divorce.

His serve soon came around again. The game was tied. He was in motion to take a swing when he noticed Kelsey standing on the edge of the field near where the pole to the net had been pushed into the ground. She had a slight smile on her face. His hand stopped in midmotion. He sucked in a breath. His gaze found hers. He remembered her all too well now. He'd seen that expression on her face before. That sweet I-only-have-eyes-for-you look.

His male pride made him want to show off. He couldn't recall purposely trying to prove his manhood through a sport ever before. Bringing his hand back, he gave the ball a hard lick. After a couple of volleys, his team earned the needed point.

"Game point, everyone," the nurse who'd invited him to play yelled. She looked at him. "Jordon, this is it."

"Thanks. No pressure."

He didn't dare look at Kelsey. He was too afraid he'd mess the serve up. Flipping the ball into the air, he punched it across the net. His male teammate tipped the returned volley back, it was returned again, and this time the nurse barely got it back over the net. It was then hit high and toward him. He had to run to get under the ball. With arms stretched out and hands fisted, he dove across the sand and popped the ball up. It just cleared the net. The other team was unable to reach the ball.

The crowd went wild. When he was on his feet again the nurse jumped into his arms, wrapping her arms around his neck. His other teammates patted him on the back.

His gaze met Kelsey's. She smiled at him and suddenly he felt like a conquering hero.

Why did her praise of all the people there have that effect on him?

Just as quickly, she turned and grabbed the arm of the man standing next to her and disappeared into the crowd. The heady feeling imploded like a building being demolished, leaving nothing but disgusted rubble.

He'd found a cold bottle of water and was coming out of the restroom after cleaning up when he heard the announcement for the water-balloon fight. He strolled over to the area of pavement where it was being held. By the time he made it to the designated area on the pavement, people surrounded it.

"Okay," Kelsey said into a bullhorn. "Teens, I want you to line up on either side of the line. Last man standing wins a cell phone. Everyone on your mark, get set, go."

Wiggly, wobbly water balloons began to fly through the air, splashing as they hit their targets. Others burst on contact with the ground and splattered the observers nearby. The kids ran from the line and back to one of the coolers he and Kelsey had loaded that morning. The crowd cheered as the number of balloon diminished. Kelsey ran up and down one side of the game field cheering the teens on and reminding them to aim for the body only. One misplaced balloon caught her on the shoulder, wetting her down one side. She laughed and kept moving.

Jordon had to give Kelsey credit. She was a dynamo. Everyone, including those surly teenagers, was having a good time.

A few minutes later the last of the balloons were gone and two dry teens still remained in the game.

Kelsey stepped out into the center of the area as if she was stepping into a boxing ring. "Well, it looks like we have a tie. Hey, Jack, could you bring that smaller cooler out here?" she called through the bullhorn. A guy walked out with a round drink cooler.

With slow, dramatic movements, Kelsey opened the screw top. The entire crowd quieted and stilled as she gently tipped over the cooler while holding the top over whatever was inside. Laying the cooler on the ground, she pulled the top away and a couple of huge water balloons rolled out like blobs of jelly.

The crowd released a universal sound of amazement.

Picking up the bullhorn again, she said, "May the best man win," then backed away.

The two teens circled the balloons before one grabbed one of the fat blobs and the other did the same with the other. Soon they were struggling to pick up their unwieldy balloons. By using their bodies, they finally managed to control the balloons enough to work them into their arms without breaking them. The crowd enjoyed the scene. Jordon was no different. One contestant became the aggressor and stalked the other then lobbed his balloon at the other. The teen sidestepped the wiggly mass and heaved the last balloon at the other teen. He moved and it hit Jordon dead center in the chest.

The water was ice cold. He sucked in a breath as his knit shirt stuck to his skin. The spectators erupted in glee but the only person Jordon could see was Kelsey, doubled over in laughter. When she stood she brought the bullhorn to her mouth. "Well, we have our winner. Dr. King, welcome to Golden Shores Hospital."

He bowed his head in her direction and she grinned. What would it be like to kiss that grin off her face and make her smile for him only? He wasn't so cold anymore.

Then she said, "Now, everyone head over to the tent for some ice cream."

The crowd shifted away. Jordon stepped through them on his way to Kelsey. She was busy picking up balloon remnants from the ground.

"You enjoyed that, didn't you?" he said, pulling his sticking shirt away from his body.

Kelsey continued what she was doing. "I did."

"Did you plan it?"

She stood, indignation written all over her face. "I did not. I couldn't have planned something so well."

Kelsey went back to what she was doing.

"Can't you leave those?" he asked, despite the beautiful view of her behind he was being given, her shorts tight across it. She had a fine derrière.

"No. They'll hurt the wildlife. I had to promise to pick it all up right away to get permission from the park service to have the balloon fight in the first place."

Where was the rest of the committee? Why wasn't someone helping her? He leaned down and started picking up broken balloon.

She stood. "You don't have to do that."

"Look at this mess. I think you can use the help."

"Your mother must have raised you right," she commented, and went back to work.

His hand faltered before he picked up the next piece of rubber. He'd never thought about that. His mother had had some positive influence in his life. All he'd remembered for years was how she had hurt his father and destroyed Jordon's trust.

Kelsey tossed the last of the broken balloons in the trash and picked up one of the coolers. He grabbed the other two empty ones. They walked to his SUV and Jordon packed the ice chests.

"How about sharing some ice cream with me?" he asked.

"I really need to check on the band." She turned toward where a group of men and a woman were setting up equipment.

His hand circled her upper arm, stopping her. She glanced at where his hand rested. He released her.

"Come on, Kelsey. You've been at it all day. Take a minute for yourself. Plus I took a balloon in your game."

"Is that an order, Doctor?"

"I would like for it not to be but if I have to make it one, I will."

She gave a resigned sigh and said, "Okay. Let me check on the band and I'll meet you over there."

"Fair enough."

Jordon circled the cake table on his way to the ice-cream tent. He needed to place a bid and help out the cause. There were a number of beautiful cakes. Beside each one lay a small card with the name of the baker and a place where a bid could be written. Looking over the offerings, he saw the cake that had sagged to one side and had a crack in it was Kelsey's. He pick up her card. The card was filled with bids.

Jordon studied the cake. They certainly weren't bidding on its merits. He looked at the card again. Kelsey didn't need his sympathy and he didn't need to be tempted by her or her cake. He was already giving her more attention that he should. Moving on, he placed his name on a couple of cards and headed to where horseshoes were being thrown.

Kelsey finished reassuring the band leader she would be around if needed and walked to where the ice cream was being served.

She had to give Jordon credit for being a good sport. For a man with his attitude toward her he seemed to take the fact in stride that her game had literally blown up on him. He'd been amazing during the volleyball game. She hadn't been able to keep her eyes off him. More than that, he'd graciously helped her pick up balloon fragments while everyone else had been having ice cream. Maybe there was still some of that guy in him that she'd had such a crush on so many years ago.

He was waiting for her when she walked up to the ice-cream line. They each got two scoops. She hadn't planned to spend any personal time with him but he hadn't given her much choice. Kelsey was searching for a place to sit when she saw her sister, China, waving her over.

"Come and sit with us," China called.

Older by two years, China had been Kelsey's best friend and protector when she'd been at home. They had grown apart after Kelsey had moved out but were making an effort to mend that gap. Kelsey had missed her sister and was glad to have her back in her life. Leaving China would be her one regret in leaving Golden Shores. Kelsey would miss her more than she wanted to admit.

Under normal circumstances she would be tickled to spend time with China and her new husband, Payton. But she worried that China might recognize Jordon. It had been too nice a day for it to be ruined by talk of Chad or, worse, their parents. Resigned, Kelsey smiled and headed her way. She was aware of Jordon following. Too aware.

The picnic table where China sat was crowded. She scooted closer to her husband and Kelsey took the spot next to her, leaving Jordon to squeeze in. His thigh brushed hers as he slipped into place. When she didn't immediately introduce him, Jordon leaned forward and looked down the table at China.

Did he know her? Somehow it would hurt if he recognized China but hadn't remembered her.

"Hi, I'm Jordon King. I work with Kelsey."

She guessed not.

China smiled at him but gave no indication that she knew him. Instead, she gave Kelsey a questioning look, as if to ask if this was her new boyfriend.

Kelsey shook her head. No one important.

"I'm China, and this is my husband, Payton." She smiled at him in complete bliss then she looked back at Jordon. "I'm Kelsey's sister."

Jordon nodded. "Nice to meet you both." His tone took on a knowing sound.

Payton asked, "So, are you new to the hospital?"

"I am. I've only been here a couple of weeks."

Kelsey was glad Payton took over the conversation so that Jordon didn't have a chance to bring up Chad. She and China had only really reconnected in the last few months. They had agreed not to discuss her parents or Chad.

"So, how do you find living in Golden Shores?" Payton asked.

Kelsey shifted. Jordon glanced at her and then said, "I'm finding it a great place to live. Stuff like this today isn't the norm around DC."

Payton grinned. "I know what you mean. I moved down here from Chicago about six months ago."

When the conversation lagged Kelsey asked, "So, China, did you bring a cake for the contest?"

"I did. A sour cream pound cake." She smiled lovingly at her husband. "It's Payton's favorite."

Would she ever find a relationship like theirs? Maybe when she got out of Golden Shores there would be someone for her who would put that sparkle in her eyes.

"Payton has placed a bid so high that I don't think anyone will match it," China said. "Did you bring one?"

"I did, but it doesn't look like much. That was always your department." Kelsey scooted back. "It's almost time for the auction to be over. I'd better go check on things."

There was no graceful way to get out from between China and Jordon without placing her hands on their shoulders for support. There was a marked difference between China's thin, petite one and Jordon's large, muscular shoulder.

"I'm tired so we won't be staying for the dance," China said.

"Are you feeling okay?" Kelsey looked down at her with concern.

"Never better. I was going to tell you Tuesday when we have lunch but I can't wait."

Payton slipped his arm around China's waist and smiled up at Kelsey.

"I'm pregnant," China announced.

Kelsey squealed and leaned over to hug her. "That's wonderful."

When she tipped forward too far, strong hands steadied her until she was on her feet again. Heat rose to her face and she glanced away from China to find her face entirely too close to Jordon's. "Thanks," she murmured.

"Now maybe you'll rethink moving to Atlanta. I want your niece or nephew to know you," China said softly, for Kelsey's ear only. The pleading tone pulled at Kelsey's heart. Still, she couldn't give up her dream.

"They'll know me. You can come visit often," Kelsey whispered.

Her name was called and she waved at the man across the park.

"Go on," China said. "I'll see you Tuesday. We'll talk more then."

Leaving them behind, she headed to see what Walter wanted. A twinge of worry ran through her. Surely Jordon wouldn't get into a personal discussion with her sister and Payton about their shared past.

An hour later Kelsey was standing behind the table where her cake sat along with all the other people who had baked one. All the final bids had been made and now the winners were being announced. Despite the awful mess her cake was, she'd had a full bid sheet when she'd last checked. Obviously there was compassion in the world. From what she could tell, the cake auction would make a nice sum of money for the children's ward redecoration.

"Alice Reynolds's cake was won by Mark Dobson.

Come up and claim your cake and the baker. All right, the next cake was made by Nancy Mitchell. And the winner of that cake is Jordon King."

Kelsey's head jerked round. The smiling Nancy from the business office. Her unofficial date competitor. Nancy was going to be sharing her cake with Jordon. Why should Kelsey care? She'd seen more of him today than she'd wanted to. Still, it bothered her on a level she didn't understand. Had he even bid on hers?

"Well…" She leaned over and said to Molly, "I guess you just lost your bet."

"Winning her cake doesn't constitute a date. Being asked out does," she whispered back.

Two cakes later it was her turn.

"And the winner of Kelsey's cake is Reid Johnson."

Reid worked in the E.R. and was a nice enough guy. He'd asked her out a number of times but she just wasn't interested. She smiled, picked up her cake and went to meet Reid. He took the cake from her and led her over to a nearby table. To her dismay, it was close to where Jordon sat with Nancy.

"Uh, wouldn't you rather sit in the shade?" she asked.

"No, this is fine," Reid said, putting the cake down.

"Then I'll get us some forks and plates and something to cut with."

"Hey, would you mind getting us some too?" Jordon called.

She couldn't say that she did mind or why, so she nodded. "Sure." The man was starting to get under her skin.

As she returned with the plates and utensils, a loud burst of laughter came from Jordon and Nancy's direction. Kelsey walked to their table and placed the things Jordon had requested on it.

"Thanks, Kelsey," Jordon said as he picked up the plastic knife, giving her no more attention.

Nancy offered a coy smile as if she thought she'd won the prize. Kelsey had never had anything against Nancy but apparently she saw Kelsey as a rival, which certainly was not the case. Kelsey had no designs on Jordon.

"You guys enjoy!" she said as brightly as she could, and went back to where Reid waited. She and Reid shared a slice of her cake while he told her a joke. Kelsey laughed. She looked up to find Jordon glaring at her. Turning her shoulder to him, she continued her conversation with Reid, which included more humor.

The sun was beginning to set when the band struck up a tune. The people still there drifted toward the dance area in front of the makeshift stage. Kelsey left Reid with the rest of her cake and went to check on an issue in the food tent. For the next couple of hours she only saw Jordon from a distance. Each time she did Nancy was beside him, even to the point of hanging on his arm. It was no big deal. Nancy could have him. So why did she keep looking around to see where they were?

Kelsey danced a few dances but spent most of the last minutes of daylight cleaning and packing up. As soon as the dance was over she would be on her way home to bed. Exhausted didn't even describe how tired she felt. She was circling the floor, picking up forgotten drink cups, when a finger tapped her shoulder.

"I wouldn't be a gentleman if I didn't dance with the one that brung me," said a voice she knew far too well after such a short period of time.

"That's not necessary and I think you distorted the saying some."

"I know, but that's beside the point. Instead of correcting me, how about being friendly enough to accept my offer to dance?" He extended his hand.

She didn't want to appear mean by not agreeing, but instead of taking his hand she walked onto the dance floor and waited. When he reached her his hand came to rest snugly on her waist, giving her the feeling of being imprisoned and protected at the same time. She placed her hands on his shoulders. Her fingertips traced the corded muscle beneath them.

She met Jordon's gaze. "You know, I can find a way home if you want to leave with Nancy."

"Jealous?" he asked with a grin.

Kelsey stopped moving. "I am not. You have to care to be jealous. I was just trying to be nice."

One of his arms slipped further around her back and pulled her closer but not so close that they touched.

"Hush and let's enjoy the dance. I brought you, I'll be taking you home," he murmured, as he slowly led her around the floor.

Being in Jordon's arms made her feel jittery, unsure and out of sorts. She rarely felt any of these and never in a combination. She'd worked too hard and for too long to lose control over her emotions. She didn't like them escaping.

They swayed to the music until the last note. She was walking away from Jordon when the bandleader called for the last dance. Nancy passed her, headed in the direction Kelsey had come from.

A half an hour later, true to his word, Kelsey was sitting beside Jordon as he pulled his vehicle out of the parking lot. "That was a lot of fun," he said, with a contented tone in his voice.

"Yeah, they always are. Picnics on the beach are one of the few things I'm going to miss about this place."

He quickly glanced at her. "Miss?"

"I'm hoping to get a job in Atlanta. I'm expecting a call to set up an interview any day."

"That's news."

"I've not told many people. I'd like you to keep it to yourself," she said, as she leaned her head against the doorframe and closed her eyes.

Kelsey eyelids opened when Jordon turned the motor off. She hadn't planned to sleep.

"You're exhausted. Why don't you go on in and I'll unload?"

"No, I'll help."

He shrugged. "I was just trying to be nice." He then went around to the back of the SUV and started pulling out the coolers. She unlocked the door to the house and flipped lights on as she walked into the kitchen. Jordon followed, setting the coolers on the floor.

Her phone buzzed against her hip. Pulling it out, she answered it. "Hey, Paul. No problem. I'm just getting home."

"I forgot to ask you if you would be willing to remain on the committee for the picnic next year?"

"I don't know. Can I give you an answer closer to the time?"

"Sure. See you soon."

"Bye." She placed the phone on the counter.

Jordon stood with his arms across his chest and a hip against the cabinet.

She propped fisted hands on her hips. "Why're you always glaring at me?"

"Glaring?"

"Yeah. Glaring. Like this." She hunched her shoulders slightly, thrust her chin out, squinted and looked pointedly at him. "Glaring. What have I done to you?"

"Maybe I'm just trying to figure you out. Like why you

have that wild hair. Why nothing is peaceful when you are around. Why men are always hanging around you."

She straightened and narrowed her eyes. "Why should it matter to you why men hang around me?"

"It doesn't."

"Then why mention it?"

"Because…aw, hell…" Jordon grabbed her and brought his mouth down to hers. It wasn't a tender kiss but one born of frustration. The entire day he'd thought of kissing her. Had watched her smile at all the men. Now it was his time to have her complete attention. Force her to really notice him.

She made a startled sound of surprise. Her mouth opened and he took advantage of the opportunity to dip into the warm cavern before backing off and nipping questioningly at her lips. They were as sweet as he'd imagined they might be.

Kelsey's hands gripped his waist as she stepped toward him.

Jordon released her as suddenly as he'd taken her. He had to remember that caring could turn and bite you. Still, he wanted her. Didn't want to want her. Wished she'd want him.

He wouldn't give Kelsey the power to hurt him like his ex-girlfriend had. Wouldn't become one of the herd of men who fell under her seductive power. His ex had woven such a perfect picture that he hadn't been able to see the truth about her and what she'd been doing until it had been far too late. Not again. That was a chance he refused to take. Kelsey could easily hurt him the same way. He would keep her at arm's length. After all, she was leaving soon.

Kelsey rocked back. His hands remained on her until she steadied then he let go. Her eyes were filled with questions.

"Don't ask me why," he growled, and stalked out.

CHAPTER FOUR

KELSEY WASN'T SURE what had just happened. Had she been kissed or punished? What wasn't she supposed to ask about? The kiss or why he'd quit?

Since she'd been fourteen boys had been attracted to her. She'd dated a lot but had never had a serious relationship. Sure, she'd had a couple of boyfriends but she'd never considered marrying them. They had been local guys. Her future plans hadn't included staying in Golden Shores. Marrying a local would have held her here. She was having nothing of that.

Until Jordon's kiss she would have said he scarcely tolerated her. He'd been helpful today but still he seemed to spend more time than not giving her disapproving looks. What had she ever done to him?

It was more like what he'd done to her. She had been the girl with the broken heart when he'd left without even saying goodbye. As irrational as she'd felt as a young girl, she'd been crushed. She'd worn the plastic ring every day for over a year and cried each night for half that time. If she wasn't careful the man would do the same thing to her again. But this time it would be her leaving with the broken heart. Because she was leaving.

As pretty as Saturday had been for the picnic, by Monday the wind had increased and the weather report sounded more ominous. As Kelsey entered the hospital a gust lifted her skirt and she pushed it back into place. She arrived at her office and unlocked it.

Molly had left early that morning for a meeting in Jackson. Kelsey fussed about her returning with the tropical depression coming in. Molly assured her that she'd be fine. The weatherman reported the worst of the storm was headed to the west of them but the area would get massive amounts of wind and rain. Golden Shores wasn't required to evacuate but, still, the weatherman recommended people stay put for twenty-four hours. Even that would bring in a boatload of patients.

Clicking on her computer, Kelsey scanned her emails and saw one she had been expecting glowing brightly. The hospital was on alert, which meant she wouldn't be going home tonight. Worse than that there was no dodging Jordon.

As the day progressed the wind increased to the point that windows rattled. The sky darkened enough that the security lights in the parking lot came on. By the time Kelsey returned to her car to claim the small bag she'd packed with extra toiletries and clothes, the air had taken on a heavy feel.

In the middle of the afternoon the rain began to fall. At every nursing station the hurricane was the topic of conversation and TVs were set to the weather channel. Minutes before four o'clock her cell phone rang. It was Jim, letting her know it was time for their team to meet in the lobby. She hurried to her office and changed from her skirt and frilly blouse into her knit shirt with the hospital staff logo, jeans and tennis shoes.

Her group was already busy setting up behind one of the support walls in the lobby for protection if the storm worsened. The area was constructed of tall all-glass windows but it was the largest area available. Since the brunt of the storm wasn't coming their direction it was being used as the emergency room overflow.

"Hey, Josh, are we expecting patients right away?" she asked.

"Not right this sec. We're the first group backing up the ER. There's been an accident on the highway and the ER is covered with incoming. We're to handle any minor injuries here."

"Okay. I'll be ready." She went in search of the paperwork she would need to fill out on each patient. Jim handed her a clipboard that he'd just pulled out of their supply box. Staff members worked setting up portable tables for patients and rearranging the lobby into a makeshift waiting area.

With clipboard in hand, Kelsey walked over to look out one of the windows. The rain pounded against the glass. She could no longer see the highway in front of the building.

"I forgot how fearsome a Gulf storm can be."

Her pulse quickened. *Jordon*.

"Yes, they are something. I've ridden out so many that I don't get too upset about them anymore."

"About the other night…"

She turned to face him. "Look, I'm not starting anything with you, Jordon. I'm hoping to move soon. I don't need the headache."

"I want to apologize for walking out like I did. I'm not looking for a relationship either."

An elderly couple coming up the walk drew her attention away from Jordon's statement. They were huddled against the sideways rain with no umbrella in sight. One of them was obviously assisting the other.

Jordon hurried to the door and she was right behind

him. He had the door open and almost pulled the couple into the building when Kelsey reached them. The woman was bleeding.

"Kelsey, get a couple of blankets," Jordon said.

As she ran to the rolling cart where the blankets were stacked, she passed Josh. "We have a patient."

"I'm on my way."

By the time she returned, Jordon had the woman in a chair. He and Josh worked to stop the bleeding from a laceration to her head. Kelsey left a blanket with Josh and went to the forlorn-looking man sitting in the waiting area.

She sank into the chair next to him.

"Hi, I'm Kelsey. How about me helping you take off your coat and let's put this dry blanket over your shoulders."

"Okay," the man murmured, his teeth chattering.

She went through the slow process of helping to remove his coat. With that done, she pulled the blanket over his back.

"Why don't you tell me what happened?" Kelsey had learned from past experience that patients or their caregivers wanted to talk first. After they had that chance she didn't have any problem getting answers to her official questions.

"I told her, my Bernice, not to go out and get that last potted plant. The wind and rain were getting too strong. But she didn't listen. She loves those blasted plants too much." He looked with such love and concern at the woman who Jordon was preparing to stitch up.

What would that kind of love feel like?

"The hanging basket swung and hit her in the head. Blood went everywhere and she felt dizzy. I knew it was bad, so we had no choice but to come here."

Kelsey patted his age-spotted hand. "You did the right

thing. Dr. King will take care of your wife." She was confident she was telling him the truth. Even though she hadn't known Jordon that long, he was a good doctor. She could say that with complete confidence.

"If it's okay with you, I'd like to get some information now." Kelsey picked up her clipboard and pen from the nearby chair where she'd left it.

The man nodded and sat a little straighter.

For the next few minutes Kelsey took down the woman's personal information. As she finished, Jordon joined them.

"Mr. Lingerfelt?"

The man nodded.

"Your wife is going to be just fine. I've had to put in a few stitches but she'll be as pretty as ever."

Mr. Lingerfelt lifted his lips in a tired smile.

"I'd like to admit her so we can make sure she doesn't have a concussion. You two don't need to be out in this weather anyway. You'll be a lot safer here. We don't have any stylish clothes for you to change into but we do have some dry ones. How does that sound?"

"I wasn't looking forward to driving in that." He glanced toward the window.

Jordon looked that direction too. "I don't blame you."

"Kelsey, would you see Mr. Lingerfelt back to where Mrs. Lingerfelt is?"

"Sure." Kelsey waited for the man to rise. Together they walked to the treatment area.

"Oh, Bernice, honey," Mr. Lingerfelt said as he approached his wife.

"I'm fine, Walter. You can say I told you so later. The nice doctor said he wants me to stay tonight. He'll let you stay too."

"I know." Mr. Lingerfelt took his wife's hand and held it.

"We'll pretend we're camping like we did on our honeymoon," Mrs. Lingerfelt said with a weak grin.

Kelsey couldn't help but smile. The image of these two spending their honeymoon in a tent in the woods gave her a warm feeling.

One of the nurses from the second floor entered the area, pushing a wheelchair.

"This nurse will be taking you to your room," Kelsey said.

"Will you be seeing that nice Dr. King?"

Kelsey nodded. Jordon *was* nice. She hadn't given him much of a chance but he'd managed anyway. "Yes."

"Tell him I said not to give up on that girl."

What girl? Did Jordon have someone in town he was interested in already? She smiled and said, "I'll tell him."

By the time she returned to the lobby, Jordon was with another patient. Hours raced by as they cared for a patient with a cut to the hand he'd received trying to keep a piece of tin from flying into another person. A broken arm had come next, followed by another patient who'd had a foreign object in her eye.

It was after nine p.m. before they got a break.

"Let's get a sandwich and a drink, and sit while we can," Jordon said. The cafeteria staff had set up a table with food toward the back of the lobby.

Jim and Josh were already moving in that direction.

"I'm coming. I have one more thing that needs to be done."

"Let it wait. You look like you could use a rest. I'd bet that, like me, you haven't eaten since lunch."

She didn't like admitting it but he was right. "You go on. I'll be right behind you."

"No, I'm going to wait because I think you'll get sidetracked doing something for someone if I don't."

Kelsey huffed and put down the clipboard and pen. "Satisfied?" She looked around. They were relatively alone. She placed her hands on her hips. "For someone who wants nothing to do with me you sure like to tell me what to do."

Something flared in his eyes. "I didn't say that I didn't want to have anything to do with you. I said I don't want a relationship."

"What does that mean?"

He took a step closer. "It means I want to kiss you but I have no intention of marrying you."

"So I'm good enough to have sex with but not to take home to your mother?"

"I don't care what my mother thinks."

That sounded a little harsh. What was the deal with his mother?

"Hey, you two had better come on and get something to eat before the next patient shows up," Josh called.

Kelsey moved towards the back, picked out a premade sandwich and pulled a canned drink out of the bucket filled with ice. There weren't enough chairs for everyone so she slid down the wall with a sigh and sat on the floor. To her dismay, Jordon joined her.

"You could have taken the last chair," she said.

"I would have felt bad about doing that while you sat on the floor."

"Go on and take the chair. I don't mind sitting here. I'm comfortable."

"If I didn't know better, I'd think you were trying to get rid of me."

If the truth be known, she was. "Suit yourself." She took a bite out of her sandwich.

Jordon settled in beside her but not within touching distance. They ate in silence. He finished before she did and leaned back and closed his eyes. A few minutes went by. Was he asleep?

"You know, you're going to miss all this kind of excitement if you leave town."

She looked at him. His eyes were still closed. The slump of his shoulders said he was tired as she was, and they still had the rest of the night to get through. The weather would get worse before it got better.

"I don't think I'll miss this or anything else for that matter."

"Ooh, that has an unforgiving sound to it. A slam on me."

"I don't know you well enough to miss you. I'm just ready to get out of Golden Shores."

"So tell me about this new job." He still hadn't opened his eyes.

"Shhh, my boss doesn't know I'm looking. I don't want him to find out some way other than from me telling him."

He opened one eye. "Sorry." He went on, "I can't imagine someone as well liked as you wanting to leave."

"So I guess since you're here you weren't well liked in Washington."

"I was liked. I just made some bad decisions. Stood behind the wrong people."

"How's that?"

"I really would rather not talk about it. There were issues."

"Well, I have some issues about being here."

"Like what?"

"Like I've been trying to get out of Golden Shores since I was eighteen. Now's my chance." Kelsey picked up her sandwich wrapper and drink can. Pushing against the wall, she stood. She looked down at him pointedly. "This place holds some bad memories for me."

She started to walk away then stopped. "By the way," she threw over her shoulder, "I forgot to give you Mrs. Lingerfelt's message. She said for you not to give up on that girl."

Kelsey didn't ask what it meant or even who the girl was. It was none of her business. Still, she wanted to know more than she was willing to admit.

Jordon didn't doubt that there were some unhappy memories for Kelsey in Golden Shores. How would there not be with her brother disappearing? It hadn't always been happy times for him in Golden Shores either but the good memories far outshone the bad. Had what had happened with Chad affected her that much or was there something more?

He didn't have time during the night to ask her. If he had he wasn't sure that she would have answered him. They were busy most of the time with minor injuries. At three thirty-five the electricity blinked off. It took a few minutes for the back-up generators to kick in and the lights flickered on again.

Around six a.m. Jordon saw Kelsey take out her phone. She stayed on the line for a few seconds then slipped the phone back into her pocket. He returned to filling out paperwork on his most recent patient. Some time later he noticed her with her phone out again. Was she worried about her parents? Sister?

Jim give him the word that the worst was over. They could all go home their last patient was taken care of. Kelsey was standing in a nearby corner with the phone to her ear when he walked up to give her the news. As he approached he noticed her brows were drawn together and she was pacing. Kelsey glanced at him. Her eyes were heavy with moisture on the verge of falling.

"What's wrong?" His tone demanded an answer.

"I can't find Molly," she blurted out, close to a sob.

"Molly?"

"My roommate. She works here."

"Isn't she on call, like the rest of us? Is she here in the hospital?"

As if she'd run out of patience she said, "No. She was out of town for a meeting. She should've been back but she's not answering her phone. I'm worried something has happened."

"So where should she be?"

"At home."

"Come on. I'll drive."

"I can go myself."

"I have no doubt that you can but I think you'll get there much faster in my SUV. I was just in the E.R. and one of the ambulance drivers said that the roads are a mess with debris and flooding. So do you want to take a chance in your low-to-the-ground car or—?"

"Let's go." She started toward the employees' entrance, pulling her cell from her pocket at the same time.

The storm still blew rain crosswise as they ran for his SUV. Kelsey hadn't even attempted to use an umbrella. It would have been a complete waste of time against the torrent. During one gust Jordon grabbed her arm to help steady her. He took her hand and held it until they reached the SUV. After climbing in they both huffed with the exertion it took to move around in the awful weather. They sat for a second or two before Jordon reached into the back-seat and pulled a towel forward.

"Hardy sits on it when he rides. I don't think he'll mind if we use it under the circumstances."

That gained him a half smile before Kelsey took a corner and started wiping water from her face. He used the opposite corner and did the same. She let the towel drop and struggled to pull her phone from her hip pocket. He didn't miss the way her wet T-shirt molded to her breasts. Despite his concern over her worry for her friend, he still had the hots for her. Maybe he didn't want a relationship, but he sure wanted her. It might be short as she was planning to leave town, but it would sure be sweet while it lasted.

Kelsey put the phone to her ear as he cranked the SUV.

"Still nothing?"

Kelsey shook her head and lowered the phone with a look of disappointment and escalating fear.

"Okay. Let's go find her. I bet she's in bed and can't hear her phone over the wind."

He maneuvered around limbs that littered the parking lot and one palm listed badly to the left near the picnic area. Main Street was deserted but he stayed toward the middle of the road to avoid the deep pockets of water. The drains were overflowing in their efforts to handle the run-off. It was slow going. Traffic lights were out and the few cars he passed were driving far too fast for the conditions.

One car threw enough water over them to cover the windshield. He cursed low as he had to strain to see. He glanced at Kelsey. She leaned forward, peering through the glass with both hands clamped to the dash. Everything about her demeanor screamed she was terrified.

"She's going to be fine."

"You can't know that," she snapped.

"No, I can't."

"I'm sorry. I'm just so scared."

He reached over and took one of her hands and squeezed it before letting it go.

As he attempted to turn right into their road he slowed to a stop. A beach oak had fallen across the road.

"I don't think I can drive across it. I'm going to see about moving some limbs so maybe we can get around it." Jordon climbed out of the SUV and was soaked completely before he reached the tree. Kelsey was there beside him to help as he picked up the second limb.

"Get back in the SUV," he yelled.

"It'll go faster with two of us working."

They pulled branches out of the way and went back for more. After moving as much as they could without a chainsaw Jordon called, "I think I can get around now."

If there had been any dry clothes on them before, there weren't now. He turned the heat on high then started slowing rolling over a large branch they hadn't been able to move. The leafy top of the tree hindered his sight. Seconds later they were on their way again down the dark road. In one area a power pole had snapped and the line lay on the ground. There was barely enough space for him to skirt it.

Kelsey hissed and jumped in his direction as sparks shot in the air when the line bounced against the pavement. He laid a hand on her back in reassurance before returning his attention back to the downed line, making sure not to touch it.

As they passed her parents' house, he glanced at it and saw she was looking too. "You want to stop and check on them?"

"No. I've already talked to China. They're fine."

Jordon said no more and continued to drive at a slow and steady pace. He worked to see through the gloom ahead. He ached between his shoulder blades. The sky was growing lighter behind them but wasn't making much headway against the heavy cloud cover and rain. He remained in the center of the road to miss the water gushing along either side. With a swift turn of the wheel he dodged a large limb in the road. They were approaching his house when Kelsey gasped. He looked further ahead. A huge oak tree lay on the roof of the back half of her bungalow.

"Molly's car is there." She pointed. He could make out a small red car sitting in the drive close to the house.

He made a quick turn into his drive.

Kelsey looked at him in shock and demanded, "What're you doing?"

"I'm going to get Hardy. You stay here." Jordon climbed out, not waiting for her to answer. He ran for the house, opened the door and Hardy almost knocked him over in his zest to go out.

"Let's go, boy."

He returned to the SUV to find Kelsey gone. Why wasn't he surprised? She'd better not have gone and done something impulsive and gotten herself hurt. He opened the door of the SUV for Hardy and they both jumped in. Seconds later, Jordon pulled into Kelsey's drive. Letting Hardy out, he grabbed his emergency medical bag from the rear floorboard and a flashlight out of the glove compartment. He and the dog ran for the open door of the house. The faint sound of Kelsey's voice calling Molly's name came from deep inside the dark house.

"Kelsey!" he yelled. "For heaven's sake, stay put. The whole place may come down on your head."

He saw a flash of light off to the right and under where the tree had hit. His heart caught in his throat.

"Over here, Jordon," she called.

He moved toward the dim light. "Did you find her?"

"No." The sound was almost a sob.

Hardy rushed past him and was now barking somewhere ahead to Jordon's left.

"Good boy. I'll be right there." Jordon headed toward Kelsey.

When he reached her she was moving her cell phone flashlight in a frantic motion backward and forward among the limbs of the tree in the area of what he guessed had been a bedroom.

"I can't find her," Kelsey said, her voice filled with panic.

Hardy continued to bark, the sound becoming more urgent.

"Hardy has found her." Jordon was afraid to say any more. "Follow me and do exactly as I tell you." He looked at her. "Do you understand?"

She nodded. Maybe her fear would keep her in check. As they moved further down what had once been a hall-way and under the tree, she grabbed on to the back of his shirt and let him be the guide. Jordon had no idea what to expect but he didn't want Kelsey to see her friend first. He helped Kelsey climb over a rain-slick branch and under another until they managed to squeeze between limbs to where Hardy stood barking.

Jordon made sure to keep his body between Kelsey and the sight ahead of him. Molly was trapped under a branch. All he could see were her legs.

He turned and Kelsey let go of his shirt. Cupping her shoulders and looking at her intently, Jordon said, "Kelsey, Hardy has found her. Don't fall apart on me. I'm going to need your help."

She stuck out her chest as if she was preparing to fight. "I'm not going to fall apart," she said in a strong, defiant voice.

"Good. Now, hold the light. I have to crawl under and get her vitals. Hardy, hush. Sit."

The dog obeyed.

He didn't need to waste any more time. How long had Molly been lying under this tree? Placing his bag on the floor, he went down on his knees. He felt along Molly's body. At least she was wearing jeans. That would have helped prevent some injuries. Finally he found her neck. With great relief he located a pulse but it was weak. "She's alive."

"Thank God."

"We've got to get her to the hospital ASAP. She isn't in good shape."

"What do I need to do?" Kelsey's voice sounded strong and sure.

She must be rattled if she was allowing him to make the decisions.

"Call 911 and have them send the wagon. Push my bag under here." Kelsey picked up his bag from where he'd dropped it and shoved it toward the sound of his voice. She was more grateful than she could express to have Jordon there. Without him and Hardy, it would have taken her much longer to find Molly.

Punching 911, she told the dispatcher she needed an ambulance at 3564 Bay Road. The dispatcher said that because of the storm all the ambulances were out and it would be a while. She relayed the information to Jordon. His expletive mirrored her concern.

"Okay, then. We'll have to do this ourselves."

"We can't move her. We might hurt her more." She could only make out a shadowed outline of Jordon beneath the fallen tree and the shambles of the roof. Rain still fell but not as hard as earlier.

"Kelsey, take a deep breath. Molly is going to be fine."

Somehow his strong presence and reassurance made her believe him.

"Find some blankets. We need to treat for shock and keep her warm. Along with blankets we also need something flat and strong to lay her on." He said the words more in a reflective tone than in one issuing orders. "Go to my SUV. There are some straps and bungee cords there. Bring them. Also, while you are there lay the seats down. It will be a job but you're going to have to pull the back one out. We'll take her to the hospital ourselves if the ambulance doesn't make it. Can you handle all that?"

"I'll get it done."

"Good. Now get going. And, Kelsey, be careful."

She was crawling over the first limb when Jordon yelled, "Take Hardy with you."

"Hardy," she called, and the dog moved past her and through the brush. She came out from under the tree and into the living area. The brunt of the damage had been to Molly's bedroom.

Kelsey snatched the throw quilts off the chair and couch. Going through the tree again, she said when she got to Jordon and Molly. "Here are the blankets."

"Great. Do you see my hand?" His arm came out of the leaves a couple of feet in front of her.

"Yeah."

"Put them as close to my hand as you can."

Kelsey did as he said. "I'll be back in a minute with the other stuff."

"Kelsey." The sound of her name carried a warm note. "You're doing great."

Frightened beyond belief, she needed those encouraging words. She had a job to do. Jordon depended on her. Molly's life rested in their hands. Kelsey would do everything in her power not to disappoint either of them. Working her way back through the tree, she hurried outside. Hardy followed.

Using her phone's flashlight so she didn't fall, Kelsey went around to the back of the house where her surfboard was stored, hoping the tree hadn't gotten it also. It had been knocked over but, thank goodness, it was still there. Putting her surfboard under her arm, she carried it to the door and leaned it against the house. Now for Jordon's SUV. Hardy stayed with her, never more than a few paces away.

She wasn't sure why Jordon had sent the dog with her, but she liked having another breathing soul around as she worked in the dark and rain. Rushing to the SUV, she open the back door and searched with her light for the straps. They lay in a pile in the corner. *Great.* She gathered them and dropped them on the ground beside the SUV. Now all she had to do was figure out how to lay the seats flat.

Opening the passenger door, she searched for a lever to pull or a button to push. Finding a lever, Kelsey managed to fold the middle passenger seat down. She ran to the other side and did the same with the other seat. Going to the back of the SUV, she climbed inside and pushed the button on top of the rear seat, folding it over onto itself. After some frustrating moments she located the handle she needed to pull to release the rear seat. Pushing, pulling and shoving, she managed to get the large, cumbersome seat to the open door. She wasn't strong enough to lift the seat so she let it slide down the bumper to the ground. Climbing out, she pulled it away from the vehicle. She gave a brief thought to the fact it might never be the same again. But that didn't matter. Molly did.

She bundled the soaked straps and cords into her arms and headed for the house. Inside it was nice to have a moment that water wasn't running down her face. Again she worked her way back to reach Jordon and Molly.

"How's she doing?" Kelsey asked, depositing the straps in the same place she'd put the blankets. If it weren't for the low glow of the flashlight she wouldn't have had any idea that Jordon and Molly were underneath.

"She's holding her own but we need to get her out of here."

CHAPTER FIVE

"I'LL BE RIGHT BACK." Kelsey made her way to the door again. *This was going to be the tricky part.* She had to get the long surfboard between the tree branches. She kicked the fin until it broke, falling to the ground. She nudged it out of the pathway space with her foot. Molly would owe her a new surfboard when she got well. She had to get well.

Taking the strap in her hand, she pulled it across the floor. The board became hung up and she had to go to the back and straighten it before it would move further. All the time Hardy was nearby, barking encouragement. It took a while but she fought her way back to Jordon.

With a huff of exhaustion and exasperation she called, "I've got the board."

"Good girl. I need you to slide it under here and then climb under and help me get Molly on it."

Kelsey took a deep breath. Sweat and rain had long ago mixed on her face. Her jeans stuck to her. Leaves and dirt covered her hair but none of that mattered. She placed the board so that it was flat on the floor and started pushing it under the limbs until she had it straight. Sliding it along the floor, she got on her hands and knees and shoved it toward Jordon.

"That's good. Keep it coming. What is this?"

"My surfboard."

"I should have known you'd be resourceful."

His amazement and admiration fueled her tired, sore muscles. This wasn't a man who tried to control her, like her father had. Jordon had faith in her.

"Okay, that's far enough. Come on in."

She had to crawl alongside the board and then squeeze into a pocket under the tree on the opposite side of the board from Jordon. She sucked in a breath. Her hands shook. Molly lay on her back, her skin pasty white even in the dim light.

"Kelsey, now is not the time to lose it," Jordon said in a firm voice. "Look at me." She did. "Molly needs us both to hold it together. I can't help her if I'm worried about you. We've got this."

He saw them as a team. She had to do her part. Would do it.

"Tell me what you need me to do."

"We're going to need to get her on a flat surface. I'm not going to lie to you and tell you this will be easy. Molly is unconscious and we'll have to lift her weight in this small area."

The worst of the rain was being averted by part of the roof and the tree limbs. For that she was grateful.

"I'll do what I have to."

He looked her straight in the eyes. "I know you will. Okay, we need to spread the straps out at a uniform distance so they're positioned under the board."

Jordon had wasted no time preparing to move Molly. He'd already untangled the mass she'd left him. They placed the straps beside and horizontal to Molly's body. Jordon laid one end across Molly at her chest, hips and thighs.

"I hate to say this but you're going to need to move as far back as you can so that we can pull the surfboard alongside Molly. Kelsey scooted back on her knees until she was under the tree as far as she could go. Limbs poked into her head and sides.

"Okay, if you can reach the board, move it alongside Molly and over the straps, making sure the straps ends can be reached." Jordon came up on his knees with his shoulders hunched in what appeared to be an uncomfortable position for someone so large. Leaning over Molly's legs, he grasped the end of the board.

Kelsey's fingers gripped the edge of the board but she managed a better hold as Jordon's greater strength pulled it forward.

"You guide while I pull," he groaned, breathing heavily.

With him tugging, she made sure the board didn't hit Molly. They managed to get it into position with it and Molly between them. Kelsey watched the straps, making sure they remained in the correct place.

"You ready for the tough part?"

She nodded.

"Now, we've got to lift Molly onto the board. I'm going to run a hand under her shoulders. I've already put a neck brace on her but I want to keep her as steady as possible. From this position it will be difficult. I need you to see that her legs and butt get on the board at the same time. Can you do that?"

"I'll do it."

He gave her a supportive smile. "I know you will. On my count of three."

Kelsey moved to the narrowest part of the board. From her awkward position, Kelsey put both arms under Molly's thighs.

"One, two, three."

She lifted. Her muscles complained but she managed to bring Molly's legs toward her chest and up over the edge of the board. She imagined that her ache and pains were little compared to what Jordon was experiencing as he lifted the heavier part of Molly's body from that cramped angle.

Kelsey slid Molly across, then went to the end of the board and adjusted her legs so that they rested on the board. Shifting back to the side again, she moved Molly's hips until they were in the middle of the board. She looked to see how Jordon was doing. He'd gotten her upper body on the board and was now lifting her eyelids, shining a penlight into them.

"Still dilated and unresponsive," he murmured.

He didn't sound pleased.

Jordon looked at her. "Good job. Now we need to cover her with the blankets and get her strapped down."

They worked together, putting the covering over her body and placing the straps and cords across it.

"Use one of these bungee cords to hold her feet in place." he said.

Kelsey wrapped the two hooked ends together across Molly's ankles. She looked at Jordon for further instructions. His gaze met hers. She didn't miss the admiration in his eyes.

"Now comes the even tougher job. We've got to get her under this unholy mess on this unbending contraption." He pushed a leaf off his face. "Then it's out to the SUV."

"We can do it."

"That's what I like to hear. A positive attitude. I'll pull from the front and you push from the back." He thrust his bag out ahead of him then crawled past Molly's feet through the opening.

With tears falling, Kelsey cupped Molly's cheek. "Oh, Molly, I'm so sorry this happened to you." She didn't have time to say more before the board started moving. Kelsey remained on her knees and pushed. The wet surface let the straps slid along the floor, instead of bunching up and coming off. They reached the first limb and by a narrow margin were able to pull Molly beneath it. The next one would be the problem. Jordon stopped.

"I'm going to see if I can lift this limb some. See if you can find a chair or something to prop it up on. We need to get it off the floor enough that we can slide her under."

Kelsey climbed out and fought her way down what had once been the hallway to her bedroom. She dumped the clothes she'd left lying on her favorite overstuffed chair on the floor and started dragging the chair down to where Jordon and Molly waited. "Will this do?"

"Yeah that should work." Jordon said, "Turn it over on its side."

She flipped it.

"When I get this high enough, I want you to push the chair under."

He wrapped his arms around the limb and began lifting. After a groan from Jordon the tree began to move. Kelsey grabbed the limb, lifting upwards. Once it was high enough she let go and shoved the chair beneath it.

Jordon let go, releasing a huff. Standing, he rubbed his back. "We've got to get her under as fast as we can. I don't know how long the chair will hold."

Kelsey crawled beneath the tree and got behind the board. Jordon started pulling and the surfboard with Molly on it moved through the opening. Kelsey crawled under the branch when the chair made cracking noises. The next second she was jerked by her arms out from under the limb and across Jordon's prone body. A moment later the tree made a thudding noise and the leaves surrounding them shook.

She shuddered and looked up. Jordon's face was inches from hers. The warmth of his breath caressed her forehead.

"Are you okay?" The words were raspy with emotion as his hand touched her face.

"I'm fine," she managed to get out.

"Good. Let's get Molly to the hospital." Jordon moved, tipping her off him. He stood and helped her stand. With him pulling and her steering, they managed to get Molly to the kitchen door.

"I'll back the SUV as close to the door as I can get."

Jordon went out, with his head down, into the stream of rain that had started again. He was something special. That hero he'd been when she'd been a kid was fast becoming shiny again.

Molly moaned. It was the first sound she'd made since they'd started to move her.

"Mol, it's Kelsey. We're trying to get you to the hospital. You should be there soon."

Red brake lights flashed as Jordon moved the SUV into position in front of the door. Seconds later he opened the back doors to the SUV wide.

"We need to lift her head in first. Then we'll slide her the rest of the way."

"She's starting to come to."

"Then we need to get moving. She'll be in a lot of pain when she does."

Jordon lifted the front end of the surfboard and Kelsey the back as they eased out the narrow door of the house. Outside, Jordon placed his end of the board in the SUV. No longer able to carry her friend, Kelsey placed her end on the ground.

"You steady her from the side while I lift and push her in."

Kelsey went to the side of the board and did as Jordon instructed.

He shook his head, removing the water from his soaked hair. "Okay, let's get her in,"

With muscles straining, Kelsey held the slippery board in place the best she could. Finally, Jordon gave a last push and Molly went in as far as the front seat would allow. Hardy barked as they worked.

"I'm going to ride with her," Kelsey lifted her knee to climb in. Strong hands lifted her and placed her inside. She crawled to Molly's head.

Jordon closed one of the doors but the other wouldn't shut. Pulling off his belt he wrapped it through the door handles and secured it. "That should hold until we get to the hospital. Hardy, go home," he said in a firm tone.

Hardy gave one last bark.

Jordon disappeared from her sight and seconds later the SUV was running. Tires spun in the wet grass then hit shell and crunched before they found pavement.

Kelsey held on to the board, steadying it, as Jordon drove through the obstacle course on the roads to the hospital. During the drive he was on the phone, letting the E.R. know that they were coming and the status of Molly's injuries. The trip seem to take hours when it couldn't have been more than ten minutes.

Jordon wheeled the large SUV under the light of the E.R. cover, honked a couple of times and pulled to a stop. Seconds later he was at the doors and the E.R. staff arrived with a gurney.

They placed Molly, surfboard and all, on the rolling bed. As she was being pushed into the hospital, Kelsey moved to the back of the SUV and Jordon helped her out. He put his arm around her shoulders and squeezed. "You did great. I've got to move the SUV. I'll be there in a minute."

Kelsey was headed inside as he pulled away. Rushing to the cubicle where they were working on Molly, Kelsey stood in the hall out of the way. Jordon joined her, standing behind her and placing a supportive hand on her waist. She leaned back against him appreciating his sturdy company. She shuddered. Without him, Molly might have died under that tree.

"Hang in there," he whispered in her ear.

One of the surgeons looked at them. "Your diagnosis was spot on, Jordon. Internal bleeding. The spleen will have to come out. Maybe a little patchwork. I'll know more when I get in there."

Kelsey slumped against Jordon. He brought his hand further around her waist and tightened it.

"We'll be in the waiting room," he said.

The surgeon nodded and went back to Molly.

"I need to call her parents." Kelsey searched her pocket for her cell. "It must be in your SUV."

Jordon pulled out his phone. "What's the number?"

As Kelsey called it out he punched it into the phone then handed it to her. Kelsey's heart was in her throat as she waited to hear one of Molly's parent's voices. Her mother answered and Kelsey explained what had happened and that Molly was in surgery. A minute later Kelsey ended the call.

"They're on their way."

"Good. Come on. We're going to the doctor's overnight room to get a shower and dry clothes. Then let's find ourselves a hot meal."

Kelsey opened her mouth to argue.

"Molly's in good hands and you can't be here for her if you don't take care of yourself."

She let Jordon lead her through the E.R. to the doctor's sleep room. She'd never been inside. Jordon shut the door behind them. He stepped into the bath and the sound of water filled the space.

Returning with a towel in his hand, he said, "You go

get a shower." He started rubbing his hair. "Don't take too long or I'll be in to join you."

Kelsey didn't hesitate before she entered the small room and closed the door.

Jordon was confident it would take him days, possibly weeks before his muscles would quit screaming. Every time he moved his body protested. He kicked off his shoes, pulled his wet shirt off and dropped it on the floor with a slosh. Next went his pants and underwear. He wrapped the towel around his hips and turned on the TV. The weather channel announcer stood in front of a map. The swath of color across the Gulf area indicated Golden Shores was in for a few more hours of rain.

The sound of the water being turned off reminded him that Kelsey was but a few feet away and nude. She'd been amazing over the last few hours. There hadn't been a single complaint from her. She'd followed his directions to the letter and had been brilliant in thinking of the surfboard. He couldn't have asked for a more able and industrious person to have as a partner during an emergency.

The door of the bath opened, letting out a cloud of steam. His breath caught. Kelsey's hair stood on end and the white towel contrasted with her late-summer tan. His manhood stirred. This wasn't the time or the place. If it were, he'd pull the towel off her, bring those gorgeous curves against him and make use of the single bed inches away.

"There are scrubs…" he cleared his throat "…in the bottom drawer of that chest." He pointed to the cabinet the TV sat on.

She moved out of the doorway. He stepped beyond her, making sure he didn't touch her, and closed the door behind him with a firm click. If he didn't get away from her soon, he wouldn't go at all.

Safe behind the door, he turned the water on. It was still running hot from her shower but he switched it to cold and stepped in. He didn't linger in the shower but Kelsey wasn't in the room when he came out.

Would he always have to hunt her down? Pretty sure where she was, he headed for the surgery waiting room. She sat curled in a chair with her head in her hands, shoulders shaking. It had been a rough enough night, caring for patients, but to add her roommate being crushed under a tree and being part of the rescue effort had taken its toll. It was too much for almost anyone. Even someone as strong as Kelsey. Going to her, he wrapped an arm around her and pulled her to him. She didn't resist. Instead, she buried her head in his shoulder and let the tears flow.

For long moments he sat with her crying in his arms as his hands glided along her back in an effort to soothe her. He hadn't heard a woman cry since his mother had said goodbye when he'd been sixteen. He'd refused to look at her and he hadn't let her tears affect him then. Now his heart hurt for Kelsey. How had Kelsey succeeded in getting to him so much? She wasn't even his type. Still, when that limb had been about to fall on her, he hadn't even stopped to think about grabbing her.

"When Molly's out of the woods, you can go home and get some rest."

"I don't have a home. There's a tree in it." She cried softly.

He hadn't known her long but she had to be at the end of her rope if she was feeling sorry for herself.

"Aw, sweetie, it's going to be fine."

He continued to hold her close. Kelsey settled and drooped against his chest. She was asleep. Something about having her in his arms felt right, even though he wanted nothing to do with a woman.

Kelsey woke to the sound of two male voices. One rumbled beneath her ear and the other was speaking above her. Her eyes blinked open and she sat up, pushing against the hard torso beneath her.

She looked at the surgeon dressed in blue scrubs. "Is Molly all right?"

Jordon released her and she sat up. She missed his warmth and security immediately.

"I had to remove Molly's spleen and repair a few ruptures in her intestines. She is still unconscious, so we don't know yet about any brain damage. We'll just have to wait and see. She'll be in Recovery for another hour or two and then in ICU. You need to go home and get some rest. You can see her later this evening."

Jordon stood. "Thanks. I'll see about Kelsey. We'll be back later."

The surgeon nodded and walked through the swinging doors and back into the surgical wing.

Where did Jordon get off, deciding what she was going to do? No man was going to take over her life. She'd had enough of that when she'd been a kid.

"I'm staying here."

Jordon frowned at her as if she'd this instant proclaimed she was a mermaid.

"No, you're not. You need rest and you're doing Molly no good here. You can call and check on her."

"I'm fine here."

"What eats you so much about me telling you to do something that is only in your best interest?"

"I don't like to be told what to do."

"This time you'll just have to get over it." He leaned

down and said in a low forbidding voice, "I'm taking you out of this hospital by choice or force. It's your decision but you're leaving."

Kelsey gulped.

"I don't have to do what you say."

"No, you don't. But you're not being rational right now and since I'm the only one here in his right mind, I'm making the decisions. So what will it be? Over my shoulder or on your own two feet?"

He sounded like he meant it. Kelsey jumped up and stomped down the hallway toward the exit. She was being childish, but she had worked so hard to get out from under her father's iron hand and her mother's obliviousness. Kelsey didn't want to go back there any time, for anyone. Still, she was almost at her breaking point after no sleep for twenty-four hours, the adrenaline rush of finding Molly and now the waiting.

"Where're you headed?" Jordon's deep voice asked in a tone of a person speaking to a child.

"Home, like you told me to."

"And how're you going to get there?"

She stopped and narrowed her eyes at him. "In my car."

"So your little car is going to make it over the tree in the road and you're going to cuddle up in your wet bed under the tree."

"You seem to have all the answers. What do you think I should do?"

Without blinking an eye or pausing, he said, "Come home with me."

Even Jordon looked stricken for a second at his statement.

"Why would I do that?"

"Do you have somewhere else you would rather go?"

Anywhere else came to mind.

"Maybe your sister's? I'll be glad to see that you get there."

To China's? No. She and Payton had worked at the clinic like Jordon and she had at the hospital. China didn't need her around. She needed to rest. There was a baby to think about now. Kelsey wouldn't go to her parents'. That wasn't even an option.

"Okay. But I'm only on the sofa until this evening then I'll find a place to stay until my house is repaired."

"For once you're being sensible."

She didn't like the sound of satisfaction in his voice.

"We need to go and get something to eat then pick up our sack of wet clothes." He passed her, going in the direction of the cafeteria.

Kelsey followed a couple of paces behind, still not in complete agreement with the plans. They shared a quiet meal eating at a two-person table in the far corner of the large room.

"You want anything else?" Jordon asked, when her plate was clean.

Kelsey shook her head. She would've said she couldn't have eaten anything but she'd had a big meal and was glad for it.

"Good." He pushed his chair back. "Then let's go get those clothes and then get some sleep. I'm beat. I know you must be also."

She waited outside the doctor's sleep room while he gathered their clothes. There was something far too intimate about their clothes being commingled in the plastic bag Jordon carried.

How had her life become so entangled with his?

A little later Kelsey climbed out of the SUV when Jor-

don stopped in his drive. It was daylight but still gloomy
and rainy. Even that had become a more steady flow instead of a frog strangler. Hardy came out of a doghouse that
sat at the rear of the house. Wagging his tail, he greeted
her first then went around to where Jordon was pulling
their clothes out of the backseat.

With the bag in hand, he head toward the door. Kelsey
moved across the yard toward her place.

"Where're you going?" The exasperation in his voice
would have been comical under other circumstances.

"I'm going to my house to get some clothes and personal things."

"You can't do that. It isn't safe."

"Maybe not, but you can't stop me."

Jordon dropped the bag and stalked toward her. "Okay,
you have ten minutes to get what you can. After that I
haul you out."

"Don't tell me what to do!"

He put up a defensive hand. "Okay, okay. I'll help you
for as long as it takes. Be careful. And for both our sakes,
work fast. You don't know if the roof could fall in at any
time."

"You didn't make a big deal of that when we were getting Molly out."

"I didn't want to scare you and we had no choice then.
Are you always so unreasonable when you're tired?"

Kelsey chose to ignore the question and kept walking.
She opened the door to her house and looked around. In the
daylight it looked even worse. She blinked back the tears
that threatened. It could have been worse. Molly could be
dead. Squaring her shoulders, she found a black plastic
garbage bag under the kitchen counter and weaved her
way through the top of the tree to her bedroom. Memories of following this path in the dark made her shudder.

Jordon remained close behind her, like a guardian angel. He waited at the door while she entered the bedroom. The floor was wet. She touched the bed and found it damp also. Jordon was right—she couldn't have stayed here. Going to her chest of drawers, she grabbed fistfuls of clothing and stuffed them into the bag. Having emptied the drawers, she went to the closet and took what clothes she could until the bag was full.

Jordon stepped forward and said, "I'll take that."

She let him have it. Was the relieved look that crossed his face been because she hadn't argued? Maybe she had been overreacting.

A creaking from above made her glance up.

"We need to get moving," Jordon said with a firm tone of urgency.

"I have to get my jewelry box." She went to her dresser and picked up the square wooden box sitting there and pulled it to her chest. "I'm ready."

Without a word, Jordon turned and walked down the hall. With one quick glance at the room, Kelsey followed. Soon they were out of the gloomy house and walking toward Jordon's.

"You were a great help this morning. The surfboard was inspired."

"Thanks." She met his gaze for a second. "I'm sorry I haven't said thank you sooner. I'm glad you were with me when we found Molly. She's alive because of you."

"I'm not sure about that, but I do appreciate the vote of confidence."

Hardy joined them.

"And you, boy, were great also." She looked at Jordon. "How did you know Hardy would find her?"

"Because he was in training to be a rescue dog before I got him. He washed out because he couldn't focus."

"Well, your focus was perfect this morning." She patted the dog on the head.

Jordon's liked Kelsey's praise. It was much nicer than her anger and indignation. Had he been so high handed to warrant her reaction when he'd said she needed to get some rest? Had an old boyfriend made her so defensive? If he remembered right, her father had been tough. Maybe it was a reaction from that.

He pushed his door open and held the screen, letting Kelsey and Hardy enter first. She wandered around the room as if surveying it all then headed for the sofa, placing the box she'd been clutching to her chest on the end table.

"I'll take care of washing the clothes after I've had a nap." She lay down on the sofa, curled up and was fast asleep almost instantly.

Jordon looked at her in amazement. He had never seen someone go out like a light before. Kelsey was exhausted in mind, body and spirit. He started the clothes washing then went to his bedroom and pulled the covers back on the bed before returning to the living room. Looking down at Kelsey, he found that even with her short hair in disarray she was quite striking. Her skin looked creamy. Unable to resist a touch, he ran a finger along one silky cheek. She sighed.

Gently, in order not to wake her, he slipped her shoes off, letting them fall to the floor. Lifting her into his arms and cradling her against his chest, he stood. She felt warm and perfect but he had to push those feelings away. Kelsey was the type of woman who would break his heart.

She cuddled against him, making her more difficult to resist. Gritting his teeth and with rock-hard control, he carried her to his bed and placed her on it. He covered her and tucked her in. She made a soft mumble and settled in, pulling his pillow to her. Jordon wished it was him. He would have to wash the bedclothes and remove her scent or he'd never get another good night's sleep.

Against his better judgment and all his efforts not to, he was falling for the woman. At the door, he looked back at her snuggled in as if she belonged there. The problem was, he wasn't with her.

Kelsey woke to darkness. She pushed against the tree leaves that surrounded her face before she realized it was the blanket around her.

She inhaled deeply.

Jordon.

Where was she? That's right, she was at his house. Where was he? She'd fallen asleep on the sofa. How had she gotten here? Had he carried her?

She turned on the bedside table lamp and looked around the room. Thank goodness Jordon wasn't with her. She was becoming far too dependent on him, growing to like having his support. He had been wonderful the night before with Molly. Even when *she* had broken down in tears. For once she'd found his high-handedness comforting.

When she'd first seen the house she'd wanted to scream. There she'd felt like she'd had a real home for the first time since Chad had left. Now it was destroyed.

Her gaze circled the room. It was masculine with unfinished wood for the walls, dark furniture and a massive bed. It was Jordon's room. Jordon's bed. One she needed to get out of.

Tossing the covers away, she stood and groaned. Her back and leg muscles were complaining. She rolled her shoulders in the hope of easing the aches but it didn't help. All the physical activity of the morning had gotten to her.

It was pitch black outside. Kelsey looked at the clock.

It was ten-fifteen at night. She'd slept the day away and missed visiting hours. She needed to call and check on Molly.

Glancing down, she saw she still wore the scrubs she'd put on at the hospital. What she wouldn't give for a long bath and her own clothes. Her stomach made a loud unsociable noise. And some food.

But first she needed to find Jordon. Tiptoeing down the hall, she found another room. It had been made into a study but there were still boxes stacked in the corner as if Jordon hadn't completely unpacked. Continuing toward the front of the house to the living area, she saw Jordon curled up on the sofa, which was much too small for his large frame.

Hardy lay on the floor beside him. The dog looked up at her. She put a finger to her lips and shushed him. The blanket that Jordon must have pulled over him had slipped to the floor. She picked it up and covered him with it. He shifted and rolled over.

He'd been her hero yesterday. What would it be like to lean over and kiss the stubble-covered jaw? Would it be as firm as it looked? Would he mind if she did?

Mentally shaking her head, Kelsey stepped away before she was tempted further. She tried to remember why she was there. Where had she'd last seen her phone? She'd been with Molly. Jordon's SUV. Making an effort not to wake Jordon, she went outside with Hardy at her heels. On bare feet she walked across the wet grass. Opening the back door of the SUV, she climb in and ran her hands around in search of the phone. She located it sandwiched between the folded seat and seat-belt holder. Her heart sank when she saw that the battery was dead.

A deep voice behind her said, "Fine thanks I get for giving a homeless woman my bed. She sneaks off without saying a word."

Kelsey shrieked and lurched upward, hitting her head on the roof of the vehicle.

"And a concussion," she mumbled, as she sat down and rubbed her skull.

"Are you okay?" His voice turned solemn with concern. "Let me have a look."

"I'm fine. I've just got a small knot." She scooted on her butt, feet first, out the door.

"I didn't mean to scare you."

Jordon hadn't sounded this worried even when they'd found Molly. "I'm fine. Really. It takes more than a bump on the head to get me down."

"I know. I've seen you in action. What're you doing out here anyway?"

"I was looking for my phone." He waited as if expecting her to say more. "I left it in here when we took Molly to the hospital." She climbed out of the SUV and faced him. "Really, I was out here, trying to hot-wire your SUV," she said sarcastically, "but I was afraid Hardy might wake you." She patted Hardy's neck.

"Funny. It would have been smarter to take the keys. Did you find your phone?" Jordon closed the doors to the vehicle.

"I did but the battery is dead. Can I use yours to call the hospital?"

"Already did that. Molly is holding her own but still in guarded condition."

Kelsey lips quivered and she pressed them together to keep from crying.

As if Jordon knew the news had upset her he put his arm across her shoulders and led her across the yard. "Hang in there. Molly's young and strong. She'll get through this."

The need to be held filled her. She wanted another human's warm touch, to forget how horrible it was to see her friend pinned under that tree. Jordon was who she wanted. To absorb his strength, have his reassurance. To be kissed, and return that kiss. She wrapped her arms around his waist and pulled him closer, laying her head against his firm chest as they walked toward the house.

CHAPTER SIX

JORDON WASN'T SURE what Kelsey's actions meant. He knew what he wished they indicated but he'd misread her a number of times and he sure hoped he wasn't doing so one more time. To begin with, he'd seen her as nothing but a teasing gadfly but Kelsey had proved there was more to her than a good-time girl. Maybe she just wanted a friend to see her through a tough time.

His arms tightened, pulling her closer then eased long enough to let her move past him through the door into the house. She brushed his chest as she went by, making his desire grow. Plenty of women had touched him on purpose and his body had never gone on the high alert he was experiencing now. Hardy followed close behind. Even his dog seemed enamored by Kelsey.

Jordon stepped inside. The living room was dark except for one small reading lamp he'd turned on when he'd woken.

Kelsey stood at the end of the kitchen bar, facing him. Hardy sat at her feet. Her gaze locked with his. What was going on? His emotions were like being on a swing bridge, unsteady and unfamiliar, fearing the next step might be the wrong one.

Jordon raised a brow then turned to close the door. He needed a few seconds to gain control. He felt more than heard Kelsey step nearer. Returning round, his breath caught as she stretched upward on her toes and kissed him. It was too brief, but it was the sweetest kiss he'd ever received. He wanted more. More kisses. More of her.

"What was that for?" His voice was raspy leaving him embarrassed. He cleared his throat.

"Really? Aren't you a little old not to know when a woman wants you?"

Her eyes held a dark come-hither look. "With you it's hard to tell. You run hot and cold too often."

She stepped closer, pressing her body against his. "I'm feeling rather hot at the moment."

Jordon growled low in his throat. He'd been approached by women before but this blatant come-on from Kelsey was the sexist. "Hey, I'm not complaining here. And I'm no superhero who's going to turn a beautiful sexy woman down, but what has changed your mind about me?"

"You were my hero yesterday." Her breath was so soft against his lips that he almost missed what she said. She wrapped her arms around his neck and pulled his mouth down to meet hers.

He groaned and circled her waist, bringing her tightly against him.

Her tongue teased his lips until he opened for her. She made a suggestive rub against him, making his desire soar and his manhood grow rigid. Her tongue met his, moved away and returned to caress his another time.

Had he ever been this turned on? He took control of the kiss, taking it deeper. She pulled away. He wanted to complain, demand she return to kissing him, but he got caught up in the movement of her lips across his cheek to his ear. She took his earlobe between her teeth and nipped, then tugged, making low cooing sounds.

The woman was killing him.

Her fingers burrowed through his hair as her lips returned to his.

Yes, this was more than he'd imagine in the middle of the night when he'd dreamed of her. Jordon pulled away and gazed down at her. "I don't know if this is a post-traumatic reaction or not but there's no going back from here."

"I'm no longer twelve so why don't you hush and stop being the chivalrous hero and take me to bed? I want to forget everything but how you make me feel."

He crushed her mouth with his, then scooped her up over his shoulder and carried her down the hall. Leaning over, he let her fall back on to the bed with a flop before pinning her body beneath his.

Kelsey shifted beneath him, creating further intimacy. "Mmm, I like this."

She cupped his face and guided his mouth to hers close enough that the tip of her tongue tormented him before she opened and accepted his entrance.

His hands went to her back and he lifted her against him, grinding his hips into her. There was too much between them. Too much need, too much heat and too many clothes.

He pushed the cotton material of her scrub top up. She wore no bra. It was in the washer where he'd put it earlier. With regret, he released her lips and pulled away. He rolled to his side then gathered the material of her top in both hands and pulled. "This has to come off."

Kelsey arched her back and raised her arms over her head, helping him. With her arms still half in and half out of the shirt, her glorious breasts were available for his viewing pleasure and he planned to take full advantage. He clasped her hands and held them in one of his.

His mouth watered as he lowered inch by inch to surround one rosy straining nipple. Could anything be this wonderful? Giving the erect tip a tug, he was rewarded with a buck of her hips. Kelsey's uninhibited reaction fueled his already raging desire. She was sunshine, sensuality and sweetness. He wanted to bask in it, feel it and taste it until his heart was content.

Jordon laid a leg across one of hers, holding her in place, making her a smorgasbord of delights displayed for him alone. Sucking at her nipple again then sweeping his tongue around it, he was rewarded with a moan. She was so responsive, accepting. His length strained and throbbed. He placed his hand on her flat stomach, spreading his fingers wide. Her skin beneath his hands was pure silk.

Kelsey trembled. The self-assured and in-control Kelsey was like putty in his hands. He'd never felt more of a man. As he moved his mouth away from one breast to the other, his gaze met her half-lidded one. Her crimson-colored mouth was partially open and a dreamy look covered her face. If he hadn't by this time been hot for her, that look of heavenly pleasure would have made him so. She was breathtaking.

Using his index finger, he twirled it around her belly button at the same time he pulled her nipple into his mouth. She arched, offering him the world. He couldn't have turned it down even if he'd wanted to, and he didn't. His hand traveled over the heated skin of her stomach to cup one breast. He hadn't been wrong. They were flawless.

"I want to touch you." His words sounded coarse with need.

She tried to sit.

Grinning, he shook his head in slow motion one way and then the other. "For once you're not running the show." Jordon lifted, kneaded and kissed her breast until she moaned for mercy. Capturing the sound with his mouth, he released her wrists. He needed her touch.

Kelsey shook her shirt away and her hands found his T-shirt, her fingers clawing to pull it up. His breath caught when her hands slid under the material and touched his skin. Yanking until he had no choice but to stop kissing her and remove his shirt, she helped him off with it then threw it to the floor. Kelsey sighed as his lips found hers again and her chest met his. The touch of her skin against his almost did him in. Jordon ran his hand down low over her belly.

She shivered.

"Like that, do you?" He watched her skin ripple as his hand traveled across her satiny surface. He brought his hand back and followed the same path again. She squirmed. His fingers crept toward the place he desired the most, this time sliding under her elastic waistband. His breath caught. She wore no panties. Those must have been tied up in her other clothes he'd put in the wash.

Kelsey sucked in a breath as he raked over her mound and retreated.

Jordon leaned forward and kissed her where her pants met skin, running small nipping kisses along that line.

Her fingers curled in his hair.

Jordon pushed away her pants until what had been hidden was revealed.

She kicked the scrub pants off and pulled at his shoulders. "I want—"

"Shush, sweetie. I have to admire you."

Her long supple legs, tanned from the sun, were spread out before him, waiting to pull him to her. He moved his hand across her springy curls to cup her. With a measured movement he slid a finger to her center, finding it damp and hot.

She clenched his finger.

He looked at her face.

Kelsey's eyes were closed tight and her shoulders curled forward. As the tenseness eased from her body, a look of pure bliss covered her face and she settled to the bed. Her eyes opened and her soft gaze met his for a second before her lids fluttered closed.

Jordon's chest swelled. How had the woman managed to make him feel like beating his chest when he hadn't even entered her?

What had just happened? Jordon had made her come with the simple touch of his finger.

Kelsey had always maintained the lead in her relationships. That way they wouldn't get out of hand. This time she'd lost it. Given it over to Jordon and had enjoyed every perfect minute. What was the man doing to her?

She opened her eyes to find him studying her with the smile of a male who knew he'd done something amazing.

"Thanks. That was nice." She ran a hand down his chest, enjoying the feel of hair over firm pectoral muscles.

"You're welcome." His lips curled into a self-satisfied grin.

She leaned up and reached for the clasp of his jeans. "How about joining me this time?"

"I do believe I will."

One of the things she liked best about Jordon was his wit. Other men she'd been with had been so serious. They had been more interested in themselves than her pleasure. Minutes ago it had been all about her. She'd come to believe that it would never be about what she wanted or needed, but Jordon had proved her wrong.

Her hand wandered over his zipper and the large bulge beneath. Jordon audibly took in a breath. So she still had some power.

He pushed her hand away and rose. Shucking his pants,

he let them drop to the floor. Jordon made her stare in amazement as he stood in all his bold and masculine glory before her. He opened the drawer of the bedside table and pulled out a foil packet. Tearing it, he covered himself.

With the look of a prowling cat that wouldn't let his prey escape, he joined her on the bed again. Nudging her back against the covers, his hair-roughened legs found their place between her legs. His hands came to cup her breast and lift them to his moist mouth. Her womb contracted in unison with each tug and pull, making her squirm with building need. She opened her mouth to complain and Jordon brought his down to meet hers. The tip of his length kissed her throbbing center.

Her fingertips massaged the skin at his waist, urging him to take her. She deepened their kiss, tangling her tongue with his while lifting her center in offering.

With the growl of a man who had held back as long as he could, Jordon thrust forward, filling her. He stilled. Then pulled back to a point she feared he'd leave. With exquisite control, he reentered her, drawing back again and again until the towering, swirling need took her and released her into a floating abyss of pleasure. Three deep plunges later, Jordon tensed and groaned his completion.

He rolled from her but his index finger touched her thigh as if he wanted to maintain their connection.

"J-man, that was nice."

Their breathing slowed in unison, something that both amazed her and sent a zing of fear through her. What was happening here? She needed to distance herself, regain some equilibrium. He turned on his side, facing her. "J-man? I haven't been called that in years."

She pushed off the bed, picking up the first thing she could use to cover herself, which turned out to be Jordon's shirt. "Remember when you used to come to my house?"

He sat beside her on the edge of the bed. "In those days I was either high or thinking about getting high. I don't remember much."

A ripple of disappointment went through her. Yet she'd still noticed a note of pain in his voice that Kelsey didn't quite understand. "I guess it's unrealistic to think you would remember someone's kid sister."

The tip of his finger grazed the length of her thigh. "I'll never forget you again."

His sexy grin made her middle turn to mush. She wanted him. For once she wasn't thinking of how she'd get out of this as soon as possible without hurting his feelings. That was something that had never happened before. She'd always seen to it that she didn't linger.

Jordon gave her a long, deep kiss. "How about we make some more memories?"

Kelsey had taken command of their lovemaking and Jordon had never been more turned on, or had a more mind-blowing release. Even now he was growing stiff, thinking of her above him.

Kelsey stirred and rubbed catlike against him. She turned and looked up at him. "Hey."

"Hi."

"I've been wondering…"

He was afraid of what might be said next. "If I know how to cook?"

She grinned. "My guess would be that you do, but that isn't it. I want to know where you and Chad went."

This wasn't what he'd expected. "When?"

"When you left."

"*We* didn't go anywhere. My father enrolled me in military school in Virginia and I left the morning I got out of jail."

"Oh." She opened her mouth to say something then closed it.

He waited, wanting to change the subject but knowing she wouldn't let him. He had to face the music. This conversation had been a long time coming.

"Do you know where Chad went?" More softly, she continued, "Where he is? If he's alive?"

There was the question he dreaded. "I haven't seen him in some time." At least that was an honest answer, of sorts.

The hope died in her eyes. Jordon's chest contracted. It was worse than he'd believed. He wasn't feeling heroic at all now.

It almost destroyed him but he had to keep his word. He'd promised Chad not to tell anyone, his parents or sisters in particular, that he was in prison. Jordon had thought nothing of the promise at the time, never imagining that he'd meet any of Chad's family again, much less become involved with one of his sisters. And involved Jordon was. Far too much so. If he allowed his feelings to go much further he was afraid he might fall in love with Kelsey.

The first chance he had he was going to visit Chad. He had to allow him to tell his family he was at least alive.

"When was the last time you saw Chad?"

"The morning after you both got into trouble."

"Really?"

"He left and we thought he was with you." She turned to look at him. "We haven't heard from him in fifteen years, three months and twenty-one days."

Chad hadn't said he'd never contacted his family. That explained some of how she felt about her parents. "You blame your parents, don't you?"

She looked away toward a picture of a fishing boat that hung on the wall. "Yeah."

"Will you tell me about it?" he asked softly.

"I don't talk about it."

"I figured as much. You haven't looked at your parents' house once when we were riding by except after the storm." For a few seconds he wasn't sure she would say any more.

She didn't look at him as she said in a tight voice, "My father was so inflexible about what we could and couldn't do. I idolized Chad. It almost killed me when he left. I can't stand the thought that he might be dead or that he was alone if he did die."

Jordon's heart constricted. He opened his mouth to tell her that Chad was alive but he couldn't. He'd given his word. That meant something to him. He'd learned the value of trust when his mother had run around on his father. Had had it driven home again when his ex had not only crushed his heart but had taken his professional integrity also. No, giving his word was too important, that bond of trust unbreakable. He wouldn't discard his commitment to Chad, not even for Kelsey.

"That had to have been tough."

"Yeah. That's an understatement. My parents drove Chad away. I made up my mind to leave home as soon as I could. I pretty much bided my time until I could get out of there. China covered for me when I became the wild child my parents feared. 'You're no better than your brother,' I heard on more than one occasion when China couldn't make what I'd done go away soon enough."

"Like what?"

"The usual stuff. Sneaking out at night, smoking, seeing boys they didn't like. They thought it, so I did it."

That explained her reputation. "You were determined to get back at them."

"I guess I was. I couldn't believe my father could tell someone he said he loved to leave. And my mother was worse, she stood by and said nothing. When I turned sixteen I got a job, and saved my money. I was out of there the day I turned eighteen."

And that explained her independence. Her need to control. She'd even worked to build a surrogate family by being the person who planned events, surrounding herself with people. "I'm impressed. To be on your own at that young an age. Then get an education."

"Hey, don't make me out as a wonder woman. I made some poor choices, lived with the wrong guy, slept on a friend's floor for months before I decided if I wanted to get out of Golden Shores I needed to find a way to do that. I remember my high school counselor telling me about an educational program the hospital offered. They would send me to school, and I'd owe them X number of years."

Jordon sucked in air as if he'd been punched. He'd forgotten. She was planning to move. The thought of Kelsey no longer being around made him want to grab her and hold on. He was stepping over a line. He'd no intention of letting her matter that much.

"And now you've paid your time, hence the job in Atlanta."

The light of a person seeing a beautiful possibility within their grasp filled her eyes. "Yes, it's my chance to leave my parents, my less than stellar past behind and start fresh. What I hate most about leaving is not seeing China regularly but she has Payton and the baby. We'll visit."

Where did that leave him? Here, now, making the most of what time he had. Reaching for Kelsey's hand, he pulled her to him. She resisted for a second then slid along him. Looking into her eyes as his hands skimmed over her bottom, he lifted her until she straddled him. "Then we don't have any time to waste."

Pleasurable minutes later, Kelsey lay wrapped in his

arms. Jordon pulled the covers over them and clicked off the light. Kelsey nestled against him, putting her head on his shoulder.

The sun was but a pink haze in the eastern sky when Jordon woke again with a warm bare behind settled against him. Life was good. What were his chances of having Kelsey in his bed nightly? Everything about her said it wouldn't be as easy as asking. He'd have to smooth-talk her, charm her before she'd give in, but she would give in. She had to for his sake.

"Tell me what happened."

Jordon started. She was awake. He knew what she referred to but he didn't want to spend their time together talking about the past.

"Good morning to you too."

She shifted to face him. "Tell me about military school."

At least she wasn't asking about his mother. "I went kicking and screaming. It was that or Dad was going to let me stay in jail. He called in a favor otherwise the school would have never taken me. Dad got a transfer so he'd be close enough that I could at least spend holidays with him."

She wrinkled her nose and asked, "Where was your mother?"

"She and Dad divorced two years before. She'd moved to California." He didn't even try to keep the bitterness from his voice.

"You haven't seen her since, have you?"

Was he that easy to read? "No."

"Why not?"

"I don't want to go into it."

"You going to military school rather than running away to live with your mother says something. Okay, if you won't tell me about that, then tell me about how you decided to become a doctor."

"You're not going to give up on the questions, are you?"

She rolled over and faced him, putting an arm on his chest. "Nope. You know about me, but I don't know much about you. So spill. I want to know it all."

"Despite my unlawful ways, I managed to keep my grades up in school. The first few months in military school were tough. I stayed in trouble, on the verge of being thrown out almost daily."

"So did you get thrown out?"

"No." For that he would be forever grateful.

"What happened?" She looked at him intently.

"One night I was sneaking in and got caught by an old sergeant who had lost his arm. He sat me down and told me about his life and how I was throwing mine away. He'd lost his arm doing something foolish and he regretted it every day. I may not have lost an arm but I might lose more if I didn't get my act together. I spent all my spare time after that with him."

"So how did you decide to be a doctor?"

"I had always wanted to be a doctor. I liked helping people. Enough talk about me."

He brought his hand to rest on her hip and nudged her closer.

Kelsey pushed his hand away.

"Nope. I've got one more question."

Jordon groaned.

"I want to know why you decided to move back here."

He tensed. His gut roiled. She really was hitting all the sore spots. If it wasn't for her unwavering gaze and the value he placed on truth he might have told her something less honest just to get off the subject. But he couldn't.

"Okay, if you really want to know. My partner was convicted of Medicaid fraud. I wasn't involved but I was close enough that my records were looked into." He broke their gaze. No longer speaking to her, he said as if in a vacuum, "I stood beside my partner but it killed all my credibility. To make it worse, we were engaged. I believed in her, trusted her. I don't ever want a relationship like that again." The pain and bitterness flowed through him like the first second he'd learned of her deceit. "There wasn't much left for me to do but to start over. I thought this would be a good place to do so."

Kelsey placed hand on his chest palm down and said in a soothing voice, "I'm sorry. That had to have been tough."

"It was." Somehow he felt better for just saying it out loud. As if he'd thrown off the ugliness of the past to truly start living in the here and now.

"Thanks for telling me. I understand your reaction to some things now." She hugged him and then scooted off the bed. "I'm sorry that happened to you. I understand how you feel the way you do."

"Where're you going? It's still early."

Jordon had never seen anything more beautiful than Kelsey standing there in her full glory in the buttery light of morning. She was bodacious, confident and alluring. An amazing combination. He wanted it all for himself.

"I need to check on Molly. See about my house." She rifled through the sack that held her clothes, pulling items from it. "Mind if I use your shower?"

She seemed to be pulling away. Had his comment about never wanting a relationship like the one he'd had with his ex made Kelsey think he did want something more with her? "No. Mind if I share? I'll dress and go with you."

"That's not necessary." She didn't even look back at him.

Jordon sat on the side of the bed. Kelsey acted as if the amazing night they'd shared meant nothing. He refused to be dismissed so easily.

"Kelsey, do you mind looking at me?"

Instead of doing so, she took her armload of clothes and headed toward the bath.

"Kelsey!"

She stopped short and whirled round to face him. "Don't you ever shout at me!"

"Hey, I'm sorry. I was just trying to get your attention. I'd like to know what's going on." He found his pants and pulled them on.

"Going on?" She looked at him in disbelief. "One, my best friend is in the hospital and I don't know how badly off she is and, two, I don't have a house anymore, which means I don't have a place to stay. So now you know what's going on."

"You know that isn't what I was talking about." Jordon stepped toward her.

"What else is there to talk about?"

"Us."

She looked at him directly. "Jordon, there is no us."

"Seemed to me there was plenty of us last night."

"Last night was about nerves, adrenaline. Right place at the right time."

Had he been slapped in the face? He'd said similar words to women before, had seen the looks on their faces. That must be on his now but this was the first time he been on the receiving end of a brush-off. He didn't like it and refused to accept it.

"That's cold even for you, Kelsey." A niggle of satisfaction went through him at her slight flinch.

"Look, Jordon, the sex was amazing, you were amazing, but I'm leaving Golden Shores as soon as the job in Atlanta opens up. I'm not going to start a relationship knowing that I'm leaving. You don't want one either. After what you said about your ex I can't blame you. I don't think it's wise for either of us go any further than this."

Jordon stepped into her personal space. She didn't budge. That was the Kelsey he knew well but after last night he was aware of her valuable side also. When she cared for someone she did so deeply, with all her heart and until the end.

"I'll tell you what. Why don't we forget about you leaving and enjoy the time we have until that happens? We're both adults. I believe we can handle that. We'll start with being friends."

"I don't know. Seems like after last night we might be stretching the meaning of the word 'friends' a bit."

Jordon pulled her into his arms, clothes and all, his hands finding the skin of her back. "Maybe so, but I don't mind if you don't." He kissed her.

Kelsey was confident that everything about being "friends" with Jordon was a bad idea. He wasn't the type of person a girl was only friends with. Even now, if it wasn't for wanting to see Molly, Kelsey would pull Jordon back into bed. She already liked him too much.

Leaving town was for her own sanity. She'd been controlled by her father and she wouldn't let Jordon manipulate her into something she didn't want to do. Still, she liked him. What would it hurt for them to spend some time together as long as they both knew the score?

She looked into his beautiful eyes. "Okay. But there have to be some rules."

"Like?" he drawled, as if he wasn't sure he liked the idea.

"Like you can't tell me what to do. You don't keep tabs on me. I go and do as I please without checking in with you. You understand I'm leaving town. That this stays on a friendly level, nothing more. No talk of us. No talk of love."

"And you're so sure I might fall in love with you."

"I don't know but I don't want it to happen."

"No worries there. Having a good time is all I'm interested in. I've had the other and it wasn't pleasant when it ended."

"I wouldn't have done you that way."

"I know that but you can't blame a guy for being gun shy."

There was a sharp squeeze in the area of her chest. All of a sudden she didn't like being just a good time for Jordon. She wanted to mean more but she refused to say that. "It's a deal."

He grinned. "Then I think we should seal it with a kiss." His lips met hers. She let go of the clothes, letting them drop between them, and wrapped her arms around his neck, returning his kiss. Jordon lifted her and carried her in the direction of the bath.

There he put her down long enough to turn on the water. Stepping into the shower, he pulled her after him. She shrieked as the cool water touched her heated skin. Jordon chuckled before he picked her up again and she wrapped her legs around his waist. "Cold? Don't worry, I'll heat you up."

His thick manhood stood between them, leaving her no reason to doubt him. He let her slide down his wet, slick body until he had fully entered her.

"Mmm, I like being friends with you," he murmured in her ear as he started to move. Kelsey closed her eyes and appreciated each thrust until she could stand it no longer. She found her pleasure and went weak against him. Supporting her against the tiles, he groaned in triumph against her neck.

Jordon guided her to her feet and helped her to stand. His eyes were still hooded with passion. "You know, this might be the nicest shower I've ever taken."

"And to think you haven't even picked up the soap yet."

Jordon gave her a light swat on the butt. "How like you to make fun after a wonderful moment."

She gave him a serious look. "I don't want you to forget we're only friends."

"You sure know how to hurt a man's ego. The least you could do is say thank you."

She cupped his face. "Last night was wonderful. A second ago was so amazing my knees are still weak. Thank you, Jordon." She kissed him with all that she felt, which was far more than she wanted to.

When they came up for air, Jordon said, "That's more like it."

Kelsey couldn't help but grin. In that moment he reminded her so much of the boy she'd had such a crush on. Now she had a crush on the man.

He picked up a bar of soap. "I think we'd better focus on bathing so I can get you to the hospital to see Molly. I'll help you then you can help me." His voice was deep with suggestion.

Kelsey laughed. "I don't think that'll work."

She was right. Twenty minutes later they emerged from the bath. If she wasn't careful it would be her feelings she'd have to worry about when she left and not Jordon's.

Dressed in the few work clothes she had that weren't too wrinkled to wear, and almost ready to go to the hospital, she asked, "Hey, can I use your phone? I want to call and check on Molly."

"Sure."

Kelsey scooped up the phone off the bedside table where it had been through the night. She punched in the number and asked for ICU. Because Molly wasn't a family member, the clerk couldn't tell her anything except that Molly was still in guarded condition. Kelsey needed to see Molly for herself.

Kelsey searched the room. Where was her jewelry box?

"Problem?" Jordon asked, from where he was pulling socks out of a drawer.

"I thought I had brought my jewelry box in here."

"It's in the living room on the table beside the sofa."

"Yeah, that's right." She headed down the hall. Hardy met her in the kitchen and gave a yelp. "Hey, boy. Thanks for being a hero yesterday."

"Please don't make his head any larger," Jordon said, coming up behind her.

"There's nothing wrong in letting someone know they are appreciated."

"I thought that was what I was doing a few minutes ago."

Kelsey would have believed that she was beyond blushing but that was what she was doing. She didn't dare look at Jordon. Instead she said, "Any chance of getting a cup of coffee?"

"Sure," he said, and headed into the kitchen area.

While he was doing that she found her jewelry box. It had been the one thing she had taken with her when she had left her parents. Opening it, she checked to see if anything had been damaged. She looked over her shoulder to see where Jordon was. He had his back to her, pouring coffee. Lifting the tray and placing it on the table, she removed the picture of Chad that rested on top of the items below. It was damp but in good shape. Placing it to the side, she pushed the other items around with the end of her finger. Beneath some bracelets lay the yellow plastic ring that Jordon had given her long ago.

"Here you go," he said behind her.

Kelsey jumped. The box fell to the floor.

"Hey, I didn't mean to startle you."

She went down on her knees and turned the box upright. Jordon placed the cups on the nearby counter and joined her.

"I can get it," she assured him.

Jordon ignored her and continued to place necklaces, rings and bracelets into the box. When everything visible was returned, Kelsey picked up the box and set it on the table.

"This is Chad." Jordon's voice sounded pained.

She turned to find him holding her picture.

"I took it out of my parents' album. It's all I have left of him."

A stricken look fluttered through his eyes before he turned away from her. He bent down and reached a hand under the edge of the sofa. "Is this yours?"

In his palm lay the plastic ring.

Kelsey gulped. Would he remember that? He didn't remember her. She put out her hand. "It's mine."

His gaze met her as he picked up her hand and placed the ring on the third finger of her left hand just as he'd done when they'd been kids. "It looks like one of those rings out of a Cracker Jack box."

"It is. You gave it to me." Why had she said that? She pulled it off and dropped it in the box. Maybe it was time for him to remember.

"I did? When?"

"The night before you and Chad were arrested. I came into Chad's room and you were eating Cracker Jacks. You came out with the ring and put it on my finger. Said that now I was your girlfriend. Chad laughed and ran me out of the room."

Jordon stood then sat on a nearby stool that belonged to the kitchen bar. "Hey, I do remember that. You kept it all this time?"

"I forgot it was even in here."

"Then why won't you look at me?"

She turned and glared at him. "Satisfied?"

"Not exactly. There's more to it than that."

"What do you want me to say? That I had a horrible schoolgirl crush on you. That I kept it because you were my first love."

He grinned and took one of her hands. "Hey, that sound nice to me."

"I shouldn't have told you."

He pulled her to him. Kelsey resisted a second then came to stand between his legs. "I'm glad you did. I'm honored you thought it important enough to keep." He gave her a kiss so tender she feared she'd cry. And she'd stopped crying long ago for things that couldn't be.

CHAPTER SEVEN

JORDON WALKED BESIDE Kelsey across the neighbor's yard to look at her house. Unfortunately, the bright morning sun didn't improve the view. They stood not saying a word. Kelsey made a step forward and Jordon stopped her with a hand on her elbow.

"I'm not letting you go in there. If I could have seen this clearly I wouldn't have allowed it then."

She pulled away. "What did I say about telling me what to do?"

"I heard you. But this is a safety issue. I wouldn't let anyone enter."

Standing side by side, they looked at the house for a few more minutes.

"We need to go if we're going to make visiting hours in the ICU," Jordon said.

Kelsey nodded. Catching a glimpse of her face, he saw moisture in her eyes. He put an arm across her shoulders and pulled her to him as they made their way to his SUV.

Kelsey had a forlorn look on her face as she peered out the window as he drove.

"It's hard to believe that today can be so beautiful after yesterday."

"It is." He didn't know what else to say. He'd never seen her so down. She was always the one encouraging people, the peppy upbeat person with a quick, smart-aleck come-back. It saddened him to see her so despondent.

The floodwaters had ebbed away. Limbs and debris lay in yards and along the road. Even the trees that had fallen over the road had been cut up, and piled to the side. Along Main Street people were already out cleaning in front of their businesses, some opening early so that people could buy supplies needed for repairs. It would merely take a few days the effects of the storm would have disappeared from sight. Though the damage would linger in the hearts and minds of the residents for a long time to come, adding to the fear that it might be worse the next time.

"You know you can stay with me as long as you wish," Jordon said, hoping to draw her out of her gloom.

"I can't do that."

"Why not? Where're you going to find a place to stay for the short time you think you will be here?"

"I don't know but I'll find a place."

He wanted to protect her, reassure her and to his won-derment keep her close.

Last night had taken their relationship to a deeper level. He hated deception. Knew what it had done to him and his father, but he couldn't break his promise to Chad. Keeping his word meant everything to him. It was the foundation of trust. When he'd moved back to Golden Shores it had been to find that foundation again. The more he became involved with Kelsey, the more she shook that.

He would never have dreamed that she'd kept a nothing trinket he'd given to her so many years ago. What was he being pulled into?

It hadn't escaped his notice that Kelsey placed impor-tance on the jewelry box. She didn't strike him as senti-mental but she'd insisted that she get it when she given nothing else a second glance in the house. She'd not give that much interest to her parents' house when they'd passed it. What she had in the box was of value to her and one of those items had been the ring he'd given her.

This time, to his amazement, she did look at her parents' home when they passed. There were a few limbs in the yard, otherwise nothing was different at the neat yard and house. Was she thinking about the past, like he was?

Kelsey stood beside Jordon as they rode the elevator up to the second floor. His strong, sturdy presence had been a blessing during the fight to get Molly to the hospital, with her sorrow over her home and during the uncertain moments the night before. He'd made her forget it all with his tender but powerful lovemaking.

There had been something far too disconcerting about sharing Jordon's room as they'd dressed that morning. But nice nonetheless. She'd had Molly as support for so many years but it was comforting to have someone strong in her corner for a change. China had been there but Kelsey had hated to unload on her. She had a new husband and a baby coming, and she didn't need to carry Kelsey's burdens also. China had such a soft heart she couldn't help but morph into big-sister mode and try to fix things for her.

Squaring her shoulders and taking a deep breath, she prepared to see Molly. She and Jordon exited the elevator. When Kelsey would have stopped at the door of ICU to use the phone to ask permission to enter, Jordon pushed the door open instead. She'd forgotten he had access to almost any area of the hospital. They walked to the bed located in a corner of the large open space. Kelsey moaned when she saw Molly. Jordon took her hand and squeezed it.

He leaned over and whispered, "Hang in there. It isn't as bad as it looks."

Kelsey wasn't good with these types of injuries. That's why she'd become a nutritionist instead of a nurse. No blood.

Molly eyes were closed and she was hooked up to monitors. The bed was elevated but she lay motionless. Red angry scratches parted her pale skin. In a couple of places fine black stitches marred her appearance. Kelsey wanted to sob. Molly was so particular about caring for her skin, having her make-up on just right.

Kelsey stepped to the bedside and took one of Molly's hands. Its warmth reassured Kelsey. "Hey, there."

Molly didn't respond but Kelsey continued to talk to her. She did glance around once when the sound of two male voices caught her attention. Jordon was speaking to the surgeon who had taken care of Molly. A few minutes later Jordon came to stand beside Kelsey.

"Rick says she's doing well. They're backing off on the meds so she should be awake by this afternoon. If she's doing well by then, they'll move her out to the floor, maybe tomorrow."

Some of the pressure in her chest eased. "That sounds wonderful."

"It's almost shift-change. Why don't we go get some breakfast in the cafeteria?"

"Okay. I'll come back later."

Kelsey let Jordon escort her out of the ICU.

"I think I'll pass on food. I'm sure I have hundreds of emails to answer. I also want to check in on Mr. and Mrs. Lingerfelt if they're still here."

"They are. I asked about them when I called. And you need to eat. You've not had anything since yesterday morning. If you're not careful, you'll be sick too."

"I can take care of myself."

"I'm not saying you can't. Even if you aren't hungry, the least you could do is keep me company."

"I think you're trying to send me on a guilt trip."

He grinned. "Is it working?"

"A little bit."

"Enough to get you to share bacon and eggs with me?"

She made a resigned huff. "If I do, can I then go to my office? I need to call the landlord and my insurance company. I've got to figure out how to salvage what I can of our stuff."

Jordon looked at his watch. "It's early yet. You've got time to eat and then start on those calls."

She was hungry and she found she rather liked sharing her meals with Jordon. "Okay. I give up."

"Good. Let's go. I'm starving."

By the middle of the morning, Kelsey had answered her emails, attended a meeting for new diabetic patients where no one showed up, which was understandable, and gone up to check on Molly. Her doctor was in the process of examining her so Kelsey wasn't allowed into the ICU. She did get to speak to Molly's parents, who assured Kelsey Molly was improving.

Kelsey had phoned her landlord, who was sending his insurance representative out to look at the house. His concern had sounded genuine. She'd asked about getting her belongings and had been told she'd have to wait until the insurance people gave the okay. That hadn't improved her spirits.

She'd also checked in with China. They were supposed to have lunch the next day but decided to wait. Instead, China had invited her to dinner at her and Payton's house. She didn't tell China about the tree, not wanting her to worry.

"I don't know. Won't that be too much work for you?"

"Come on, Kelsey. I want to show you what I'm thinking about using in the baby's room."

"That's so not fair. You knew that would get me."

"Yeah, I thought it might. Why don't you bring Jordon too? He seemed to be a nice guy and he's new to town. He might like a home-cooked meal."

"That's China. Mothering everyone. Hey, you're not doing the cooking, are you?"

"No, Payton will. Part of our marriage vows were that he cooks, I help."

Kelsey laughed. "I'll think about asking Jordon and let you know."

"I'll expect you both Sunday night, six o'clock."

How like China to give her no choice. "Just because you're my big sister doesn't mean you get to tell me what to do." A few short months ago China being high-handed would have been cause for Kelsey to hang up. Now somehow it felt good to know her sister was in her corner.

"What're big sisters for? I miss you. Come on, say you'll be here."

"Okay."

"And bring Jordon?"

"I'll ask him, that's all I can do. But no matchmaking between Jordon and me, do you understand?"

"I don't have to matchmake. I saw the way he looked at you the other day. The job is already done. Bye." There was click on the line.

How like China not to give her a chance to refute that statement. Did Jordon's feelings for her go further than being his bed partner? Had things between them already gone too far?

Jordon went looking for Kelsey around five o'clock that afternoon. He'd been so busy with the new patients admitted during the storm he'd not had a chance to check on her. But she had been on his mind. Other than his ex-partner and girlfriend before the FBI had become involved, he'd never given another woman as much thought or concern as he did Kelsey.

She wasn't in her office and he was pretty sure where he'd find her. Pushing through the doors of ICU, he saw her sitting beside Molly's bed. Her eyes were still closed but she lay in a more natural position, as if she had woken up some time. An older couple sat on the other side of the bed from Kelsey.

As he approached the man rose and Kelsey did also. "Mr. Marks," she said quietly, "this is Dr. Jordon King, the man I was telling you about."

Mr. Marks put out his hand. "I understand that we..." he glanced toward the woman beside him "...owe you a large thanks for saving our daughter."

"Not at all. It was a team effort. Kelsey more than did her part."

"Either way, we're grateful."

"So how is Molly doing?" Jordon asked.

"She was awake a few minutes ago and knew who we were. Even got on to Kelsey for coming into the house to get her," Mr. Marks said.

"I'm glad to hear it."

"They plan to move her to the floor tonight," Kelsey added.

"That sounds like she is improving." Jordon looked at Kelsey. "May I speak to you a minute?"

She nodded and they stepped away from Molly's area.

Jordon said, "I wanted to let you know that I'm headed home. Do you want to ride with me? I'm in no rush."

"I've got my own car. I'll see you in a little while."

"I'm not leaving until you do because I think you'll be right here in the morning if I don't see that you go home."

"Jordon, I don't need a keeper."

"No, you don't but you do need someone to remind you to take care of yourself. Why don't you page me when you're ready to go?"

With a huff, she said, "I'm ready now. Let me say good-bye to Molly's parents."

Jordon watched as she walked over and gave first Molly's mother then her father a hug. "I'll see y'all and Molly in the morning. Let me know if anything changes."

Molly's parents assured her that they would.

Kelsey walked beside him through the ICU doors. He wanted to touch her badly, something as simple as hold her hand, but she wouldn't like that. It would be too personal. Would imply more than they were both willing to admit. He'd learned she was anti-involvement. Get too close, act like you cared too much and she'd start pushing away. This time he wasn't going to let her.

Last night had meant something to him and he refused to let her run from him now. "I'm worn out. You have to be also," he said casually.

"Yeah, but I still have to find a place to stay tonight."

Jordon stopped in the middle of the hall and glared at her.

Kelsey pursed her lips questioningly. "You're glaring at me again."

"I should be. I thought we'd talked about this already and that you would stay at my place."

She looked up and down the hallway. "This isn't the place to talk about this."

He followed suit, seeing no one. "Maybe not, but we're going to."

In a low voice Kelsey hissed, "Look, just because we

had one night of mad, passionate sex doesn't mean we're going to start living together."

"I would agree to your description of the sex and normally the moving-in part, but where else are you planning to go? You've already said it wouldn't be your parents' or sister's place."

Both were out of the question.

"Hotel?"

She didn't have that kind of money. What she did have she needed to use to set up in Atlanta.

"At least at my house you can keep an eye on what is being done at yours."

He had a point.

"You've said more than once you're leaving town soon so neither of us should be inconvenienced long."

Did he consider her an inconvenience? That idea kind of hurt. "I'll only agree if I take the sofa. You're too big for it. You looked like a sardine in a can curled up on it. And the minute I find another place there will be no argument about me leaving. Understood?"

"Something tells me that having you for a roommate isn't going to be easy. I'll most likely be glad to see you go."

Kelsey flinched. Her father had pretty much said the same thing when she'd moved out of her parents' home. She was afraid she was going to miss living with Jordon far more than she'd ever missed anything. He was beginning to fill that spot that had been empty since he and Chad had left town.

He placed a hand at her waist and gave her a slight nudge. "Come on. I'm starving for a fat, juicy burger. We can stop by the Beach Hut for some takeout and head home. I owe Hardy some attention after the last two days."

Less than an hour later she pulled her car up behind

Jordon's SUV. He got out, carrying a white sack. As she got out of her own car he called, "Hey, can you get the drinks?"

Pulling her purse up on her shoulder, Kelsey reached into his SUV and took the two soft drink cups out of the holders. Using her hip, she closed the door.

They walked to the house and Jordon unlocked the door. Once inside Kelsey placed the drinks on the counter. "Before I eat I want to go over to the house. I think I saw my landlords' car."

"Give me a sec and I'll walk with you."

"No. Stay here. I'll be back in a few minutes. Eat your burgers before they get cold." She started out the door. Jordon was beginning to encroach on her life too much.

"Are you trying to get rid of me?"

She turned back and looked at him. "If I was?"

His gaze didn't waver. "Not going to happen. If you're not back in fifteen minutes I'm coming to look for you, and I'd better not find you inside that death trap."

"Yes, sir," she snapped, but with a grin on her face. For once she didn't feel dominated by being told what to do. Jordon was concerned for her well-being. To her surprise, she rather liked being protected.

What would it be like to have that feeling all the time?

When Kelsey returned to Jordon's, he was sitting in a recliner with his feet propped up and his eyes closed. The TV was tuned to a sports channel.

Kelsey closed the door, making a low click. The burger bag sat on the counter next to the drinks, unopened. He'd not eaten without her. Her father wouldn't have thought twice about having a meal without waiting.

She'd take a shower and let him sleep. Pulling off her shoes so they wouldn't make any noise, she walked down the hall to his bedroom. Gathering her clothes and toiletries, she came back up the hall to the small second bath.

She placed her things on the counter. If she was going to have to stay here, she might well make the small place her own.

After a hot shower, she pulled on an extra-large T-shirt with a blue umbrella on it that almost covered the entire shirt and some black leggings that went to midcalf. She mussed her hair, encouraging it to dry standing up every which way.

Kelsey looked into the mirror. There were dark rings under her eyes. Sleep had been scarce over the last few days. She'd read somewhere that emotional upheaval wasn't good for your complexion. Goodness knew, she'd lived through mayhem. First Molly, then her house, then spending the night with Jordon, and now staying at his house indefinitely. Much more and she would qualify for the funny farm.

Leaning her head against the mirror, she groaned. When had her life spun so out of control? She needed the woman in Personnel in Atlanta to call before she got in too deep with Jordon.

Two quick raps to the door made her jerk straight up.

"Hey, supper is on the table when you're ready," Jordon called.

"Be there in a minute."

Even the sound of his voice through a door made her stomach flutter. She had never reacted to a guy that way before. Though that wasn't true. She'd felt the same way about Jordon when she'd been a kid.

Waiting a minute, she opened the door and headed toward the kitchen. Jordon stood with his hip against the counter and one foot crossed over the other, watching the TV and drinking through a straw. He'd changed and now wore a snug-fitting T-shirt that clung to his well-developed chest. Well-worn jeans with a straight hole at one knee rode low on his hips. All things considered, he was the sexist man she'd ever laid eyes on. Her mouth watered.

"What team do you pull for?"

He put his drink down. "I'm a Washington Redskins fan. Can't live around Washington and not become one. I thought we'd sit outside. Give Hardy a chance to run while we eat. I'll get the burgers and you carry the drinks."

"Sure."

She watched as he pulled their burgers, still in the foil wrap, out of the oven. He put them on a plate. Picking up the drinks, she led the way to the sliding glass door that faced the bay.

"I'll get the door." He came up beside her close enough that his familiar scent filled her nostrils. She was in so much trouble. Jordon pulled the door open and stepped out. There was a small round table with two chairs sitting on the cement patio.

Kelsey took one seat and he the other. The sun was still above the horizon but the sky was fast turning pink in the west.

"When I get someplace permanent I'm making sure that it has the porch facing west so I can watch the sun set every night. Even better, a sleep porch. You know, the ones with a swing bed."

"That sounds kind of kinky."

Jordon's gaze met hers and he had a quirky lift to one corner of his mouth. "Maybe you could come over and try it out with me."

"I'll be in Atlanta."

Jordon chose not respond to that remark. Kelsey seemed to use leaving as a defense mechanism and he plain wanted to forget it might happen.

"Did you talk to your landlord?" He took a bite of his food.

"Yeah. The insurance company doesn't want anyone in the house. The damage is bad enough that the house will have to be demolished."

He reached across the table and took her hand. "I'm sorry."

"Molly is the one I feel sorry for. She's in the hospital and has lost everything. It's so unfair."

"What about you? You've lost everything."

"I got the thing that truly matter the other night."

"Your box."

"Yes."

They were both quiet for a few minutes as they ate.

"Did your sister have any damage at her house?"

"They seemed to have weathered the storm pretty well. She said they lost a couple of hanging plants that they couldn't take inside because they were working at the clinic."

"I'm glad that was the worst of it."

"I haven't told her about the tree. I didn't want her hurrying over here to take care of me. We were supposed to meet for lunch this week but canceled so instead she invited me to dinner Sunday night. She wanted me to ask you to come also."

"So, are you inviting me to go to your sister's for dinner?" He grinned.

"Yes, and you don't have to make a big deal out of it."

He leaned back, stretched his legs and crossed them at the ankles. "I'm not making a big deal out of it. I'm honored."

How did the man always know the right thing to say?

They'd finished their burgers when Hardy rose from where he lay at Jordon's feet. "You ready to play, boy?"

The dog ran in a circle then picked up his stick, which was lying near him.

Kelsey laughed. "It looks like he is." It was the first real laugh she'd had in a couple of days. It felt good.

"While I clean up here, would you mind taking Hardy down to the water and playing a little fetch?" Jordon piled the leftover paper and cups on the plate.

"I can clean up."

"We'll take turns. Tomorrow night will be yours."

That was nothing like it had been growing up. Her father would never have thought of helping in the kitchen. Her mother wouldn't have thought to even ask him to. Jordon was different than any other man she knew.

"Agreed." She stood and started toward the bay.

Hardy ran ahead then turned and came back to her. When they reached the dock he raced to the end. Kelsey followed. She threw the stick into the water and in a flash Hardy was swimming after it.

Kelsey was sitting on the pier, dangling her feet over the water, when Jordon joined her.

"I left you the chair," she said, glancing at him. He had evening shadow along his jaw, which gave him a bit of a bad-boy look. She wanted to run her hand along his face to feel the prickliness. Instead, she gripped the edge of the rough wood beneath her.

"You made a beautiful picture out here. I wished I was enough of photographer to do you justice."

She narrowed her eyes at him. "That was a smooth line, Doctor."

He moved his face in close, his nose touching hers. "I'll have you know that I don't have to use lines."

"Ooh, such confidence."

He leaned back and shrugged as if he was well aware of his masculine appeal.

Kelsey looked out over the bay. The slight breeze made the water ripple. Pink, orange and yellow reflected off the water in a half circle. Her attention turned to the place she'd called home for the last three years. It looked perfect across the front but was a mangled mass from the back. Even the beautiful tree that had shaded the place for what seemed like forever was gone. It lay half in and half out of the house.

"Hey, don't be looking over there." Jordon took her hand.

"I can't help it."

Hardy returned with his stick and this time Jordon threw it, without letting go of her hand.

"Tell me about your mother."

The second she mentioned his mother he let go of her hand. Jordon didn't look her way. He seemed to focus on Hardy swimming to his stick.

"Why do you want to know about her?"

"I guess I'm curious because you don't want to talk about her," she said softly.

"There's no big mystery. Her name is Margaret and she lives in Arizona with her new husband." His tone was as flat as the now-still water.

"New? You say the word like you don't like him."

"I don't know him. Can't even tell you what he looks like." His focus still remained on Hardy.

"You've never met him?"

"Don't want to."

She turned toward him. "Why not?"

After some time he looked away from the dog and said in a hard tone, "You're not going to let it go, are you?"

"No."

Hardy returned to them, shook himself and settled behind them.

"Since you're determined to know everything then I'll tell you," he said in a harsh voice. "My mother was having an affair and I found out. I knew before my father did. I heard her talking on the phone with the man who's her new husband."

She hadn't expected that or she might not have pushed. She reached for his hand but he wouldn't allow her to take it. "Oh, Jordon, that's a horrible burden to carry."

"Yeah, it was. I didn't know whether or not to tell my dad or tell my mother that I knew. For over six months I kept it to myself. I wanted to forget. I started skipping classes, started hanging out with a different crowd."

"Chad."

"Yes, he was part of the crowd."

"After a call from one of my teachers my mother asked me what was going on. I told her that I didn't see why I had to follow the rules and do the right thing when she didn't. I could tell by the look on her face she knew what I was talking about. I explained about the phone call. That night, when Dad came home, she told him she wanted a divorce. Dad was devastated. He never said it but I think he'd guessed about the affair. He loved her so much he'd kept hoping it wasn't true. Mother left the next day. I often wondered if they'd still be together if I'd kept my mouth shut."

Kelsey took his hand between both of hers, not letting him avoid it this time. She waited until he looked at her. "That had nothing to do with you. It was between your parents."

He ran his fingers between hers and held hers on top of his thigh. "I know that now. But it took me years to place the blame where it belonged. On her."

"So that's why you don't see her."

"Yes."

"So how long has it been?" She didn't see her parents

regularly but she did keep up with them through China. She also saw them occasionally in town, driving by or in the grocery store.

"Ten years maybe. She calls on my birthday every year. Sends a present at Christmas."

She'd thought her relationship with her parents was cold. Jordon's with his mother was at subzero. "And your dad? Do you see him often?"

"Dad is great. I'll always be grateful to him for getting me straightened out. Even when he was hurting so deeply, he saw about me. He made changes in his life because he loved me and I mattered to him."

"Unlike your mother."

"Yeah. Hey, Dad is coming down next month for a visit. I want him to meet you."

Ho, that sounded like something too close to a meet-the-parents moment in a real relationship. Still, she liked the idea of meeting Jordon's father. "I'd like that, but I may be in Atlanta by then."

"Would it be so bad to stay here?"

She tugged at her hand but Jordon wouldn't release it. "Please, don't start. I've been working and dreaming for years of moving to a bigger city. This is my chance and I'd appreciate you not making it harder."

He was quiet for a moment. "I promise not to mention it again."

They sat in peace until the last ray of the sun had been swallowed up by darkness. Jordon released her hand and stood, then helped her up. He wrapped an arm around her waist and pulled her close as they walked back to the house. He pushed back the sliding screen and let Kelsey enter first. Hardy squeezed past her.

"Hardy, you're not much of a gentleman," Jordon said, as he closed the glass door.

Kelsey laughed, something she seemed to do more when she was around Jordon. She like to laugh. In fact, sitting on the pier, watching the sunset and talking had been one of the nicest things she'd done in a long time. Despite all the turmoil in her life, Jordon seemed like a safe spot in the storm.

"You want something to drink? Watch some TV?"

"You don't have to treat me like I'm a guest."

"Tonight I've decided you are a guest. Tomorrow you can clean the bathrooms. I hate cleaning bathrooms."

She smirked. "You do know how to make a roommate feel at home."

His chuckle warmed her from the inside out.

"So what about that drink?"

"I don't think so. But I wouldn't mind watching some TV."

"The remote is over by the recliner. Pick out whatever you like except a home-decorating show."

"That sounded a little chauvinistic."

"I'm not. I just don't get into that stuff."

She picked up the remote and turned on the TV. Flipping through the channels, she said, "I like those decorating shows. I'd love to have a place of my own to decorate. I've never lived where I could make a place my own." She stopped at a crime drama. "Hey, I love this show."

"That's one of my favorites too."

Kelsey took a seat on the sofa and curled her legs under her. Jordon didn't join her. Instead, he took the recliner. A tickle of disappointment went through her that he didn't sit beside her. They spent the next hour watching the show and talking about what had happened over the season and where they thought the show was going during the commercial.

After the show, Jordon put the footrest on the recliner

down and stood. "I've got an early morning so I'm going to call it a night. I'll get you some sheets and a blanket."

Well, at least he was going to follow her rules without an argument.

He returned with an armload of bed linen. "I was going to tell you to make yourself at home in the spare bath but I can see you've done that already. Tomorrow evening I'll move some things around in the closet in my office and you can hang your clothes there."

She took the items from his arms. "Thanks. You have been great and I appreciate it."

"It's the least I can do for a neighbor."

Last night she had been his lover and now she was only his neighbor.

She was tucking the sheet in around the cushions of the sofa when Jordon said, "Kelsey."

"Uh." When he said nothing more she looked at him.

"I want you to know I'd like to have you in my bed next to me more than anything. Don't think that because I don't ask, it's not what I want. I'll respect your requests but know all you have to do is walk down the hall. Rest well, Kelsey."

She watched Jordon's broad back as he headed for his bedroom. Yeah, right. After that speech he thought she'd rest well? He left the door wide open, as if to say he was there if she wanted him.

Kelsey shoved down the desire to go after him and throw her arms around his neck. That wouldn't help her keep her heart from breaking when she had to leave. She picked up the blanket and gave it a sharp shake, opening it.

Going to the bathroom, she washed her face and brushed her teeth. The water was running on the other side of the wall as well. Jordon must be taking a shower. Water would be rolling over his handsome face, across his chest, down his muscled thighs.

Kelsey put her toothbrush down and all but ran back to the sofa. She crawled under the sheet and blanket and pulled them both up to her neck. Tomorrow she'd start looking for another place to stay.

She tried not to listen as he pulled out a drawer, pushed it back, the squeak of the bed as he lay down, and the click of the light switch before the house was washed in darkness.

Each tick of the clock sounded like a gong as she forced herself to sleep. If she slept she couldn't think about the warm, hard body that would curl around her if she went to him or the tender kisses Jordon would place along the curve of her ear. Worse, the feel of his lips on her breasts that would cause her to throb and tremble with need.

Jordon wanted her. Had said it. Shown it. She wanted him. That was the real problem. She was desperate for him. So why was she fighting it? Because she'd have a devil of a time leaving him behind. Still, a short time with Jordon was better than no time.

Kelsey threw the covers back. She was going to spend every night in Jordon's arms that she could. Padding down the hall, she paused at the door for a second before going to stand beside the bed.

Suddenly a hand grabbed her wrist and jerked her downward. She yelped seconds before she came in contact with the warm skin of Jordon's chest.

"It's about damn time you showed up," he growled, before his mouth took hers.

CHAPTER EIGHT

SUNDAY DAWNED A bright warm fall day on the coast. Jordon declared his life better for his move back to Golden Shores. He and Kelsey had slept in and together cooked a huge breakfast. Now they sat on the pier. He in the chair and her on his lap, Hardy beside them.

Since the night she'd come to him, Kelsey hadn't backed away once. One morning she'd even allowed him to kiss her goodbye when he'd walked her to her office. He'd like to have a chance to do that always. He felt good about himself around Kelsey, as if life was a rich playground and she was his playmate. If he could only convince her to stay in Golden Shores just a little bit longer, but that was a subject he'd promised not to bring up and one he didn't want to talk about anyway.

"Hey, what time are we supposed to be at your sister's?"

"Around six."

"Great. I'll have time to see the game. The Redskins play today."

"So I'm going to be a football widow?"

"Don't sound so pitiful. I'll let you watch it with me."

She sat up so he could see her eyes. "Why, that's mighty big of you."

"I thought so. Come on." He pushed on her butt, nudging her off his lap. "We don't want to miss the kickoff."

"Ooh, I can hardly wait." She wiggled all over.

Jordon hugged her close until she giggled. "You're such a funny woman."

Thirty minutes later Jordon looked at Kelsey in disbelief and admiration. She could carry on an intelligent conversation about football, even knowing the names of a number of men on the Redskins' team. Kelsey was a woman after his own heart. In fact, he was afraid that she might already have it.

At halftime he said, "Want some popcorn?"

"Sure. I've not had any in a long time."

Jordon found a boiler, placed it on the stove then added oil. He was looking through the cabinet when Kelsey asked, "What're you doing?"

"I'm looking for the popcorn."

"No, I mean with the boiler."

"That's how I cook popcorn. The old-fashioned way."

"I've never seen it popped like this before. Microwave is the way I go."

"My grandmother made it this way, so did my mother and now I do."

"I know you don't like to talk about your mother but this isn't the first time you've mentioned her when you were doing something."

There was some truth to that statement. As much as he wanted to believe his mother meant nothing in his life, she still influenced him. He poured the corn into the boiler. "I guess she was a good mother at one time."

"We all can't be perfect all the time."

By the time the game started again they were seated on the sofa, munching on popcorn with soft drinks in glasses nearby. Kelsey yawned widely at the beginning of the third quarter, mumbled a comment about someone keeping her up all night, laid her head on his thigh and seconds later was asleep.

Jordon pulled down the blanket that stayed on the back of the sofa and covered her. He rested a hand at her waist. What a perfect way to spend a Sunday afternoon—the Redskins on TV and Kelsey close. What would it take to make this happen all the time?

He had to see Chad and remove the proverbial elephant from between them if he wanted any kind of future with Kelsey. Jordon didn't look forward to telling her. The scene would be ugly. Still, it had to be done. It was long overdue. If he waited any longer it would be worse. Maybe with that part of her life truly behind Kelsey he could convince her they belonged together. That staying in Golden Shores with him was worth the risk.

At five minutes to six Kelsey said, "Make a right into the drive of that yellow house. It's China and Payton's."

"Nice place." Jordon followed Kelsey up the long stairs. "I've got to start looking for a place before my lease is up. I've put off doing anything about it because I'm not good with the details. Like are there enough bathrooms. Would you go house-hunting with me some time this week?"

It sounded too permanent. Like something a couple did together. "I don't know."

"Kelsey, I could really use your opinion."

She would enjoy seeing inside homes and looking at how they were decorated. Having a chance to imagine what she would do with one if it was hers. "I guess I could, if you really want me to."

"Of course I do. Having someone along to help would at least get me moving in the right direction. Do you think you could take off on Tuesday afternoon if I can get a real estate person to set some places up?"

"I guess. I have time coming for the other night during the storm."

"Good. Then it's a date."

Kelsey smiled. She'd had to look at three places in town to find a hot pink bikini this late in the season. She'd carried it to Molly who had been moved to a room two days earlier. Kelsey had broken the bad news about the house and Molly had seemed to take it well, just relieved to be alive. Kelsey had dangled the bag with the bikini in it off the end of her index finger.

"What's in that?"

"Your winnings."

"Winnings?"

"Yeah, you won the bet about who the new doctor would date."

Molly had squealed, then winced. "So he asked you out?"

"Well, not exactly." Kelsey had smiled and drawn the last word out.

Molly had given her a quizzical look then her eyes had widened and her mouth had formed an O. "You've been to bed with him!"

"Hey, what're you thinking? You have a huge smile on your face," Jordon said, bringing her back to the present as they waited on someone to answer China and Payton's door.

"I was just thinking about Molly's reaction to winning a bet."

"You mean the one about who I would ask out first?"

She stepped back and looked at him with narrowed eyes. "Who told you?"

"No one really. I kind of figured it out."

"Why didn't you say something?"

He grinned and said in a low voice, "It didn't matter.

You've been my pick since you asked me to dance the night we met."

"Why, that's one of the nicest compliments I've ever received." She went up on her toes and kissed him.

She broke the kiss to find China standing in the open doorway, looking from her to Jordon and back again with a grin on her face. "Well, I was going to say come in but if you'd rather wait awhile I'll understand."

Kelsey stepped away from Jordon and beamed at China. Jordon's hand remained at her waist. "No, we're ready to come in."

China opened the door wider. "Welcome."

"Thanks for inviting me to dinner," Jordon said as he stepped into the house.

"Payton will be glad to have another male around while Kelsey and I chat." She pointed to the right and through the living room. "He's in the kitchen, finishing up the meal and watching the football game. Why don't you go in and keep him company? I'm going to show Kelsey's the baby's room."

Kelsey watched Jordon walk away with a knowing grin on his face then she turned to her sister. "That wasn't remotely subtle."

"I had no intention of it being subtle. Come on, I'll show you where we plan to put the baby then you can spill."

Should she tell China that Jordon had been Chad's friend? That wasn't a secret she should be keeping.

China led her down the hall and into the small room across from the master bedroom. The second they stepped into the room China turned and faced Kelsey with an eager look on her face. "Okay, tell all."

"There's not much to say." She made a point of looking out a window at the ocean.

"Oh, come on, Kelsey. I thought we were trying to be

sisters like we once were. You used to share everything with me."

Kelsey decided she might as well tell China what had been happening between her and Jordon. She would badger her until she did. Even when they had rarely seen each other China hadn't given up on her. Kelsey faced her. "He's from the Washington area. He's a doctor—"

China put her hands on her hips. "That's not what I'm talking about and you know it! Start with that hot kiss on my porch."

"He moved in two doors down. A tree went through mine and Molly's house during the storm. Molly was trapped and Jordon saved her life."

"What? Why I'm I just hearing about this now? Were you at home when it happened?"

"No, I was working at the hospital. I'm on Jordon's team and he saw that I was worried. We went in search of Molly."

"How is she?"

"She's doing well but still in the hospital."

"Good," China said, relief in her voice. "But we're getting sidetracked. I want to know about *you* and Jordon."

"My house was condemned and he's letting me stay at his house." Warmth filled her cheeks. "One thing led to another…"

China raised her brows. "It did, did it?"

Kelsey looked away. "Yeah."

"I knew there was something going on between the two of you at the picnic. You really like him, don't you?"

"I do. More every day."

"So-o-o, are you planning to stay around here after all?"

The eagerness in China's voice made Kelsey wince and her heart constrict. She truly sounded like she wanted

Kelsey to remain close. "No, I'm still planning to take the job in Atlanta if they want me."

"I had hoped that Jordon might change your mind where I couldn't."

Kelsey met her gaze again. "China, there's something else I need to tell you. Jordon used to live in Golden Shores. He was Chad's friend."

China said nothing for a moment. "I told Payton that Jordon looked familiar for some reason. Now I remember." China's voice went higher. "He called himself J-man. He gave you that yellow ring you wore forever. You had such a crush on him."

"I did and I'm afraid that I still do."

China laughed. "It's about time some man got past that ten-foot-high electric fence you have built around you."

"Enough about me. Tell me what you have planned for this room."

Fifteen minutes later they joined the men in the kitchen. They were standing in front of the TV, screaming at the football game on the screen. She and China looked at each other. There was a catch in Kelsey's chest. This was what it felt like to have a happy family circle.

Before they disturbed the men, China put her hand on Kelsey's arm and stopped her. "I don't want this to ruin the evening but I have to ask, does Jordon know where Chad is, what happened to him?"

Kelsey shook her head.

China gave her a sad smile. "I guess that was too much to hope for," she said, before she put on a happy face. "Okay, men, it's time for dinner."

"Aw, honey, we're under the two-minute warning," Payton called over his shoulder.

"Okay, you're the chef. Kelsey and I will be out on the porch. Call us when you're ready."

"Will do," Payton said, already focused on the game again.

Jordon's gaze met Kelsey's and he winked, sending a tingle along her spine, before he joined Payton at the game again.

There was a momentary lull in the conversation at the dining table and China looked at Jordon. "I remember you now."

Jordon chest constricted. Was this how an animal felt when it was trapped? Had Kelsey told her about his and Chad's relationship? "I didn't recognize you at first either."

"What're y'all talking about?" Payton asked, looking from China to Jordon.

"Jordon was Chad's friend."

"Chad? Your brother."

"Yes," China said. "I wish we knew where he was." She looked a Kelsey.

Jordon shifted in his seat. Guilt washed over him. Chad's disappearance had affected China as strongly as it had Kelsey. Deception didn't appeal to him on any level. He was keeping a secret that directly affected someone he cared about and he didn't see a blameless way out. Had his mother felt the same way? Been unable to tell the truth because she'd feared the hurt she'd inflict? It didn't make what she'd done right but it did help to explain her actions.

He had to ease their suffering. Last week he'd called the prison and been told he couldn't visit for another week. When he did get to see Chad he would insist he agree to let him tell his family he was alive. He couldn't keep it from them any longer. He'd already kept the secret far too long.

Payton took China's hand. "Honey, maybe one day you'll know something."

The evening was no longer enjoyable for Jordon.

An hour later he and Kelsey said their goodbyes. Jordon drove and Kelsey leaned her head on his shoulder, placed her hand on his thigh. He laid a hand on top of hers.

Could the weight on his chest feel heavier? What he and Kelsey had was tentative at best and he held an explosive secret that could tear them apart more effectively than her moving to Atlanta. When she found out he'd been keeping knowledge of Chad from her she would never speak to him again. How had he managed to get himself in such a mess?

"You're mighty quiet," Kelsey said, her breath tickling his neck.

"I was just thinking how glad I am that you invited me to your sister's." What a liar he was. Something he detested. He was becoming his mother.

"I didn't really. It was China's idea."

Jordon glanced at her and saw her smirk.

"I'm glad you came too." She squeezed his thigh before her fingers wandered upward.

"You know, if you don't stop that I'll have to pull over. I can see it now, the policeman with his flashlight shining on your cute bare tush."

"How do you know it wouldn't be yours?"

"Either way it might be embarrassing."

She giggled. "It might at that. Knowing our luck, it'll be one of the old-timers and he'll recognize both of us."

He couldn't help but smile at that idea. "Why don't you behave and I'll drive a little faster."

Her hand moved on his leg. "Why don't you just drive faster," she cooed.

* * *

Tuesday afternoon Kelsey was finishing her last notes on a patient when Jordon stepped through the open doorway of her office. The man made her heart beat a little faster every time she saw him. It would kill her to leave him, but she would. Maybe they could work it out to see each other on weekends. Spend vacations together. Who was she kidding? After a while that would become more difficult, and soon they would grow apart. That thought made her sad.

"Hey, you okay?" Jordon asked.

He always seemed to read her so well. She'd have to start covering her emotions better around him. She plastered a smile on her face. "Yeah."

"Great. Are you ready to go house-hunting?"

"I am. Give me a sec to put these files away."

He leaned a shoulder against the door and crossed one foot over the other. "Take your time but we have to meet the agent in fifteen minutes."

"You're too funny. Have you thought about giving up your day job and going into comedy?" Kelsey asked, as she gathered up her folders and filed them in a cabinet.

"No, but I thought about becoming a professional dancer."

She turned to face him with a grin on her face. "Ooh, I wouldn't do that. I've seen you dance. You're a much better doctor."

He bowed. "Why, thank you, ma'am. I do believe that was a compliment."

"I think it was more of a statement of fact."

Jordon stepped further in the room. "You know, you can give me a compliment."

"I don't think so. It might go to your head."

Jordon's hands found her waist and pulled her close.

His lips met hers seconds before his tongue demanded entrance. He shifted, widening his stance to bring her into more intimate contact. He lifted his lips but his mouth remained a hair's breathe from hers. She moaned with need.

"There, you can compliment me."

She pushed back and he let her go. "You were playing with me."

"No, I wasn't. You looked so delicious I wanted to kiss you and if I could get a compliment from you at the same time, even better."

"What compliment?"

"That moan was a loud and clear one."

She huffed. "I did not!"

He grinned. "Would you like to ask the man in the office down the hall?"

She turned and picked up her purse. "Don't we have somewhere to be?"

Two hours and three houses later Kelsey sat beside Jordon as he pulled his SUV next to the real estate woman's car in yet another drive. This two-story home was painted a light blue and trimmed in white, with wide steps leading to a dark oak front door. The entire look was welcoming. The expansive porch had long windows that looked as if they could be opened. The yard had been beautifully landscaped with foliage along the porch and beside the handrails. Large chrysanthemums filled the urns on either side of the entrance. Kelsey let out a small sound of awe.

"Like the look of this one, do ya?"

She'd worked hard to keep her opinions to herself as they'd looked at the other houses. It had only been when Jordon had asked what she thought that she'd voiced her view of a home. Even then she was uncomfortable doing so. She shouldn't be helping him make a decision on something as important as a house. His wife should do that.

His wife. A sick feeling filled her stomach. The wife who wouldn't be her.

"Are you coming?" Jordon asked, as he opened the door.

She pasted a smile on her face and climbed out of the car. "I am."

The real estate woman unlocked the front door with a flourish. "This one you could move right into. It was only finished a couple of months ago. Unfortunately the family was transferred out of the state and never got to live here." She walked further into the large open living area. "There are five bedrooms. Plenty of space for a family. Let me show you the rest of the house."

Family? Kelsey lagged behind as the other two moved though the rooms. She ran her fingertips along the Italian tile counter in the kitchen. She might start cooking if she had a wonderful place like this one to do it in. The master bedroom and bath were larger than her and Molly's whole bungalow. What would it be like to live in this grand home, have children running around who looked like Jordon?

"Kelsey?"

"Uh?"

"I asked you what you think."

"Oh, it's nice." What she wanted to stay was that it was the most perfect house she'd ever seen.

"You still need to see the outside. You'll love it," the real estate woman fussed.

Kelsey couldn't imagine that being the case. But it was wonderful. The back of the house was similar to the front, with a large porch running the length of it with a screened-in area at one end.

Jordon leaned over and whispered, "This would be a perfect spot for a swinging bed."

The woman moved further ahead of them and down the steps into the yard. He made it sounded so cozy and sensual that Kelsey shivered. It would be heaven to spend a rainy night gently swaying in a bed with Jordon. She shook herself mentally. Those thoughts had to stop.

The real estate woman waited on the half circle slate patio at the bottom of the steps. The manicured yard lay between them and the bay beyond. There was a T-shaped pier with a white gazebo on one section of the T. Thank goodness the real estate woman's chatter covered Kelsey's quietness. This place was the home of her dreams. But it wasn't to be hers. Jordon's maybe, but never hers.

"How many acres again?" Jordon asked.

"Two point five."

Jordon looked at Kelsey. "There would be plenty of room for Hardy to run."

Kelsey nodded, looking out over the space.

The real estate woman's phone buzzed. "Do you two mind walking down to the pier without me? I need to return this call."

"Sure, that's fine," Jordon told her. He took Kelsey's hand and they strolled to the water. "It's more than I had really planned to start out with, but I like it. What do you think?"

"It's nice," Kelsey said in a flat voice.

He stopped her short of stepping onto the dock. "You don't like it?" Disbelief filled his voice.

"It's beautiful, Jordon, but it really doesn't matter if I like it or not. It will be your house. I won't be living here."

They walked to the end of the dock. "You could if you wanted to."

"I'm planning to move to Atlanta."

"So you can leave just like that?" He sounded hurt.

"I'm not leaving 'just like that'. I told you when we started this that I planned to leave."

"I know, and I agreed to keep things simple between us.

I'm sorry if I was applying pressure. I want what's best for you. If that's moving out of Golden Shores then I'll have to accept it. Maybe right now isn't the right time for me to be thinking of buying a house."

"You shouldn't let what I'm doing affect your decisions."

"There's no hurry on this house idea. Who knows, I might become so enamored with you I can't live without you and decide to move to Atlanta."

An ache filled her chest. What had she let happen? Would she want that for him? Jordon had moved back to Golden Shores to find peace and start over, and he had. Could she, would she, want to take him away from that? She smiled up and him. "Come on, let go and see the gazebo."

They were walking around the side of the house on their way back to the SUV when her cell phone this be the call she'd been waiting for?

"I need to answer this. I'll just be a minute." She stepped away from where Jordon and the real estate woman stood.

Jordon was half listening to the ongoing prattle of the real estate woman about other homes she wanted to show him. Instead, his focus was on Kelsey. He'd hardly noticed when the real estate lady had said she'd call him soon. Kelsey's face lit up. Jordon knew without asking this was the phone call from Atlanta she'd been expecting and he'd been dreading.

That was the moment he knew. He'd fallen hopelessly in love with Kelsey and he was destined for the same heartache as his father. Even if he could convince Kelsey to stay or if he moved with her, the issue of Chad would still tear them apart. Their days were numbered.

She'd finished her conversation and was now coming

toward him with a bright smile on her face. He made an effort to match it. "Hey, is everything all right?"

"Better than all right. They want me in Atlanta on Friday for an interview."

His world wasn't fine. It was falling apart again. It had happened when his mother had left and one more time when he'd had to give up his job in Washington. The difference was this time his heart was involved and it would be far more devastating.

"But if you care for someone you support them, want the best for them, and you let them go." That's what his father had said when he had asked why he hadn't fought for his mother to stay. His father had cared so much that he'd put her happiness above his own.

Jordon put his arm around Kelsey's shoulders and squeezed her to him. "That's wonderful, honey."

She gave him a narrow-eyed look. "I didn't think you'd be happy."

"If this is what you think you need to do then I think you need to go. I want what's best for you."

Kelsey wrapped her arms around his waist and hugged him. "That means a lot to me. I've spent years with a father who micromanaged everything I did and most times told me what to do. So I appreciate the support."

Jordon was thankful for his father's wisdom that was now serving him well. He only hoped he could remember it as he watched Kelsey leave for Atlanta that final time.

CHAPTER NINE

THURSDAY AFTERNOON KELSEY was paged to the second-floor heart wing. She walked up to the nursing desk. "Some-one need me?"

A woman who Kelsey had known since high school said, "Yes. Dr. King. He's in Room 207."

"Thanks."

"Hey, Kelsey." She turned to look back at the nurse. "You know we're all jealous. He's a keeper."

Kelsey couldn't deny the feeling of pride that filled her. "Yeah, I know."

At the door of the room Kelsey knocked then pushed it open. She heard the soft sound of Spanish being spoken by a female and the return of a deeper voice in the same language. To her surprise there was a middle-aged, dark-skinned man in the bed, a woman standing beside it and Jordon. The patient was hooked up to monitors but other-wise looked fine. All too well, Kelsey knew that was the case for most heart patients.

The woman spoke and Jordon answered. Kelsey had had no idea he spoke fluent Spanish. The man continued to surprise her. Since his initial response to her going to Atlanta he'd made only encouraging remarks. Their love-making had been nothing short of phenomenal. Anna, the nurse, was right. He was a keeper. So why was she so willing to leave him? She wasn't but getting a job in a city and moving away from Golden Shores had been her dream forever. What if she stayed to be with him and he left? He'd done that years ago. He'd not said anything about making their relationship permanent. If he did, would she agree?

"Ms. Davis," Jordon said, looking her direction. "This is Mr. and Mrs. Sanchez. They are from Colombia. Mr. Sanchez has had a mild heart attack. We're going to keep him here for a few days for monitoring." Jordon paused and translated what he'd said then looked at Kelsey again. "I would like you to work with him on his diet while he's here." He spoke to the couple and they nodded.

Kelsey smiled at the man and woman. "Nice to meet you. I'll be glad to help." She looked at Jordon. "May I see you in the hall for a moment, Dr. King?"

He spoke to the couple and then followed her out into the hall. "Is there a problem?"

"Here's a big one. I don't speak Spanish and the translator is out sick today."

Jordon seemed to think then he said, "I'll do the translating. You do have your handouts in Spanish, don't you?"

"Of course."

"Good. Can you meet me here in an hour? That should give me enough time to find someone to cover for me for a while."

"I'll be here. What's the urgency?"

"I'm just afraid that Mr. Sanchez might not stay long enough to hear this if we don't do it right away."

"If that's the case, do you think he'll pay attention to what we say?"

"No, but I think his wife will and she'll see that he follows it."

"You are a smart man, Dr. King."

He grinned. "I like to think so but it is always nice to hear it from you."

She jutted her jaw. "See, I *can* give an unsolicited compliment."

"You can and I shall reward you for it later this evening." He gave her a wolfish look that made heat rush to places it shouldn't when she was at work.

"I'll see you in an hour."

Jordon was taking to Anna at the nurses' station when she returned to the floor. Another young nurse hovered nearby. Every once in a while she would glance at Jordon as if she'd like to have his attention. Never before had Kelsey wanted to walk up and kiss a man in front of everyone just to prove that he was hers. She'd never cared enough before for it to matter. Resisting the urge to make a public spectacle of herself, she walked up and stood by Jordon. Anna's lips curved up and the other nurse picked up a chart, gave Jordon one last glance and headed down the hall.

Jordon looked at Kelsey and smiled. The one she recognized as hers alone.

"I'm ready when you are," Kelsey said, smiling back.

"Then let's get started."

Mr. and Mrs. Sanchez greeted them as she and Jordon entered the room. Kelsey pulled a spare chair from the corner and placed it next to the bed. "Please, ask Mrs. Sanchez to pull her chair around next to mine," she told Jordon, but smiled at Mrs. Sanchez.

He did as she requested.

"Now, I know this may be overwhelming but you can stop me any time if you have a question."

Jordon translated as Kelsey opened a notebook with Mr. Sanchez's name on the front. So it went for the next hour. When they finished Jordon looked tired and she knew she was. It had taken twice as long to explain the heart-smart diet because she had to stop and let Jordon repeat what she'd said. They managed to get through everything and the Sanchezes had even ask a few questions.

As they left the room Jordon said, "I'll be in to see you tomorrow."

Kelsey started to say the same but stopped herself. She wouldn't be here. She'd be in Atlanta. On Monday she'd check in on Mr. Sanchez if he hadn't already been discharged. She smiled and gave a slight wave before she headed toward the door. Mr. Sanchez said something. Kelsey turned and saw him taking his wife's hand. He spoke to Jordon. He smiled and looked at Kelsey and said something back to Mr. Sanchez.

"Thanks for helping out there," Jordon said, as they walked down the hall.

"Hey, I was doing my job. You were the one helping me out. Do you think he'll stay in the hospital long enough to have the test he needs?"

"I think he will now."

"Why?"

"Because of you."

"Me?"

"He told me that if everyone was as nice as you then maybe he should stay. You made the difference."

"I didn't do anything special."

"You just being you is special."

She placed her hand on his arm. He stopped and looked at her. "Thank you. That's the nicest thing anyone has said to me."

"Honey." His voice was soft with sincerity. "There's a lot of special things about you. Let's get out of here and I'll name them for you."

Jordon kept his promise. During the night he told her

something special about herself as he kissed the back of her knee, as he nuzzled the sweet spot behind her ear and just before they became one. He whispered more qualities when he woke her in the wee hours of the morning and made love to her again.

The next morning, as he drove her to the airport in Jackson, they were both quiet. Jordon had insisted that she not drive to Atlanta but fly. She complained she didn't have the money for a ticket and he wouldn't take no for an answer, insisting he buy it. She'd admitted she'd never flown before and Jordon had assured her it was a short flight and she'd be fine. After much discussion back and forth, she'd relented and let him have his way. The truth was she dreaded leaving Jordon any sooner than she had to, and flying would give her more time with him.

He pulled to the curb in front of Departures. Kelsey met him at the back of the SUV to get the small overnight bag she'd brought for the trip.

"Call me when you get to the hotel so I'll know you're safe," Jordon said.

It was nice to be worried over. That was one of the things her father had done to the extreme and she'd found she had missed that to a certain extent. "I will. You don't have to worry about me. I'm a big girl."

"I know. But when you care about someone you tend to worry."

Had that been how her father had felt?

"I'll be here waiting tomorrow evening. Just give me a call when you land and I'll pull around to get you."

"I will." She smiled at him. "After all, you're my only way home."

"You remember that and don't take off with just any man." He hugged her close for a second then gave her a tender kiss. "I'll miss you."

"I'm only going to be gone overnight."

"I know but that doesn't mean I won't miss you."

"I'll miss you too. Bye." Kelsey took the handle of her luggage and pulled the bag through the door of the airport. She had to go now or she never would. Moisture filled her eyes. If she got this job she was afraid it would tear her heart out when she left Jordon for good.

Maybe with this separation she could get some perspective. Heaven knew, she had none when he was close.

Before daylight the next day Jordon driving up the interstate on his way to the state prison. He had called ahead so Chad would know he had a visitor. Jordon had to make him understand that his family must be told where he was. If not for their sakes then for his own. Jordon couldn't keep that knowledge to himself any longer.

As promised, Kelsey had phoned when she'd arrived at her hotel room. She'd sounded excited and said the plane ride had been a wonderful experience. Jordon wished he'd had the opportunity to share that with her. To see her eyes light up with wonder. Hold her hand for reassurance when they landed. He hadn't volunteered to go with her. Seeing Chad had been more important.

She'd called him again later that evening to tell him she thought the interview had gone great. The person she'd spoken to had promised to let her know something by the beginning of the week. She'd sounded so excited that he was both thrilled for her but pained for himself. Could he let her go? He had no interest in being involved in large hospital politics again, but if that was what it took to have Kelsey in his life, he would seriously consider moving to Atlanta.

He couldn't spend another night like the night before. Tossing and turning for hours, he'd finally moved to the recliner. That hadn't been much better. Without Kelsey nothing seemed to suit.

Three hours later, Jordon faced Chad through the window of the visiting cubicle of the state penitentiary.

"Hey, bud, this is an unexpected visit. I thought you wouldn't be back for a couple of months," Chad said.

Jordon hated seeing a human being locked up but was pleased to see Chad looking well. "I know, but something has come up that I need to talk to you about."

Chad's forehead wrinkled. "What's that?"

"I've met your sisters. I came to tell you that I can no longer keep it a secret that I know you're here. I have to tell them you are alive."

Chad sat forward. "How did you meet them?"

"Kelsey and I work together at the hospital. I met her the third day I was in town. She introduced me to China at a hospital picnic."

"So what do they do?"

Chad seemed eager to know everything about his sisters, asking questions until Jordon told him all he knew.

"So China's going to be a mother," Chad said with a smile on his face. "And does Kelsey have a husband?"

For once in Jordon's life he wanted to say yes and it was him. "No, but I am hoping some time soon that I can convince her that I would make a good one."

Chad leaned back in his chair, crossed his arms over his chest and grinned. "Well, well. You have the hots for my sister."

"That, and I love her. So you can see why I need to tell her about you. China has to know. Your parents too. I didn't want to break a promise without telling you first that I was going to do it. I'm already afraid Kelsey may not speak to me again. I've kept the secret too long."

"I'm sorry I put you in that position, man. I just didn't

want my family to know that they had a jailbird for a member. I never really thought you would ever meet them. I didn't even know they still lived in Golden Shores."

"I'm going to tell Kelsey tonight or no later than tomorrow."

"Okay."

Jordon was relieved to have Chad's agreement, but he would have told Kelsey anyway. He visited a few more minutes with Chad then said goodbye. He still had to drive to Jackson to pick Kelsey up at the airport. Maybe the hours he was on the road would give him the time to configure a plan to approach the subject of Chad and keep her from hating him. He feared he could use all the drive time and more, and still not make that happen.

Kelsey stood at the curb of the airport pick-up area, shifting from one foot to the other. Despite the interview going well, she'd missed Jordon so much she'd been unhappy the entire time she'd been gone. The plane ride had been exciting but the whole time she'd been wishing Jordon had been beside her. She'd never been to a city as large as Atlanta. Overwhelmed would be an understatement of how she'd felt. Could she live there? Was this really what she wanted?

The three interviewers had been impressed by her answers. She'd seen it on their faces. She felt good about being offered the job. Would she take it if they did? Just a few short weeks ago she would have jumped at it. Now she wasn't so sure. Somewhere during that time she'd started wanting Jordon more. Her new relationship with China made Golden Shores feel more like home. With Jordon there, it might be the only place for her.

A thrill of joy ran through her as she watched the big blue SUV pull to the curb. Seconds later Jordon had her wrapped in his arms, her feet dangling above the ground.

Kelsey enfolded his neck and squeezed him as tightly as he was her.

"I missed you," he said into her hair.

"I missed you too." She had. It felt wonderful being in his arms again.

"Let's go home. I'd like to show you how much." He gave her a quick kiss on the lips then put her bag in the vehicle.

She grinned. "I think I'd like that."

Jordon couldn't bring himself to ruin the blissful reunion he and Kelsey had by talking about Chad or even asking if she would take the job if it was offered to her. As if by agreement, she didn't mention her trip outside of saying Atlanta was a huge city.

"Would you like to stop for a nice dinner?" he asked, before they left the city limits of Jackson.

"No." She placed her hand on his thigh. "I'd rather just go home."

He liked the fact she called his place home, even if she might not have meant it in the same context as he wished. "Then home it is."

Kelsey slept part of the way, as if her night hadn't been much more restful than his. Satisfaction filled him to think she might have been as lonely without him as he had been without her. Even after she woke, she didn't say much. He didn't either, just happy to have her beside him.

In Golden Shores he went through a fast-food restaurant and ordered them a takeout meal. It was dark by the time he pulled into his drive.

Inside Kelsey said, "Let me have my bag and I'll unpack."

"Are you ready to eat?"

"I'd like to get a shower and change clothes first. Go on without me." She headed down the hall.

There was a tension in the air, as if they were both circling subjects that neither wanted to talk about. She had no idea about his and he didn't want to know about hers. He wished he could turn the clock back twenty-four hours to the way it had been between them before she'd left. Once they talked, nothing would be the same. Had his mother and father felt the same way? Was that why they'd never faced their problems?

The water was no longer running and Jordon expected Kelsey to join him any minute, but instead she called, "Hey, Jordon, could you come here a minute?"

"Sure." He rose from the recliner and went down the hall. As he went through the door of the bedroom he went statue still. Kelsey stood beside the bed in a long pink satiny negligée with only the thinnest of lace covering her breasts. She was gorgeous.

His mouth went dry. His manhood rose in reaction to the sexy and desirable picture before him. He was never a man at a loss for words, but this time he could only stare.

"I bought you a present." She shifted, which made the flowing fabric move, giving him a glimpse of a long trim thigh and hot-pink painted toenails.

That proved to heat his body's reaction more. She was seducing him and he loved it.

"I saw it and thought you might like it, but…" Kelsey looked away as if insecure.

Had he ever seen Kelsey look anything but confident? He couldn't remember a time.

He stalked toward her. "Oh, honey, I love it."

She smiled then kissed him with enough passion that he couldn't remove his clothes fast enough.

Some time later, with her snuggled in his arms, he said, "Thank you for the gift. I hope you buy them for me often."

"Mmm." Seconds later she slept.

It was late afternoon the next day when he and Kelsey were walking to the dock that he blurted, "Kelsey, we need to talk."

He couldn't put it off any longer. It was eating him alive not to tell her about Chad, though he was worried sick that it might kill him when he did. He had kept a secret that had broken his father's heart and now he'd been keeping one that would break his.

She looked away for a second then met his gaze and said, "I know. I need to talk to you too."

"Let's go out on the pier."

Since there was only one chair Jordon sat on the pier and she took a place beside him but at arm's length. Kelsey let one leg dangle over the edge and brought the other into a ninety-degree angle onto the boards to face him. Hardy left them to sniff around the edge of the water.

"Kelsey, I need to tell you something. I don't know a good way to do this so I'm just going to say it."

She gave him probing look.

"Chad is alive."

She leaned toward him, her eyes wide. "How do you know?"

"I've seen him."

"Where?"

"He's in the state prison about three hours from here, doing five years for drug trafficking. He contacted me when I was in med school. He was in trouble and looking for money. We've been in touch off and on since then." Kelsey just stared at him for what felt like hours. Her face was unreadable. "How long have you known this?"

"Before I came to Golden Shores."

She looked at him with disbelief before she jumped up and scowled down at him. "And you've said nothing!"

"I couldn't. I made a promise."

"A promise! How could you keep this from me? I thought you knew how screwed up my family is over what happened to Chad. Not knowing if he was dead or alive. Couldn't you see China's reaction to you the other night?"

Jordon stood. "I made a promise and I take those seriously. I went to visit Chad when I drove down here from Virginia. When I told him I was moving back to Golden Shores he asked me not to tell his family where he was if I ran into any of them. I thought that would never happen. I certainly never dreamed that I would fall in love with his sister."

Kelsey's heart jumped. Her head jerked back, her gaze locking with his. Jordon loved her. Could she trust him to really mean it? "You expect me to believe you love me after you've lied to me for weeks?"

"I've never lied to you. I just didn't speak up." His eyes pleaded with her.

"That's semantics. You expect me to trust you with my heart and life after this? To think I was going to give up my dream job for you!"

"I love you, Kelsey. This isn't the time or place I would've picked to say this but I want to marry you."

"Is that a demand or request? It doesn't matter. What I want to know is if you have been keeping the knowledge that Chad is alive to yourself to use when you had to so that you could keep me in town and in your bed," she spat. "I've wanted out of Golden Shores most of my life. This is my chance and I'm going to take it. Don't try to hold me here by trying to give me what you think I want.

If you care about me you would have told me the minute you knew who I was that my brother was alive."

"I've explained why I didn't. And I don't think you know what you want. You've been running for so long from the loss of Chad, anger at your parents, your reputation as a teen that I don't believe you have any idea what you really want. You were so hurt when Chad left, and me," he said more softly, "you've remained so much that child who was trying to figure out how to get back what she had that you can't recognize what you have in front of you now. You want family around you, that's why you always have to be so involved in planning events.

"All of that is here for you. A sister who loves you and wants you here to help raise your niece or nephew. Parents who I would guess still love you deeply." He put up a hand. "No, don't say it. I know they love you. As an adult I can look back and see that they loved Chad. That's why your father did what he did and your mother agreed. They may not have handled the situation correctly and they made mistakes, like everyone does. You just haven't given them a chance to do any differently. Chad is alive. You can see him for yourself. And you have me heart and soul."

"So what you're saying is Jordon King has ridden in on his shining white horse and tied my world up with a perfect bow?"

Had he sounded that holier than thou? That hadn't been his intent.

His gaze locked with hers. "What I want is your happiness, more than anything else in the world."

"I think if you were that interested in my happiness you would have told me long ago about Chad. Instead of spending so much time trying to fix my life, you might use your time more wisely and work on your own. For all the failings in my family, yours isn't much better. When was the last time you truly spoke to your mother? Maybe you should work on the bow-tying in your own life!"

With that she turned and stalked up the pier toward the house, with Hardy following.

That had gone about as well as he had expected. Except he hadn't thought she'd leave with such a stinging parting shot about his mother. When Kelsey cooled off he'd talk to her again. Make her understand.

He entered the house as she was coming up the hall, pulling her bag and with the wooden box tucked under her arm. "Where're you going?"

She didn't stop as she made the turn toward the kitchen entrance. "To my sister's to let her know that her brother is alive," she hissed, with enough venom to kill if she had bitten.

"Kelsey, don't leave. Let's talk this out." Jordon hated begging. He hadn't even done that when his mother had left.

"Goodbye, Jordon," he heard through the screen door as it slammed shut.

CHAPTER TEN

KELSEY HADN'T WANTED to, had even tried to force herself not to, but she'd cried all the way to China's. This was the first time she'd gone to China in tears in years. When she opened the door to her house Kelsey fell into her arms.

"What's wrong?" China asked, fear etching the words.

"Chad is alive!"

"What?" China let Kelsey go and looked at her. "How do you know?"

"Jordon told me. He's known all along."

"Come in and sit down." China shoved the door closed and pulled Kelsey to the sofa. "Tell me all."

"Chad's in the state prison."

"Chad's alive." China breathed the words. "I can't believe it."

"I can't either."

China threw her arms around Kelsey and hugged her tight. "This is wonderful."

As China let her go she said, "It's wonderful but I just don't understand why Jordon didn't tell us sooner. He should have told us."

"He did tell you."

"Yes, but he has known for weeks. Sat at your table and didn't say anything when we talked about Chad."

"Did he explain why he didn't?"

"He said he promised Chad to keep it a secret."

"So what changed his mind?"

"I don't know. I was so angry I packed my things and left."

China looked at her in disbelief. "Why didn't you ask him?"

Kelsey stopped short. Why hadn't she listened? Because she'd felt like he was being high-handed. Because she had been willing to give up her dream to be with him and he had kept something so important a secret for so long. Because she had been hurt by him before and she was afraid she would be hurt again. Because he'd said things she'd needed to hear but hadn't wanted to. All of the above. Bottom line, she was scared. Scared of life, scared of loving him, scared she'd never find the happiness she'd once had.

But over the last few days with Jordon she'd felt that bliss again. "I don't know," she answered China. But she did.

"We need to tell Mother and Daddy." China stood. "But we can't tonight because they're out of town until Wednesday. We have to come up with the best way to do it between now and then. It'll be such a shock."

"You can tell them."

"Kelsey, this is something we have to do together. It's time you were part of the family, good or bad," China said in the firmest voice Kelsey had ever heard her use. "Come on, you look awful. Stay the night or as long as you need to."

Kelsey went to her car and retrieved her bag and box. She climbed the steps to the door with shoulders hunched like the wrung-out woman she was. Not since Chad had left had her emotions been so shattered. All she wanted to do was curl into a ball, close her eyes and forget.

* * *

Hours later Jordon had no choice but to haul himself out of the recliner to get ready to go to work. He headed to his room. He hadn't gone there last night, knowing the smell of Kelsey and the memories would only make his heart-ache more painful. Kelsey's negligée lay neatly across his bed. His agony grew as if he had been stabbed with a knife and had it twisted in his chest. The silky material was just as empty as his life would be without her.

The peace he had found by moving back to Golden Shores had disappeared like the summer crowds. Now he was at work glassy-eyed from lack of sleep. Thank good-ness it was a busy day, leaving him little time to dwell on Kelsey. A number of times he'd opened charts to see her notes. Disgusted with himself for letting something as small as her initials affect him, he'd click the charts from the screen as soon as he'd been able to.

That afternoon he'd been walking down the hall toward Mr. Sanchez's room. His heart had jerked to a stop for a second when Kelsey had come out of the patient's room along with a woman Jordon assumed was the translator. Glancing at him, Kelsey had said something to the woman beside her, turned, pulled the door to the stairwell open and had been gone. He'd been crushed. Things were so bad be-tween them that Kelsey couldn't bring herself to face him.

He was as lost and angry as he had been when his mother had left. This time he couldn't disappear into drugs and a wild time. He had to face the situation. But could he really do that when he couldn't have a simple conversation with his mother? Had Kelsey been right? Shouldn't he see about his own life before he started messing in hers? Was it time for him to start mending the bridges between him and his mother?

Jordon looked out the windshield at his empty and

lonely bungalow. How had he let his happiness become dependent on Kelsey being in his life? She consumed it. Even Hardy, who lumbered out to meet him instead of running and jumping, seemed as depressed as he was over the absence of Kelsey. It was time he did something about the situation. Past time to start getting his own house in order. He would call his mother.

Half an hour later, with his heart beating fast and with shaking hands he'd never admit to, Jordon punched his mother's number into his phone. He didn't know why but years ago he had saved it in his phone. Had he subconsciously known that one day he would want it?

A voice that was familiar yet different, happy in some way he couldn't explain, answered the phone.

"Mother, it's Jordon."

"Jordon!" The excitement in her voice was almost tangible.

"Mother, why did you do it?"

There was a pause. "Honey, I wasn't happy," she said softly. "I handled things all wrong. I should have been honest with your daddy, with you, but I was scared. I'm so sorry that I hurt you. That you had to carry the burden of knowing for so long. I stayed because I hoped I'd change. Instead, I made it worse for you and your daddy.

"He loved you." Jordon couldn't keep the bitterness out of his voice.

"I know he did. But I just didn't love him back the same way he loved me." She paused then said, "Our hearts don't always let us take the easy road."

He knew that all too well.

"You were a horrible wife, but I realize now that you had been a good mother."

"Thank you for that, Jordon. You don't know how much

that means to me. Not having you in my life has been my greatest regret. I never intended to hurt you."

"Why would you think that having an affair, breaking Daddy's heart and leaving wouldn't have hurt me?"

"Sometimes people make mistakes. Big and small. Mine was big."

Had she said this before and he just hadn't listened or hadn't wanted to? He could understand making mistakes. He'd made them as a teen, professionally and again with Kelsey.

"Jordon, I've miss you."

"I've missed you too." To his surprise, he meant it.

"I'd like to see you some time."

"I'm not ready for that."

"I understand." The disappointment and pain were loud and clear in her voice.

"I'll call."

"Thank you for that, Jordon."

"Bye, Mother."

Kelsey sat in the middle of the bed in the crisp white room that was the direct opposite of the dark emotions that swirled within her.

Her treasure box lay open. She held Chad's picture. The yellow plastic ring was on her finger. She couldn't seem to get past the idea that Jordon had kept such an important secret from her. The one time she'd let a man into her heart and he had disappointed her.

In the next few days she would need to make a major decision. She'd received the phone call she'd hoped for today. The job in Atlanta was hers, if she wanted it. To her astonishment, she hadn't told them immediately that she'd take it. Falling in love with Jordon had taken the luster off the idea of moving away. She was letting a man control her life, something she'd sworn she'd never do again after getting out from under her father's thumb.

A soft knock came at the door and Kelsey said, "Come in."

China entered. "I just wanted to check on you. You came home, headed straight in here and haven't come out. I was getting worried about you. Are you hungry?"

A slight smile teased the corner of her mouth. "Ever the mother. That baby is going to be so spoiled."

"I sure plan to. But right now I'm concerned about you." China sat on the edge of the bed. "Is that a picture of Chad?"

"I stole it out of the photo album." Kelsey handed it to China.

"I'm not surprised. I remember when this was taken." She put the picture down on the bed and picked up Kelsey's hand and touched the piece of plastic circling her finger. "You love him, don't you?"

"Yes, but I don't want to."

"I've been there, done that. But then you find out that you'd rather forgive them than live without them."

"I'm not there yet."

"You will be. I just hope you don't wait too long."

"I got the job offer in Atlanta."

"You did?" China's face remain emotionless. "What did you tell them?"

"That I'd let them know in a few days."

"I think that was wise. I spoke to Mother and Daddy. They're expecting us Wednesday evening."

"You told them I was coming? I bet Daddy is blowing a gasket."

China gave wry smile. "No, I said it would be Payton and I. They would know something was wrong if I said you were coming."

Wednesday afternoon Kelsey rode with Payton and China to her parents' house. She wasn't sure she would have made it if she hadn't been with them. More than once she'd wanted to back out. The only reason she hadn't was because it was time for her to start facing her past and the issues with her parents was a large part of that past.

"What's he doing here?" she said, when she saw Jordon's SUV sitting alongside the road in front of her parents'. She'd not seen him in the last three days outside that one time in front of Mr. Sanchez's room. Not proud of herself for it, she had hidden in her office most of the time, handling the majority of her work over the computer. If she needed to see patients, she did it when she thought Jordon would be having lunch or seeing patients elsewhere. The hospital was small but became tiny when trying to dodge someone.

"I asked him to come," China said. "He should be here to answer any questions Mother and Daddy have. We have."

"I don't want to see him." Even to her own ears she sounded childish. He'd said some things she hadn't wanted to admit were accurate. She needed to deal with Chad being alive. Then she'd figure out how to handle her feelings for Jordon. She was in emotional overload.

"That's not true," China said with the patience of a mother settling a willful child. She was right, but Kelsey wasn't willing to admit it out loud. In truth, she wanted to run to him, bury her head in his strong shoulder and hide. But she had been hiding for too long, from too many problems.

Payton pulled the new minivan to a stop in the drive. Kelsey opened the door to find Jordon standing nearby. He looked haggard, as if he hadn't slept in days, maybe even a little thinner.

It had been at least ten years since she'd been in her parents' home. The thought of facing them was staggering. She stumbled as they walked along the shell drive. Jordon's hand at her elbow steadied her then was gone.

China led the way up the length of steps to the front door of the home built on stilts. Payton followed her then Kelsey.

Jordon moved closer as they climbed and whispered, "I know you don't want me here. I also know how tough it is for you to face your parents. I'm here for you if you need me."

Before Kelsey could form a response her mother opened the door. She bit her lip and her hands shook. As if time had rolled back, Kelsey was once again the young girl who only wanted her mother to show she cared. Jordon stood close enough that she felt heat from his body.

"Well, what's all this?" Her mother scanned the group. A look of shock covered her face when she gaze rested on her. "Kelsey." The wistful note in her mother's voice almost brought tears to Kelsey's eyes.

"Mom, we need to talk to you and Father," China said.

"What's wrong?" Kelsey's mom's face turned anxious.

"Nothing. It's good news."

"Come in." She led them into the living area where her father sat in his favorite spot in front of the TV. Apparently little had changed.

Jordon took a seat next to Kelsey on the sofa. China sat beside her on the opposite side. Payton stood like a protective warrior beside China.

Her father looked straight at Kelsey. "What're you doing here?"

"Good to see you too, Father."

Jordon shifted so that his thigh came in contact with hers. She appreciated the reassurance.

"And who are you?" He looked directly at Jordon.

"I'm Jordon King."

"King." He rolled the name around his mouth. "I know that name. Did you used to live around here?"

China rose. "Let me turn the TV off."

"I was watching a show," her father groused.

Payton put his hand on China's shoulder. "I'll get it."

Kelsey watched in amazement as Payton walked to the TV and pushed a button. Her father said nothing.

"I know you now. You're that King kid that got Chad in trouble." Her father put the foot of the recliner down as if intending to come after Jordon.

To his credit Jordon's voice remained calm as he said, "Yes, I was Chad's friend."

"How dare you come into my house?" Her father moved to stand.

"You need to hear Jordon out," Payton said.

"I don't want to hear anything from him," her father growled.

Payton returned to his spot behind China and she said, "Chad is alive."

"What?" Her mother sat on the edge of her seat.

"It's true, Mrs. Davis," Jordon said.

"Why should we believe you?" Her father continued to scowl at Jordon.

Jordon ignored him and continued. "Chad's in the state prison on drug charges." Her mother groaned but Jordon went on to tell them how he'd come to know where Chad was. "He's fine but has a few more years to serve."

"Chad's alive," her father whispered, as if the truth had finally sunk in. Her father leaned back in his chair. He looked at them. "I did the best I knew how with the boy. It was my job to teach him right from wrong. He had to learn." He look at each of them in turn as if for confirmation he'd done the right thing.

To her amazement there were tears in his eyes.

Her father hung his head. His shoulders jerked. He was sobbing. She watched in shock. Going to her father, her mother put an arm across his shoulders and hugged him.

"I know this is too late but I have never forgiven myself for how I drove him from this house," he said between sniffs. "I was doing what I thought was right at the time."

"That didn't make it hurt less," Kelsey said.

"I know you girls were hurt by my decisions, especially you, Kelsey. I couldn't let Chad hurt our family."

"Yeah, but instead of it just being Chad hurting the family it was you too."

"I know that now. I'm truly sorry for what I've done to this family."

Kelsey wouldn't have thought it possible but she felt sorry for the broken man before her. He'd been big and imposing all her life and now she saw him as a sad, aging man who had hurt like the rest of them.

Her mother looked at Jordon. "Will Chad see us?"

"I think he will. He didn't want me to tell you where he was because he was ashamed. You'll have to call the prison to see when you can visit. I think he'll be glad to see you all. Mr. Davis, I'm sorry for any part you think I played in Chad leaving. I was a kid with my own problems."

Kelsey felt for that scared kid who hadn't known how to handle his life any more than she had known how to handle hers.

"So how do you know my daughters?" her mother asked.

"I'm a doctor at Golden Shores Regional. I have moved back here. Kelsey and I work together."

She needed to get out of there. They had done what

she'd come for. She needed to get away from her father and away from Jordon. Her whole world was squeezing in on her. She had to figure out where she went from here.

"I need to go." Kelsey stood and Jordon did also.

He looked at China. "I'll take care of her."

Kelsey didn't glance right or left on her way to the door. Her mother beat her there.

"You will come back soon, won't you?" Her mother gave her a pleading look.

"I don't know."

"He has changed over the last few months. Knowing Chad is alive will make even more of a difference. He's carried such a burden of guilt over Chad, over you. Maybe he'll become more like the man I married now. He loves you, Kelsey. He didn't know how to show it all the time."

"I know that now, Mom. But I can't forgive all the years of injury all in one day. Give me time."

"We would love to see you any time."

In an impulsive move Kelsey wrapped her arms around her mother and hugged her. Her mother returned the embrace. It felt wonderful being in her mother's arms again.

"Thank you so much, Dr. King," her mother said, as Jordon followed Kelsey out.

"I'm glad I had good news."

As she went down the steps, Kelsey said over her shoulder, "I don't need you to take care of me."

"I know you don't but I want to."

Jordon said the words in such a calm voice she gritted her teeth not to snap at him. She looked up at him when she reached the ground. He stood two steps above and towered over her. This wasn't her best ground for defense but she forged ahead. "I can't do this right now. I can't handle you and my parents in the same day."

"Okay."

"That's all you've got to say?"

He shrugged. "How about where would you like me to drive you?"

Kelsey blinked and looked around. She'd forgotten she'd ridden out with China and Payton.

"You can take me…" The reality that she had no house and no key to China's home left her in confusion.

"Come on, we'll ride around for a while until China and Payton return home. I know you don't want to go back in there and I sure don't." He started toward his SUV.

Kelsey looked back at her parents' door then at Jordon's back. She had no choice but to take the least of the two evils. "I don't want to talk."

"Okay."

Jordon didn't even open the door for her. Instead he climbed in on the driver's side and waited patiently while she joined him. He started the vehicle and pulled on to the road. Kelsey had never been more exhausted in mind, body and soul. She closed her eyes and slipped into sleep.

Jordon turned the engine off and looked at Kelsey. She was so beautiful but more than that she was remarkable in so many ways. People loved her and she loved furiously in return. It must have taken all she'd had to enter her parents' house, having been gone so long. She'd held herself together admirably. If he'd not known her so well he would never have noticed the slight tremor to her hands or seen the flinch she'd made when her father had questioned why she was there. For once in his life he'd wanted to hit an older man.

Kelsey's hair was standing on end in her preferred style that so suited her little left-of-center personality. Her lips were parted and he wanted to lean across and kiss her awake, beg her to see reason. His desire to touch her, do something as simple as run the tip of his finger across her cheek almost took control of him. He climbed out and closed the door behind him. Kelsey needed rest and time then they would talk. He had to get her to listen.

Jordon climbed the steps to the front entrance of the house. He'd seen the look on Kelsey's face. She'd loved the place. He'd put down earnest money on it the day before because the real estate woman had said someone else was interested in it. If he couldn't convince Kelsey that staying in Golden Shores with him was the thing to do, he would willingly forfeit the money and live wherever she wanted.

He ambled from empty room to empty room without paying much attention to where he was. Ending up in the spacious window-filled living area that stretched across the back of the house, he opened the full-length glass door and walked out onto the porch. He glanced at the screen porch then strolled to the dock. Going to the gazebo, he sat on one of the benches and put his head in his hands.

"Hey. I've been looking everywhere for you."

The sound of Kelsey's voice had him jerking upright.

"What're you doing out here? More to the point, what are we doing here?" She gestured toward the house.

"The real estate woman gave me the key so I could look around again."

"So you've decided this is the one?" Her voice had a wispy note that gave him hope.

"It depends."

She came to stand in the entry way of the gazebo. "On what?"

"On you."

"Me? Why?"

"Because I can only live here if you share it with me."

"Jordon, I thought we weren't going to go into all of that now."

He shrugged. "You're the one who asked."

"I guess I did."

Jordon captured her gaze. "I know you don't want to talk but would you be willing to listen for a minute?"

She sighed. "I guess you won't take no for an answer."

"This is something you really need to hear or I wouldn't insist."

She sat down on the bench closest to the opening as if she wanted to make sure she had an escape route. "Okay, I'm listening."

Kelsey was going to be a tough sell. He had hoped she'd softened some over the last few days but apparently not. "When I found out my mother was having an affair I swore then that I would always keep my promises. That trust was the most important thing in a relationship. Because of that I couldn't tell you or your family about Chad. It was too ingrained, too important to who I am to break a promise. I refuse to be like my mother and hurt someone by not keeping my word. But that didn't happen. I did hurt you. I'm sorry for that, but if I had to do it over again I would make the same decision. I hope you can understand why I did what I did."

She just looked at him. Why didn't she say something? At least she wasn't walking off.

"Thank you for telling me. I can't say it still doesn't hurt to know you lied to me."

"If you'll forgive me, I promise that it'll never happen again."

"I guess I can accept that, knowing how strongly you stand by your word."

"Thank you." Relief flooded him. Boosted by her positive reaction and the fact she'd not walked away yet, he asked, "So are you going to take the job?"

Her eyes narrowed. "How do you know they offered me the job? Did China tell you?"

"No. I just know they would be crazy not to want you."

Her lips curled a little before she said, "They do want me."

"So when are you leaving?"

She hesitated a second. "I'm not sure that I am. I told them I needed a few days to think about it."

His heart lightened, hope soared. "Why's that?"

"I wanted to make sure I'm making the move for the right reasons. I have spent so many years planning a way out of Golden Shores that I haven't stopped to think in a long time why I wanted to leave."

He propped his elbows on this knees, trying to give a nonchalant appearance when his happiness hung on her every word. "And do those reasons for leaving still exist?"

"Yes, but I'm no longer carrying them around like a chip on my shoulder. I've reestablished a relationship with China. I have a job that I love, people I enjoy working with. I did have a place to live."

"You will again."

"Today I faced my biggest fear, seeing my parents again. I survived. You were right, I've been running. I've been planning to for so long it was difficult but freeing to face the past. I can move on now. It isn't where I live, it's who I am. Even if I moved to Atlanta the same issues would follow me. Then China said something to me that made a lot of sense."

Where was she going with this? Dared he dream? He kept his voice even. "That was?"

"Sometimes it's easier to forgive them than to live without them."

"Like your parents?"

"Yeah. But more like you."

"Me?" He croaked then cleared his throat. "What does that mean?"

"It means I love you."

Jordon was on his way to her before she finished the words. Grabbing her, he pulled her against him and brought his mouth down to hers. He poured all his love into that one meeting of lips. Kissing the corner of her mouth, he murmured, "I don't think there has been a man more unhappy than I've been since you left my house. I thought I had lost you."

"It's time I grew up. Time to accept the decisions my parents made. Some that Chad made. I'm not going to live in the past anymore. I want to create a future. Hopefully with you."

Was she really saying all the words he'd dare to hope for? "That can be arranged. Starting right now. I want to do this right this time."

He pulled the circle of gold out of his pocket and went down on one knee.

"Jordon…" Kelsey said his name in that breathy way he adored when he was making love to her.

Kelsey held her breath. Jordon was holding a ring that looked like the plastic one he'd given her so many years ago. But this one glistened in the light. It was made of solid yellow diamonds.

"This came in a smaller box than the last one but I hope you'll accept it anyway. Will you marry me?"

"Oh, just try and stop me!" Kelsey put out her finger and he slipped the ring into place.

EPILOGUE

"KELSEY KING, I thought you got everything you needed yesterday before you left for China's," Jordon said, as they pulled into the drive of their new home.

She leaned over and kissed him. "You already sound like a husband. This won't take but a minute and we really don't have to be at the airport until tomorrow. The hotel room will keep for a few more minutes."

"Speak for yourself. I'm ready for the honeymoon to begin. I missed you last night."

"I missed you too but I bought the dress especially to take to Italy. If I hadn't pulled that casserole out of the oven and gotten a spot on it when I was trying it on we wouldn't have to be doing this."

He chuckled. "I think that's one thing I've enjoyed most about you since you started planning a wedding. You've turned more scatterbrained."

"Scatterbrained? Is that how a new husband should talk about his wife on her wedding day?"

"Maybe not, but it has sure been fun watching you rattled during the last few weeks. Kind of makes me feel loved."

He didn't give her a chance to retort before he climbed out and came around to help her out. Kelsey gathered her full white dress in an arm and Jordon lifted her out of the high SUV.

"The dress is on the porch. I hung it out there to dry."

"While you're getting it I'll double-check that the alarm is set."

"Okay."

Kelsey opened the door to the back porch with a grin on her face. She'd planned this surprise down to the last detail. And Jordon thought her scatterbrained. She'd had the carpenter come in after Jordon had left for the church, Molly's mother had seen to the new luxurious sheets, comforter and pillows. Her father had surprised her by supplying the champagne. "Hey, Jordon, could you come and help me?" she called.

"I'm on my way," he said from the other room. "They say getting married changes you but I had no idea how quickly you would become needy."

Kelsey hurried to get into place on the swing bed inside the screened area of the porch. She lay on her side and adjusted her dress around her.

Jordon stepped out onto the porch. "Now what's the—?"

"Hey, Dr. King, how about you come and start your honeymoon over here on your wedding present," Kelsey called in her most seductive voice.

"When? How? I was just here a few hours ago."

"Instead of asking questions, why don't you kiss me and rock my world?"

He chuckled and came down to join her on the bed. "That I'll be more than happy to do."

Later, with her dress and Jordon's tux lying in a pile on the floor of the porch, Kelsey snuggled under the bedcovers next to Jordon as a light rain fell in the dark.

"You know that if you ever decide you want to live elsewhere else, all you have to do is say the word." Jordon's words rumbled beneath her ear. "I promise."

"And you keep your promises." She shifted so she could look at him. "I don't want to go anywhere. I have everything I've ever wanted right here, J-man."

* * * * *